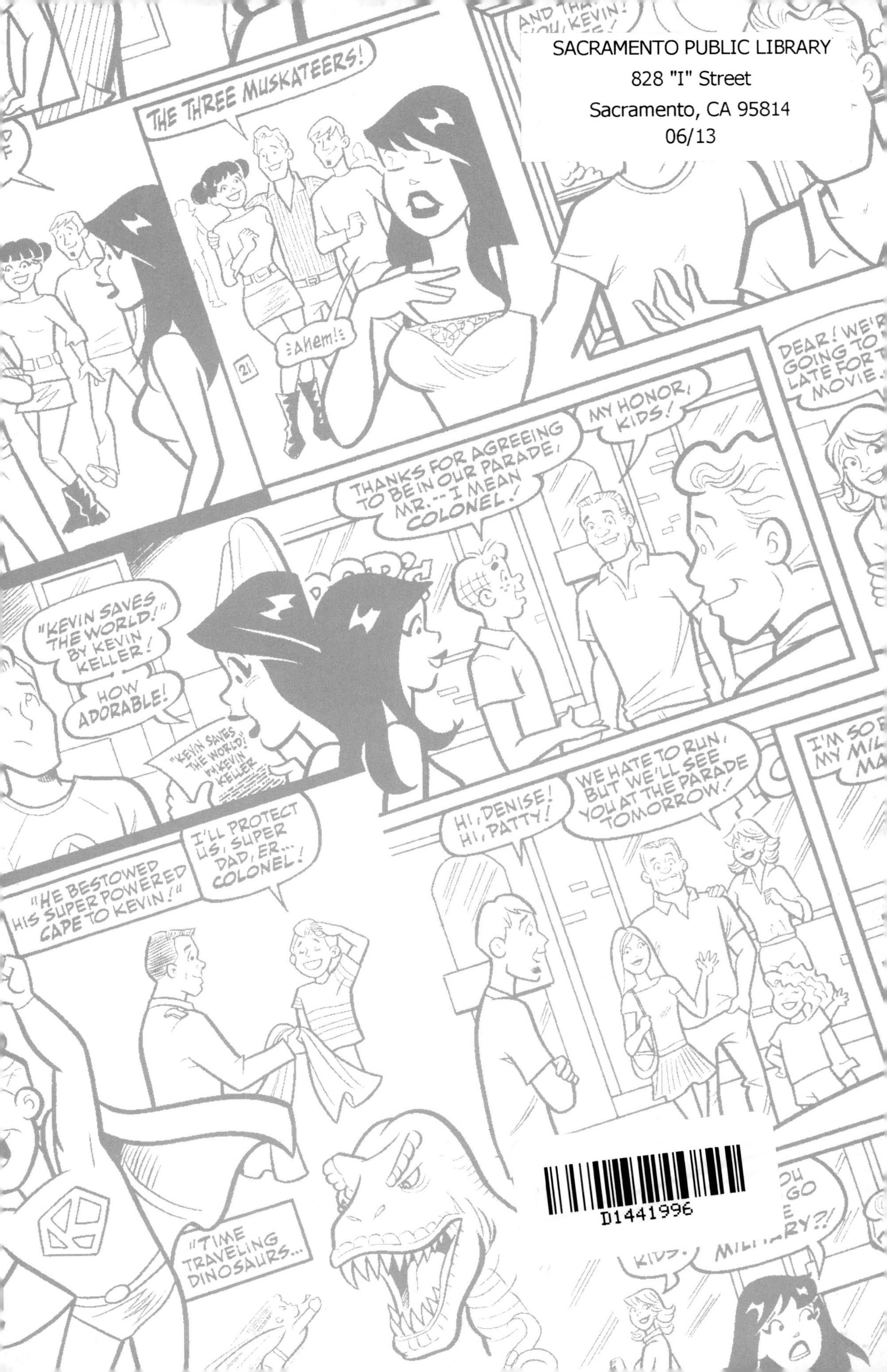
THE THREE MUSKATEERS!
AHEM!
THANKS FOR AGREEING TO BE IN OUR PARADE, MR.--I MEAN COLONEL!
MY HONOR, KIDS!
"KEVIN SAVES THE WORLD!" BY KEVIN KELLER!
HOW ADORABLE!
"KEVIN SAVES THE WORLD!" BY KEVIN KELLER
HI, DENISE! HI, PATTY!
WE HATE TO RUN, BUT WE'LL SEE YOU AT THE PARADE TOMORROW!
"HE BESTOWED HIS SUPER POWERED CAPE TO KEVIN!"
I'LL PROTECT US, SUPER DAD, ER... COLONEL!
"TIME TRAVELING DINOSAURS...

ARCHIE'S PAL

KEVIN Keller™

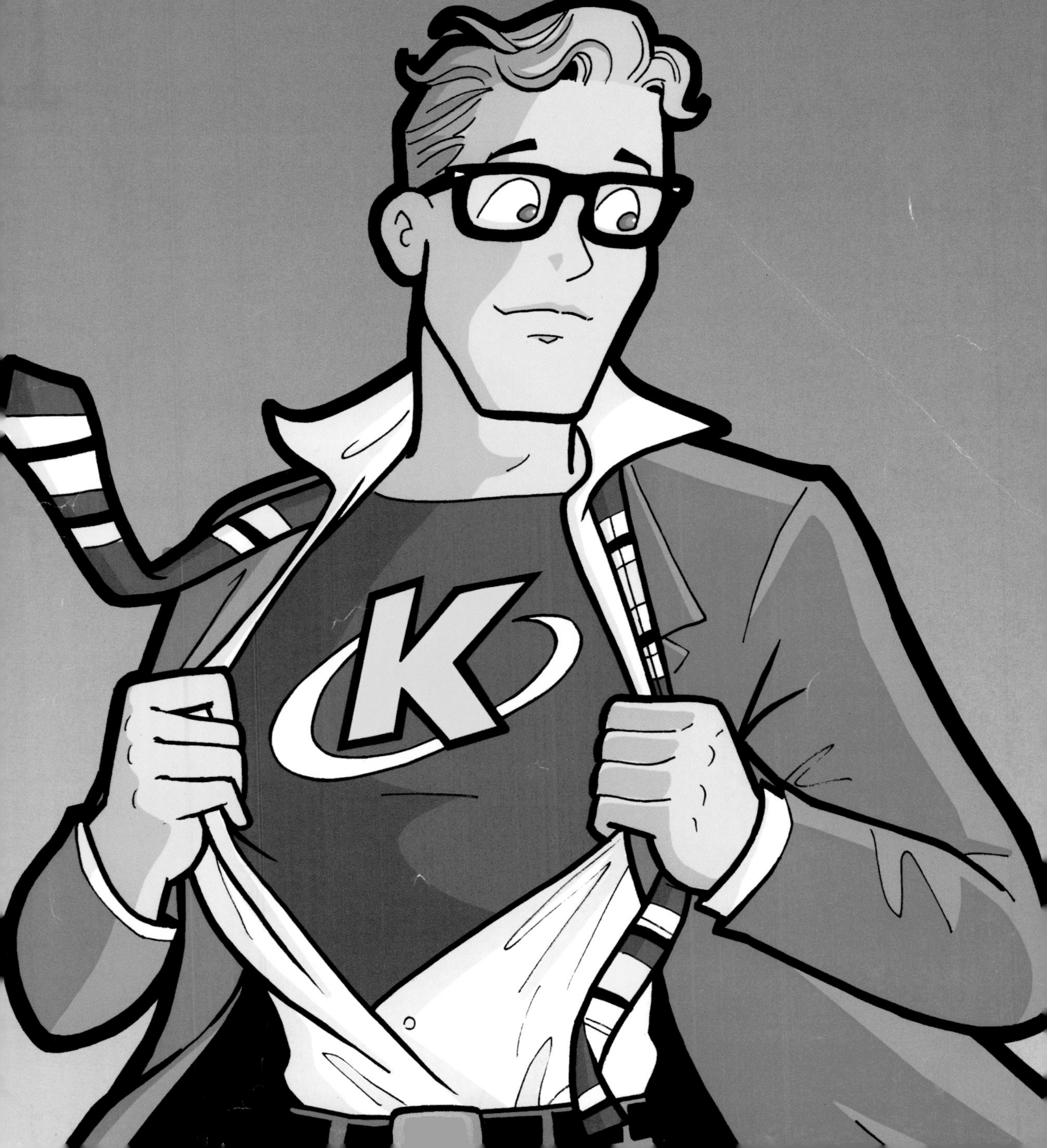

K

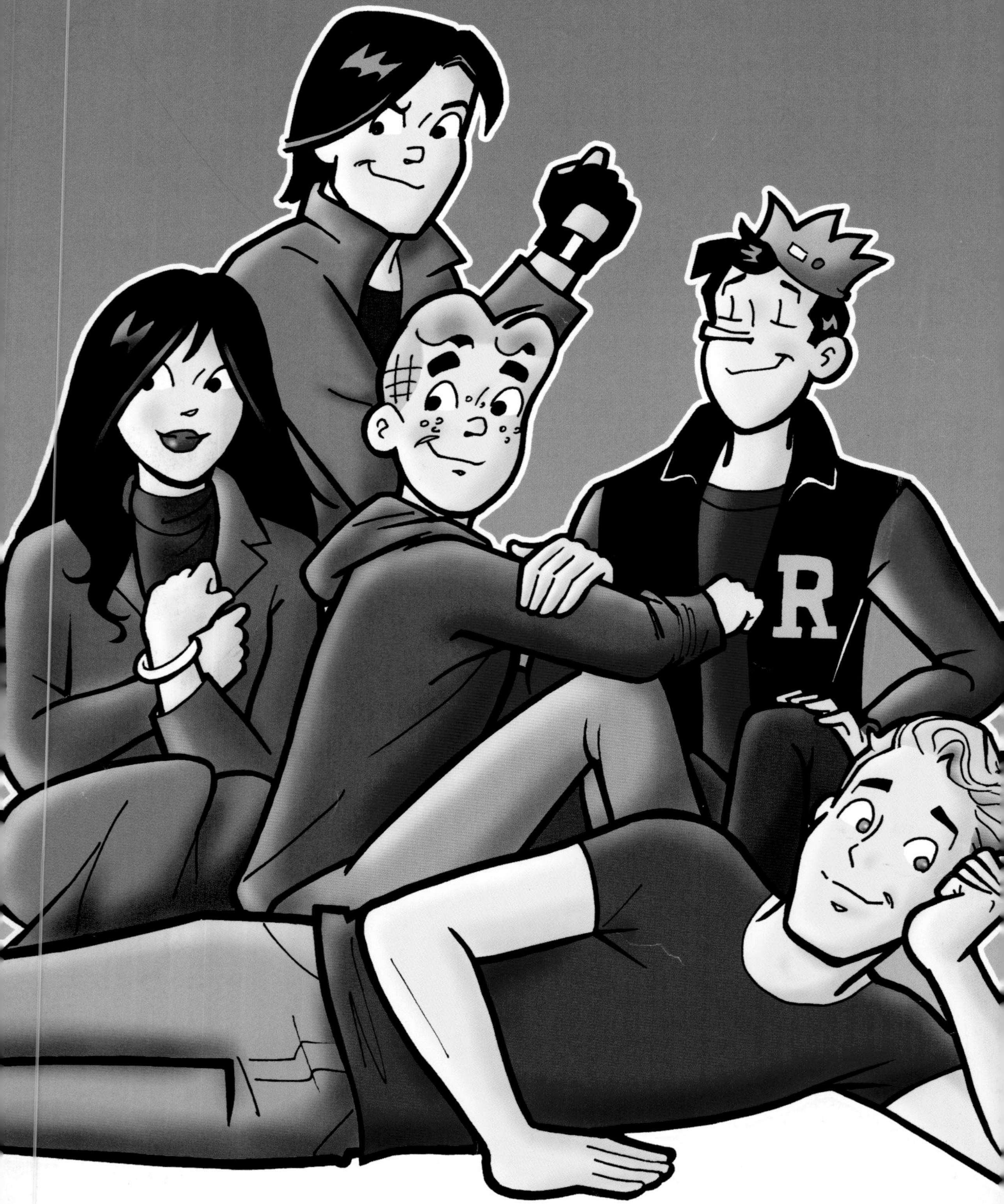

KEVIN KELLER. Published by Archie Comic Publications, Inc. 325 Fayette Avenue, Mamaroneck, New York 10543-2318. FIRST PRINTING. Printed in Canada. ISBN: 978-1-879794-93-1

ARCHIE'S PAL
KEVIN Keller™

Story and Pencils by:
DAN PARENT

Inking by:
RICH KOSLOWSKI

Lettering by:
JACK MORELLI

Coloring by:
DIGIKORE STUDIOS

Publisher / Co-CEO: Jon Goldwater
Co-CEO: Nancy Silberkleit
President: Mike Pellerito
Co-President/Editor-In-Chief: Victor Gorelick
Director of Circulation: Bill Horan
Executive Director of Publicity & Marketing: Alex Segura
Executive Director of Publishing/Operations: Harold Buchholz
Project Coordinator & Book Design: Joe Morciglio
Production Manager: Stephen Oswald
Production: Jon Gray, Pat Woodruff, Duncan McLachlan
Proofreader: Jamie Lee Rotante

GET TO KNOW KEVIN Keller™

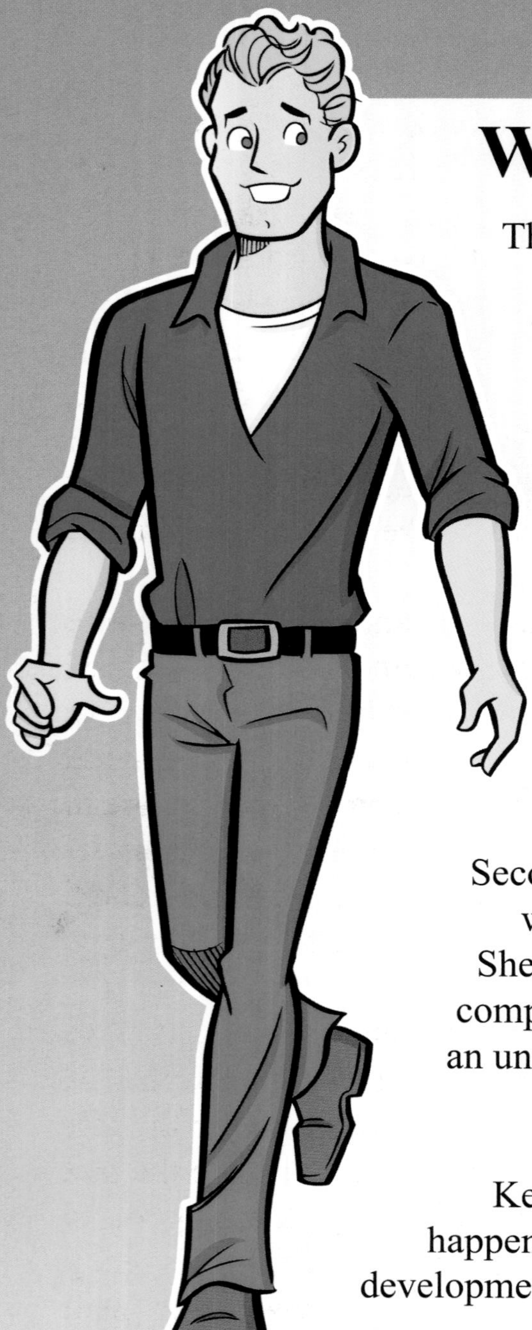

Who is Kevin Keller?

That question seems to come up more often then you'd think. There were a couple of factors that brought Kevin into Riverdale.

First, there was already a movement to actively expand the world of Archie by adding more diverse characters; the feeling was that Riverdale needed to reflect the current world we live in. Since we live in a melting pot of diversity, it would be hard to imagine a current world for Archie, Jughead, Betty & Veronica without reflecting this concept.

Second, Dan Parent had come up with a story where Veronica had finally met her match. She would fall for the "hot new guy in town" completely unaware that she was chasing after an unobtainable guy. From there it clicked, and Kevin was born!

Kevin is the all-American teenager who just happens to be gay. It's an important factor in the development of the character, but it is just one of the many aspects that make up Kevin.

The regular Archie readers are like one big happy family, and this family has accepted Kevin into its life as you would any other family member. It's been very encouraging to see such love and acceptance. However, as with any announcement of this magnitude, there is always bound to be some sort of backlash. Now you really can't do anything about negativity, it's a fact of life. You just have to accept it and move forward, focusing on all of the positives. One positive is that bringing Kevin into the forefront of the Archie universe has propelled the world of Riverdale and all of its residents light-years into the future.

Many of the issues in Archie's world revolve around the timeless romantic entanglements that many of the Riverdale teens become involved in. Whether it's the classic love triangle of Archie, Betty, and Veronica; Reggie being chased by Midge's jealous boyfriend Moose, or Cheryl Blossom sticking her nose in everyone's business, Riverdale has always been a place where readers could live vicariously through the characters. With that said, dating will be a whole new world for Kevin. As far as a gay romance being difficult or controversial, most people will want to see Kevin advance in the romance department. But for now, Kevin's focus will be on his friends, family and, most importantly, his education. He has a bright future in Riverdale and the best is yet to come!

It's important to use the words "normal" and "gay" in the same sentence. Many of our friends in the gay community have shared stories about the importance of being represented in Riverdale. We've been supported by so many people over the years - gay and straight - that is nice to see Archie working towards representing everyone in Riverdale equally! We are also seeing a ton of support from parents of gay teens, as more and more gay teens are finding the courage to come out to their parents, friends and families every day.

Archie is truly for EVERYONE! In Riverdale, you can be a part of an average all-American town no mater your race, orientation or gender; even if you're not from America! Part of Kevin's appeal lies in the fact that he's your typical everyday teen, the boy-next-door. Sure the fact that he's gay is important to the ever-growing and expanding world of Riverdale, but it's more important to remember that he's really no different from most teenagers, and that he - and many others - will always find a welcome home in Riverdale, and in all of Archie Comics.

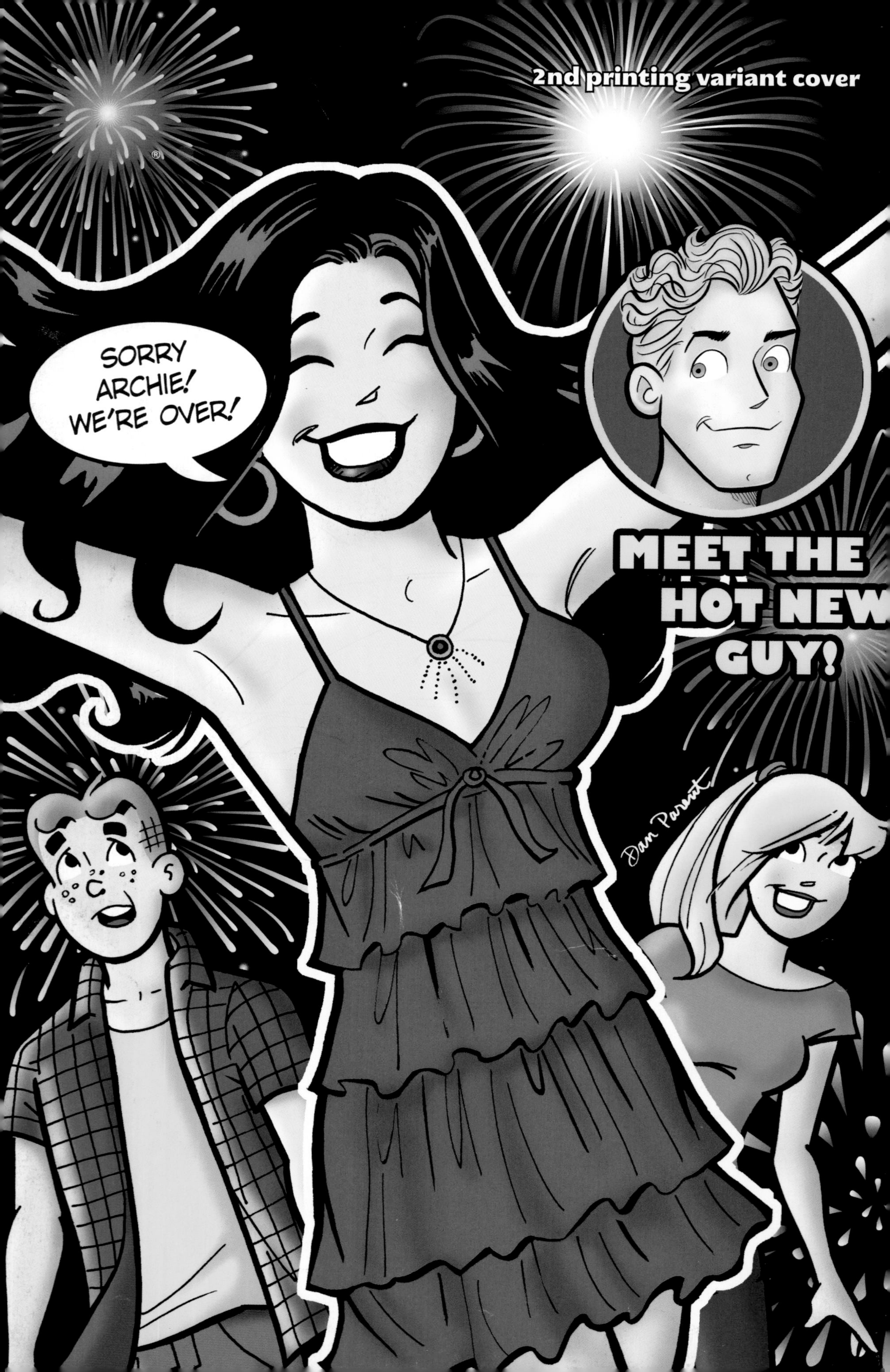
2nd printing variant cover
SORRY ARCHIE! WE'RE OVER!
MEET THE HOT NEW GUY!
Dan Parent

Part 1: Isn't it Bro-mantic?

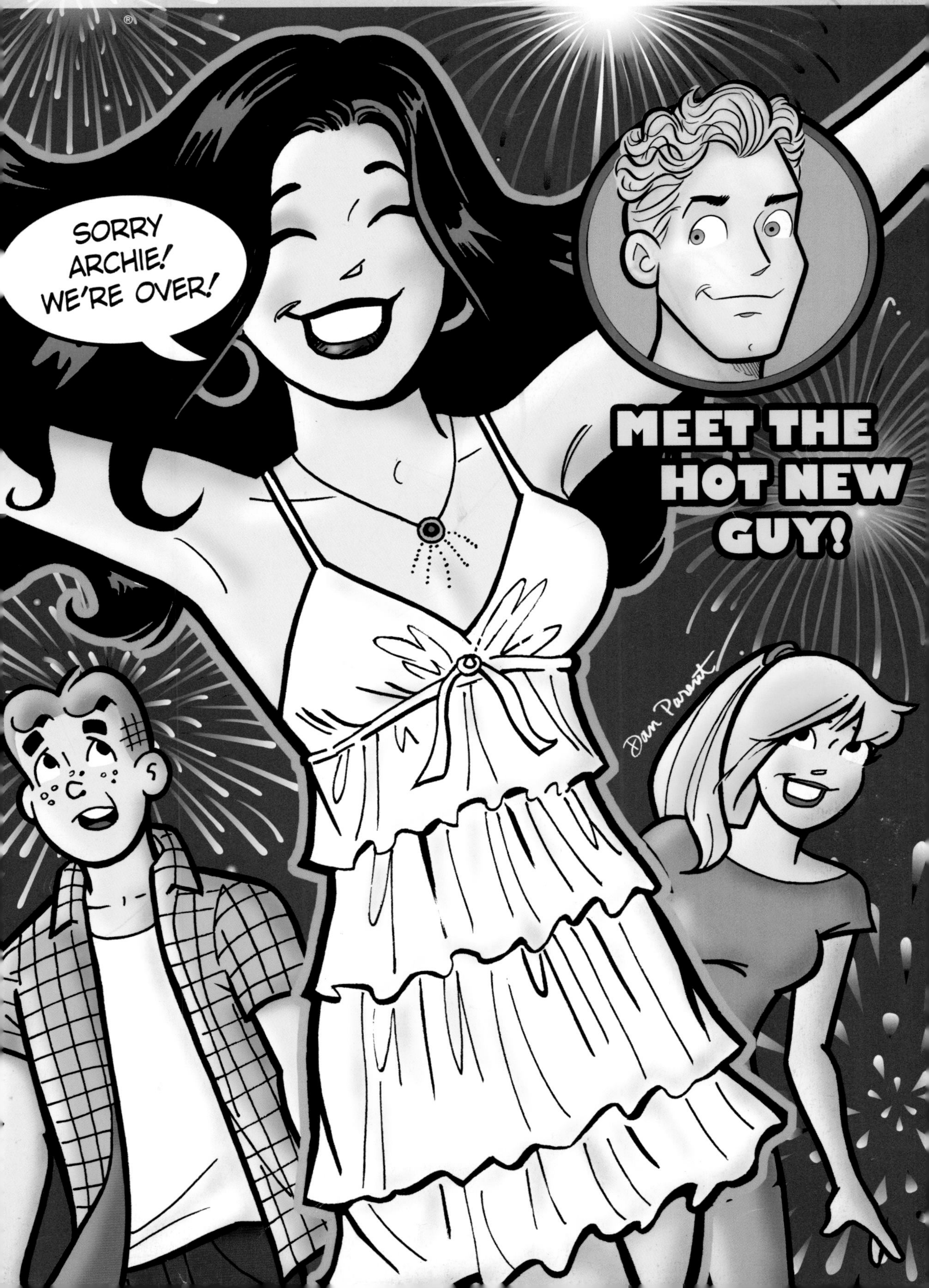
SORRY ARCHIE! WE'RE OVER!
MEET THE HOT NEW GUY!
Dan Parent

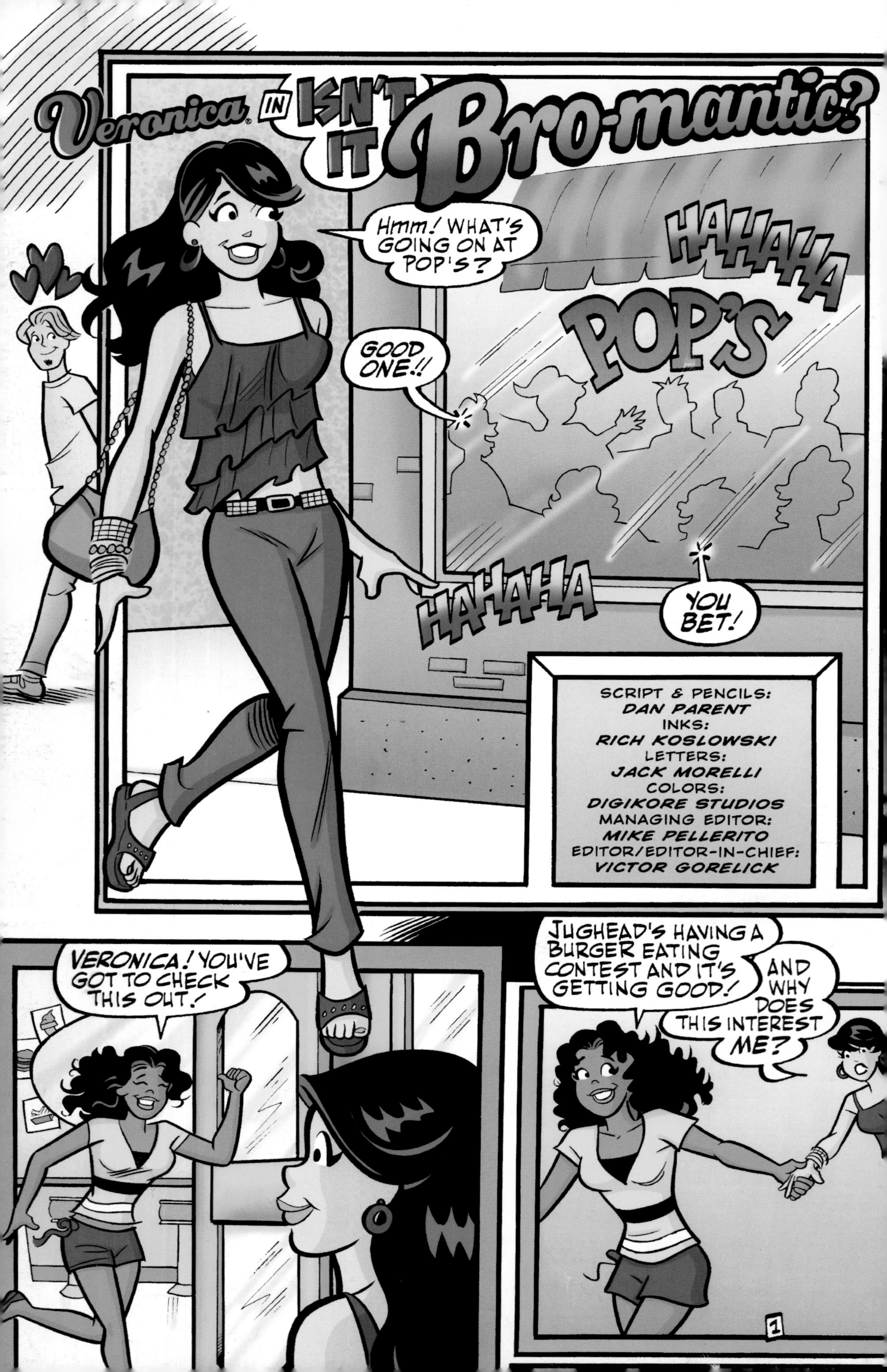
Veronica® IN ISN'T IT Bro-mantic?
Hmm! WHAT'S GOING ON AT POP'S?
HAHAHA
POP'S
GOOD ONE!!
HAHAHA
YOU BET!
SCRIPT & PENCILS: DAN PARENT
INKS: RICH KOSLOWSKI
LETTERS: JACK MORELLI
COLORS: DIGIKORE STUDIOS
MANAGING EDITOR: MIKE PELLERITO
EDITOR/EDITOR-IN-CHIEF: VICTOR GORELICK
VERONICA! YOU'VE GOT TO CHECK THIS OUT!
JUGHEAD'S HAVING A BURGER EATING CONTEST AND IT'S GETTING GOOD!
AND WHY DOES THIS INTEREST ME?
1

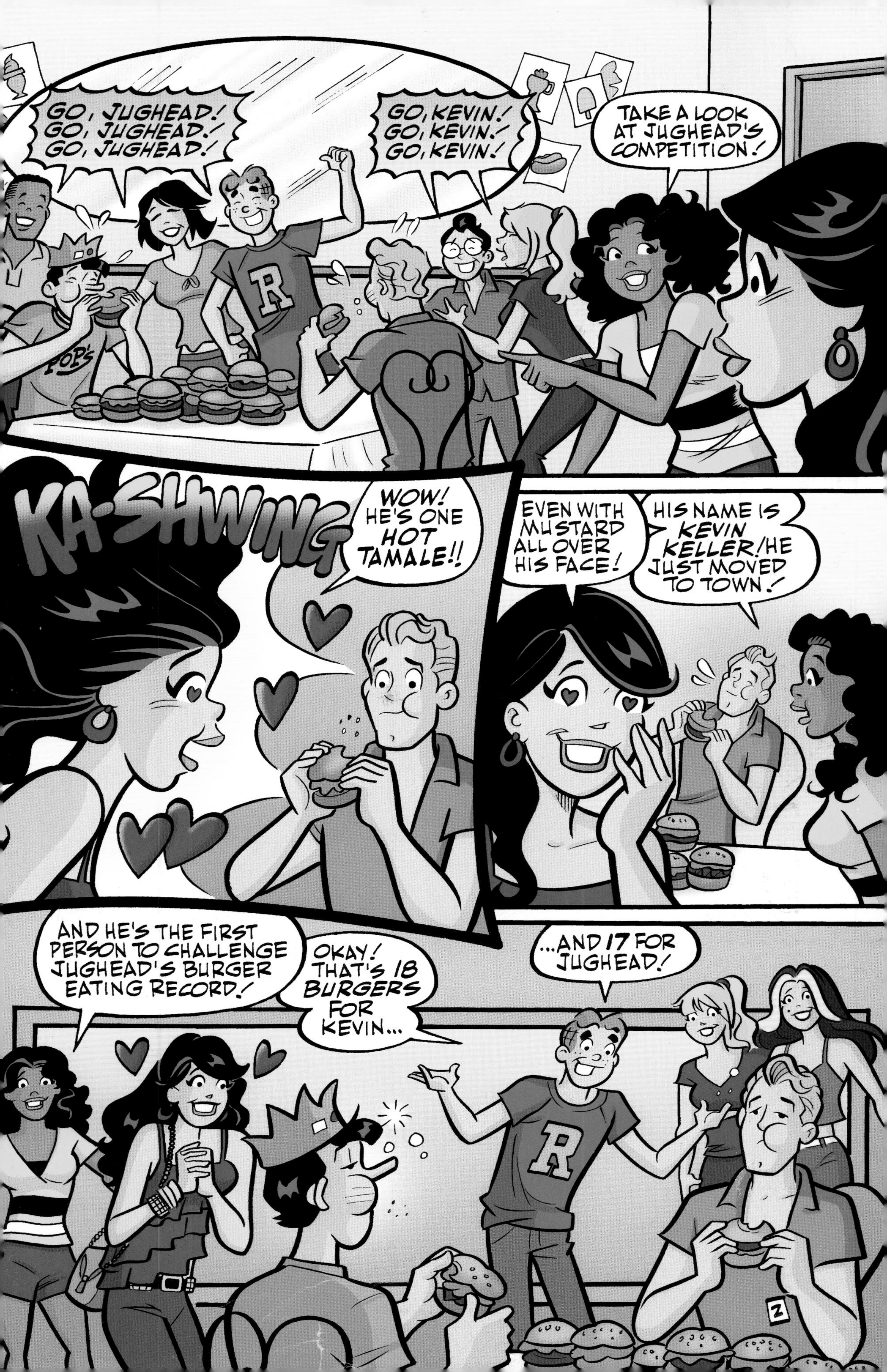
GO, JUGHEAD! GO, JUGHEAD! GO, JUGHEAD!
GO, KEVIN! GO, KEVIN! GO, KEVIN!
TAKE A LOOK AT JUGHEAD'S COMPETITION!
KA-SHWING
WOW! HE'S ONE HOT TAMALE!!
EVEN WITH MUSTARD ALL OVER HIS FACE!
HIS NAME IS KEVIN KELLER! HE JUST MOVED TO TOWN!
AND HE'S THE FIRST PERSON TO CHALLENGE JUGHEAD'S BURGER EATING RECORD!
OKAY! THAT'S 18 BURGERS FOR KEVIN...
...AND 17 FOR JUGHEAD!
POP'S
R
R
2

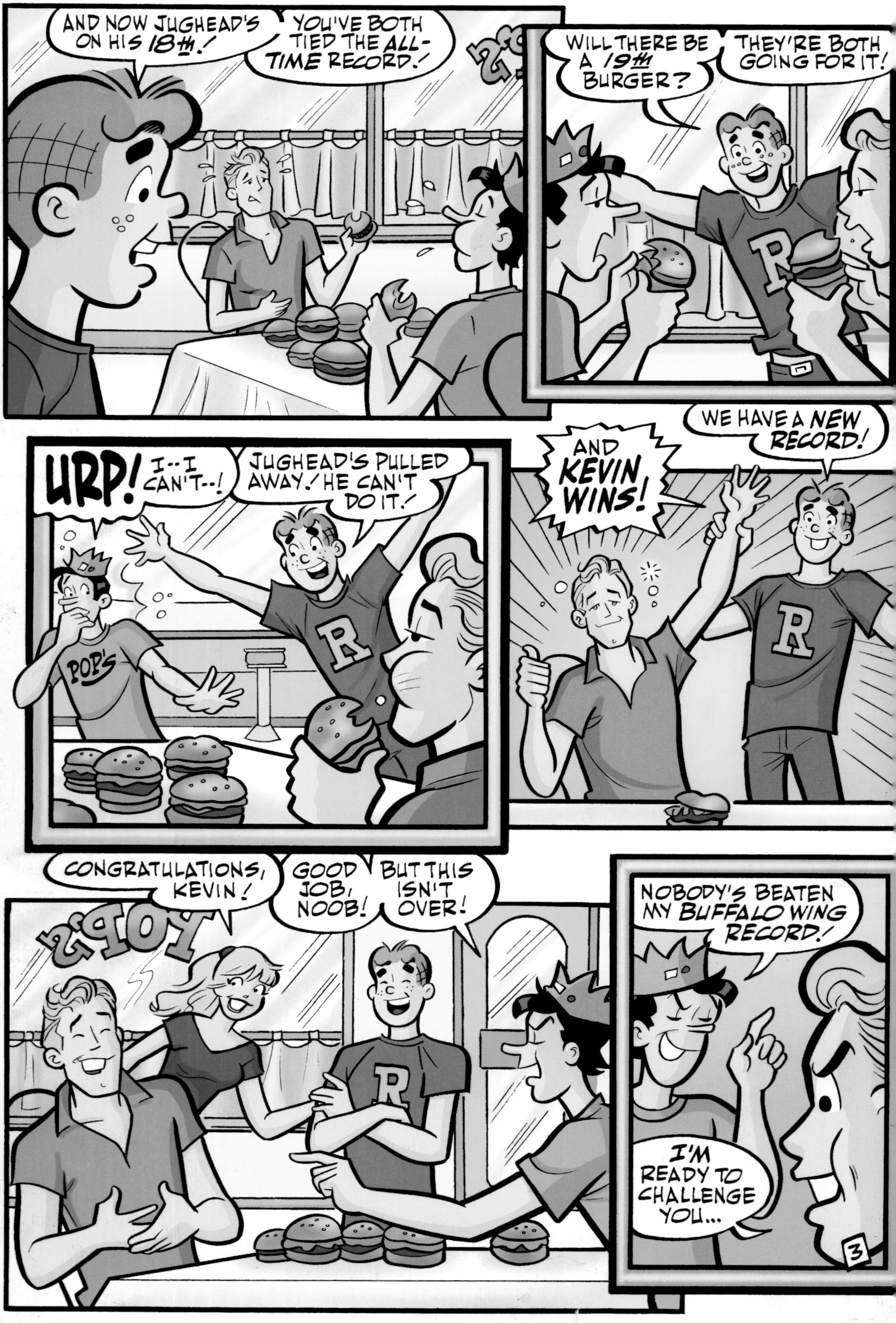

AND NOW JUGHEAD'S ON HIS 18th!
YOU'VE BOTH TIED THE ALL-TIME RECORD!
WILL THERE BE A 19th BURGER?
THEY'RE BOTH GOING FOR IT!
URP!
I--I CAN'T--!
JUGHEAD'S PULLED AWAY! HE CAN'T DO IT!
POP'S
AND KEVIN WINS!
WE HAVE A NEW RECORD!
CONGRATULATIONS, KEVIN!
GOOD JOB, NOOB!
BUT THIS ISN'T OVER!
POP'S
NOBODY'S BEATEN MY BUFFALO WING RECORD!
I'M READY TO CHALLENGE YOU...
3

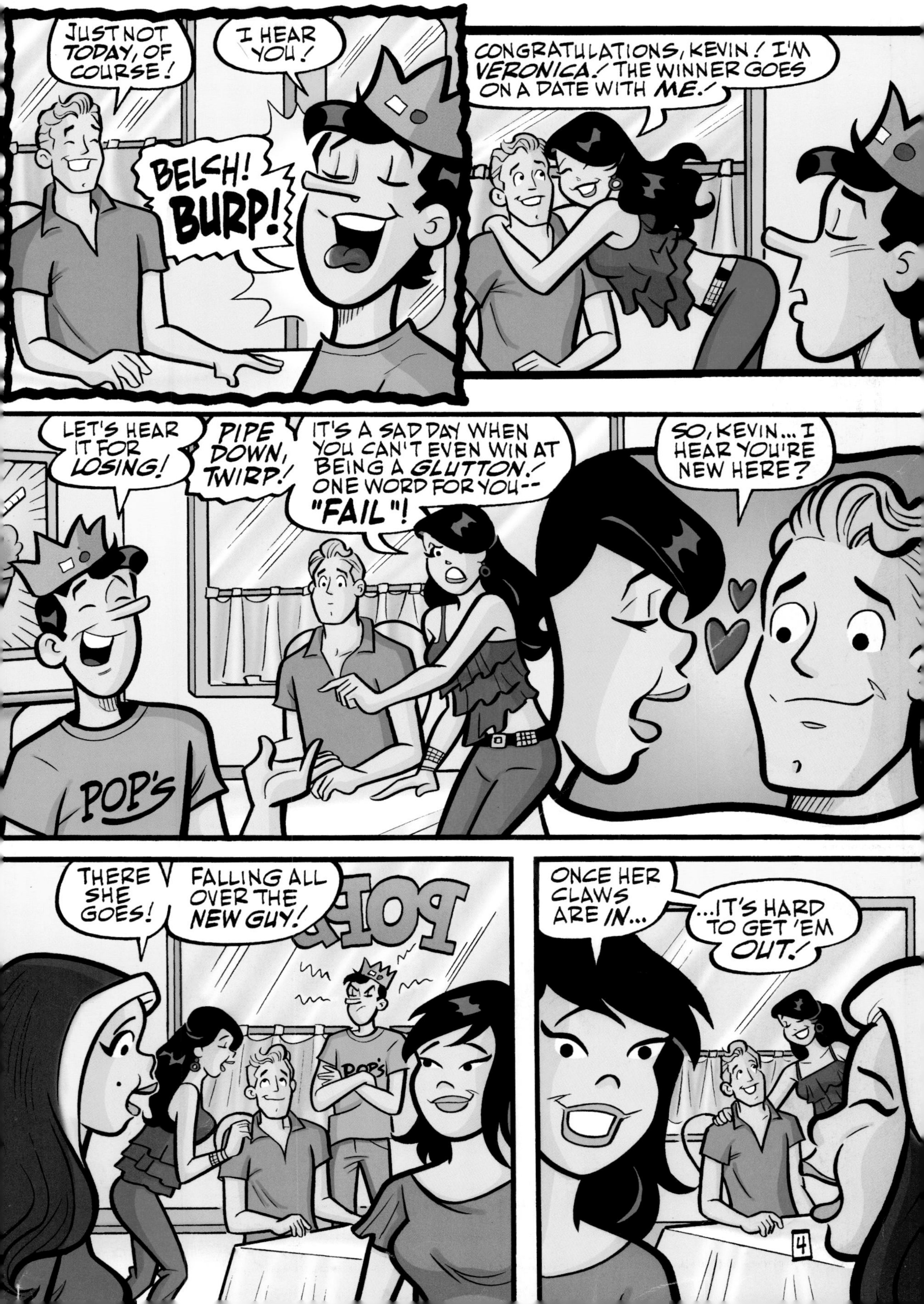
JUST NOT TODAY, OF COURSE!
I HEAR YOU!
BELCH! BURP!
CONGRATULATIONS, KEVIN! I'M VERONICA! THE WINNER GOES ON A DATE WITH ME!
LET'S HEAR IT FOR LOSING!
PIPE DOWN, TWIRP!
IT'S A SAD DAY WHEN YOU CAN'T EVEN WIN AT BEING A GLUTTON! ONE WORD FOR YOU-- "FAIL"!
SO, KEVIN... I HEAR YOU'RE NEW HERE?
THERE SHE GOES!
FALLING ALL OVER THE NEW GUY!
POP'S
POP'S
ONCE HER CLAWS ARE IN...
...IT'S HARD TO GET 'EM OUT!
4

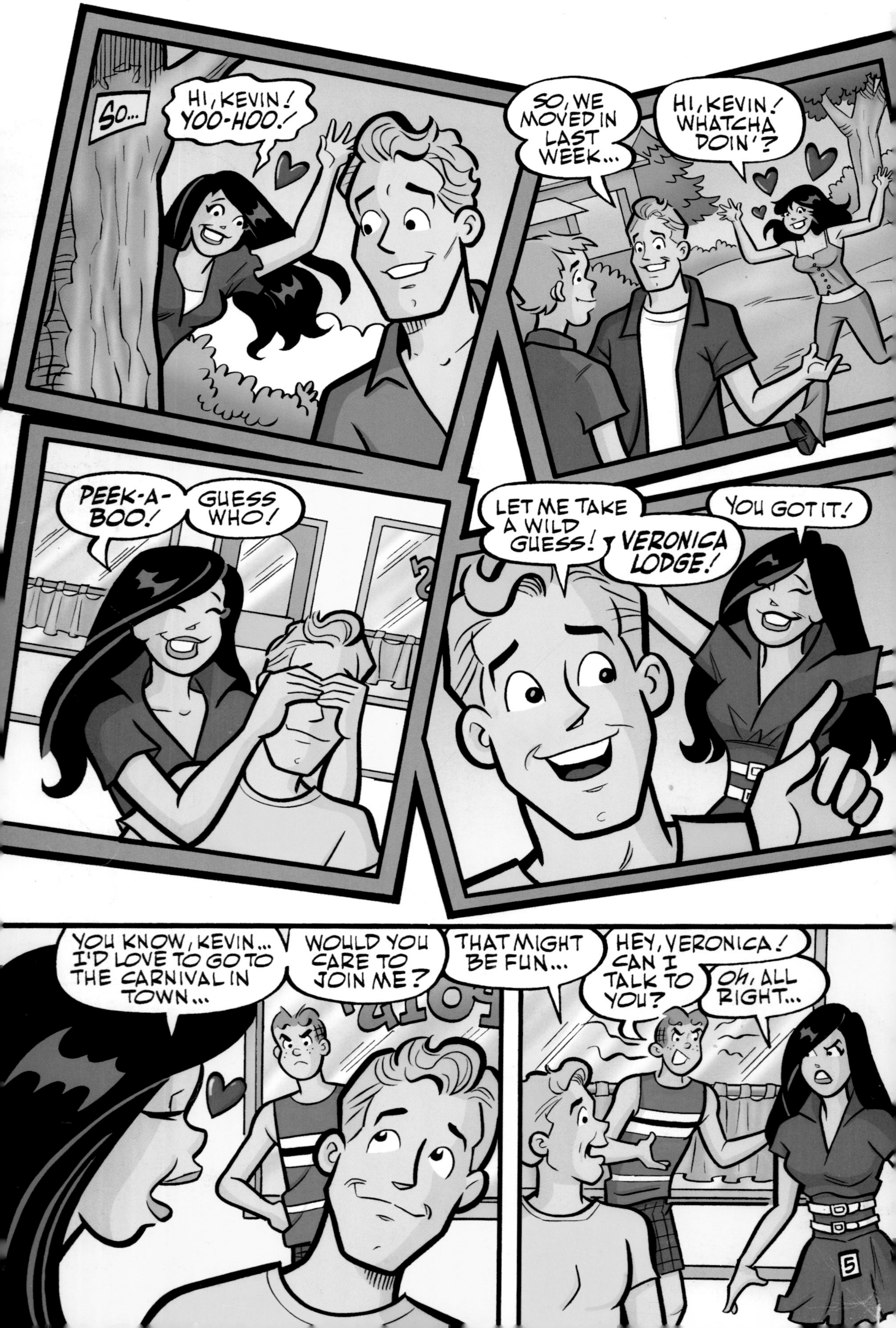

SO...
HI, KEVIN! YOO-HOO!
SO, WE MOVED IN LAST WEEK...
HI, KEVIN! WHATCHA DOIN'?
PEEK-A-BOO!
GUESS WHO!
LET ME TAKE A WILD GUESS!
VERONICA LODGE!
YOU GOT IT!
YOU KNOW, KEVIN... I'D LOVE TO GO TO THE CARNIVAL IN TOWN...
WOULD YOU CARE TO JOIN ME?
THAT MIGHT BE FUN...
HEY, VERONICA! CAN I TALK TO YOU?
OH, ALL RIGHT...
5

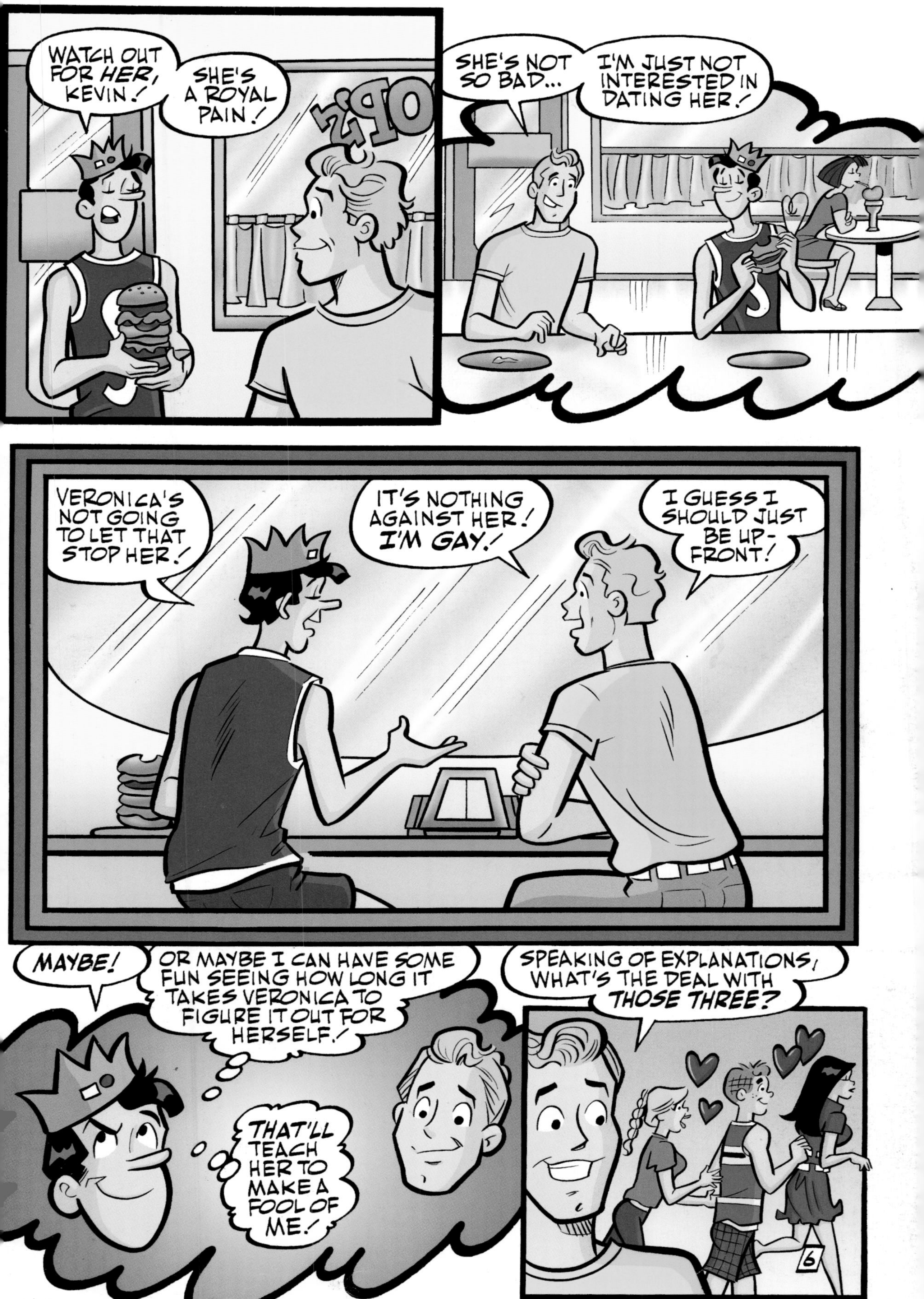
WATCH OUT FOR HER, KEVIN!
SHE'S A ROYAL PAIN!
POP'S
SHE'S NOT SO BAD...
I'M JUST NOT INTERESTED IN DATING HER!
VERONICA'S NOT GOING TO LET THAT STOP HER!
IT'S NOTHING AGAINST HER! I'M GAY!
I GUESS I SHOULD JUST BE UP-FRONT!
MAYBE!
OR MAYBE I CAN HAVE SOME FUN SEEING HOW LONG IT TAKES VERONICA TO FIGURE IT OUT FOR HERSELF!
THAT'LL TEACH HER TO MAKE A FOOL OF ME!
SPEAKING OF EXPLANATIONS, WHAT'S THE DEAL WITH THOSE THREE?
6

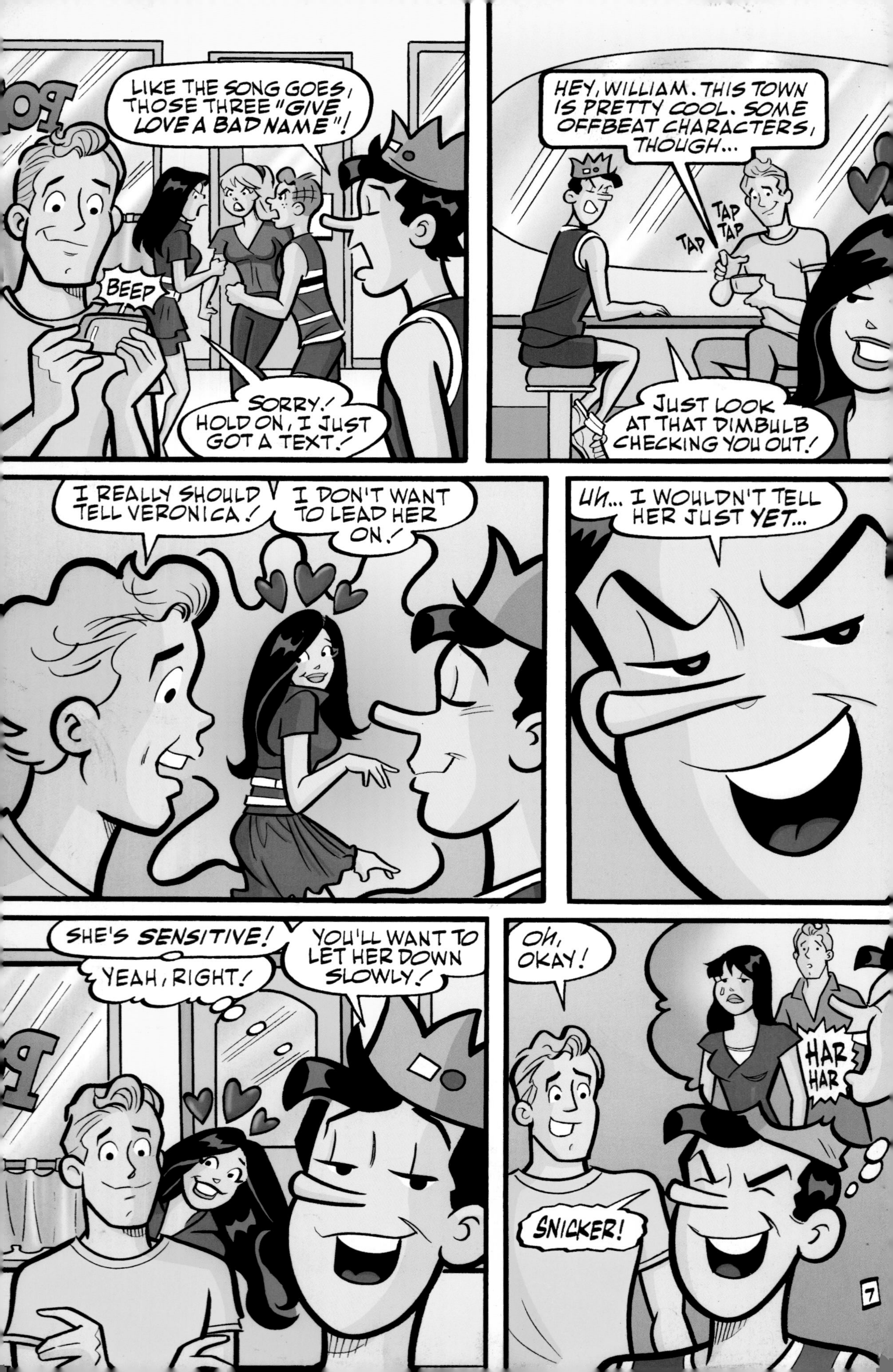
LIKE THE SONG GOES, THOSE THREE "GIVE LOVE A BAD NAME"!
BEEP
SORRY! HOLD ON, I JUST GOT A TEXT!
HEY, WILLIAM. THIS TOWN IS PRETTY COOL. SOME OFFBEAT CHARACTERS, THOUGH...
TAP TAP TAP
JUST LOOK AT THAT DIMBULB CHECKING YOU OUT!
I REALLY SHOULD TELL VERONICA!
I DON'T WANT TO LEAD HER ON!
UH... I WOULDN'T TELL HER JUST YET...
SHE'S SENSITIVE!
YEAH, RIGHT!
YOU'LL WANT TO LET HER DOWN SLOWLY!
OH, OKAY!
HAR HAR
SNICKER!
7

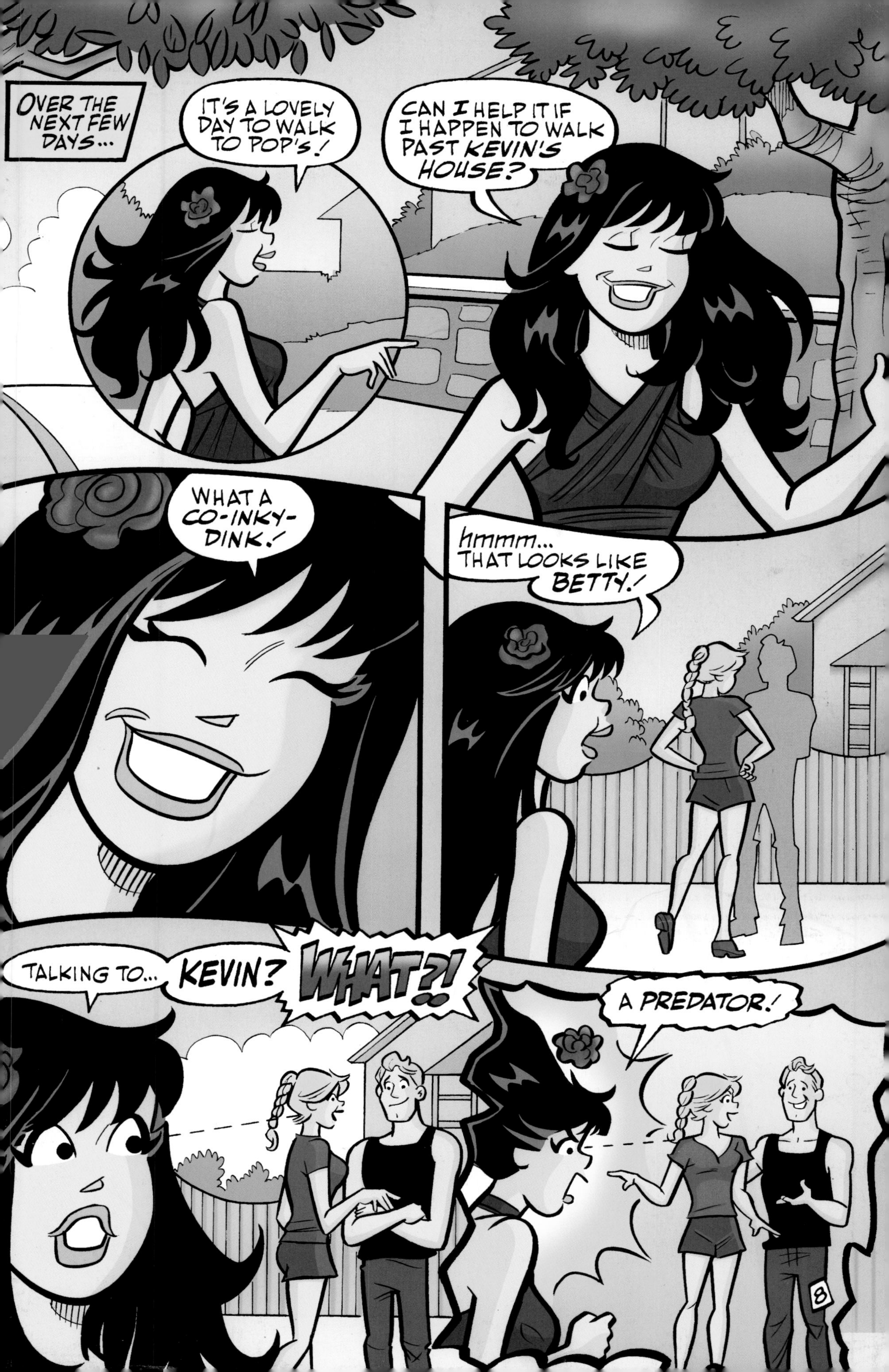
OVER THE NEXT FEW DAYS...
IT'S A LOVELY DAY TO WALK TO POP'S!
CAN I HELP IT IF I HAPPEN TO WALK PAST KEVIN'S HOUSE?
WHAT A CO-INKY-DINK!
hmmm... THAT LOOKS LIKE BETTY!
TALKING TO... KEVIN?
WHAT?!
A PREDATOR!
8

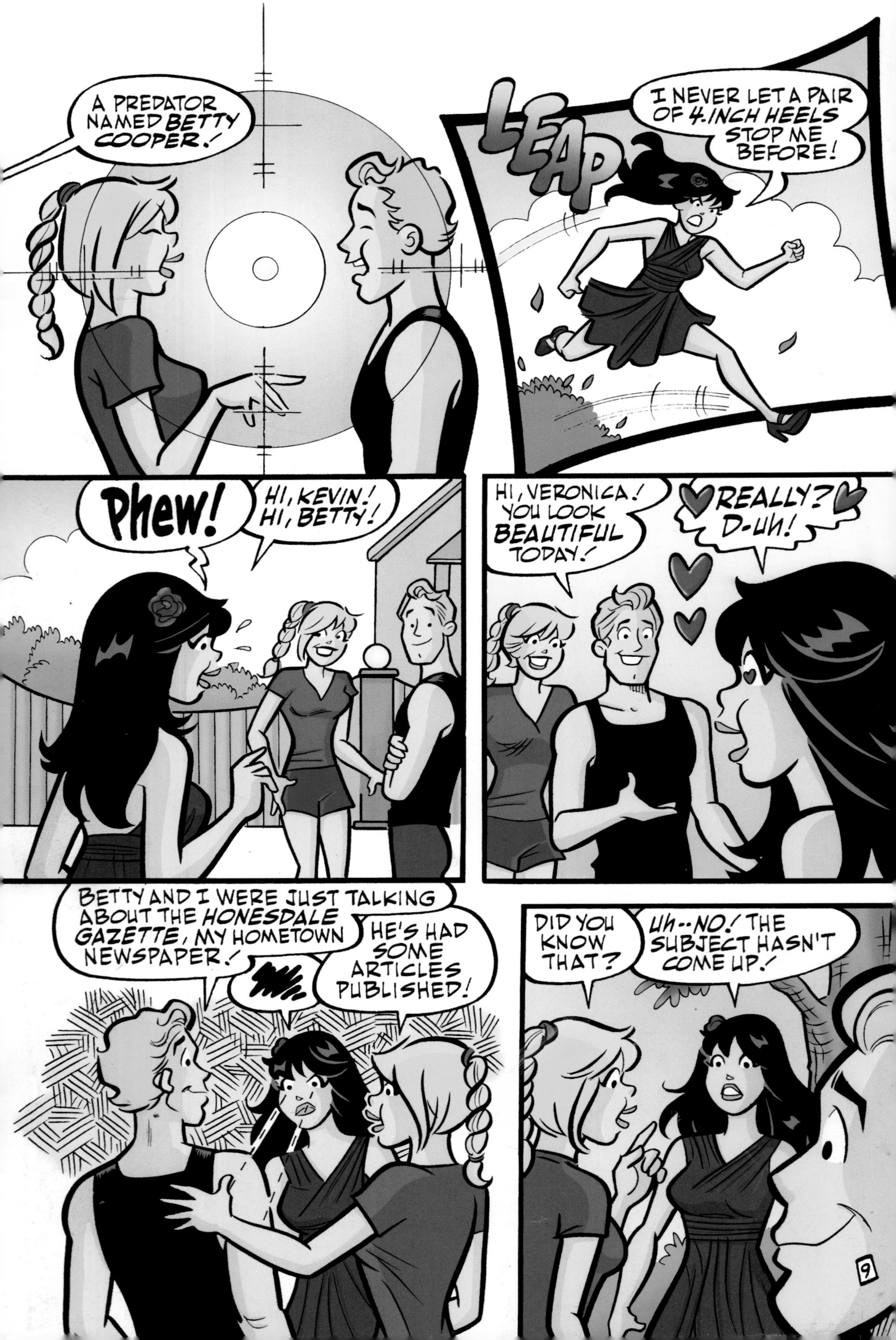
A PREDATOR NAMED BETTY COOPER!
LEAP
I NEVER LET A PAIR OF 4-INCH HEELS STOP ME BEFORE!
Phew!
HI, KEVIN! HI, BETTY!
HI, VERONICA! YOU LOOK BEAUTIFUL TODAY!
REALLY? D-UH!
BETTY AND I WERE JUST TALKING ABOUT THE HONESDALE GAZETTE, MY HOMETOWN NEWSPAPER!
HE'S HAD SOME ARTICLES PUBLISHED!
DID YOU KNOW THAT?
UH--NO! THE SUBJECT HASN'T COME UP!
9

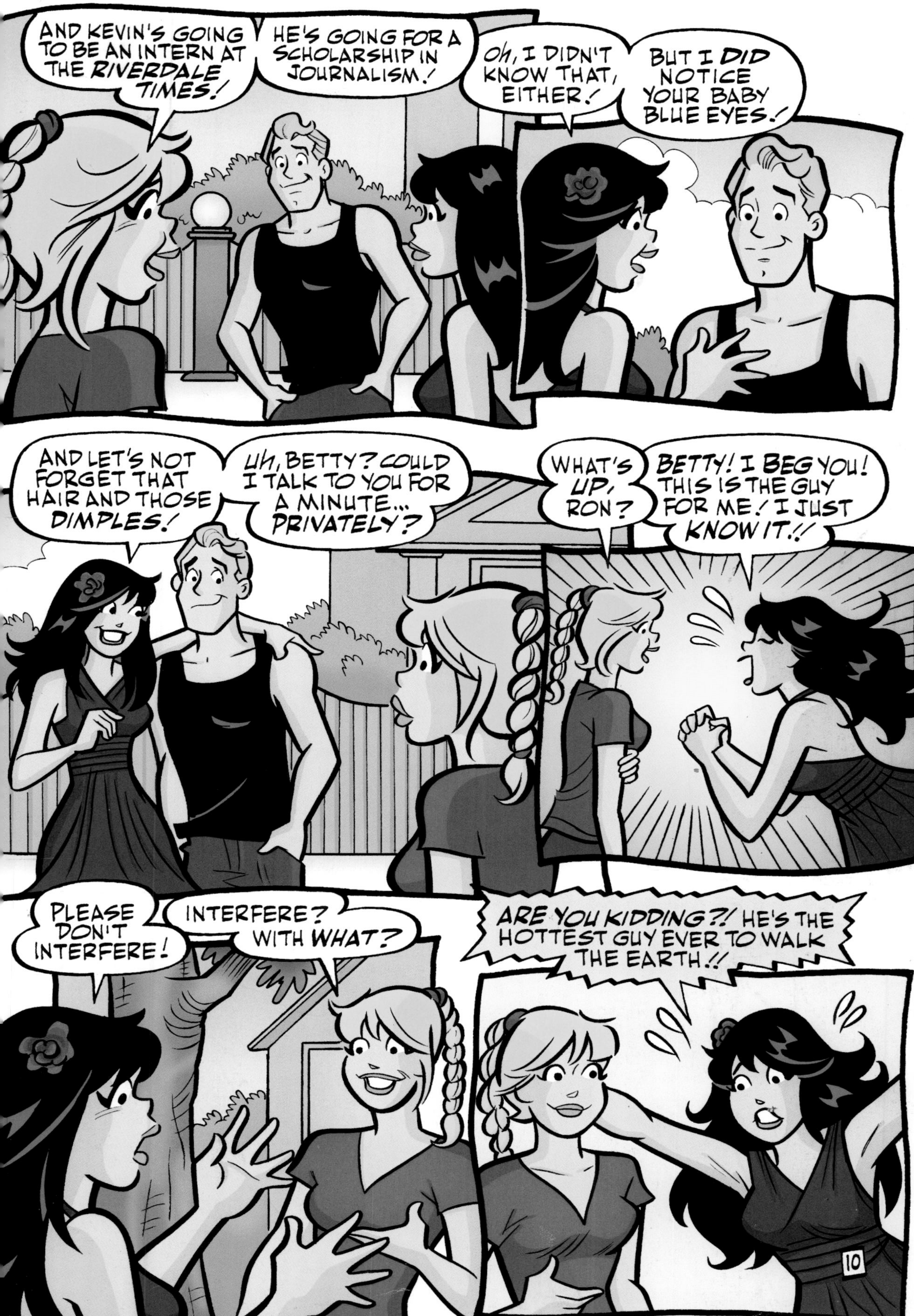
AND KEVIN'S GOING TO BE AN INTERN AT THE RIVERDALE TIMES!
HE'S GOING FOR A SCHOLARSHIP IN JOURNALISM!
OH, I DIDN'T KNOW THAT, EITHER!
BUT I DID NOTICE YOUR BABY BLUE EYES!
AND LET'S NOT FORGET THAT HAIR AND THOSE DIMPLES!
UH, BETTY? COULD I TALK TO YOU FOR A MINUTE... PRIVATELY?
WHAT'S UP, RON?
BETTY! I BEG YOU! THIS IS THE GUY FOR ME! I JUST KNOW IT!!
PLEASE DON'T INTERFERE!
INTERFERE? WITH WHAT?
ARE YOU KIDDING?! HE'S THE HOTTEST GUY EVER TO WALK THE EARTH!!
10

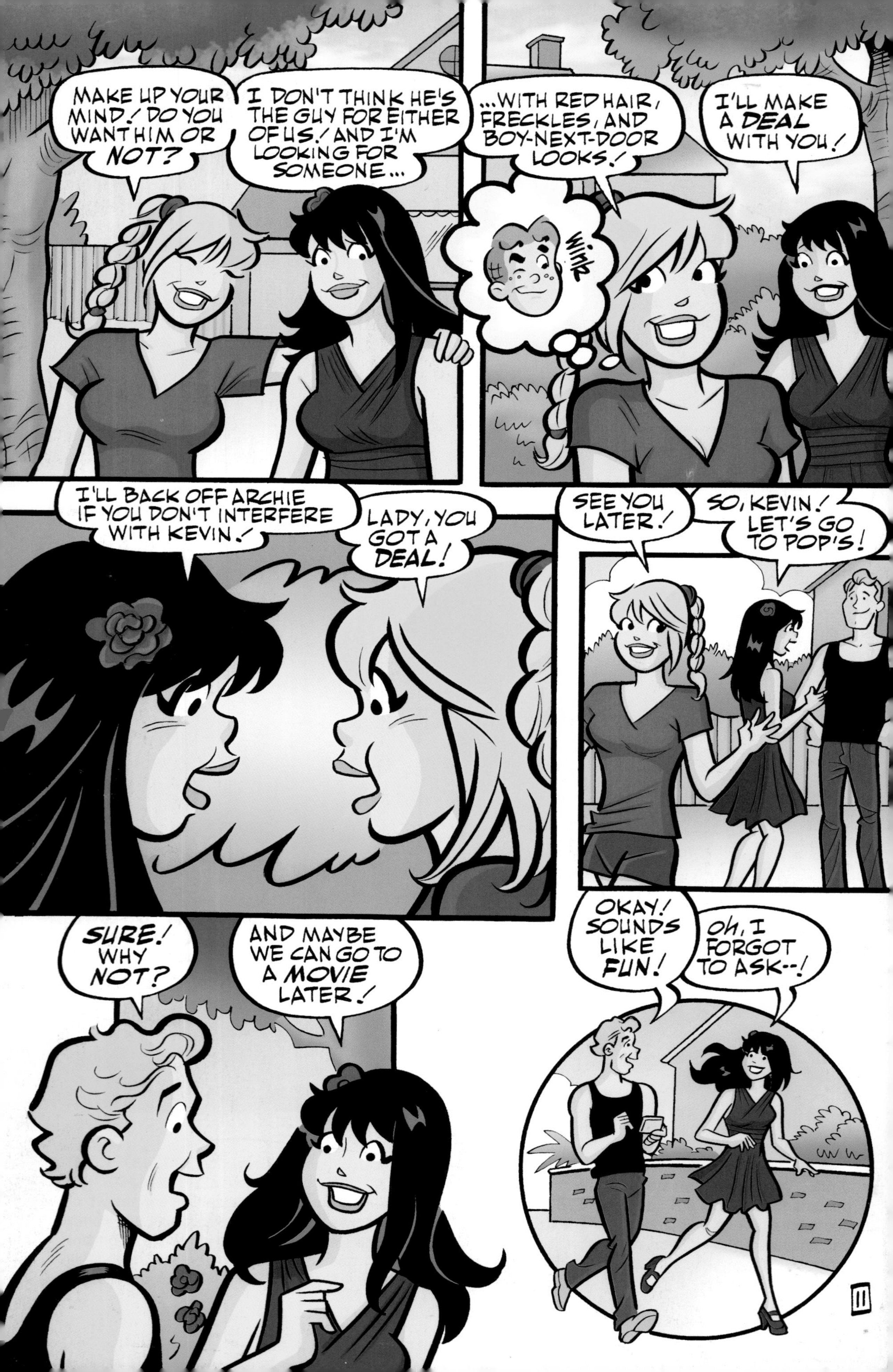
MAKE UP YOUR MIND! DO YOU WANT HIM OR NOT?
I DON'T THINK HE'S THE GUY FOR EITHER OF US! AND I'M LOOKING FOR SOMEONE...
...WITH RED HAIR, FRECKLES, AND BOY-NEXT-DOOR LOOKS!
WINK
I'LL MAKE A DEAL WITH YOU!
I'LL BACK OFF ARCHIE IF YOU DON'T INTERFERE WITH KEVIN!
LADY, YOU GOT A DEAL!
SEE YOU LATER!
SO, KEVIN! LET'S GO TO POP'S!
SURE! WHY NOT?
AND MAYBE WE CAN GO TO A MOVIE LATER!
OKAY! SOUNDS LIKE FUN!
Oh, I FORGOT TO ASK--!
11

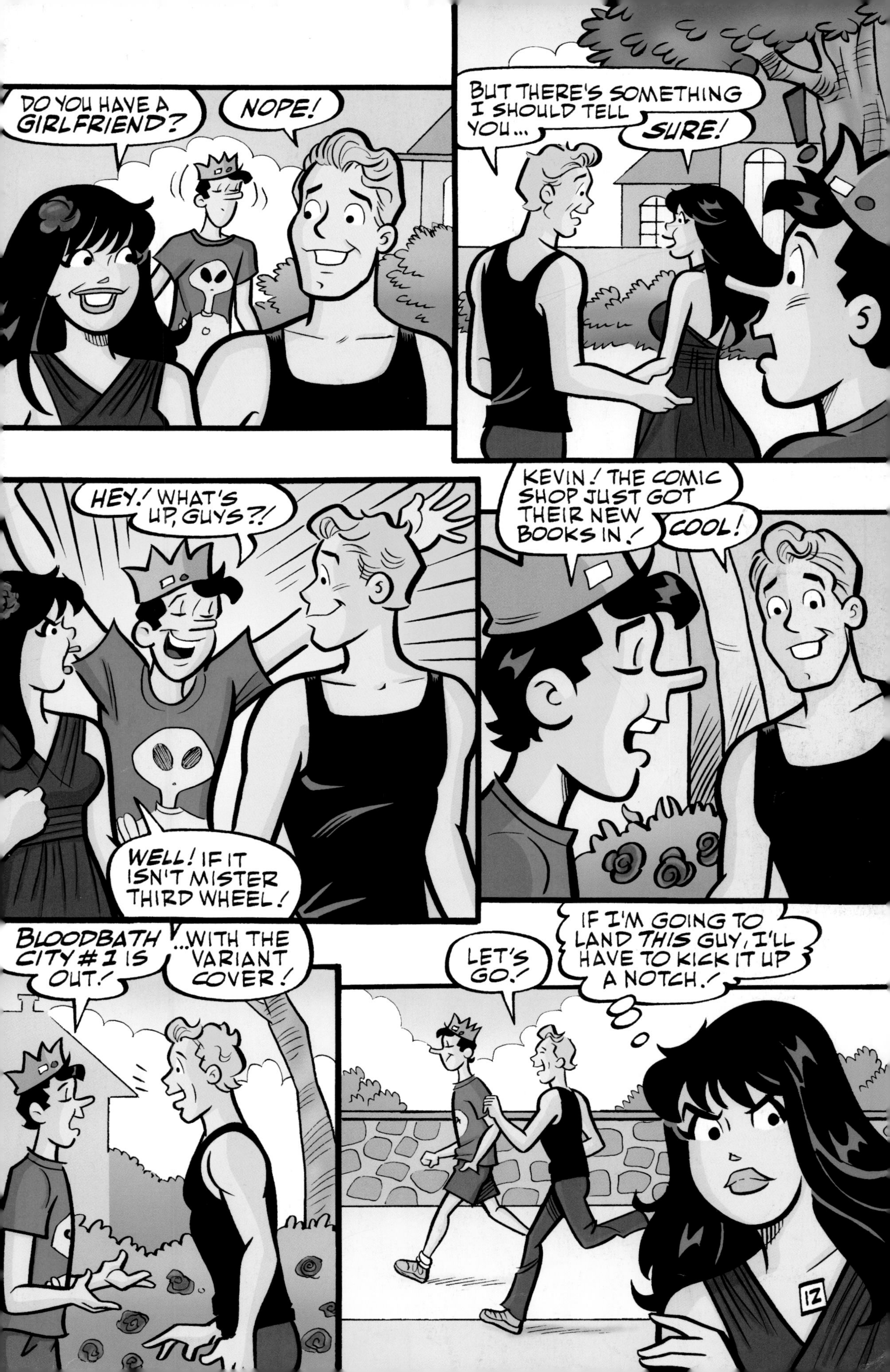
DO YOU HAVE A GIRLFRIEND?
NOPE!
BUT THERE'S SOMETHING I SHOULD TELL YOU...
SURE!
HEY! WHAT'S UP, GUYS?!
WELL! IF IT ISN'T MISTER THIRD WHEEL!
KEVIN! THE COMIC SHOP JUST GOT THEIR NEW BOOKS IN!
COOL!
BLOODBATH CITY #1 IS OUT!
...WITH THE VARIANT COVER!
LET'S GO!
IF I'M GOING TO LAND THIS GUY, I'LL HAVE TO KICK IT UP A NOTCH!
12

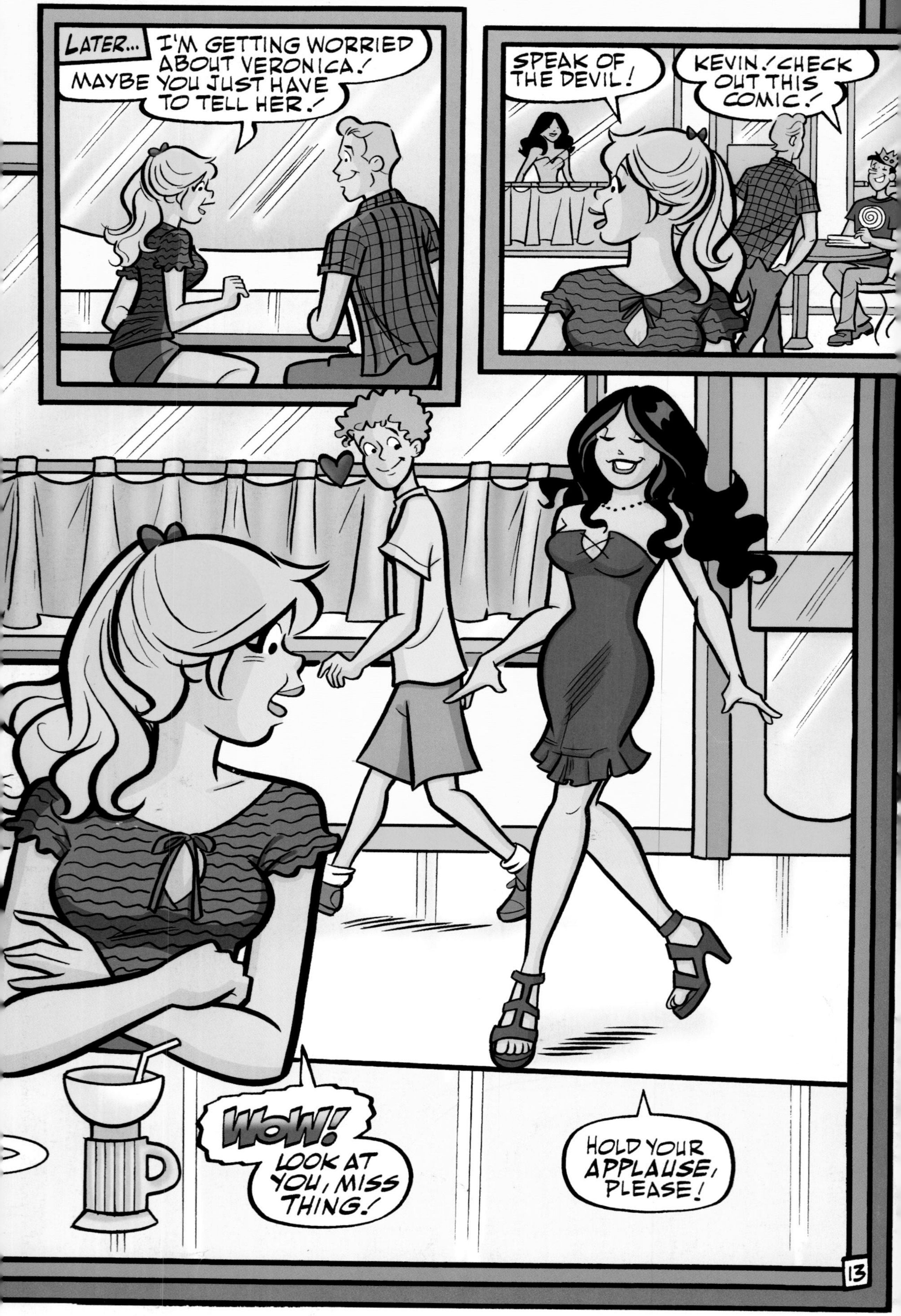
LATER...
I'M GETTING WORRIED ABOUT VERONICA! MAYBE YOU JUST HAVE TO TELL HER!
SPEAK OF THE DEVIL!
KEVIN! CHECK OUT THIS COMIC!
WOW! LOOK AT YOU, MISS THING!
HOLD YOUR APPLAUSE, PLEASE!

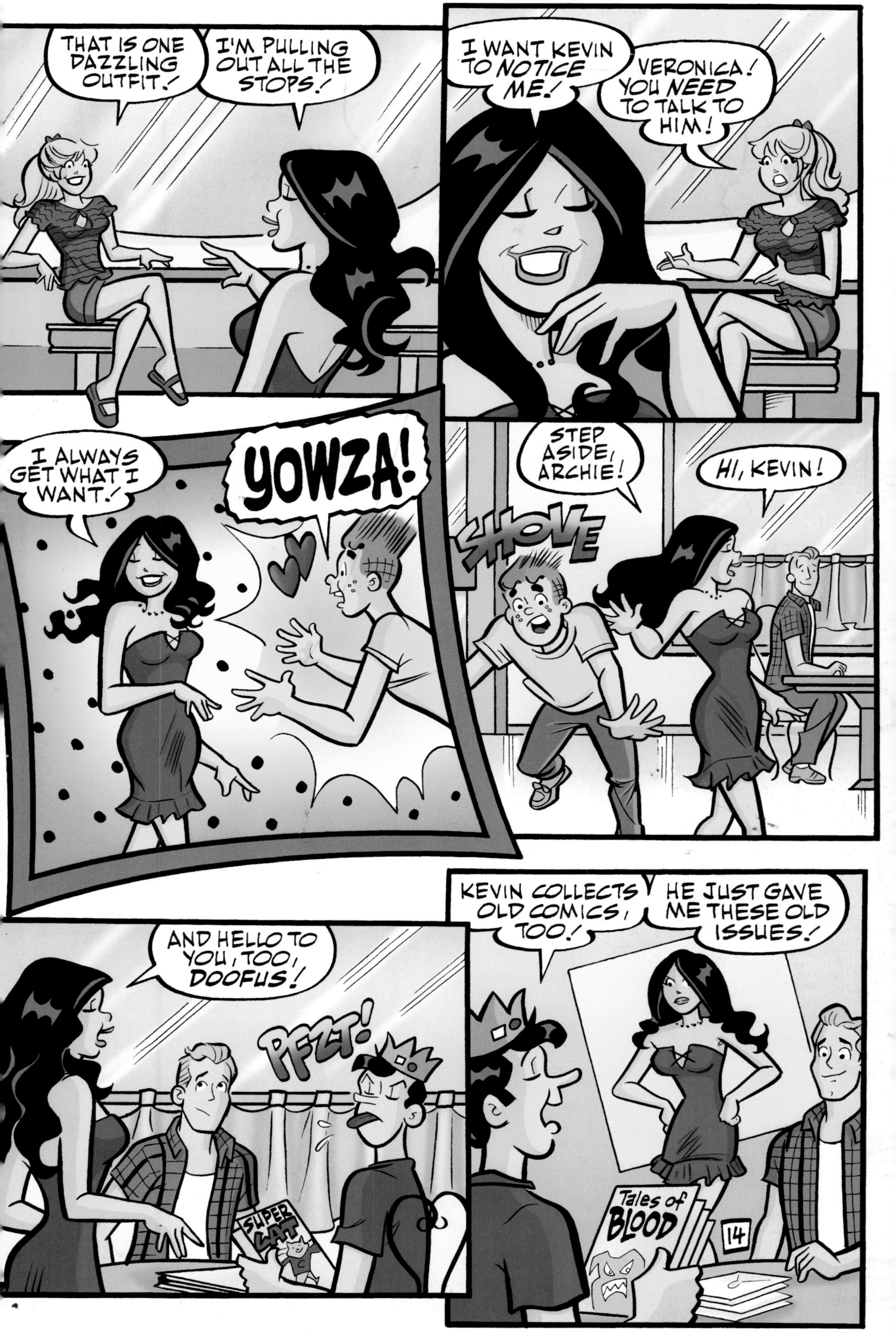
THAT IS ONE DAZZLING OUTFIT!
I'M PULLING OUT ALL THE STOPS!
I WANT KEVIN TO NOTICE ME!
VERONICA! YOU NEED TO TALK TO HIM!
I ALWAYS GET WHAT I WANT!
YOWZA!
STEP ASIDE, ARCHIE!
SHOVE
HI, KEVIN!
AND HELLO TO YOU, TOO, DOOFUS!
PFZZT!
SUPER CAT
KEVIN COLLECTS OLD COMICS, TOO!
HE JUST GAVE ME THESE OLD ISSUES!
Tales of BLOOD
14

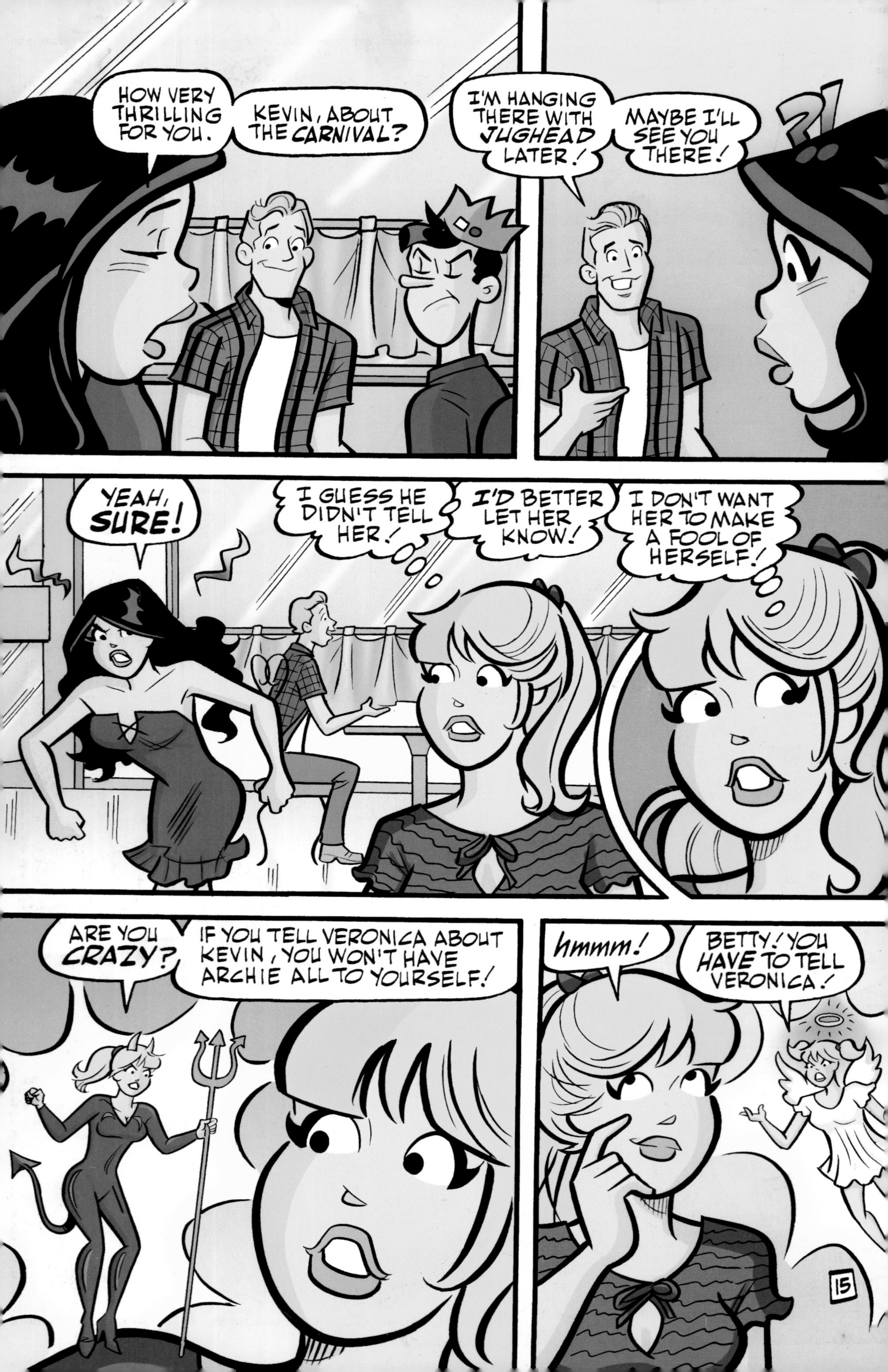
HOW VERY THRILLING FOR YOU.
KEVIN, ABOUT THE CARNIVAL?
I'M HANGING THERE WITH JUGHEAD LATER!
MAYBE I'LL SEE YOU THERE!
?!
YEAH, SURE!
I GUESS HE DIDN'T TELL HER!
I'D BETTER LET HER KNOW!
I DON'T WANT HER TO MAKE A FOOL OF HERSELF!
ARE YOU CRAZY?
IF YOU TELL VERONICA ABOUT KEVIN, YOU WON'T HAVE ARCHIE ALL TO YOURSELF!
hmmm!
BETTY! YOU HAVE TO TELL VERONICA!
15

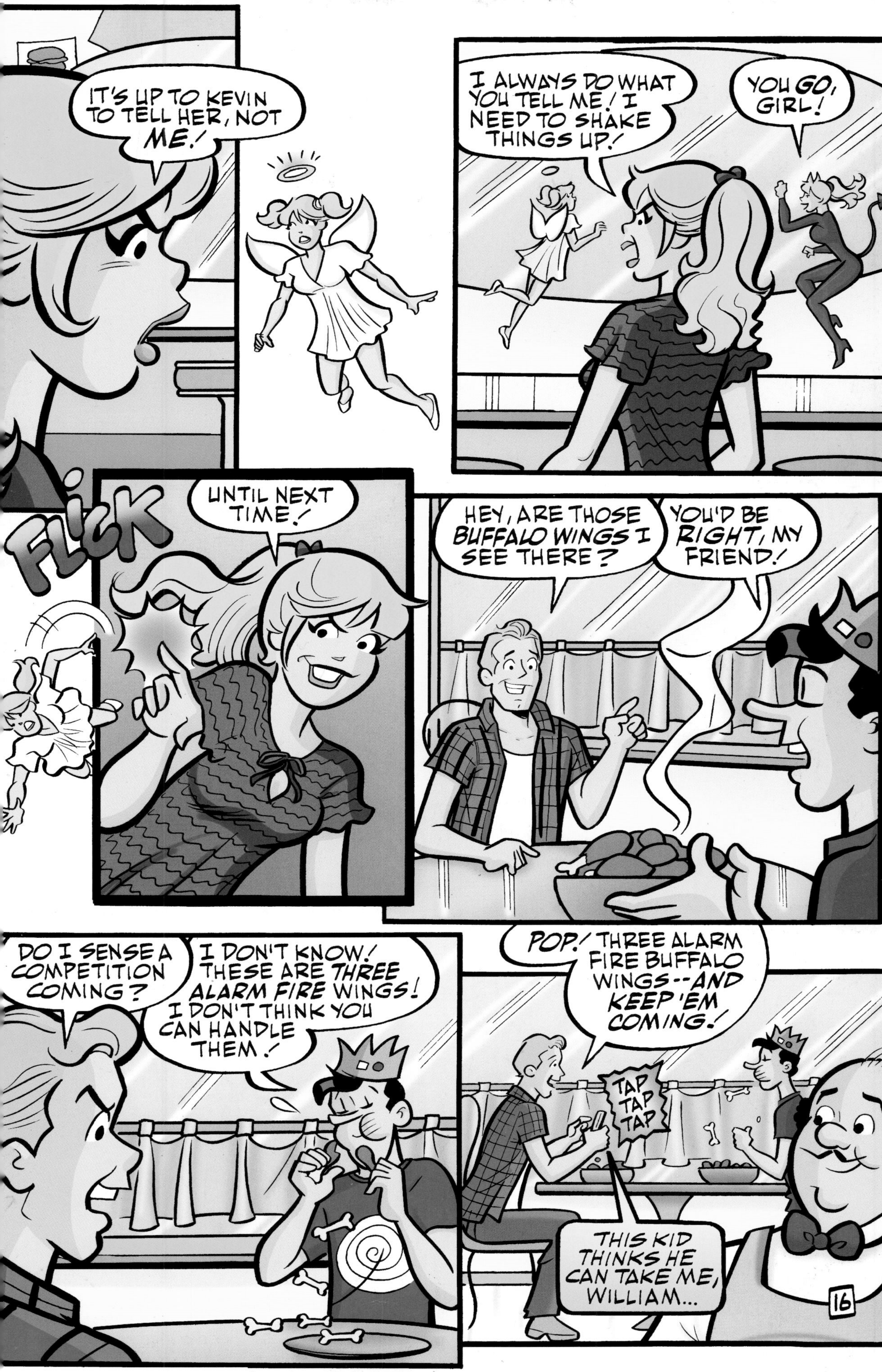
IT'S UP TO KEVIN TO TELL HER, NOT ME!
I ALWAYS DO WHAT YOU TELL ME! I NEED TO SHAKE THINGS UP!
YOU GO, GIRL!
FLICK
UNTIL NEXT TIME!
HEY, ARE THOSE BUFFALO WINGS I SEE THERE?
YOU'D BE RIGHT, MY FRIEND!
DO I SENSE A COMPETITION COMING?
I DON'T KNOW! THESE ARE THREE ALARM FIRE WINGS! I DON'T THINK YOU CAN HANDLE THEM!
POP! THREE ALARM FIRE BUFFALO WINGS--AND KEEP 'EM COMING!
TAP TAP TAP
THIS KID THINKS HE CAN TAKE ME, WILLIAM...
16

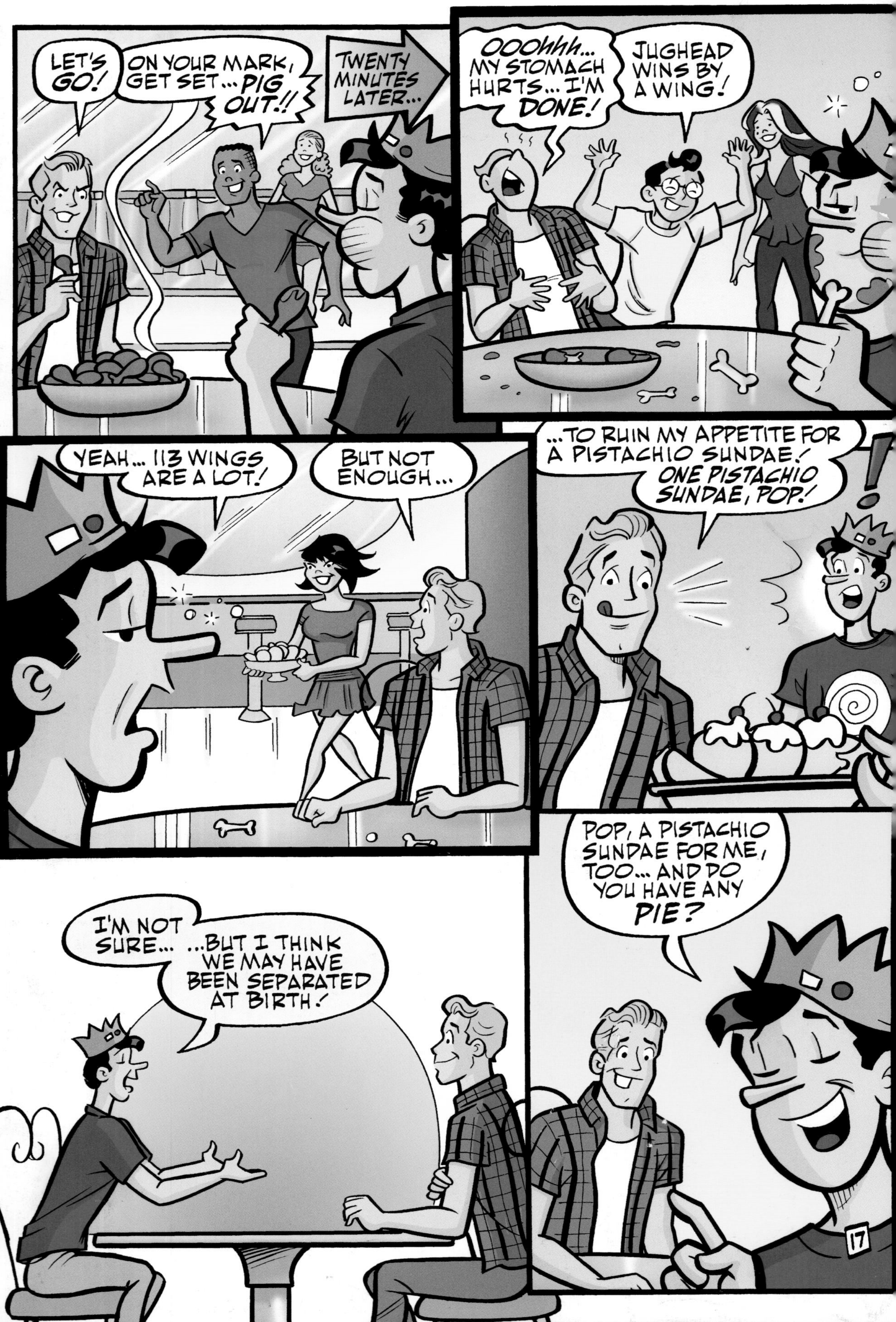
LET'S GO!
ON YOUR MARK, GET SET... PIG OUT!!
TWENTY MINUTES LATER...
OOOhhh... MY STOMACH HURTS... I'M DONE!
JUGHEAD WINS BY A WING!
YEAH... 113 WINGS ARE A LOT!
BUT NOT ENOUGH...
...TO RUIN MY APPETITE FOR A PISTACHIO SUNDAE!
ONE PISTACHIO SUNDAE, POP!
I'M NOT SURE...
...BUT I THINK WE MAY HAVE BEEN SEPARATED AT BIRTH!
POP, A PISTACHIO SUNDAE FOR ME, TOO... AND DO YOU HAVE ANY PIE?
17

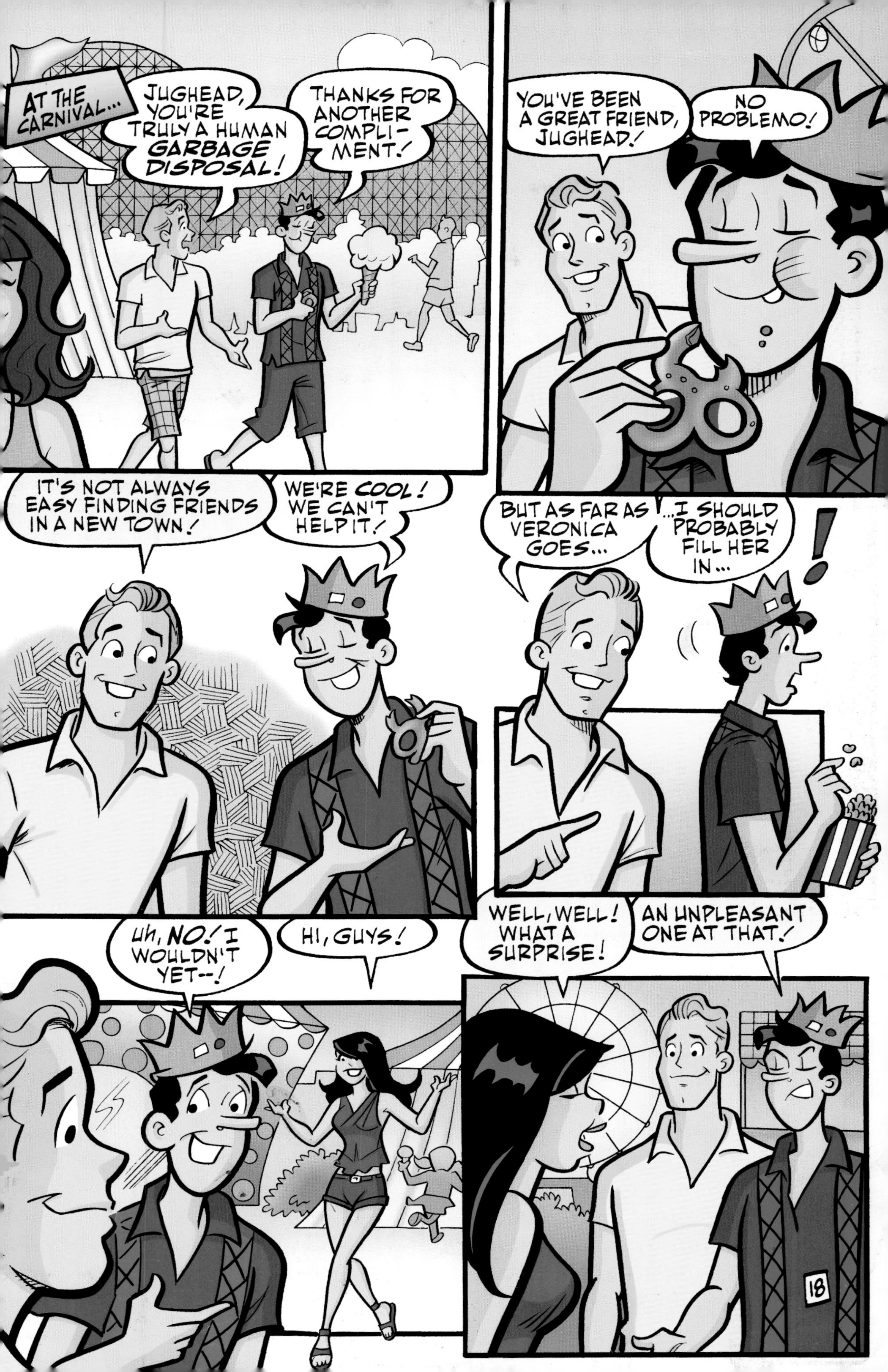
AT THE CARNIVAL...
JUGHEAD, YOU'RE TRULY A HUMAN GARBAGE DISPOSAL!
THANKS FOR ANOTHER COMPLI-MENT!
YOU'VE BEEN A GREAT FRIEND, JUGHEAD!
NO PROBLEMO!
IT'S NOT ALWAYS EASY FINDING FRIENDS IN A NEW TOWN!
WE'RE COOL! WE CAN'T HELP IT!
BUT AS FAR AS VERONICA GOES...
...I SHOULD PROBABLY FILL HER IN...
!
UH, NO! I WOULDN'T YET--!
HI, GUYS!
WELL, WELL! WHAT A SURPRISE!
AN UNPLEASANT ONE AT THAT!
18

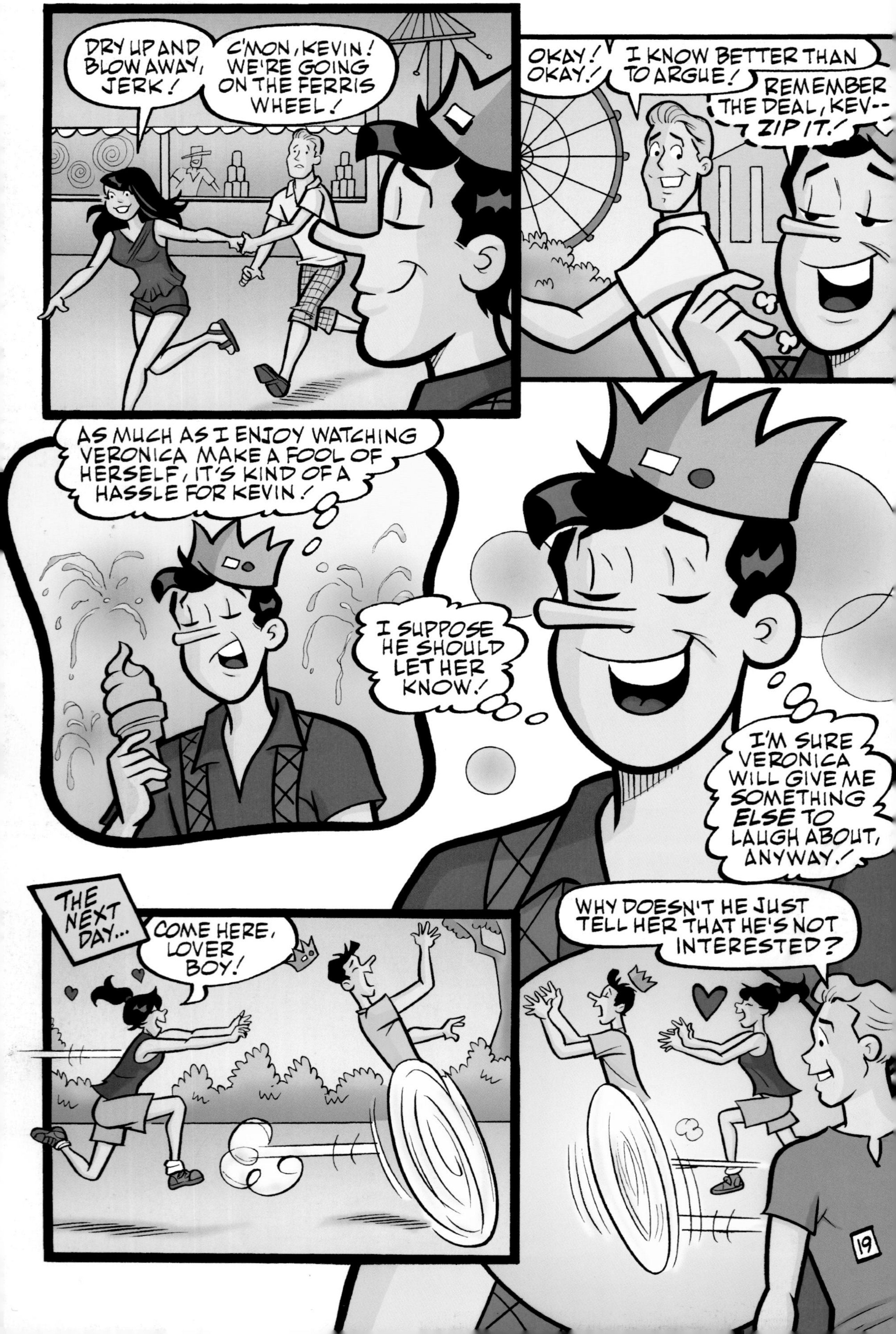

DRY UP AND BLOW AWAY, JERK!
C'MON, KEVIN! WE'RE GOING ON THE FERRIS WHEEL!
OKAY! OKAY!
I KNOW BETTER THAN TO ARGUE!
REMEMBER THE DEAL, KEV-- ZIP IT!
AS MUCH AS I ENJOY WATCHING VERONICA MAKE A FOOL OF HERSELF, IT'S KIND OF A HASSLE FOR KEVIN!
I SUPPOSE HE SHOULD LET HER KNOW!
I'M SURE VERONICA WILL GIVE ME SOMETHING ELSE TO LAUGH ABOUT, ANYWAY!
THE NEXT DAY...
COME HERE, LOVER BOY!
WHY DOESN'T HE JUST TELL HER THAT HE'S NOT INTERESTED?

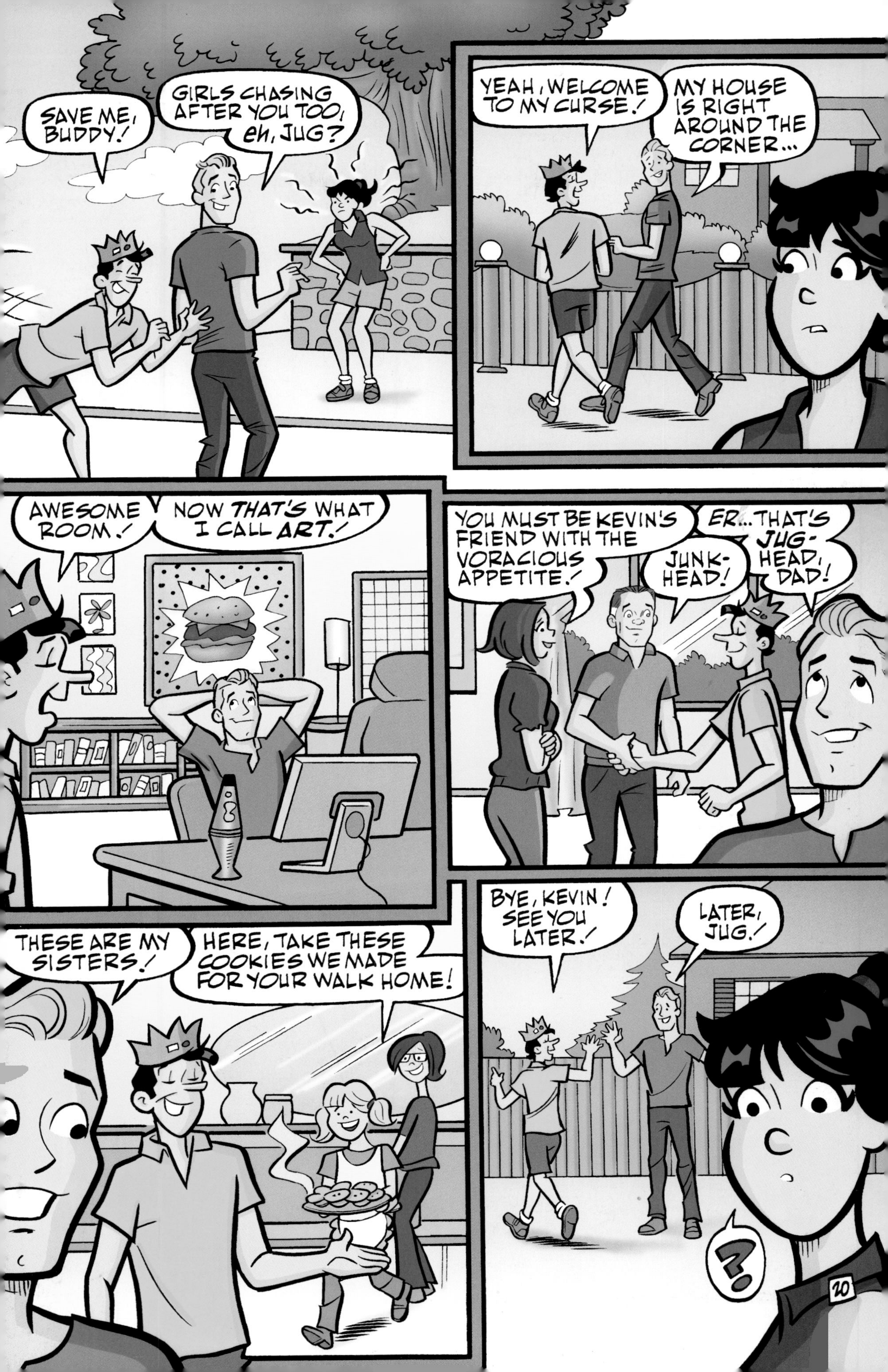
SAVE ME, BUDDY!
GIRLS CHASING AFTER YOU TOO, eh, JUG?
YEAH, WELCOME TO MY CURSE!
MY HOUSE IS RIGHT AROUND THE CORNER...
AWESOME ROOM!
NOW THAT'S WHAT I CALL ART!
YOU MUST BE KEVIN'S FRIEND WITH THE VORACIOUS APPETITE!
JUNK-HEAD!
ER...THAT'S JUG-HEAD, DAD!
THESE ARE MY SISTERS!
HERE, TAKE THESE COOKIES WE MADE FOR YOUR WALK HOME!
BYE, KEVIN! SEE YOU LATER!
LATER, JUG!
?
20

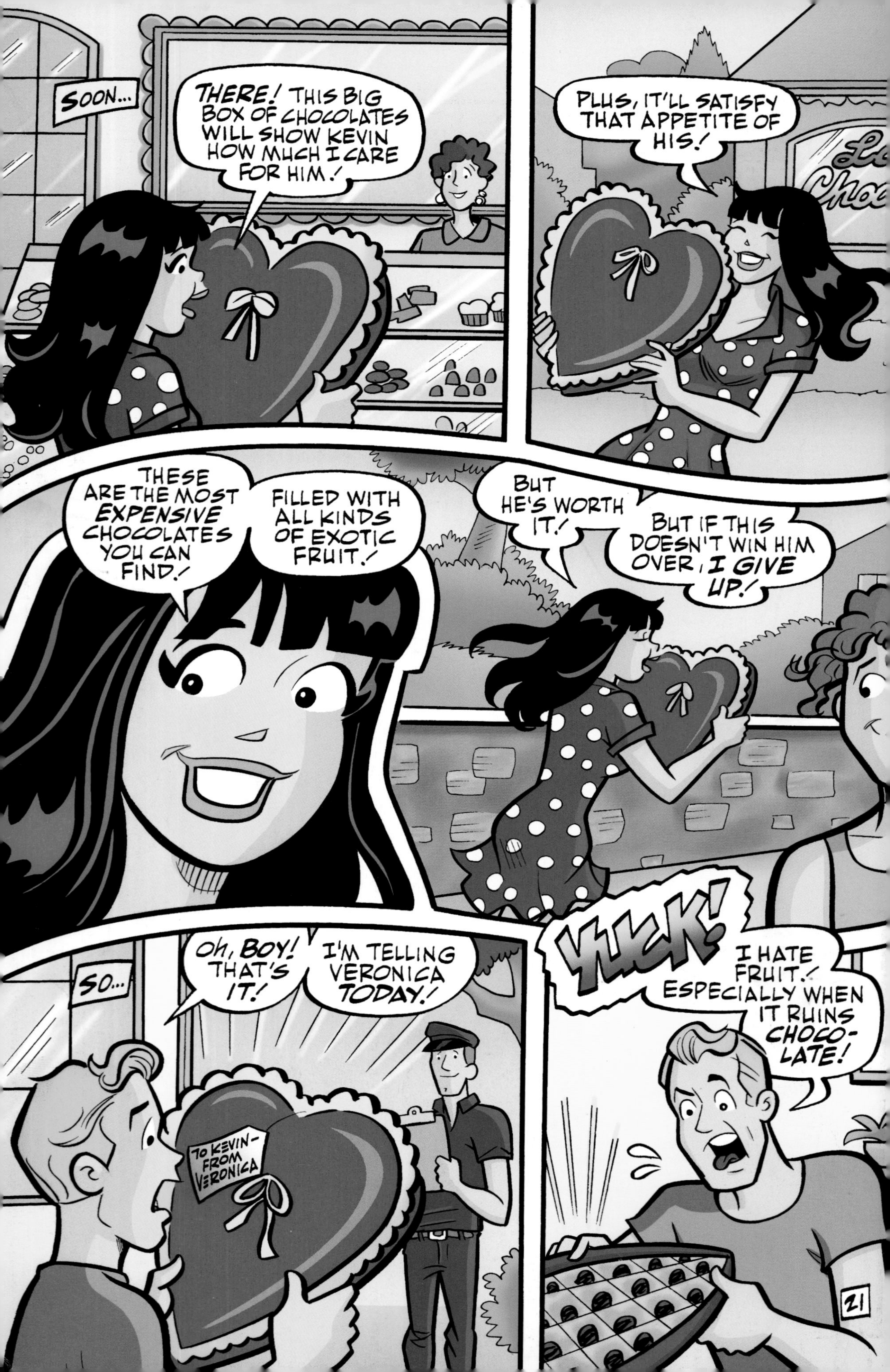
SOON...
THERE! THIS BIG BOX OF CHOCOLATES WILL SHOW KEVIN HOW MUCH I CARE FOR HIM!
PLUS, IT'LL SATISFY THAT APPETITE OF HIS!
THESE ARE THE MOST EXPENSIVE CHOCOLATES YOU CAN FIND!
FILLED WITH ALL KINDS OF EXOTIC FRUIT!
BUT HE'S WORTH IT!
BUT IF THIS DOESN'T WIN HIM OVER, I GIVE UP!
SO...
OH, BOY! THAT'S IT!
I'M TELLING VERONICA TODAY!
TO KEVIN- FROM VERONICA
YUCK!
I HATE FRUIT! ESPECIALLY WHEN IT RUINS CHOCO-LATE!

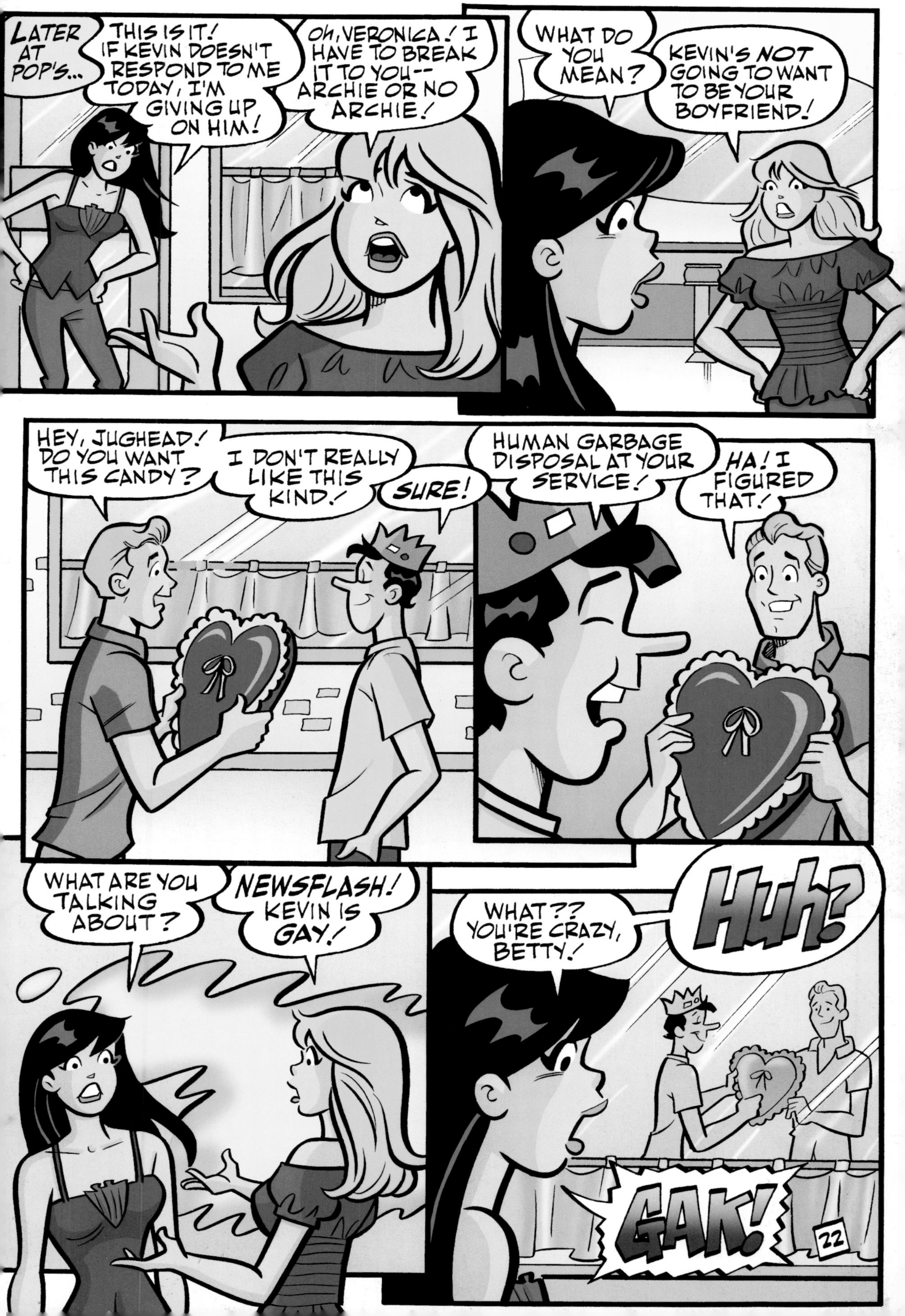
LATER AT POP'S...
THIS IS IT! IF KEVIN DOESN'T RESPOND TO ME TODAY, I'M GIVING UP ON HIM!
OH, VERONICA! I HAVE TO BREAK IT TO YOU-- ARCHIE OR NO ARCHIE!
WHAT DO YOU MEAN?
KEVIN'S NOT GOING TO WANT TO BE YOUR BOYFRIEND!
HEY, JUGHEAD! DO YOU WANT THIS CANDY?
I DON'T REALLY LIKE THIS KIND!
SURE!
HUMAN GARBAGE DISPOSAL AT YOUR SERVICE!
HA! I FIGURED THAT!
WHAT ARE YOU TALKING ABOUT?
NEWSFLASH! KEVIN IS GAY!
WHAT?? YOU'RE CRAZY, BETTY!
Huh?
GAK!
22

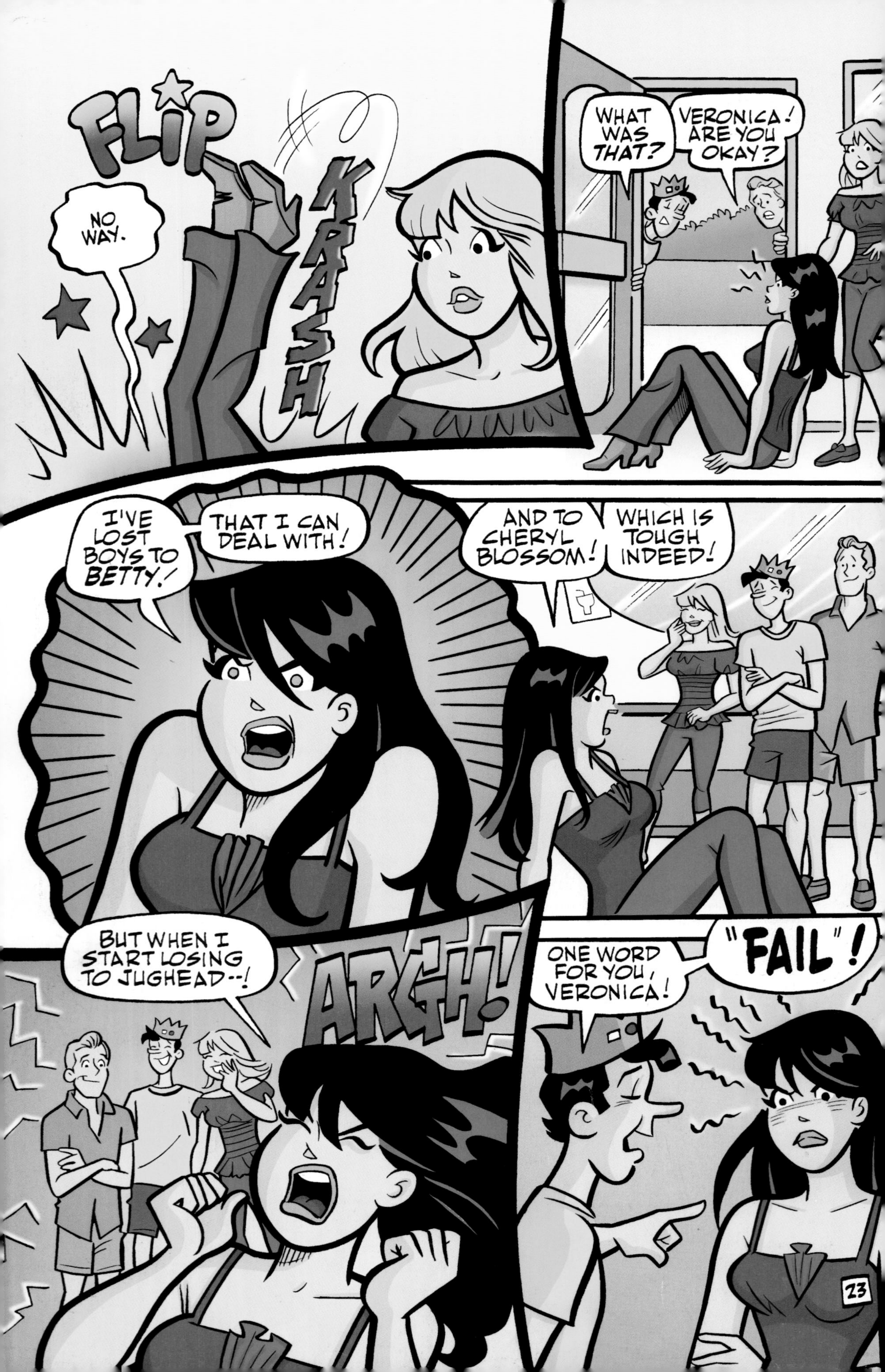
FLIP
NO WAY.
KRASH
WHAT WAS THAT?
VERONICA! ARE YOU OKAY?
I'VE LOST BOYS TO BETTY!
THAT I CAN DEAL WITH!
AND TO CHERYL BLOSSOM!
WHICH IS TOUGH INDEED!
BUT WHEN I START LOSING TO JUGHEAD--!
ARGH!
ONE WORD FOR YOU, VERONICA!
"FAIL"!
23

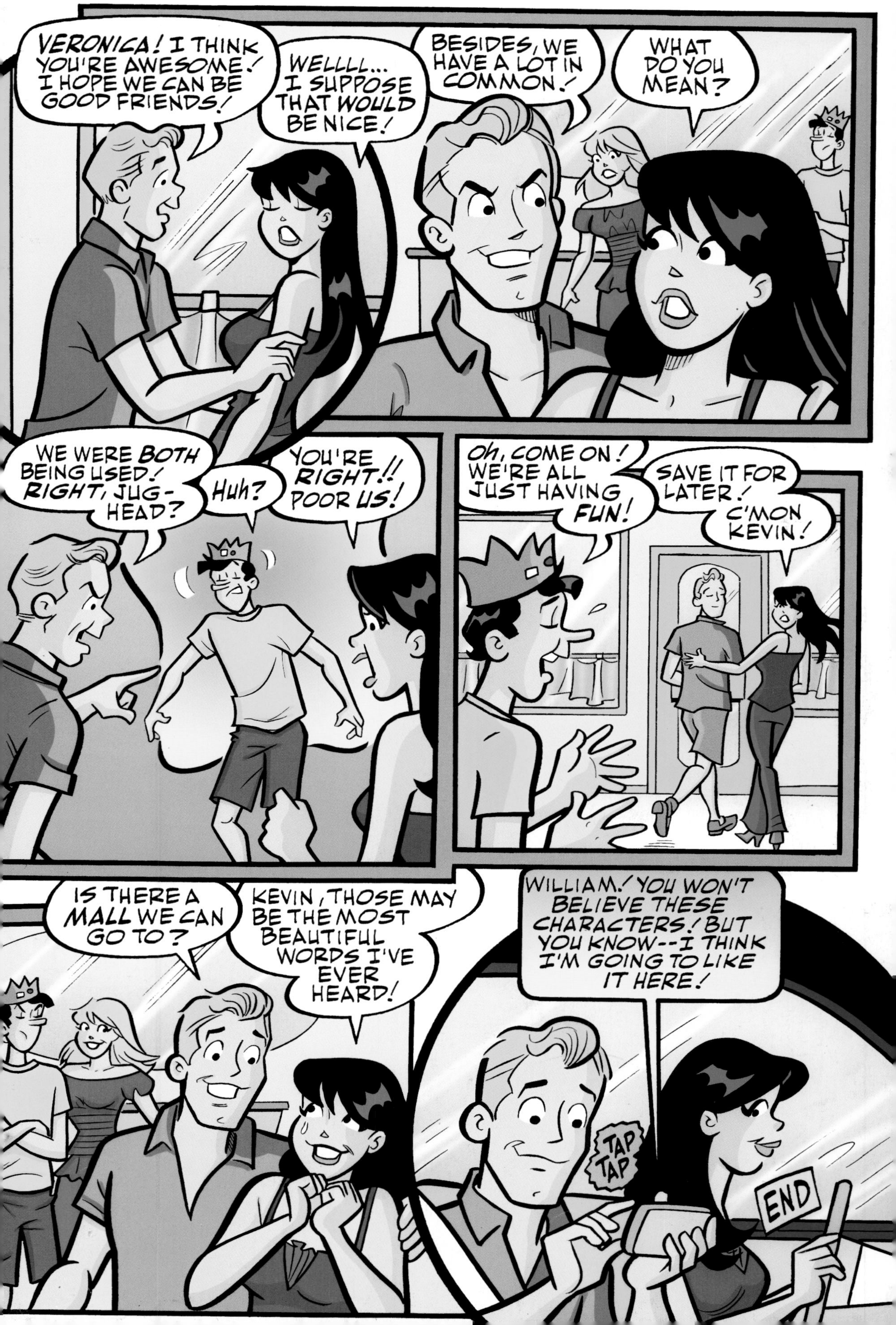
VERONICA! I THINK YOU'RE AWESOME! I HOPE WE CAN BE GOOD FRIENDS!
WELLLL... I SUPPOSE THAT WOULD BE NICE!
BESIDES, WE HAVE A LOT IN COMMON!
WHAT DO YOU MEAN?
WE WERE BOTH BEING USED! RIGHT, JUG-HEAD?
Huh?
YOU'RE RIGHT!! POOR US!
Oh, COME ON! WE'RE ALL JUST HAVING FUN!
SAVE IT FOR LATER!
C'MON KEVIN!
IS THERE A MALL WE CAN GO TO?
KEVIN, THOSE MAY BE THE MOST BEAUTIFUL WORDS I'VE EVER HEARD!
WILLIAM! YOU WON'T BELIEVE THESE CHARACTERS! BUT YOU KNOW--I THINK I'M GOING TO LIKE IT HERE!
TAP TAP
END

Part 2: The Buddy System!

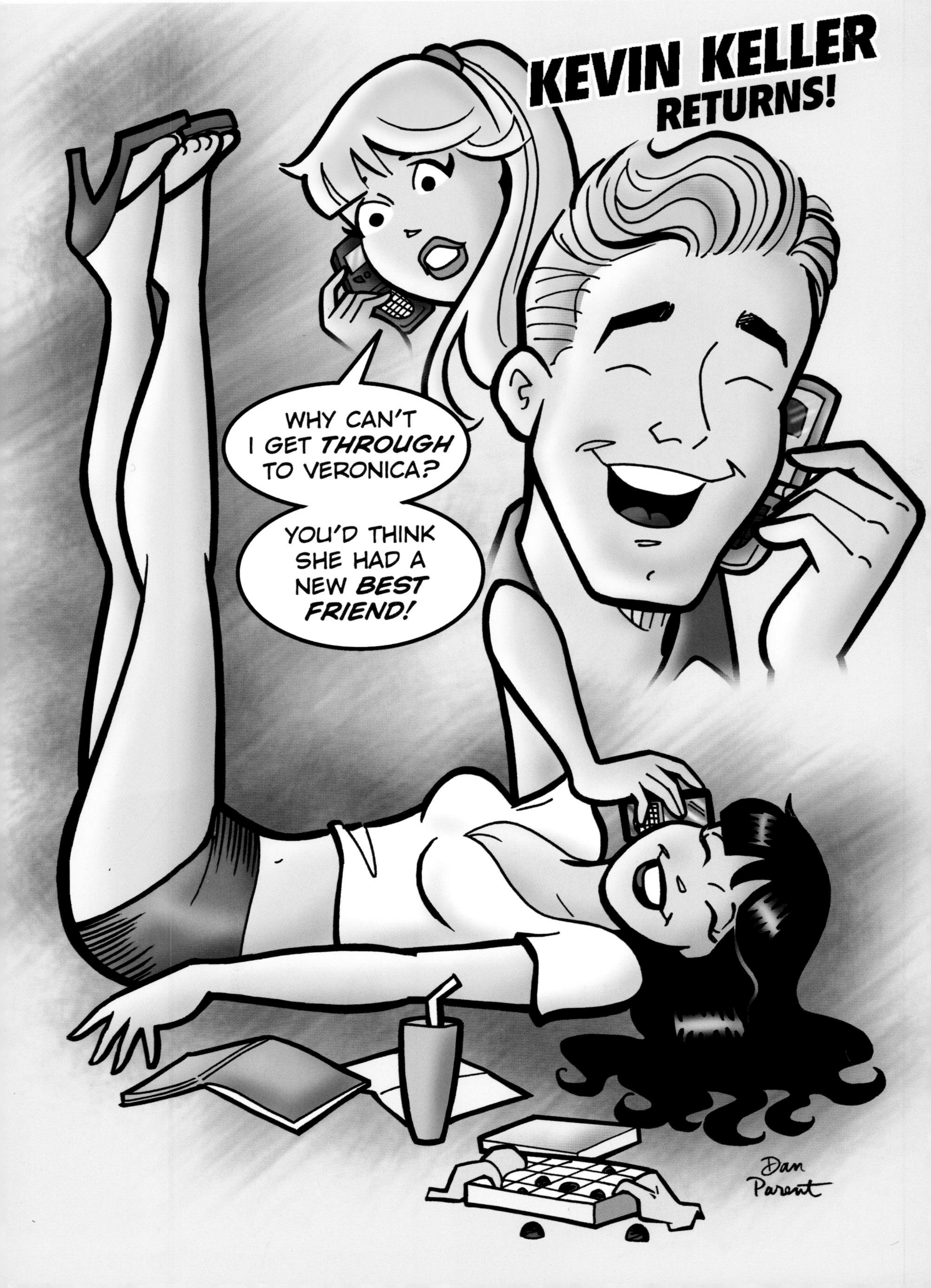
KEVIN KELLER
RETURNS!
WHY CAN'T I GET *THROUGH* TO VERONICA?
YOU'D THINK SHE HAD A NEW *BEST FRIEND!*
Dan Parent

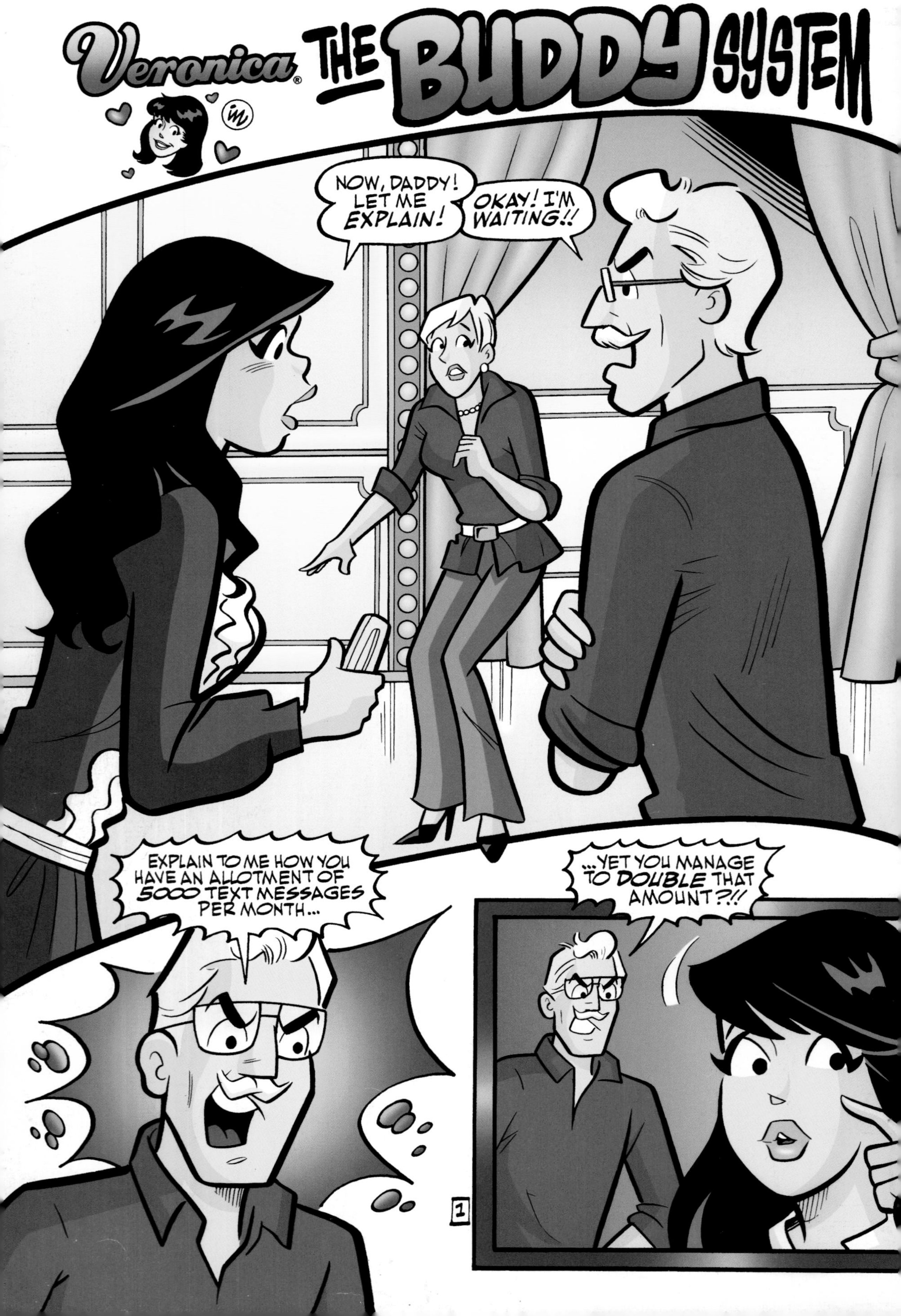
Veronica in
THE BUDDY SYSTEM
NOW, DADDY! LET ME EXPLAIN!
OKAY! I'M WAITING!!
EXPLAIN TO ME HOW YOU HAVE AN ALLOTMENT OF 5000 TEXT MESSAGES PER MONTH...
...YET YOU MANAGE TO DOUBLE THAT AMOUNT?!!

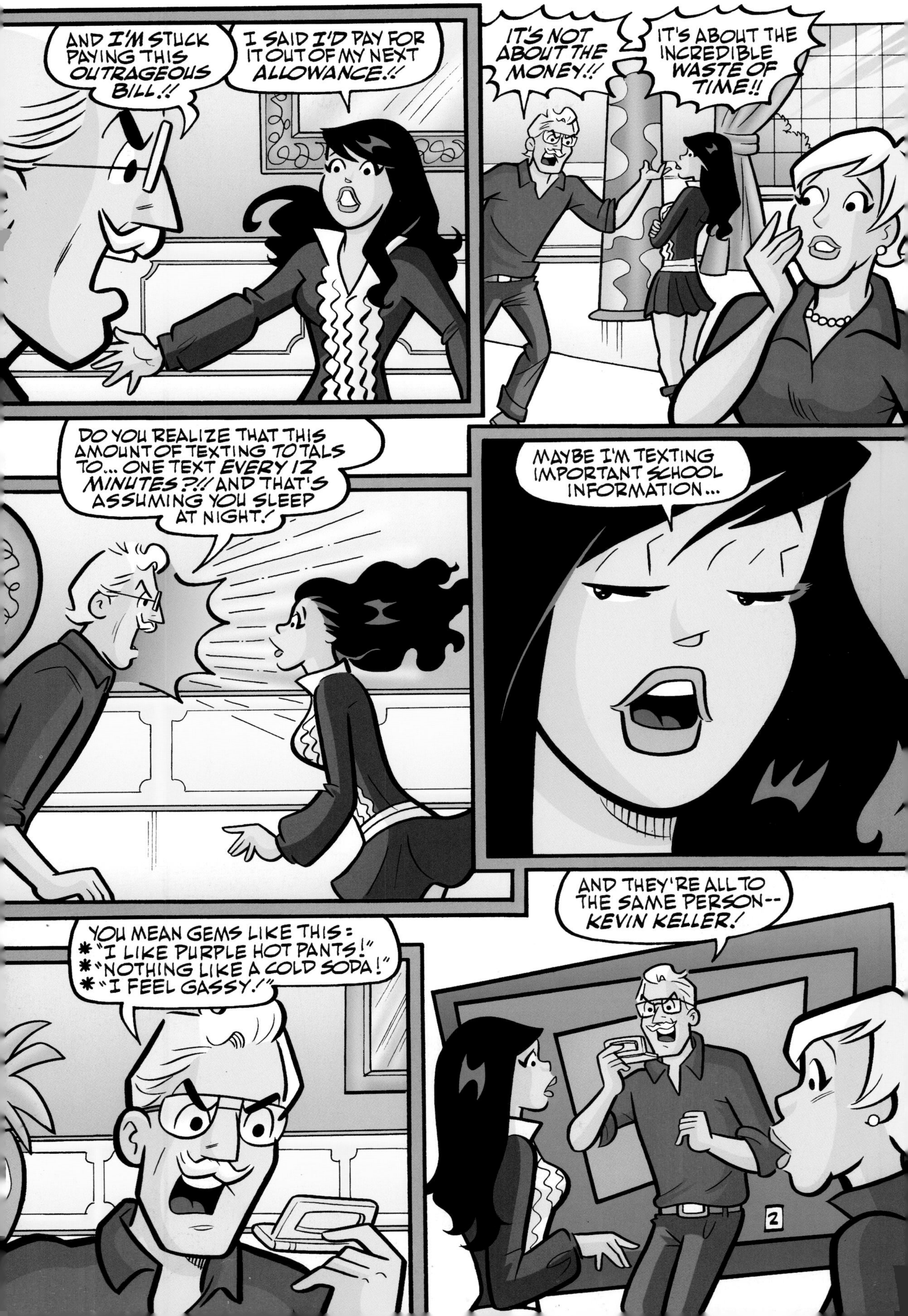
AND I'M STUCK PAYING THIS OUTRAGEOUS BILL!!
I SAID I'D PAY FOR IT OUT OF MY NEXT ALLOWANCE!!
IT'S NOT ABOUT THE MONEY!!
IT'S ABOUT THE INCREDIBLE WASTE OF TIME!!
DO YOU REALIZE THAT THIS AMOUNT OF TEXTING TOTALS TO... ONE TEXT EVERY 12 MINUTES?!! AND THAT'S ASSUMING YOU SLEEP AT NIGHT!
MAYBE I'M TEXTING IMPORTANT SCHOOL INFORMATION...
YOU MEAN GEMS LIKE THIS:
* "I LIKE PURPLE HOT PANTS!"
* "NOTHING LIKE A COLD SODA!"
* "I FEEL GASSY!"
AND THEY'RE ALL TO THE SAME PERSON-- KEVIN KELLER!
2

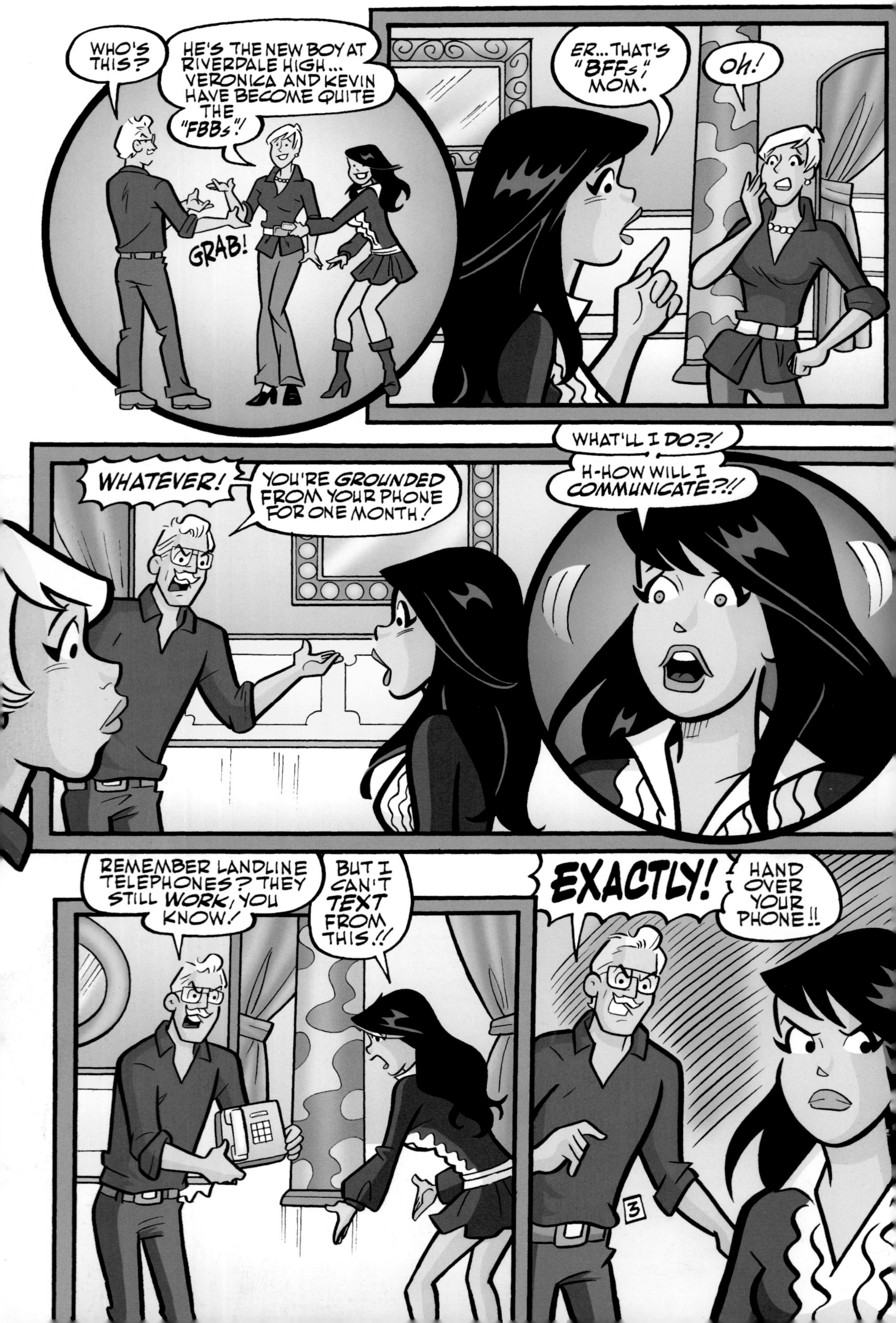

WHO'S THIS?
HE'S THE NEW BOY AT RIVERDALE HIGH... VERONICA AND KEVIN HAVE BECOME QUITE THE "FBBs"!
GRAB!
ER... THAT'S "BFFs," MOM.
oh!
WHATEVER!
YOU'RE GROUNDED FROM YOUR PHONE FOR ONE MONTH!
WHAT'LL I DO?!
H-HOW WILL I COMMUNICATE?!!
REMEMBER LANDLINE TELEPHONES? THEY STILL WORK, YOU KNOW!
BUT I CAN'T TEXT FROM THIS!!
EXACTLY!
HAND OVER YOUR PHONE!!
3

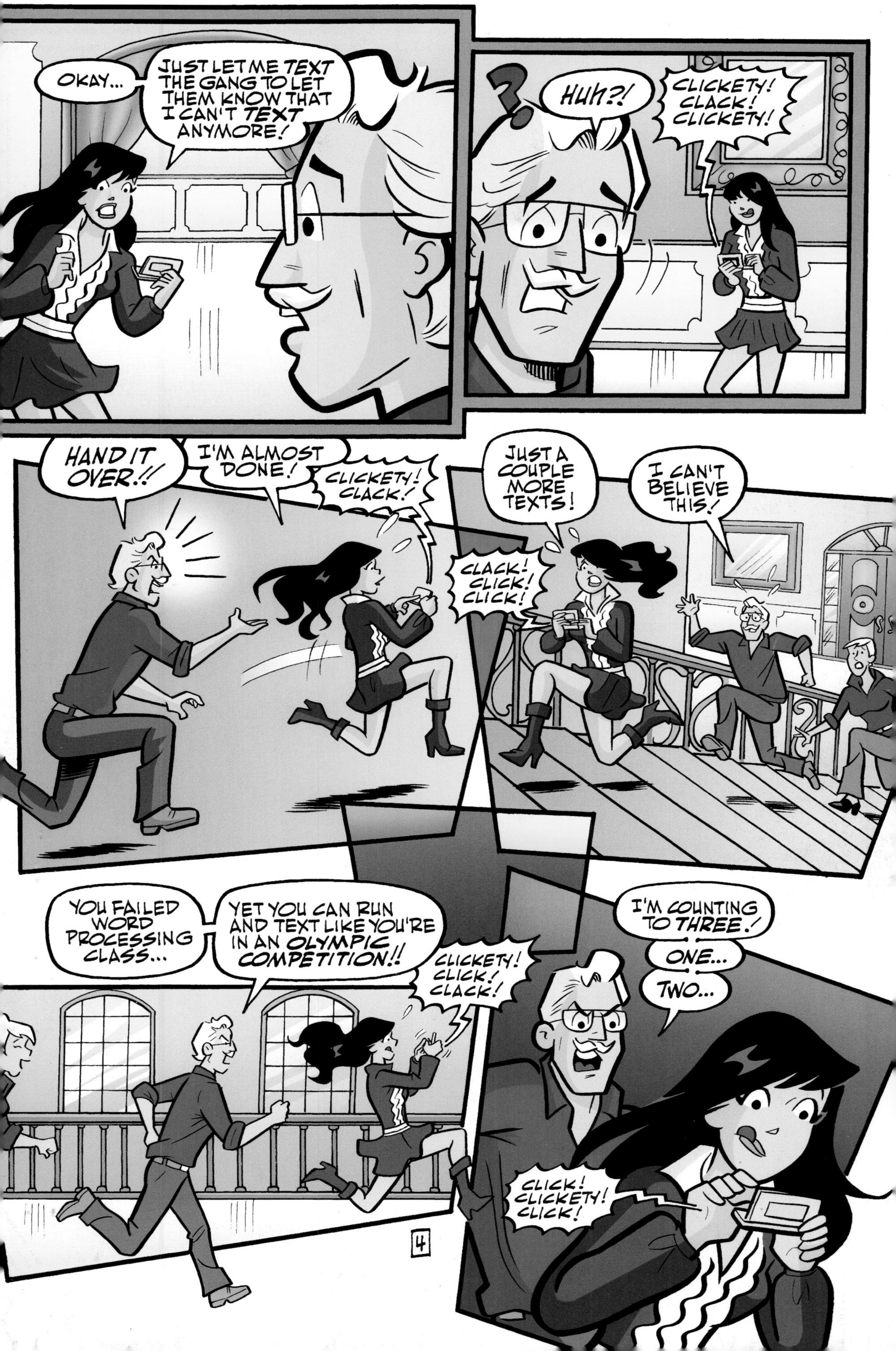
OKAY...
JUST LET ME TEXT THE GANG TO LET THEM KNOW THAT I CAN'T TEXT ANYMORE!
?
HUH?!
CLICKETY! CLACK! CLICKETY!
HAND IT OVER.!!
I'M ALMOST DONE!
CLICKETY! CLACK!
JUST A COUPLE MORE TEXTS!
CLACK! CLICK! CLICK!
I CAN'T BELIEVE THIS!
YOU FAILED WORD PROCESSING CLASS...
YET YOU CAN RUN AND TEXT LIKE YOU'RE IN AN OLYMPIC COMPETITION!!
CLICKETY! CLICK! CLACK!
I'M COUNTING TO THREE.!
ONE...
TWO...
CLICK! CLICKETY! CLICK!
4

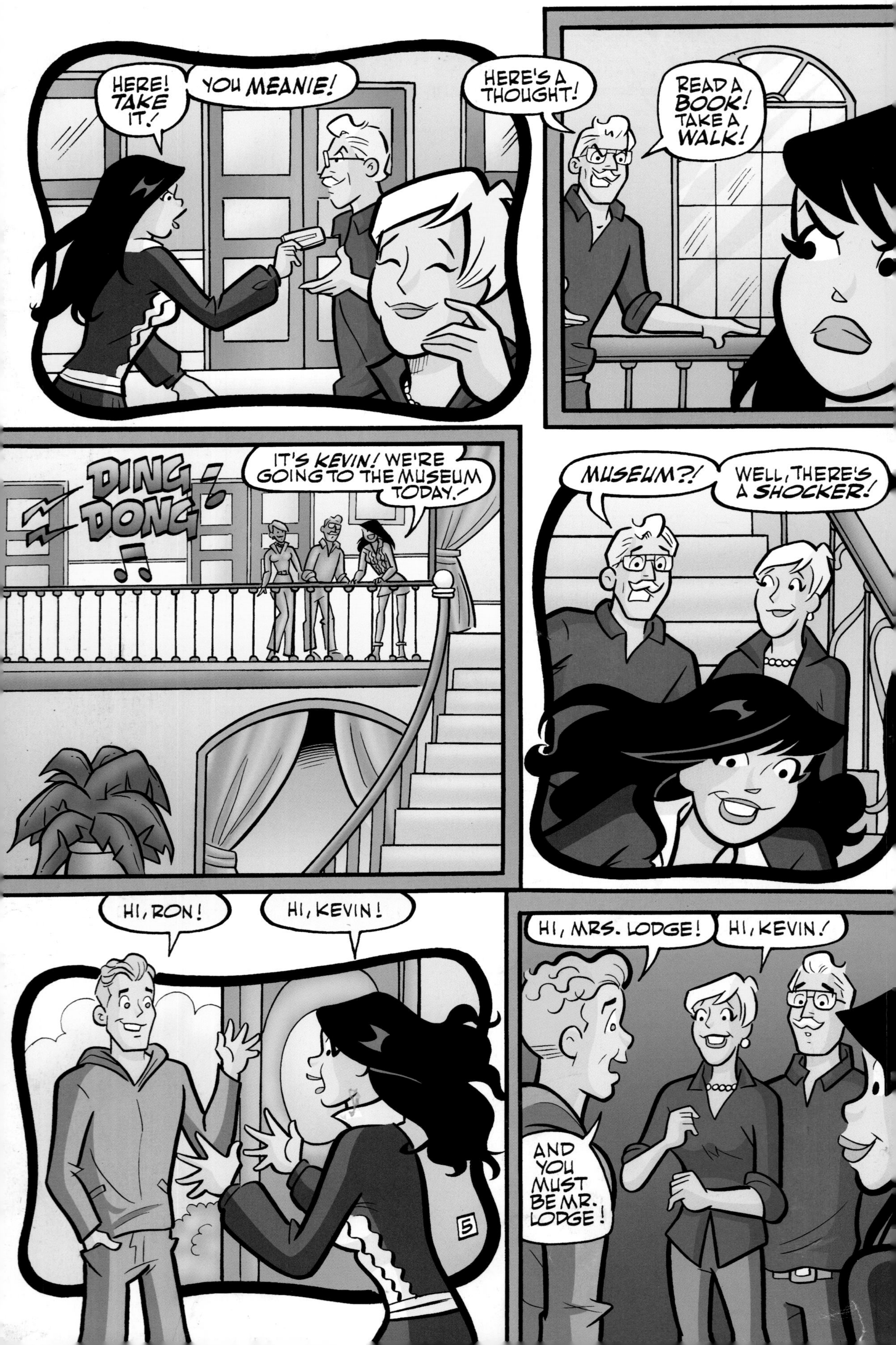
HERE! TAKE IT!
YOU MEANIE!
HERE'S A THOUGHT!
READ A BOOK! TAKE A WALK!
DING DONG
IT'S KEVIN! WE'RE GOING TO THE MUSEUM TODAY!
MUSEUM?!
WELL, THERE'S A SHOCKER!
HI, RON!
HI, KEVIN!
5
HI, MRS. LODGE!
HI, KEVIN!
AND YOU MUST BE MR. LODGE!

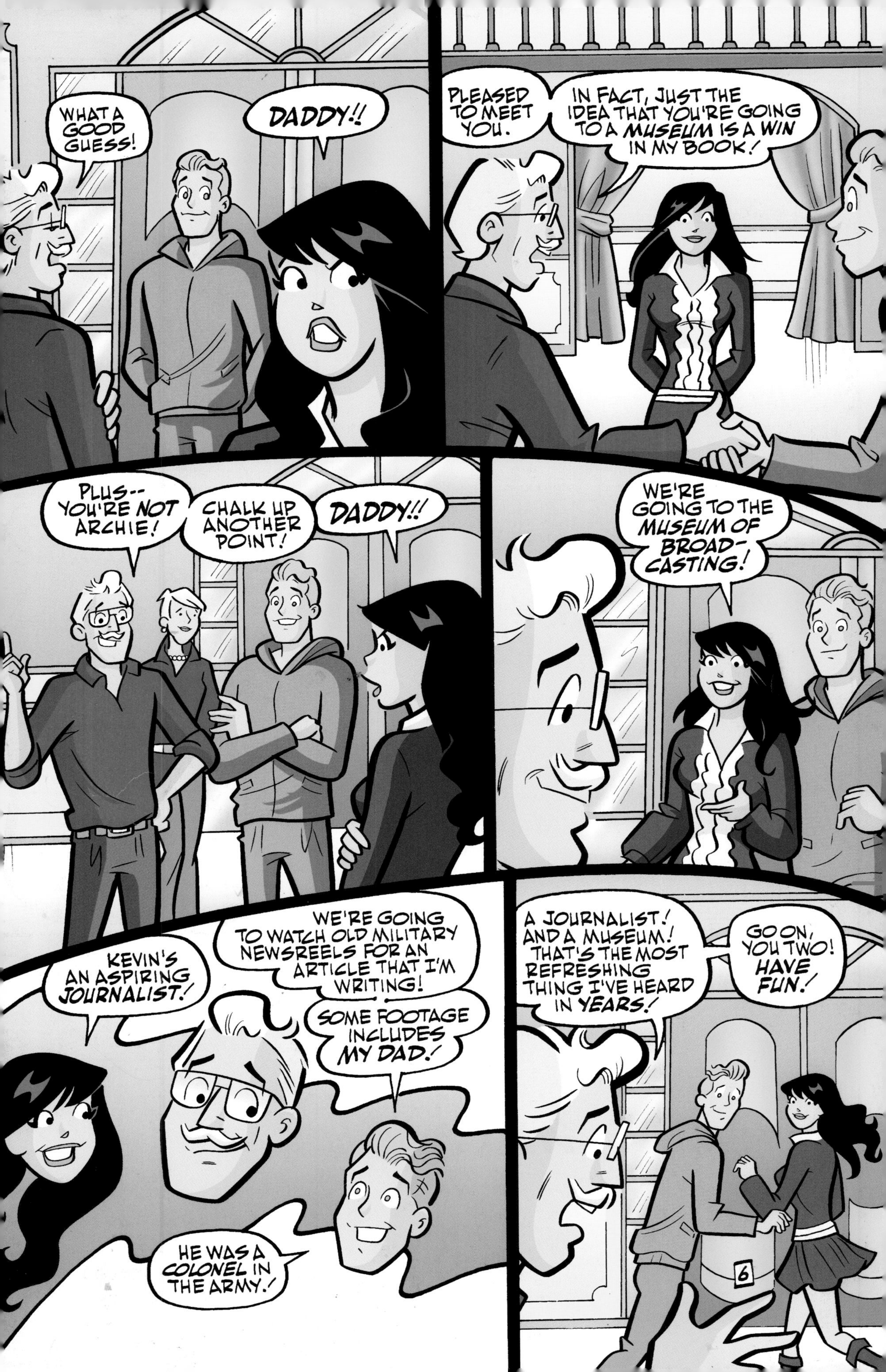
WHAT A GOOD GUESS!
DADDY!!
PLEASED TO MEET YOU.
IN FACT, JUST THE IDEA THAT YOU'RE GOING TO A MUSEUM IS A WIN IN MY BOOK!
PLUS-- YOU'RE NOT ARCHIE!
CHALK UP ANOTHER POINT!
DADDY!!
WE'RE GOING TO THE MUSEUM OF BROAD-CASTING!
KEVIN'S AN ASPIRING JOURNALIST!
WE'RE GOING TO WATCH OLD MILITARY NEWSREELS FOR AN ARTICLE THAT I'M WRITING!
SOME FOOTAGE INCLUDES MY DAD!
HE WAS A COLONEL IN THE ARMY!
A JOURNALIST! AND A MUSEUM! THAT'S THE MOST REFRESHING THING I'VE HEARD IN YEARS!
GO ON, YOU TWO! HAVE FUN!
6

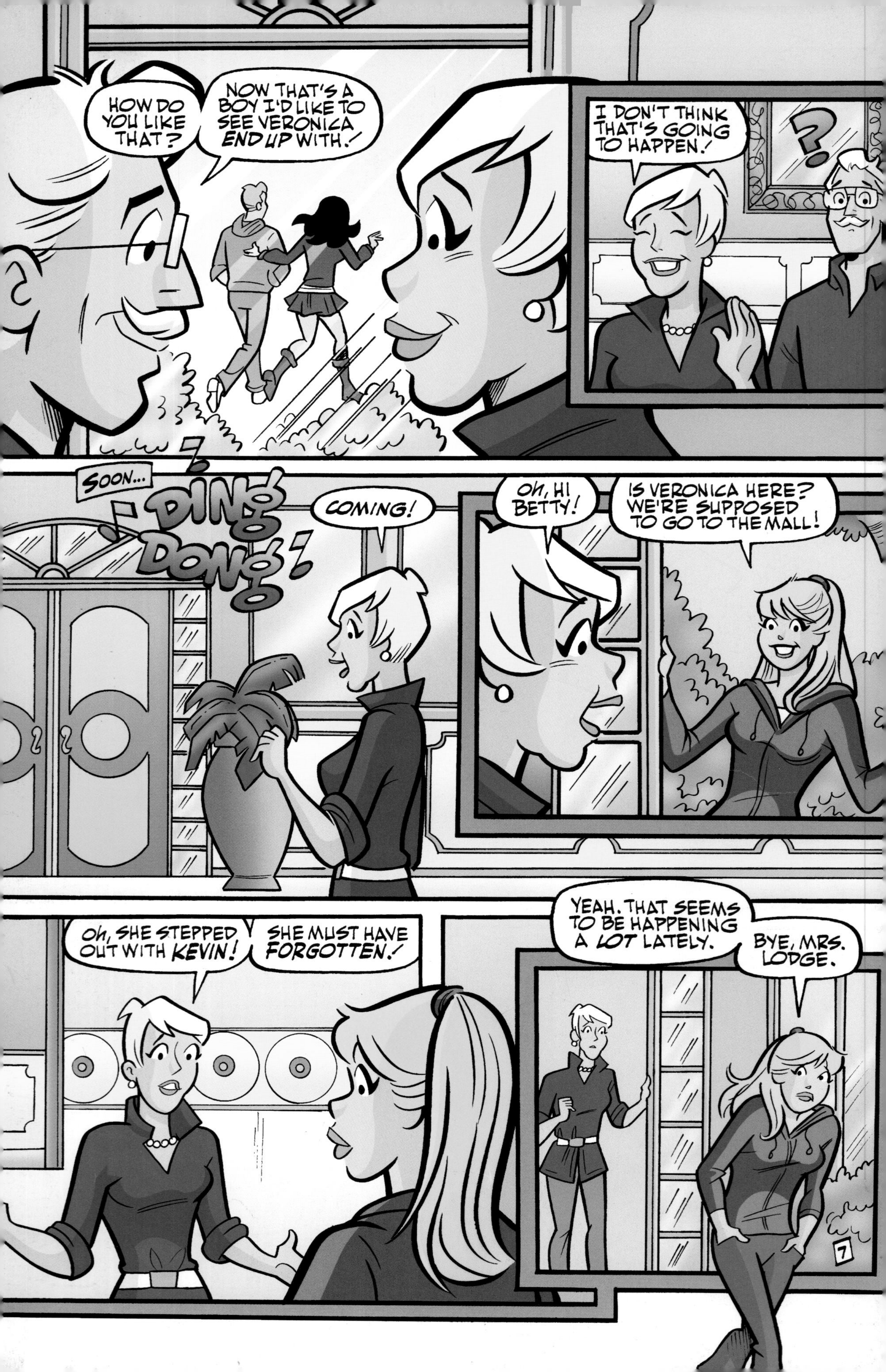
HOW DO YOU LIKE THAT?
NOW THAT'S A BOY I'D LIKE TO SEE VERONICA END UP WITH!
I DON'T THINK THAT'S GOING TO HAPPEN!
?
SOON...
DING DONG!
COMING!
Oh, HI BETTY!
IS VERONICA HERE? WE'RE SUPPOSED TO GO TO THE MALL!
Oh, SHE STEPPED OUT WITH KEVIN!
SHE MUST HAVE FORGOTTEN!
YEAH. THAT SEEMS TO BE HAPPENING A LOT LATELY.
BYE, MRS. LODGE.
7

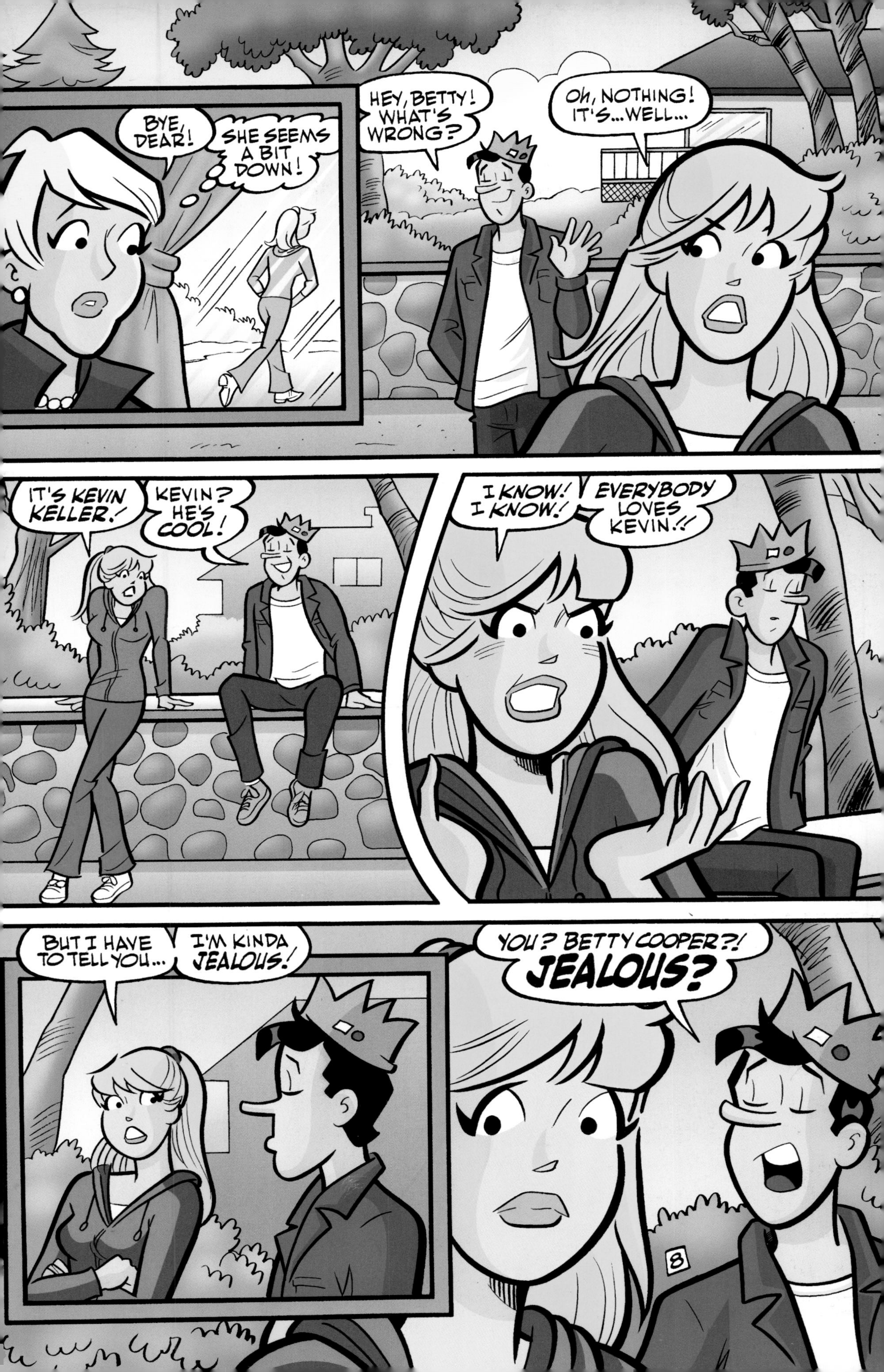
BYE, DEAR!
SHE SEEMS A BIT DOWN!
HEY, BETTY! WHAT'S WRONG?
Oh, NOTHING! IT'S...WELL...
IT'S KEVIN KELLER!
KEVIN? HE'S COOL!
I KNOW! I KNOW!
EVERYBODY LOVES KEVIN!!
BUT I HAVE TO TELL YOU...
I'M KINDA JEALOUS!
YOU? BETTY COOPER?! JEALOUS?
8

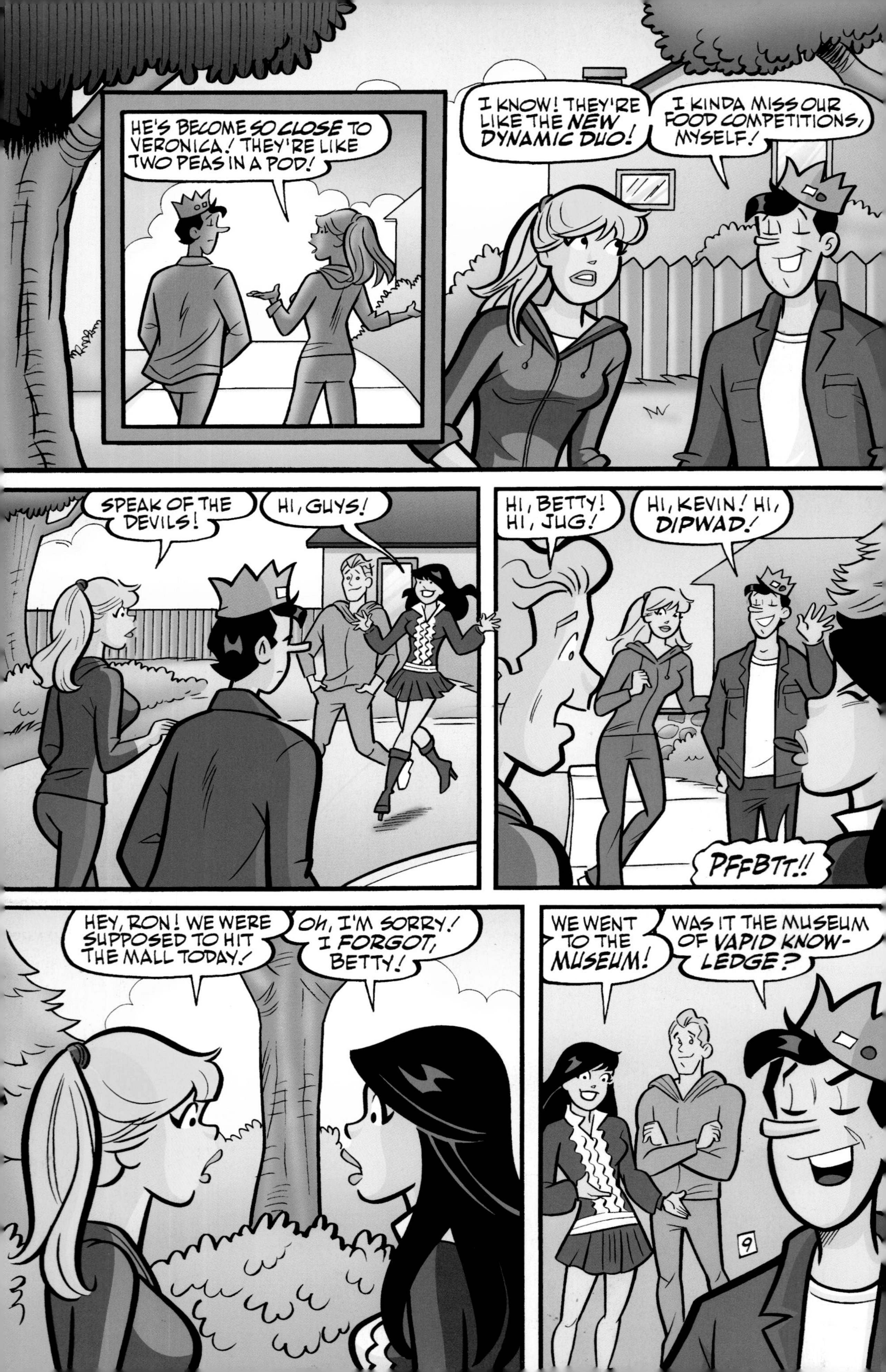
HE'S BECOME SO CLOSE TO VERONICA! THEY'RE LIKE TWO PEAS IN A POD!
I KNOW! THEY'RE LIKE THE NEW DYNAMIC DUO!
I KINDA MISS OUR FOOD COMPETITIONS, MYSELF!
SPEAK OF THE DEVILS!
HI, GUYS!
HI, BETTY! HI, JUG!
HI, KEVIN! HI, DIPWAD!
PFFBTT!!
HEY, RON! WE WERE SUPPOSED TO HIT THE MALL TODAY!
Oh, I'M SORRY! I FORGOT, BETTY!
WE WENT TO THE MUSEUM!
WAS IT THE MUSEUM OF VAPID KNOW-LEDGE?
9

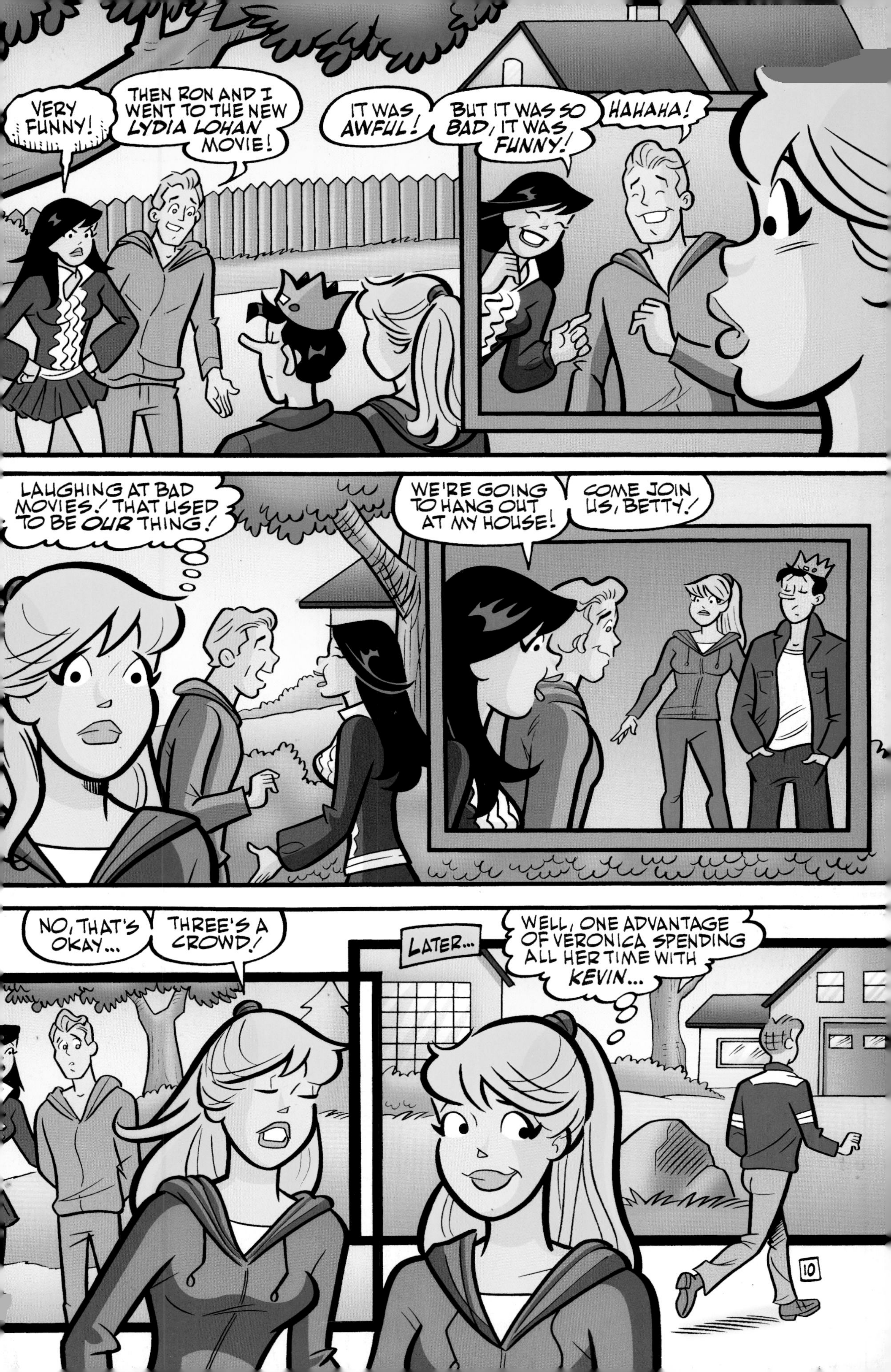
VERY FUNNY!
THEN RON AND I WENT TO THE NEW LYDIA LOHAN MOVIE!
IT WAS AWFUL!
BUT IT WAS SO BAD, IT WAS FUNNY!
HAHAHA!
LAUGHING AT BAD MOVIES! THAT USED TO BE OUR THING!
WE'RE GOING TO HANG OUT AT MY HOUSE!
COME JOIN US, BETTY!
NO, THAT'S OKAY...
THREE'S A CROWD!
LATER...
WELL, ONE ADVANTAGE OF VERONICA SPENDING ALL HER TIME WITH KEVIN...
10

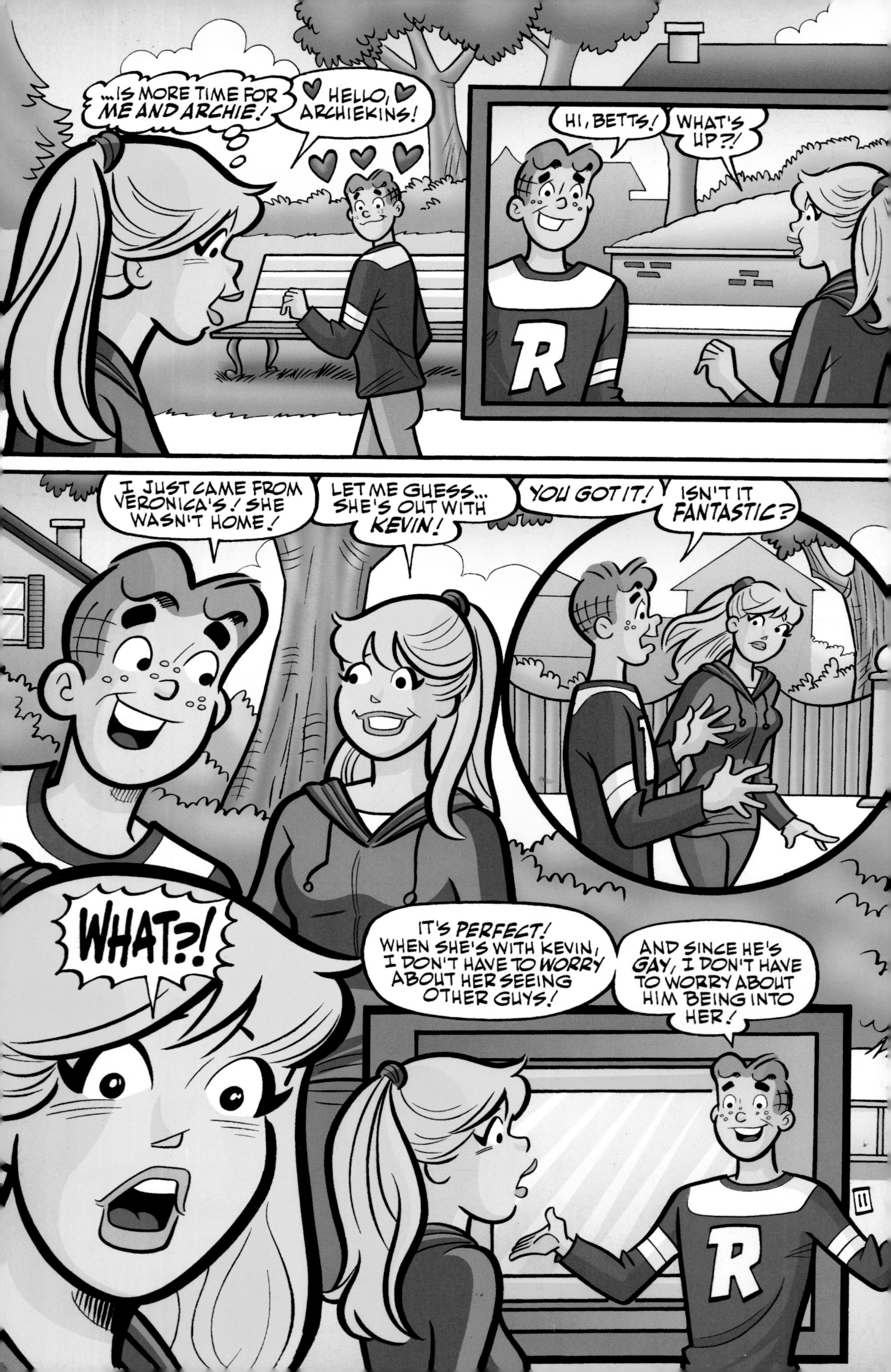
...IS MORE TIME FOR ME AND ARCHIE!
HELLO, ARCHIEKINS!
HI, BETTS!
WHAT'S UP?!
I JUST CAME FROM VERONICA'S! SHE WASN'T HOME!
LET ME GUESS... SHE'S OUT WITH KEVIN!
YOU GOT IT!
ISN'T IT FANTASTIC?
WHAT?!
IT'S PERFECT! WHEN SHE'S WITH KEVIN, I DON'T HAVE TO WORRY ABOUT HER SEEING OTHER GUYS!
AND SINCE HE'S GAY, I DON'T HAVE TO WORRY ABOUT HIM BEING INTO HER!
11

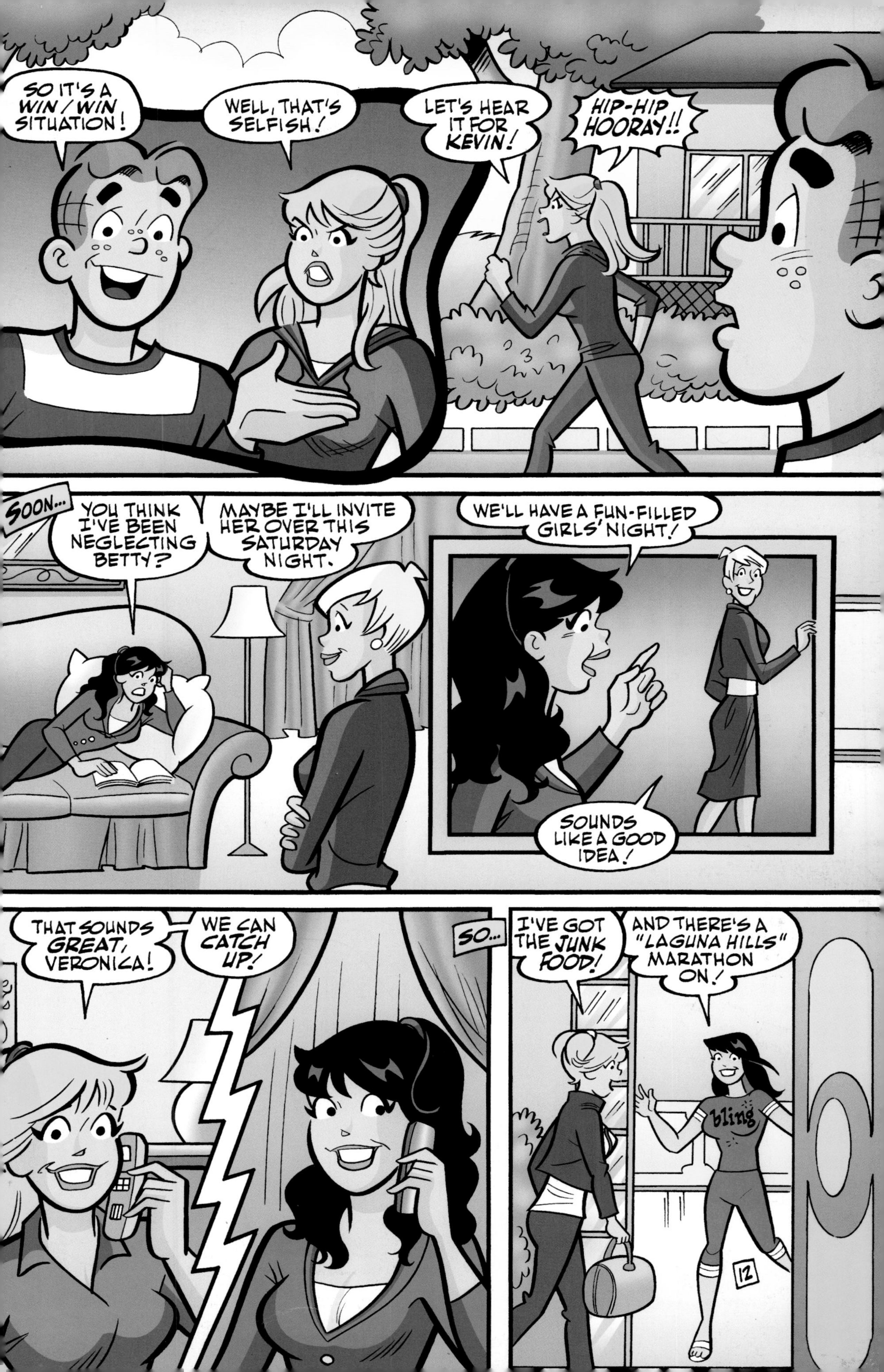
SO IT'S A WIN / WIN SITUATION!
WELL, THAT'S SELFISH!
LET'S HEAR IT FOR KEVIN!
HIP-HIP HOORAY!!
SOON...
YOU THINK I'VE BEEN NEGLECTING BETTY?
MAYBE I'LL INVITE HER OVER THIS SATURDAY NIGHT.
WE'LL HAVE A FUN-FILLED GIRLS' NIGHT!
SOUNDS LIKE A GOOD IDEA!
THAT SOUNDS GREAT, VERONICA!
WE CAN CATCH UP!
SO...
I'VE GOT THE JUNK FOOD!
AND THERE'S A "LAGUNA HILLS" MARATHON ON!
bling
12

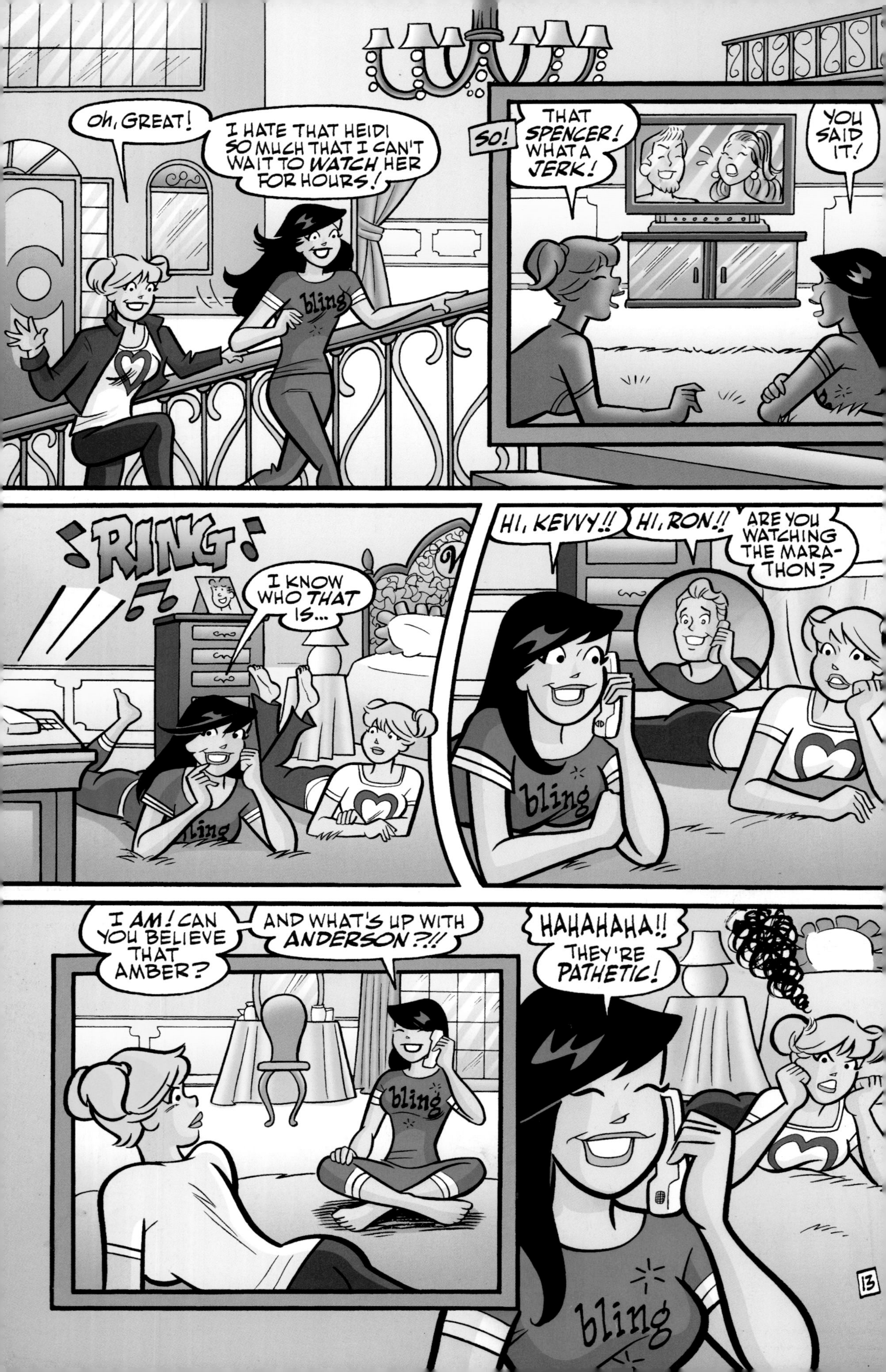

Oh, GREAT!
I HATE THAT HEIDI SO MUCH THAT I CAN'T WAIT TO WATCH HER FOR HOURS!
SO!
THAT SPENCER! WHAT A JERK!
YOU SAID IT!
RING
I KNOW WHO THAT IS...
HI, KEVVY!!
HI, RON!!
ARE YOU WATCHING THE MARA-THON?
I AM! CAN YOU BELIEVE THAT AMBER?
AND WHAT'S UP WITH ANDERSON?!!
HAHAHAHA!! THEY'RE PATHETIC!
bling
13

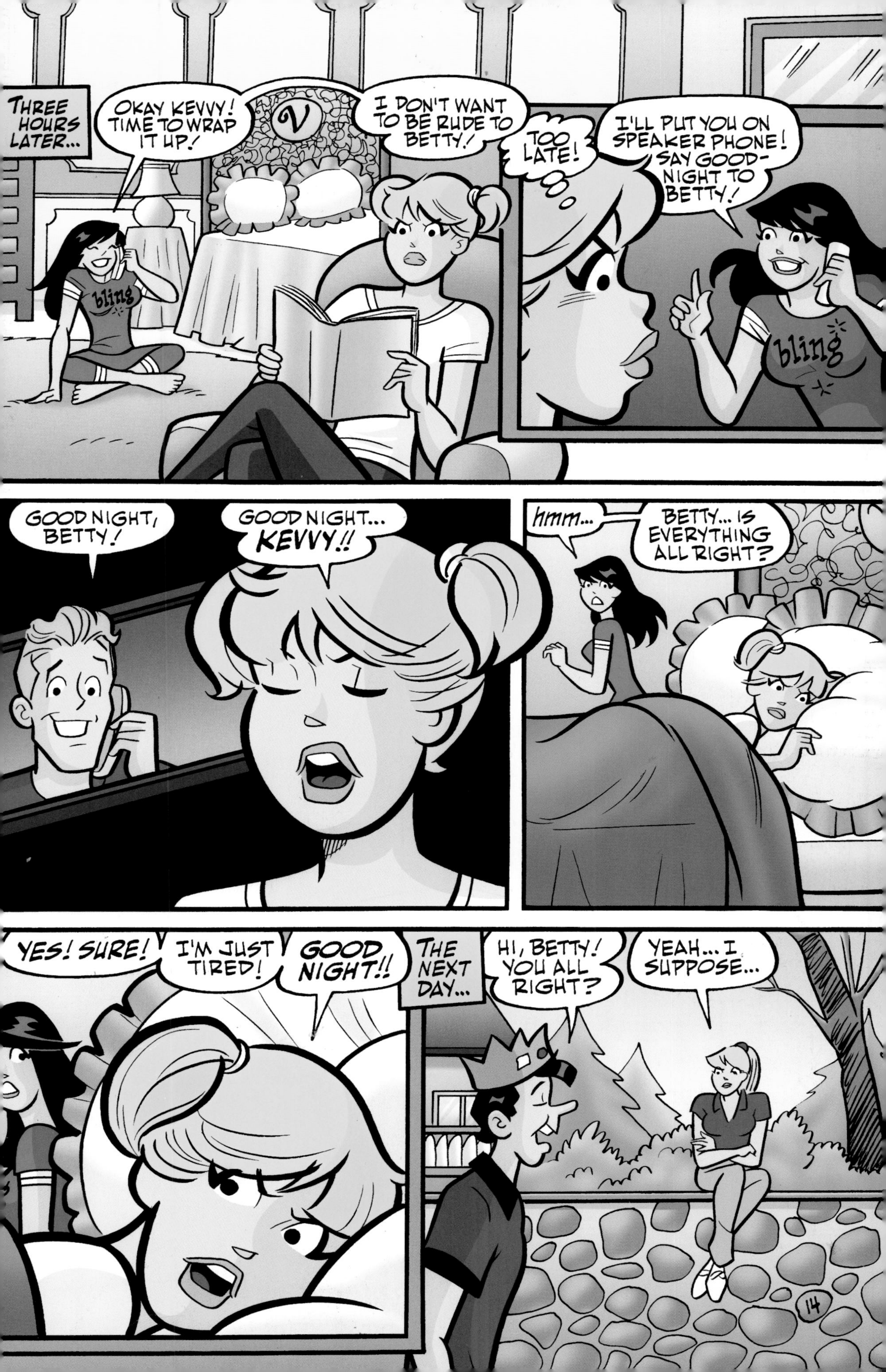
THREE HOURS LATER...
OKAY KEVVY! TIME TO WRAP IT UP!
I DON'T WANT TO BE RUDE TO BETTY!
TOO LATE!
I'LL PUT YOU ON SPEAKER PHONE! SAY GOOD-NIGHT TO BETTY!
bling
bling
GOOD NIGHT, BETTY!
GOOD NIGHT... KEVVY!!
hmm...
BETTY... IS EVERYTHING ALL RIGHT?
YES! SURE!
I'M JUST TIRED!
GOOD NIGHT!!
THE NEXT DAY...
HI, BETTY! YOU ALL RIGHT?
YEAH... I SUPPOSE...

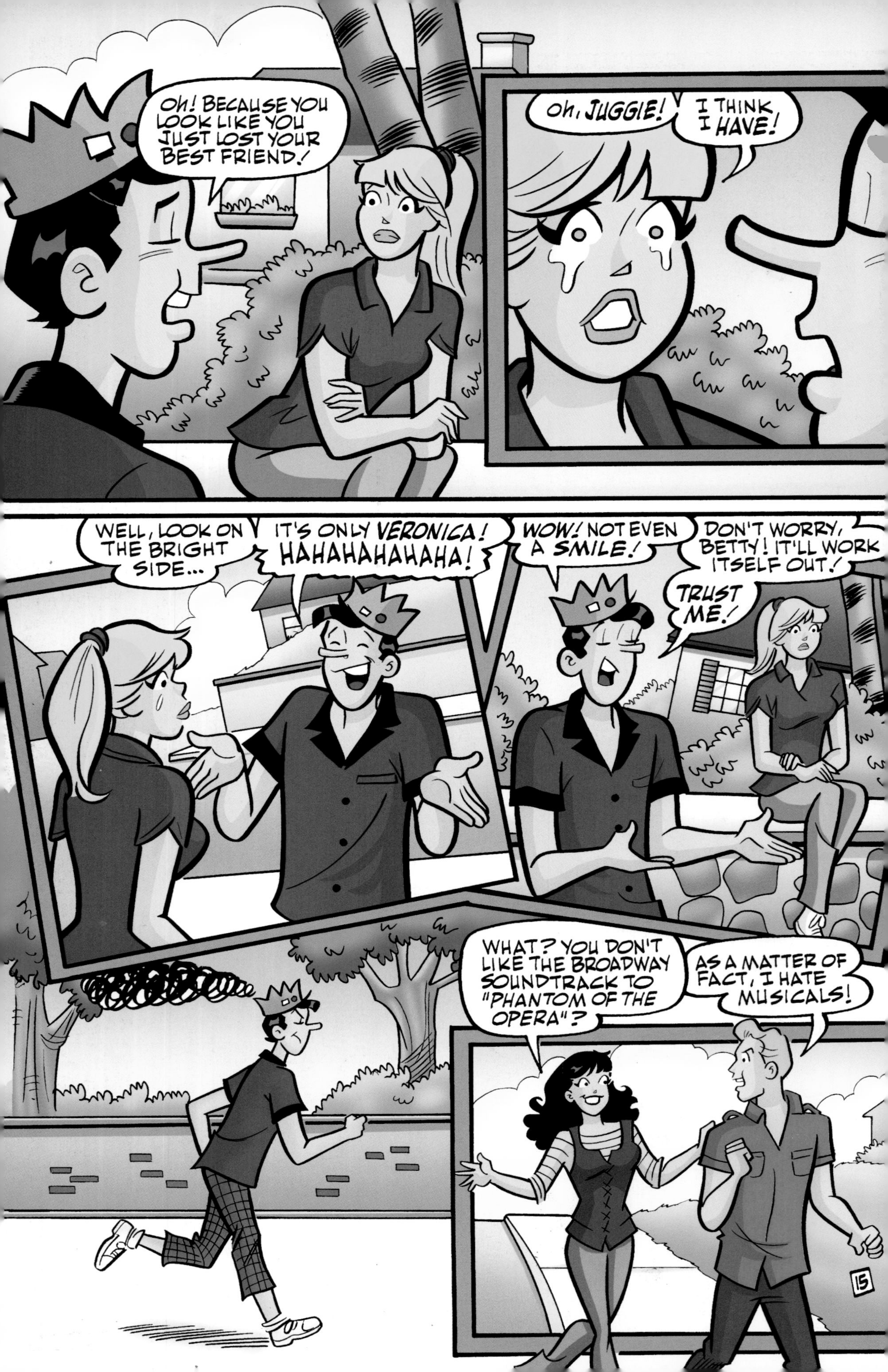

OH! BECAUSE YOU LOOK LIKE YOU JUST LOST YOUR BEST FRIEND!
OH, JUGGIE!
I THINK I HAVE!
WELL, LOOK ON THE BRIGHT SIDE...
IT'S ONLY VERONICA! HAHAHAHAHAHA!
WOW! NOT EVEN A SMILE!
DON'T WORRY, BETTY! IT'LL WORK ITSELF OUT!
TRUST ME!
WHAT? YOU DON'T LIKE THE BROADWAY SOUNDTRACK TO "PHANTOM OF THE OPERA"?
AS A MATTER OF FACT, I HATE MUSICALS!

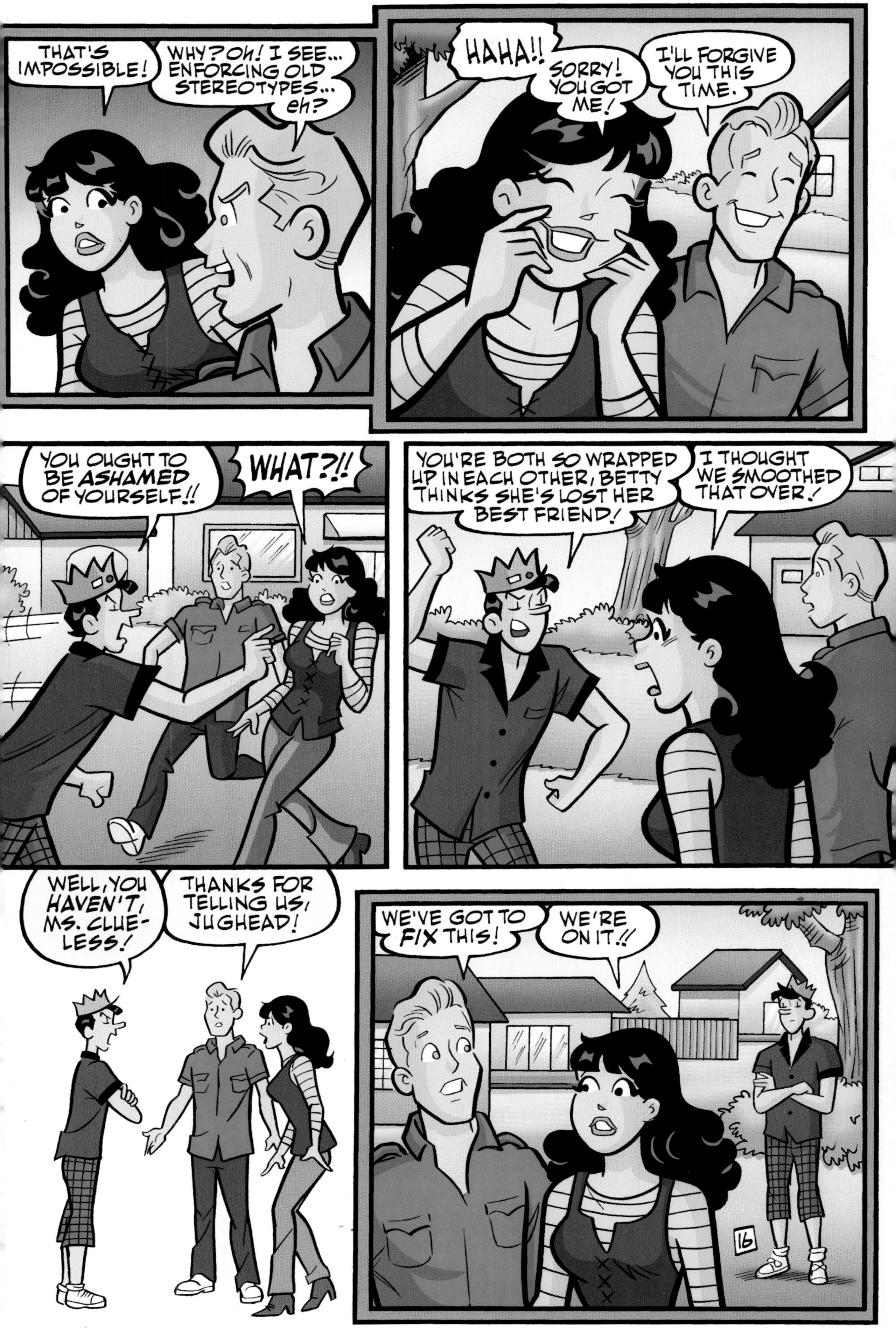
THAT'S IMPOSSIBLE!
WHY? Oh! I SEE... ENFORCING OLD STEREOTYPES... eh?
HAHA!!
SORRY! YOU GOT ME!
I'LL FORGIVE YOU THIS TIME.
YOU OUGHT TO BE ASHAMED OF YOURSELF!!
WHAT?!!
YOU'RE BOTH SO WRAPPED UP IN EACH OTHER, BETTY THINKS SHE'S LOST HER BEST FRIEND!
I THOUGHT WE SMOOTHED THAT OVER!
WELL, YOU HAVEN'T, MS. CLUELESS!
THANKS FOR TELLING US, JUGHEAD!
WE'VE GOT TO FIX THIS!
WE'RE ON IT!!
16

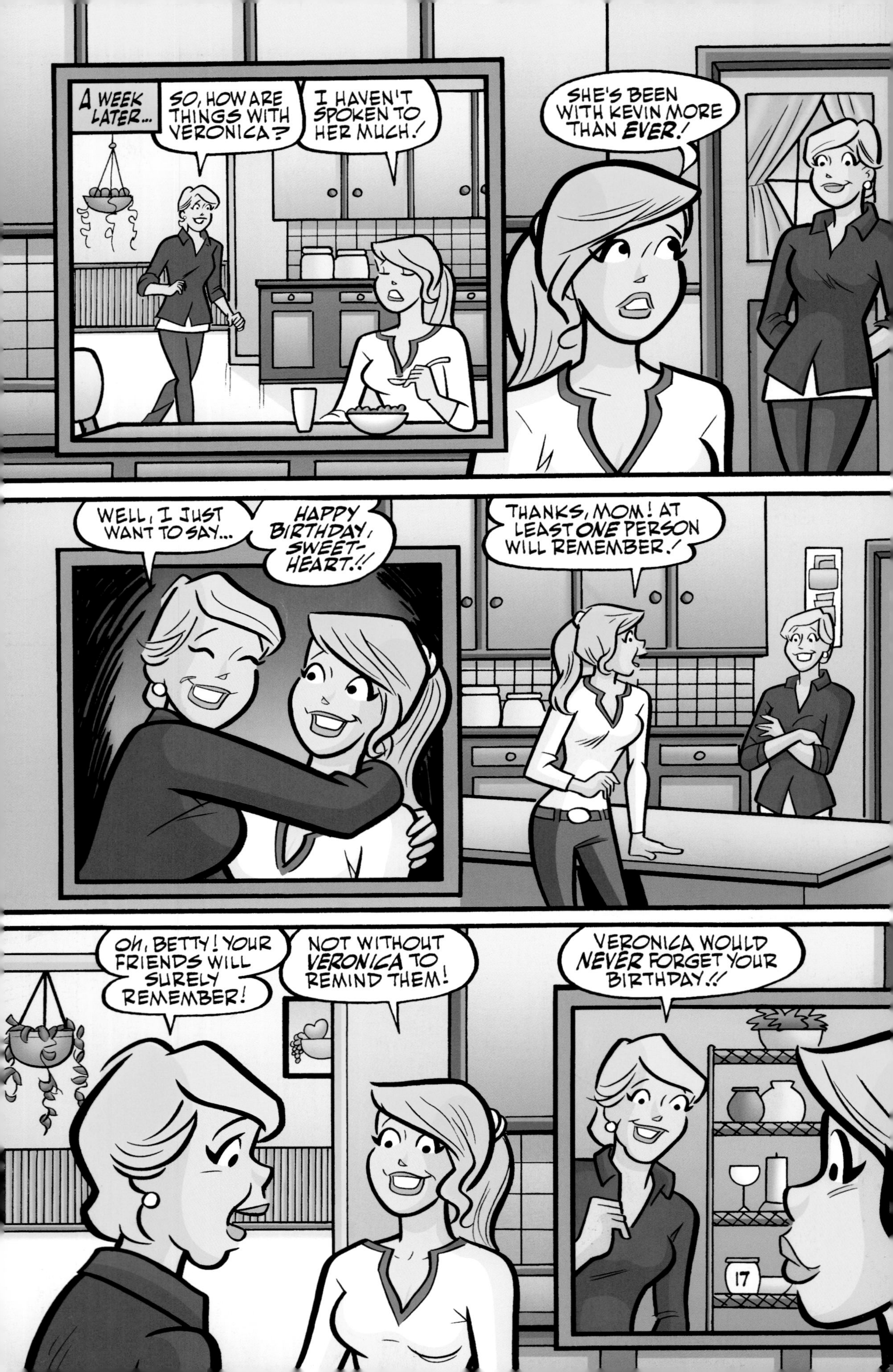
A WEEK LATER...
SO, HOW ARE THINGS WITH VERONICA?
I HAVEN'T SPOKEN TO HER MUCH!
SHE'S BEEN WITH KEVIN MORE THAN EVER!
WELL, I JUST WANT TO SAY...
HAPPY BIRTHDAY, SWEET-HEART!!
THANKS, MOM! AT LEAST ONE PERSON WILL REMEMBER!
Oh, BETTY! YOUR FRIENDS WILL SURELY REMEMBER!
NOT WITHOUT VERONICA TO REMIND THEM!
VERONICA WOULD NEVER FORGET YOUR BIRTHDAY!!
17

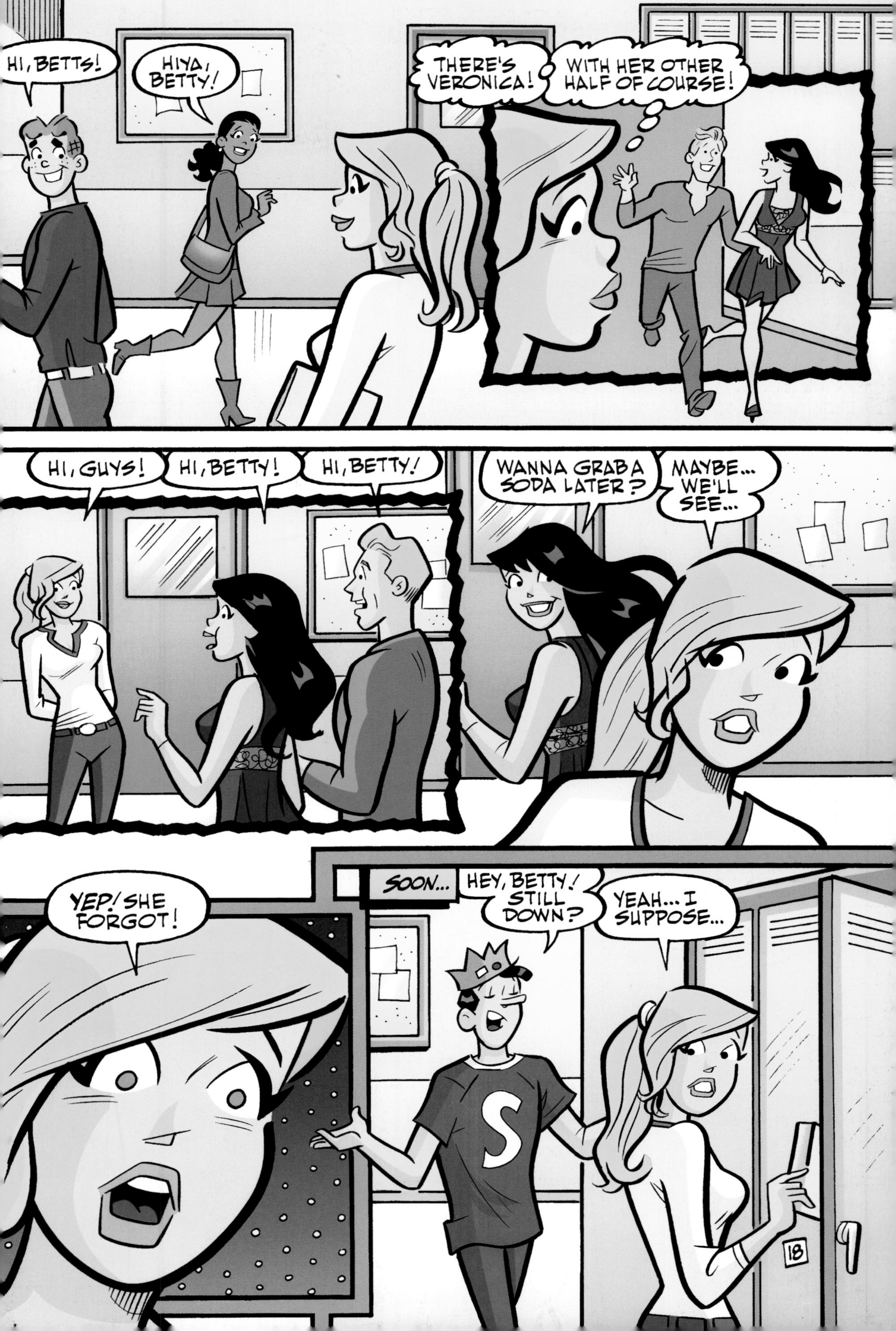
HI, BETTS!
HIYA, BETTY!
THERE'S VERONICA!
WITH HER OTHER HALF OF COURSE!
HI, GUYS!
HI, BETTY!
HI, BETTY!
WANNA GRAB A SODA LATER?
MAYBE... WE'LL SEE...
YEP! SHE FORGOT!
SOON...
HEY, BETTY! STILL DOWN?
YEAH... I SUPPOSE...
18

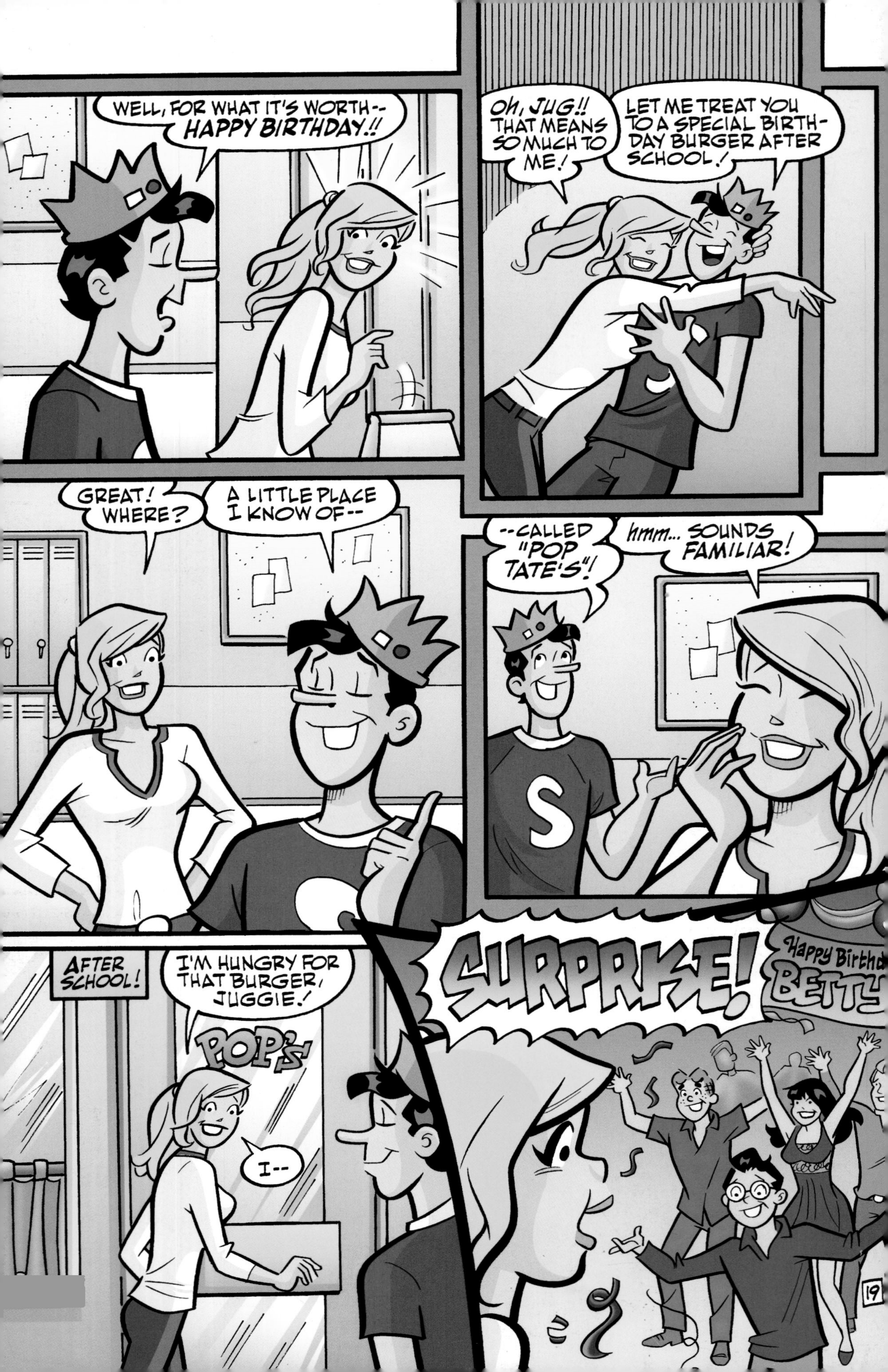
WELL, FOR WHAT IT'S WORTH-- HAPPY BIRTHDAY!!
Oh, JUG!! THAT MEANS SO MUCH TO ME!
LET ME TREAT YOU TO A SPECIAL BIRTH-DAY BURGER AFTER SCHOOL!
GREAT! WHERE?
A LITTLE PLACE I KNOW OF--
--CALLED "POP TATE'S"!
hmm... SOUNDS FAMILIAR!
AFTER SCHOOL!
I'M HUNGRY FOR THAT BURGER, JUGGIE!
POP'S
I--
SURPRISE!
Happy Birthd
BETTY
19

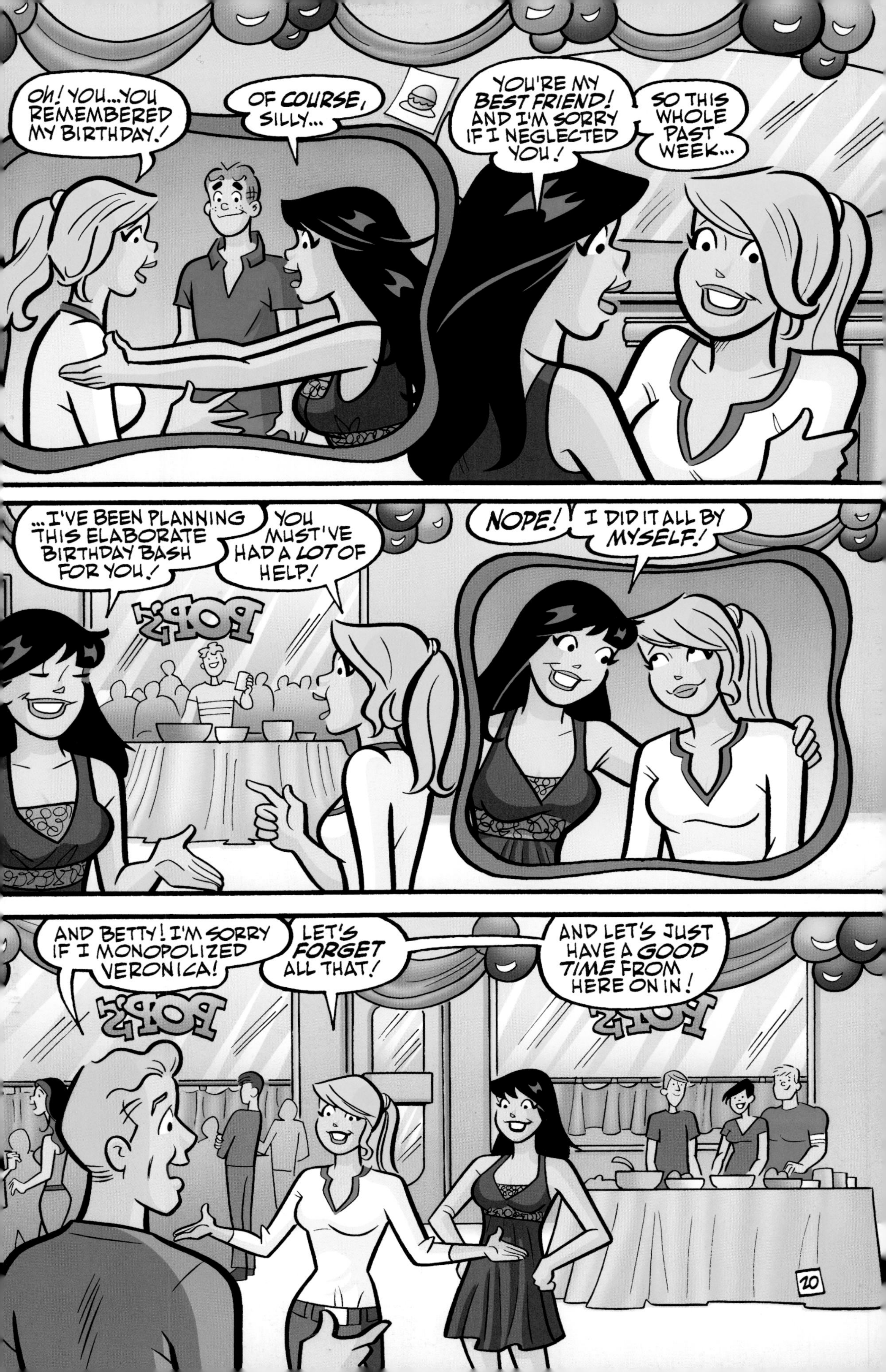
OH! YOU...YOU REMEMBERED MY BIRTHDAY!
OF COURSE, SILLY...
YOU'RE MY BEST FRIEND! AND I'M SORRY IF I NEGLECTED YOU!
SO THIS WHOLE PAST WEEK...
...I'VE BEEN PLANNING THIS ELABORATE BIRTHDAY BASH FOR YOU!
YOU MUST'VE HAD A LOT OF HELP!
POP'S
NOPE!
I DID IT ALL BY MYSELF!
AND BETTY! I'M SORRY IF I MONOPOLIZED VERONICA!
LET'S FORGET ALL THAT!
AND LET'S JUST HAVE A GOOD TIME FROM HERE ON IN!
POP'S
POP'S
20

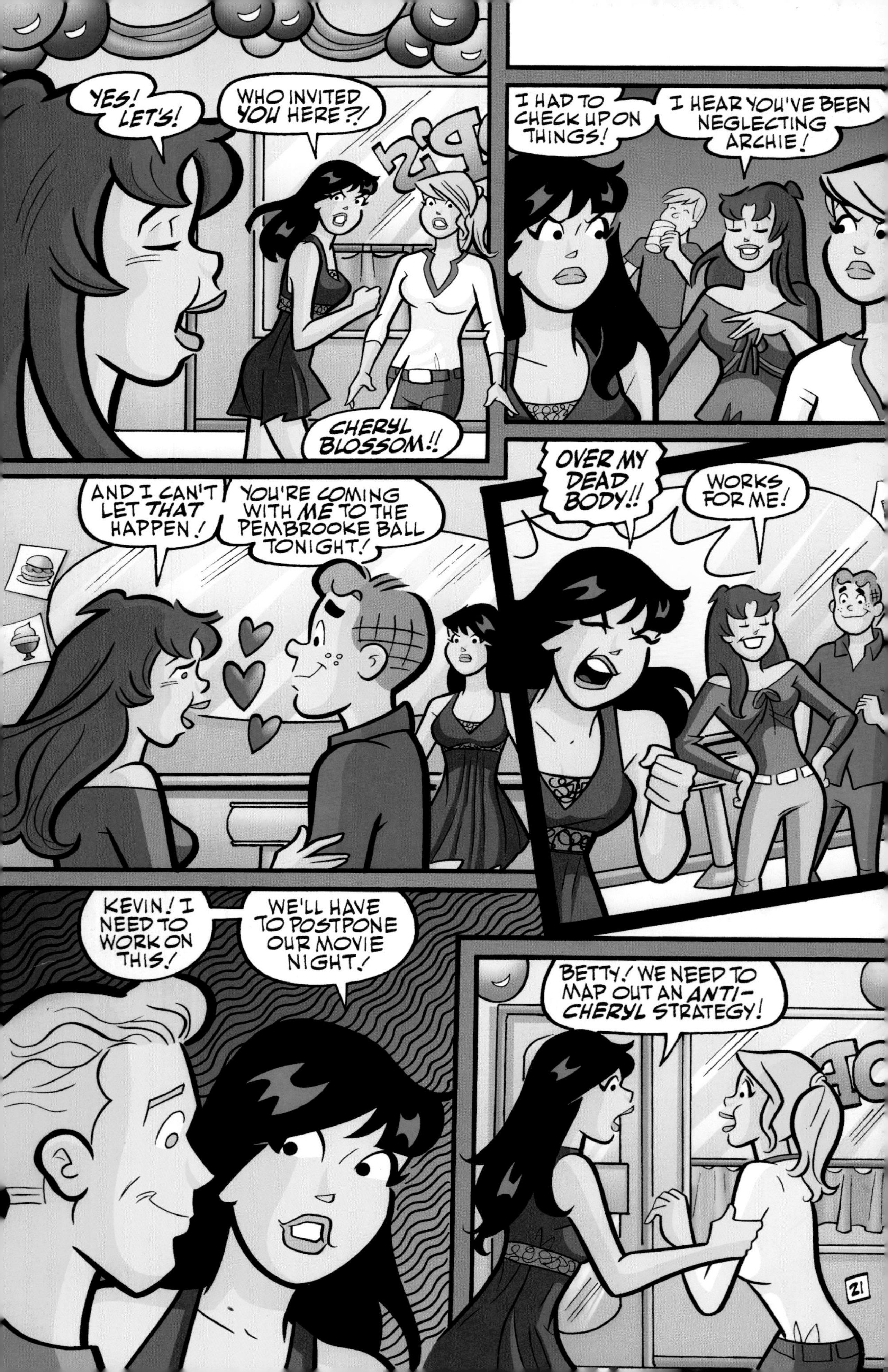
YES! LET'S!
WHO INVITED YOU HERE?!
CHERYL BLOSSOM!!
I HAD TO CHECK UP ON THINGS!
I HEAR YOU'VE BEEN NEGLECTING ARCHIE!
AND I CAN'T LET THAT HAPPEN!
YOU'RE COMING WITH ME TO THE PEMBROOKE BALL TONIGHT!
OVER MY DEAD BODY!!
WORKS FOR ME!
KEVIN! I NEED TO WORK ON THIS!
WE'LL HAVE TO POSTPONE OUR MOVIE NIGHT!
BETTY! WE NEED TO MAP OUT AN ANTI-CHERYL STRATEGY!
21

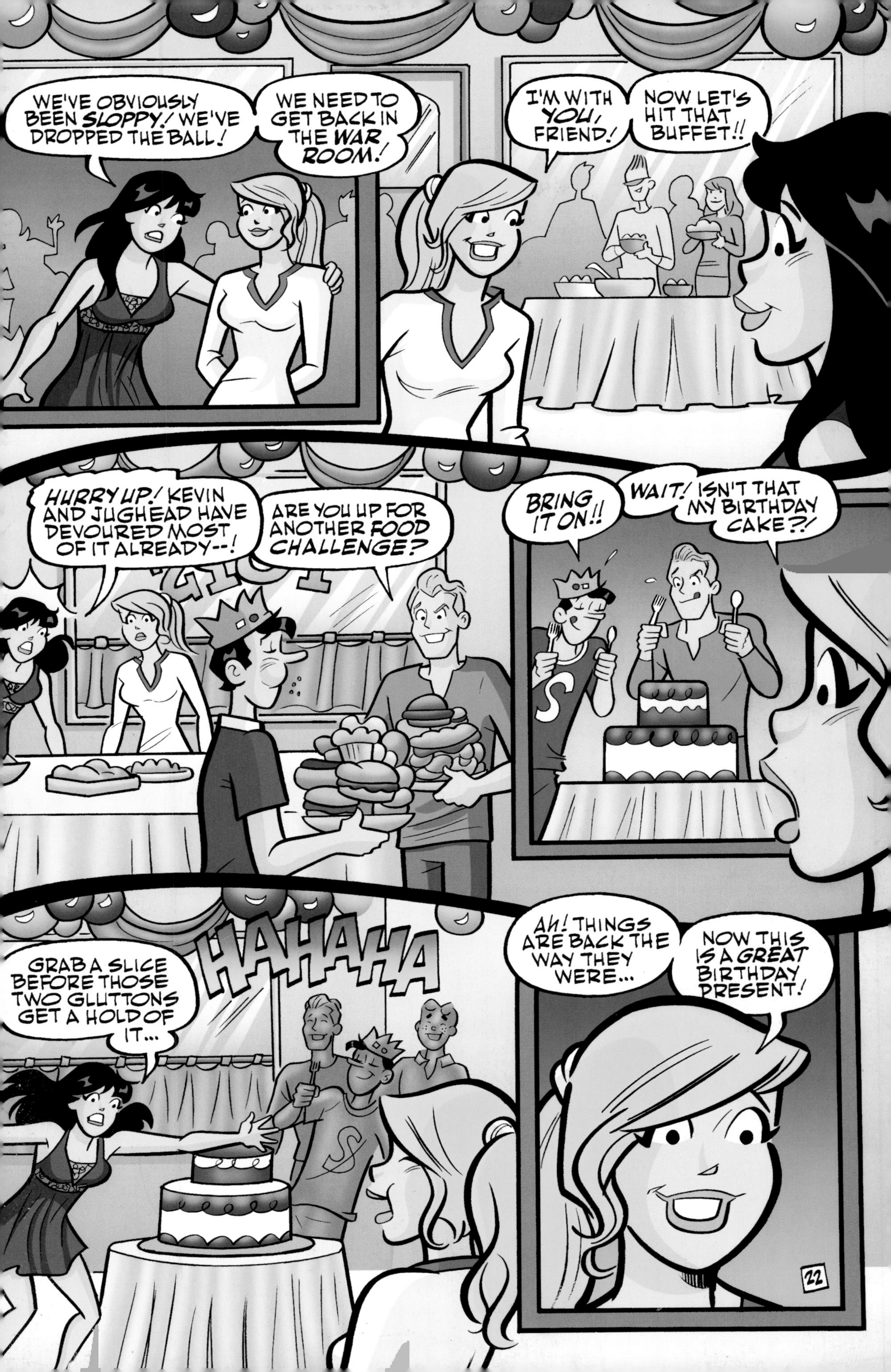
WE'VE OBVIOUSLY BEEN SLOPPY! WE'VE DROPPED THE BALL!
WE NEED TO GET BACK IN THE WAR ROOM!
I'M WITH YOU, FRIEND!
NOW LET'S HIT THAT BUFFET!!
HURRY UP! KEVIN AND JUGHEAD HAVE DEVOURED MOST OF IT ALREADY--!
ARE YOU UP FOR ANOTHER FOOD CHALLENGE?
BRING IT ON!!
WAIT! ISN'T THAT MY BIRTHDAY CAKE?!
HAHAHA
GRAB A SLICE BEFORE THOSE TWO GLUTTONS GET A HOLD OF IT...
AH! THINGS ARE BACK THE WAY THEY WERE...
NOW THIS IS A GREAT BIRTHDAY PRESENT!
22

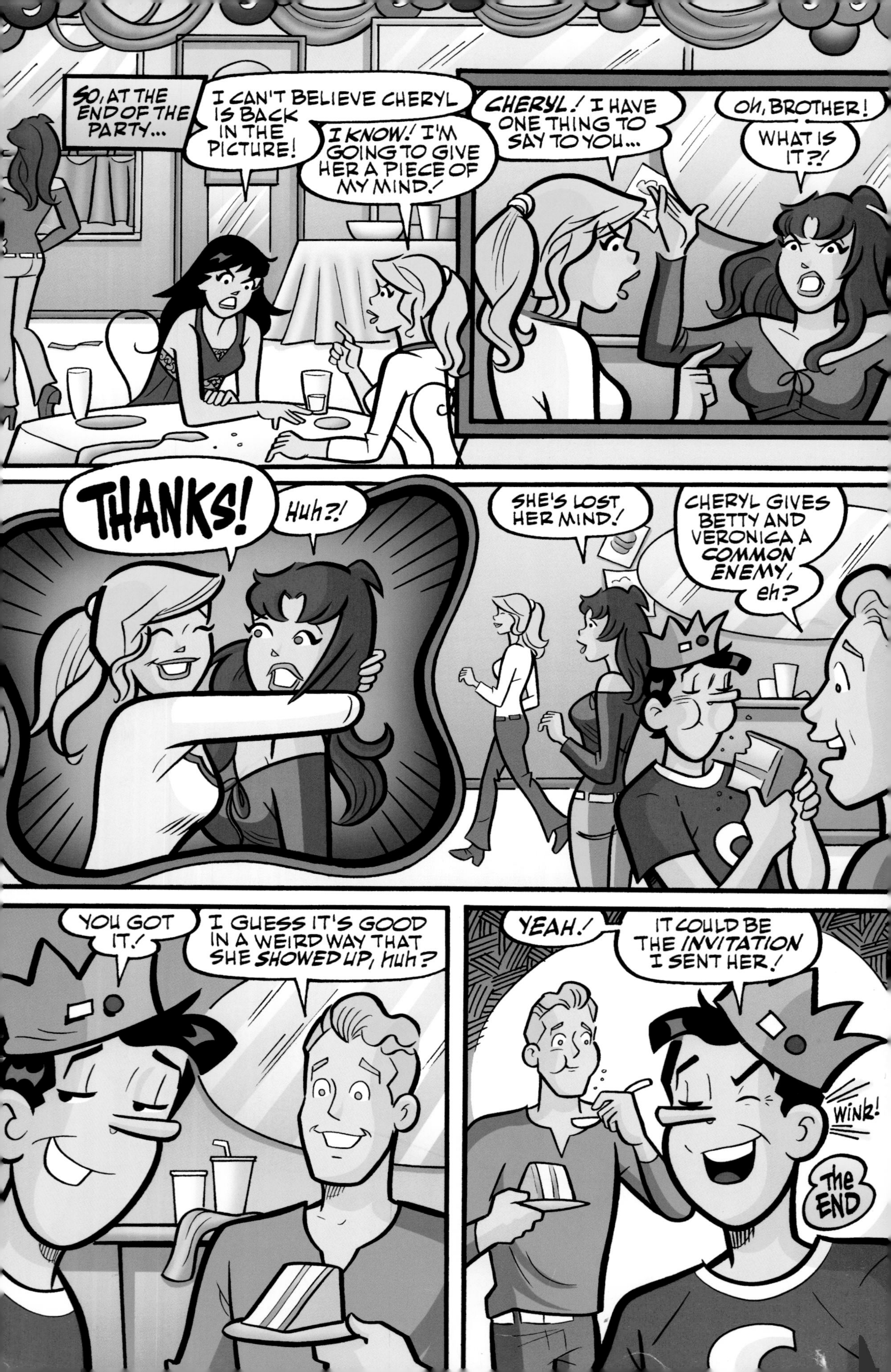

SO, AT THE END OF THE PARTY...
I CAN'T BELIEVE CHERYL IS BACK IN THE PICTURE!
I KNOW! I'M GOING TO GIVE HER A PIECE OF MY MIND!
CHERYL! I HAVE ONE THING TO SAY TO YOU...
OH, BROTHER!
WHAT IS IT?!
THANKS!
HUH?!
SHE'S LOST HER MIND!
CHERYL GIVES BETTY AND VERONICA A COMMON ENEMY, EH?
YOU GOT IT!
I GUESS IT'S GOOD IN A WEIRD WAY THAT SHE SHOWED UP, HUH?
YEAH!
IT COULD BE THE INVITATION I SENT HER!
WINK!
THE END

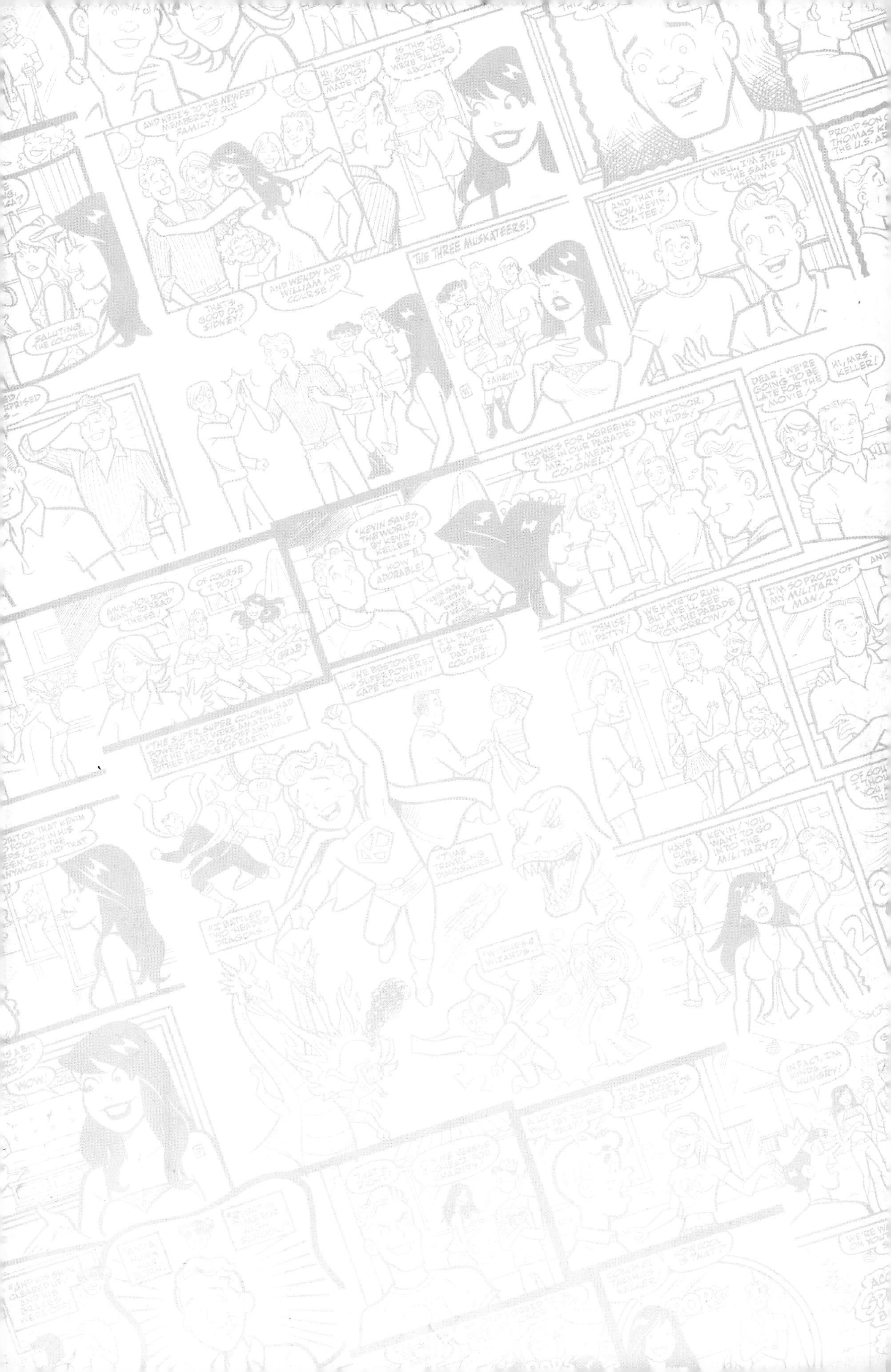
AND HERE'S TO THE NEWEST MEMBERS OF OUR FAMILY!
HI, SIDNEY! GLAD YOU MADE IT!
IS THIS THE SIDNEY YOU WERE TALKING ABOUT?
AND THAT'S YOU, KEVIN! TO A TEE!
WELL, I'M STILL THE SAME KEVIN...
SALUTING THE COLONEL!
THAT'S GOOD OLD SIDNEY!
AND WENDY AND WILLIAM, OF COURSE!
THE THREE MUSKATEERS!
DEAR! WE'RE GOING TO BE LATE FOR THE MOVIE!
HI, MRS. KELLER!
THANKS FOR AGREEING TO BE IN OUR PARADE, MR.-- I MEAN COLONEL!
MY HONOR, KIDS!
"KEVIN SAVES THE WORLD!" BY KEVIN KELLER!
HOW ADORABLE!
AWW, YOU DON'T WANT TO READ THESE!
OF COURSE I DO!
GRAB
HI, DENISE! HI, PATTY!
WE HATE TO RUN, BUT WE'LL SEE YOU AT THE PARADE TOMORROW!
I'M SO PROUD OF MY MILITARY MAN!
"HE BESTOWED HIS SUPER POWERED CAPE TO KEVIN!"
I'LL PROTECT US, SUPER DAD, ER... COLONEL!
"THE SUPER SUPER COLONEL HAD POWERS THAT WERE AMAZING! BUT HE HAD TO GO OFF AND HELP OTHER PEOPLE OF EARTH.
"TIME TRAVELING DINOSAURS...
HAVE FUN, KIDS!
KEVIN! YOU WANT TO GO INTO THE MILITARY?!
"I BATTLED TWO-HEADED DRAGONS...
"WITCHES & WIZARDS...
WOW!
IN FACT, I'M KINDA... HUNGRY!

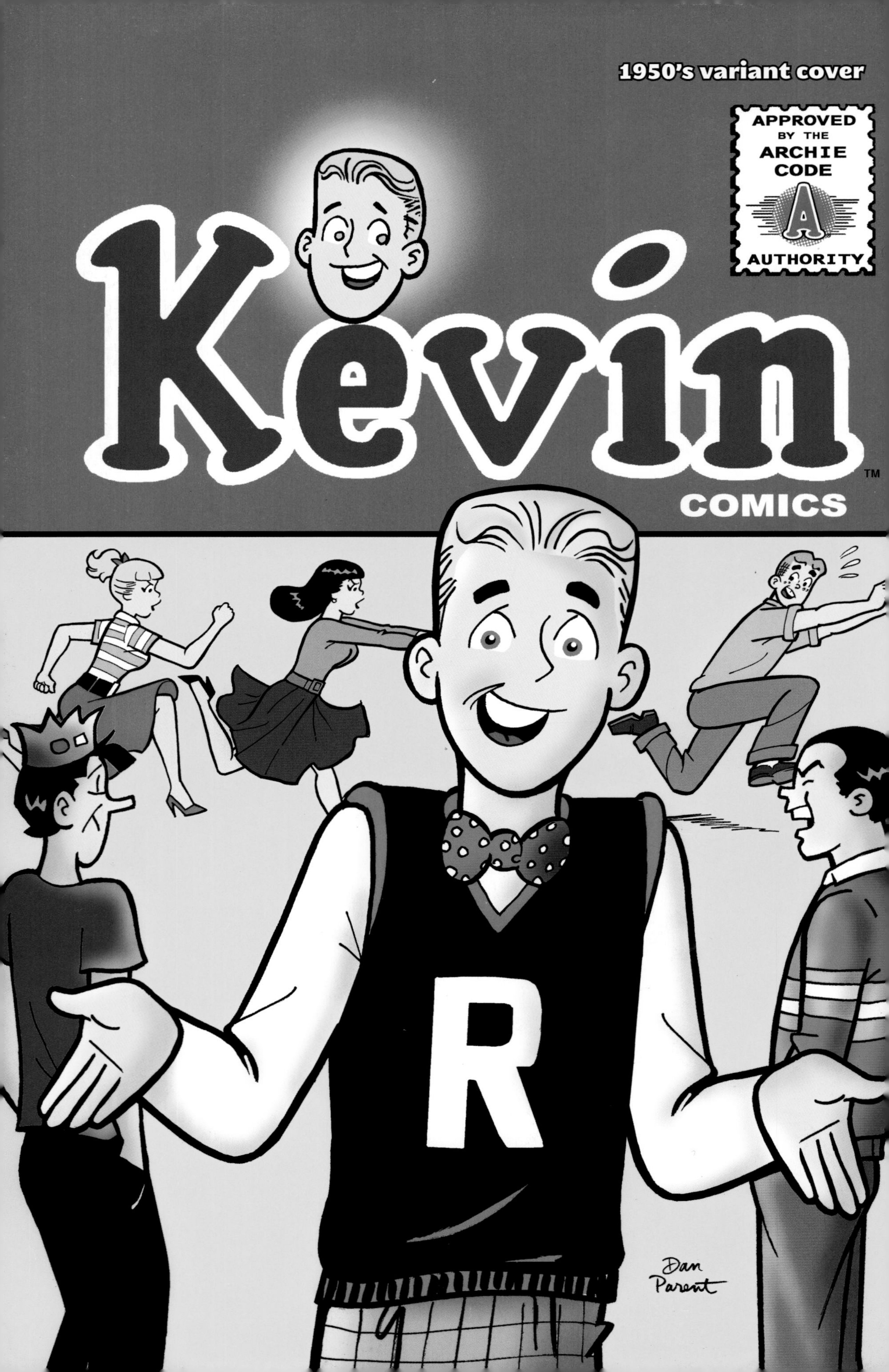
1950's variant cover
APPROVED BY THE ARCHIE CODE AUTHORITY
Kevin
TM
COMICS
Dan Parent

Part 3: Meet Kevin Keller!

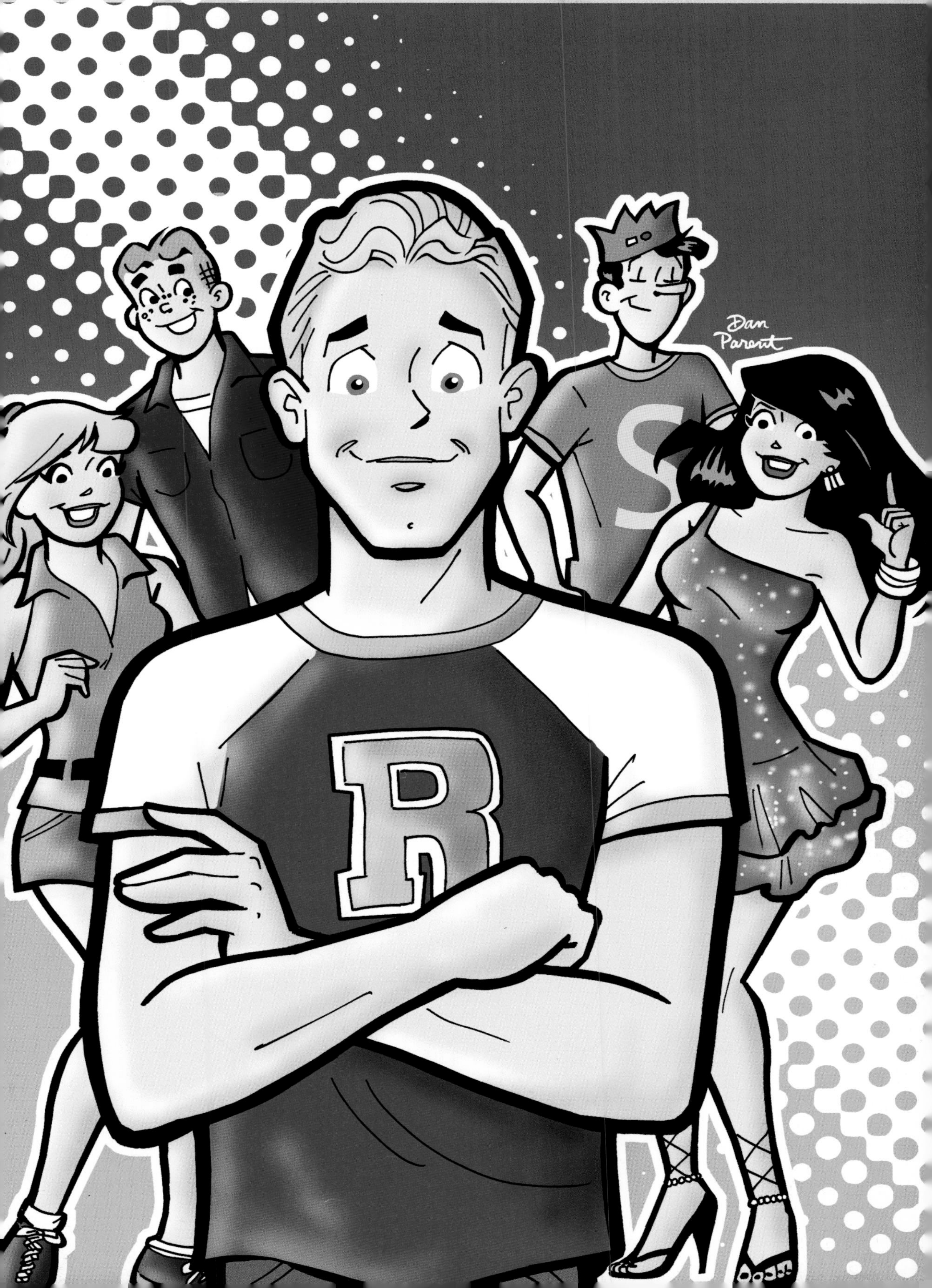
Dan Parent

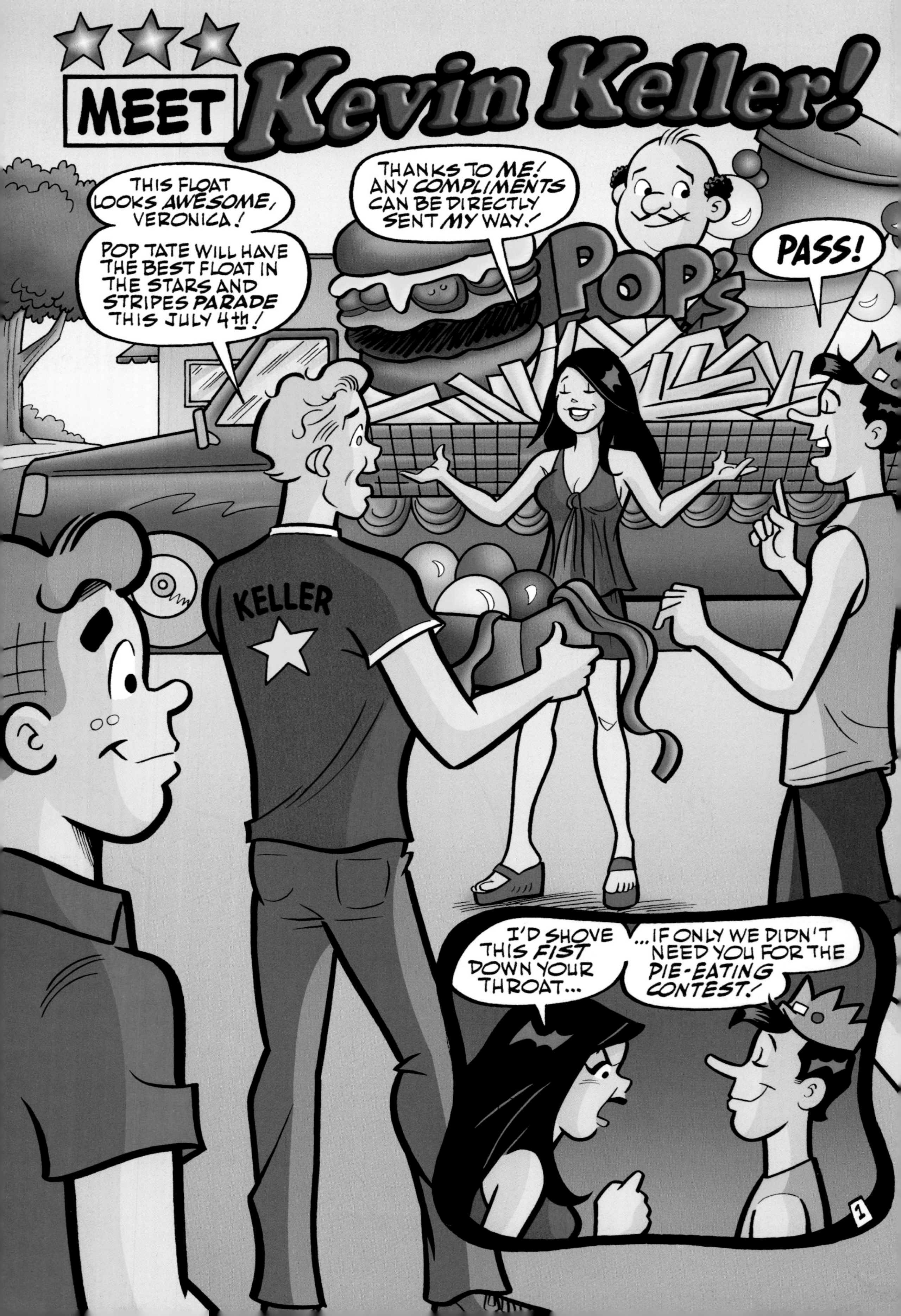
MEET Kevin Keller!
THIS FLOAT LOOKS AWESOME, VERONICA!
POP TATE WILL HAVE THE BEST FLOAT IN THE STARS AND STRIPES PARADE THIS JULY 4th!
THANKS TO ME! ANY COMPLIMENTS CAN BE DIRECTLY SENT MY WAY!
POP'S
PASS!
KELLER
I'D SHOVE THIS FIST DOWN YOUR THROAT...
...IF ONLY WE DIDN'T NEED YOU FOR THE PIE-EATING CONTEST!
1

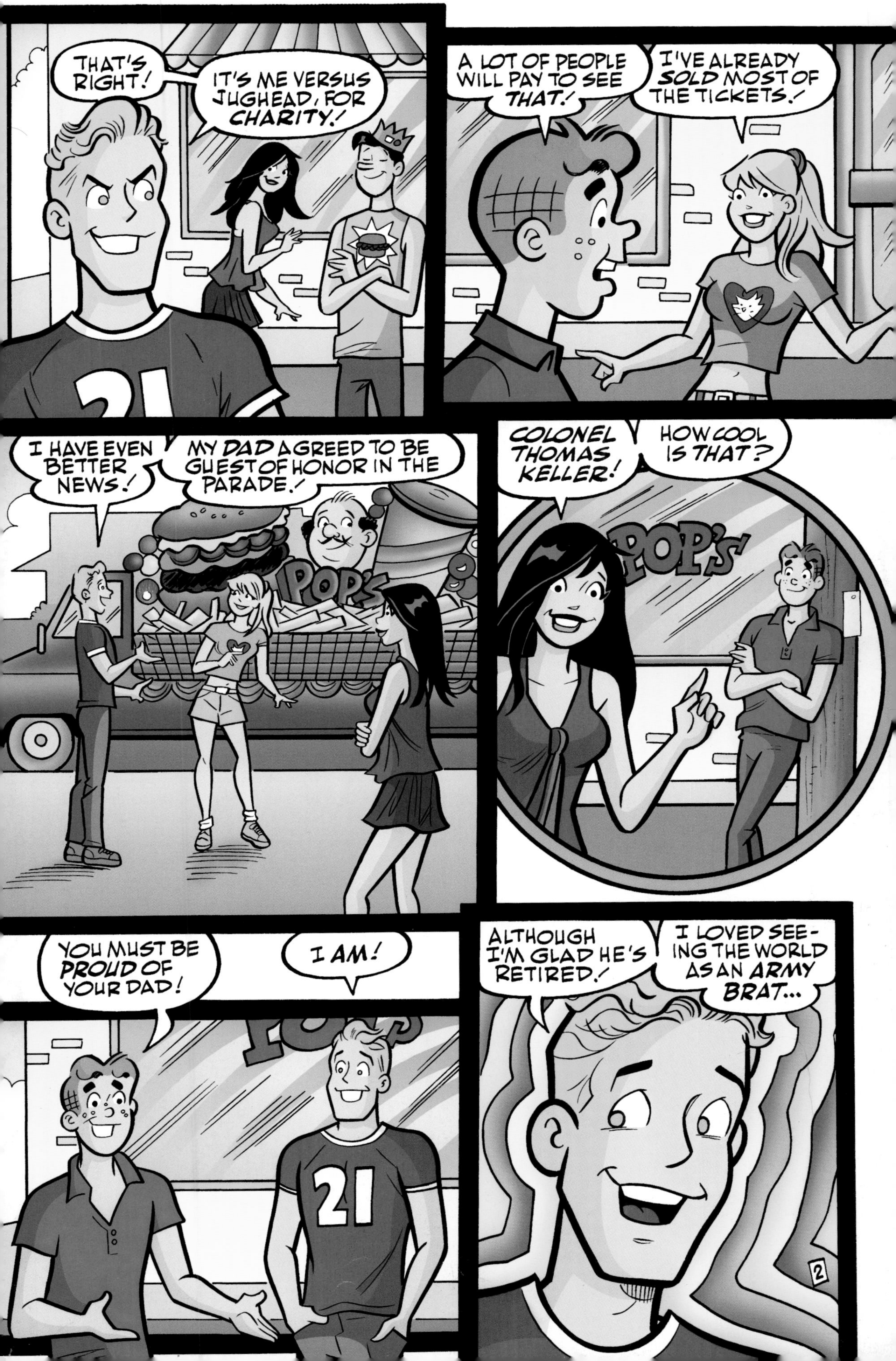
THAT'S RIGHT!
IT'S ME VERSUS JUGHEAD, FOR CHARITY!
A LOT OF PEOPLE WILL PAY TO SEE THAT!
I'VE ALREADY SOLD MOST OF THE TICKETS!
I HAVE EVEN BETTER NEWS!
MY DAD AGREED TO BE GUEST OF HONOR IN THE PARADE!
POP'S
COLONEL THOMAS KELLER!
HOW COOL IS THAT?
POP'S
YOU MUST BE PROUD OF YOUR DAD!
I AM!
ALTHOUGH I'M GLAD HE'S RETIRED!
I LOVED SEE-ING THE WORLD AS AN ARMY BRAT...
2

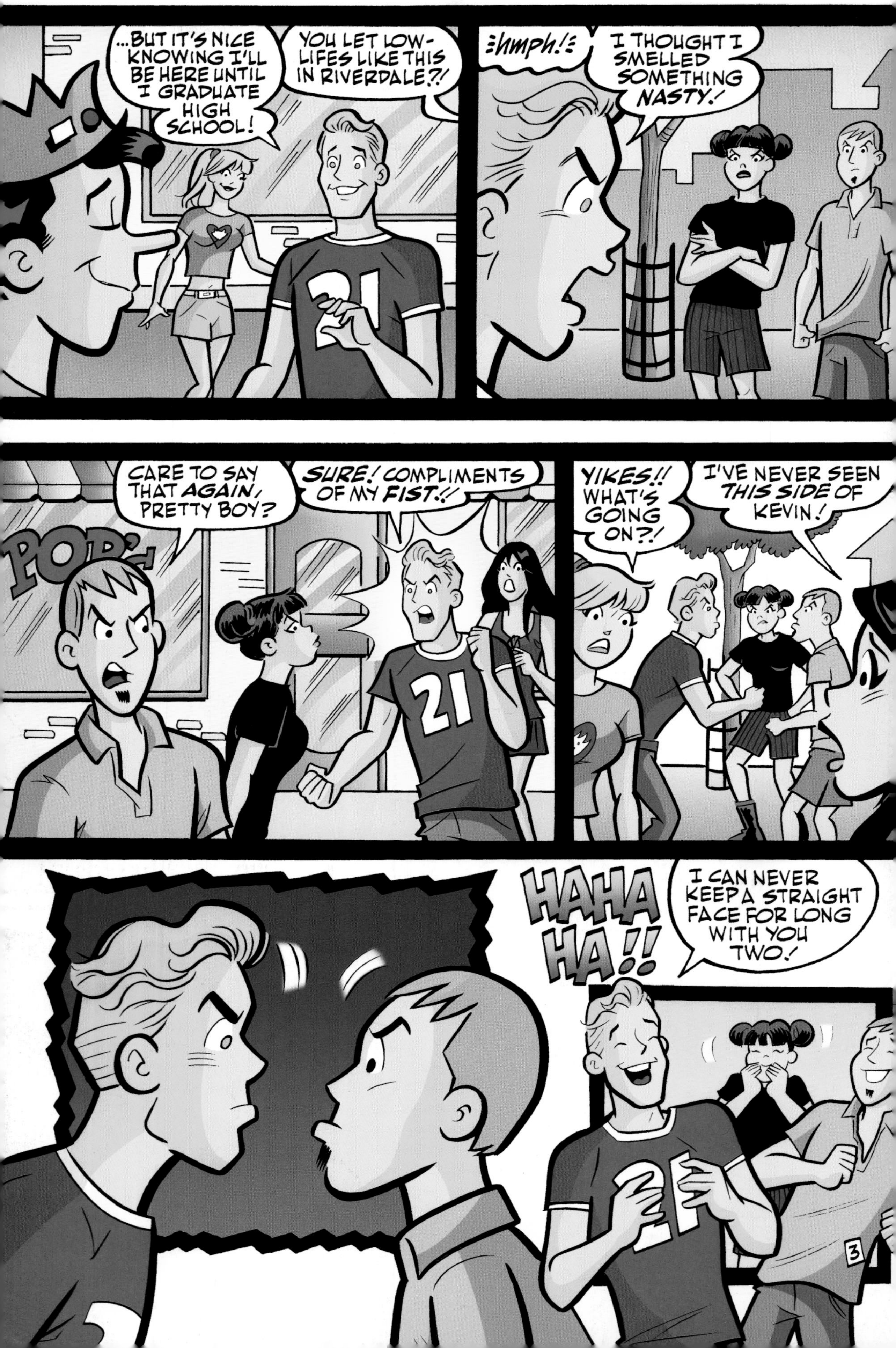
...BUT IT'S NICE KNOWING I'LL BE HERE UNTIL I GRADUATE HIGH SCHOOL!
YOU LET LOW-LIFES LIKE THIS IN RIVERDALE?!
:hmph!:
I THOUGHT I SMELLED SOMETHING NASTY!
CARE TO SAY THAT AGAIN, PRETTY BOY?
SURE! COMPLIMENTS OF MY FIST!!
POP
YIKES!! WHAT'S GOING ON?!
I'VE NEVER SEEN THIS SIDE OF KEVIN!
HAHA HA!!
I CAN NEVER KEEP A STRAIGHT FACE FOR LONG WITH YOU TWO!
3

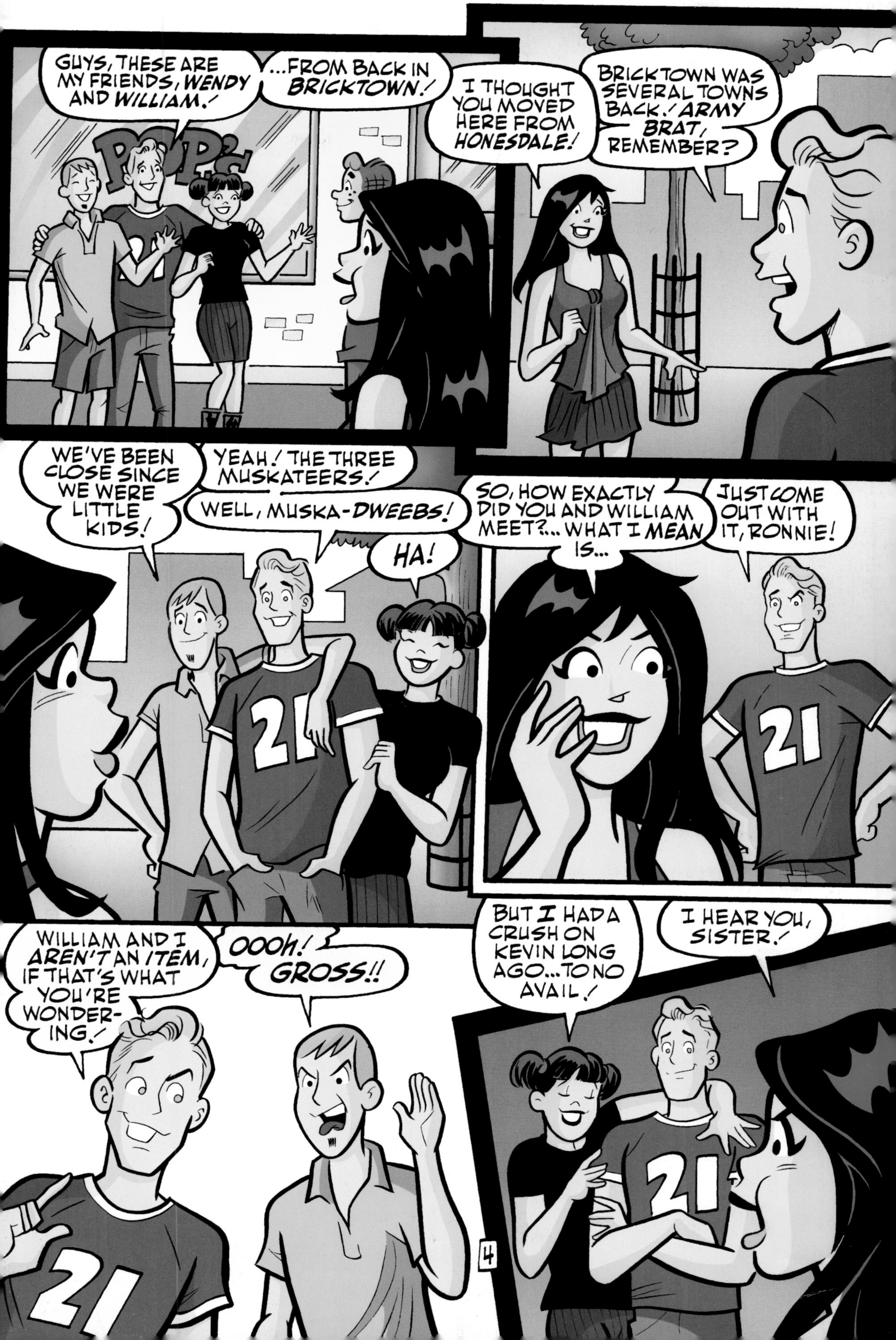
GUYS, THESE ARE MY FRIENDS, WENDY AND WILLIAM.!
...FROM BACK IN BRICKTOWN!
POP'S
I THOUGHT YOU MOVED HERE FROM HONESDALE!
BRICKTOWN WAS SEVERAL TOWNS BACK.! ARMY BRAT, REMEMBER?
WE'VE BEEN CLOSE SINCE WE WERE LITTLE KIDS!
YEAH! THE THREE MUSKATEERS!
WELL, MUSKA-DWEEBS!
HA!
SO, HOW EXACTLY DID YOU AND WILLIAM MEET?... WHAT I MEAN IS...
JUST COME OUT WITH IT, RONNIE!
WILLIAM AND I AREN'T AN ITEM, IF THAT'S WHAT YOU'RE WONDERING.!
OOOH! GROSS!!
BUT I HAD A CRUSH ON KEVIN LONG AGO...TO NO AVAIL!
I HEAR YOU, SISTER.!
4

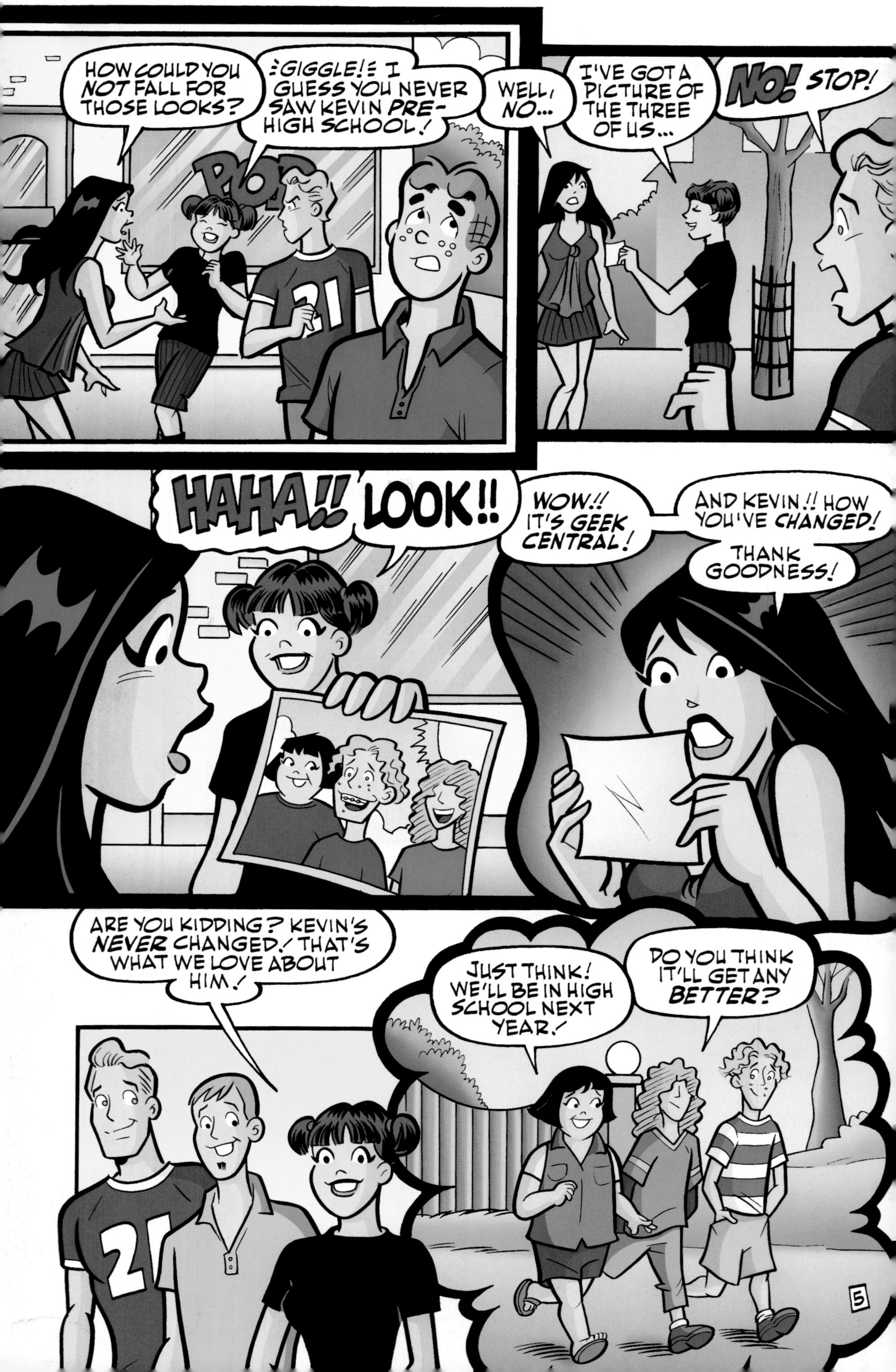
HOW COULD YOU NOT FALL FOR THOSE LOOKS?
:GIGGLE!: I GUESS YOU NEVER SAW KEVIN PRE-HIGH SCHOOL!
POP
WELL, NO...
I'VE GOT A PICTURE OF THE THREE OF US...
NO! STOP!
HAHA!! LOOK!!
WOW!! IT'S GEEK CENTRAL!
AND KEVIN!! HOW YOU'VE CHANGED!
THANK GOODNESS!
ARE YOU KIDDING? KEVIN'S NEVER CHANGED! THAT'S WHAT WE LOVE ABOUT HIM!
JUST THINK! WE'LL BE IN HIGH SCHOOL NEXT YEAR!
DO YOU THINK IT'LL GET ANY BETTER?
21
21
5

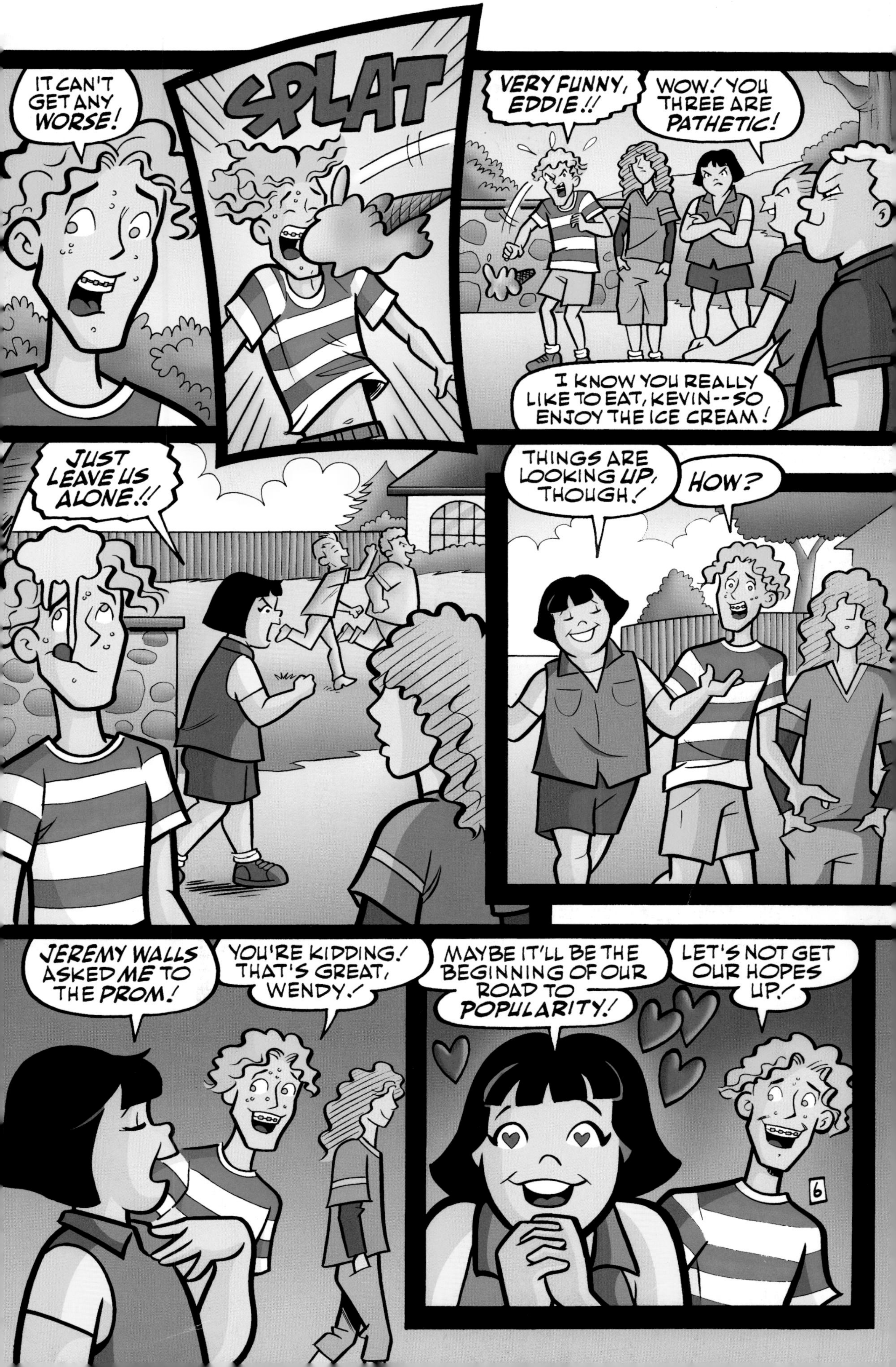
IT CAN'T GET ANY WORSE!
SPLAT
VERY FUNNY, EDDIE!!
WOW! YOU THREE ARE PATHETIC!
I KNOW YOU REALLY LIKE TO EAT, KEVIN--SO ENJOY THE ICE CREAM!
JUST LEAVE US ALONE!!
THINGS ARE LOOKING UP, THOUGH!
HOW?
JEREMY WALLS ASKED ME TO THE PROM!
YOU'RE KIDDING! THAT'S GREAT, WENDY!
MAYBE IT'LL BE THE BEGINNING OF OUR ROAD TO POPULARITY!
LET'S NOT GET OUR HOPES UP!
6

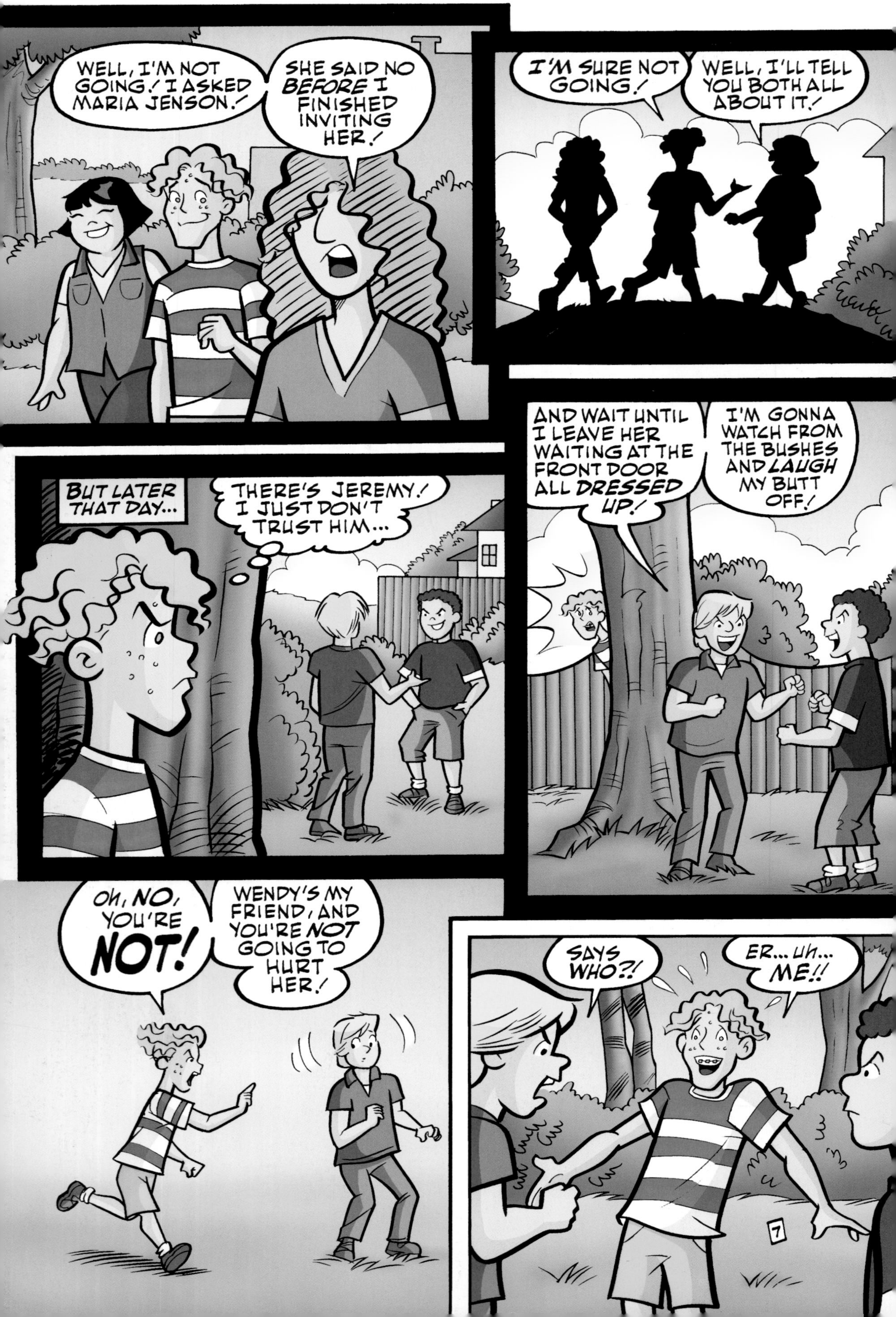
WELL, I'M NOT GOING! I ASKED MARIA JENSON!
SHE SAID NO BEFORE I FINISHED INVITING HER!
I'M SURE NOT GOING!
WELL, I'LL TELL YOU BOTH ALL ABOUT IT!
BUT LATER THAT DAY...
THERE'S JEREMY! I JUST DON'T TRUST HIM...
AND WAIT UNTIL I LEAVE HER WAITING AT THE FRONT DOOR ALL DRESSED UP!
I'M GONNA WATCH FROM THE BUSHES AND LAUGH MY BUTT OFF!
Oh, NO, YOU'RE NOT!
WENDY'S MY FRIEND, AND YOU'RE NOT GOING TO HURT HER!
SAYS WHO?!
ER... uh... ME!!
7

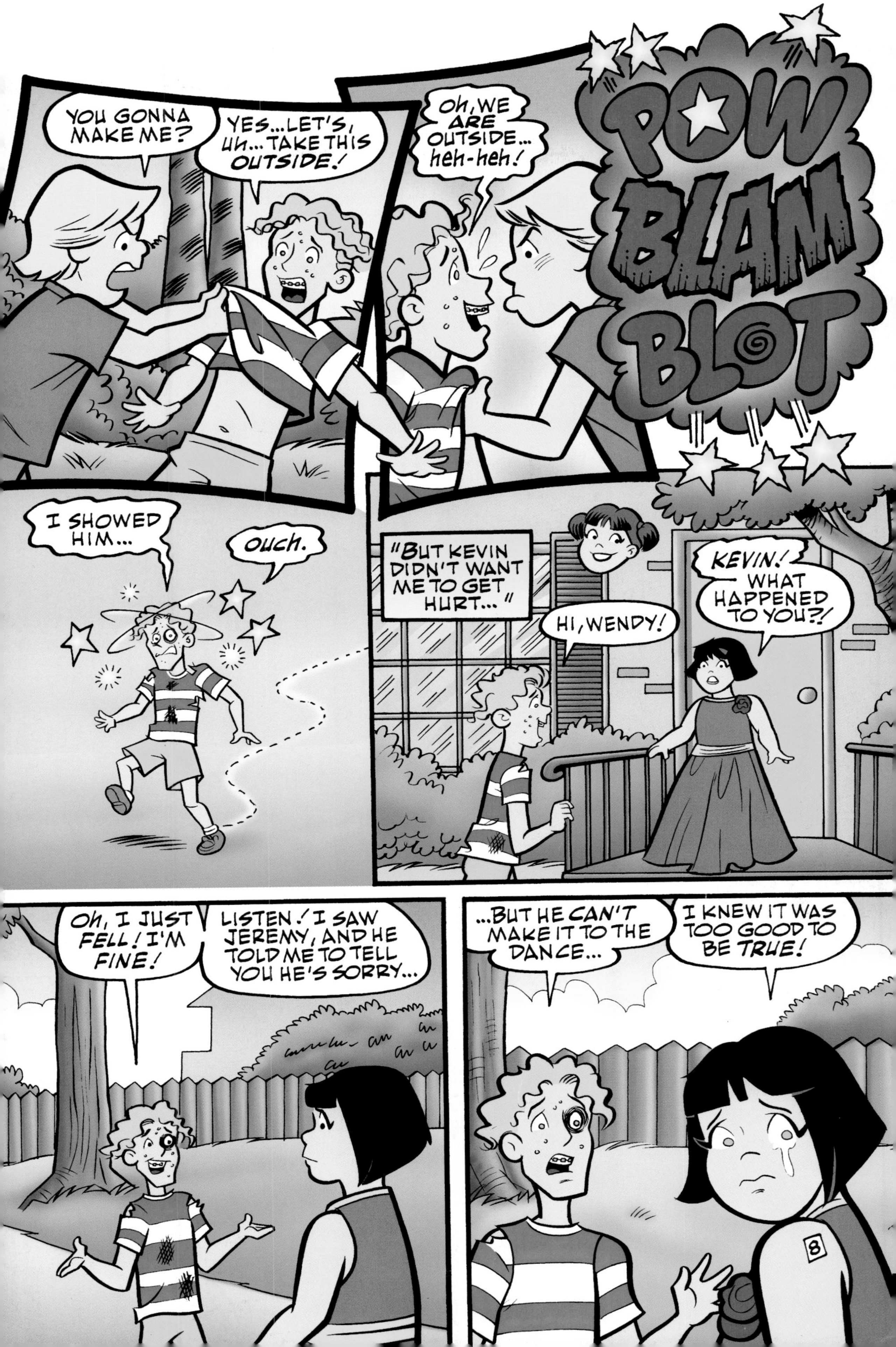
YOU GONNA MAKE ME?
YES...LET'S, uh... TAKE THIS OUTSIDE!
Oh, WE ARE OUTSIDE... heh-heh!
POW
BLAM
BLOT
I SHOWED HIM...
ouch.
"BUT KEVIN DIDN'T WANT ME TO GET HURT..."
HI, WENDY!
KEVIN! WHAT HAPPENED TO YOU?!
Oh, I JUST FELL! I'M FINE!
LISTEN! I SAW JEREMY, AND HE TOLD ME TO TELL YOU HE'S SORRY...
...BUT HE CAN'T MAKE IT TO THE DANCE...
I KNEW IT WAS TOO GOOD TO BE TRUE!
8

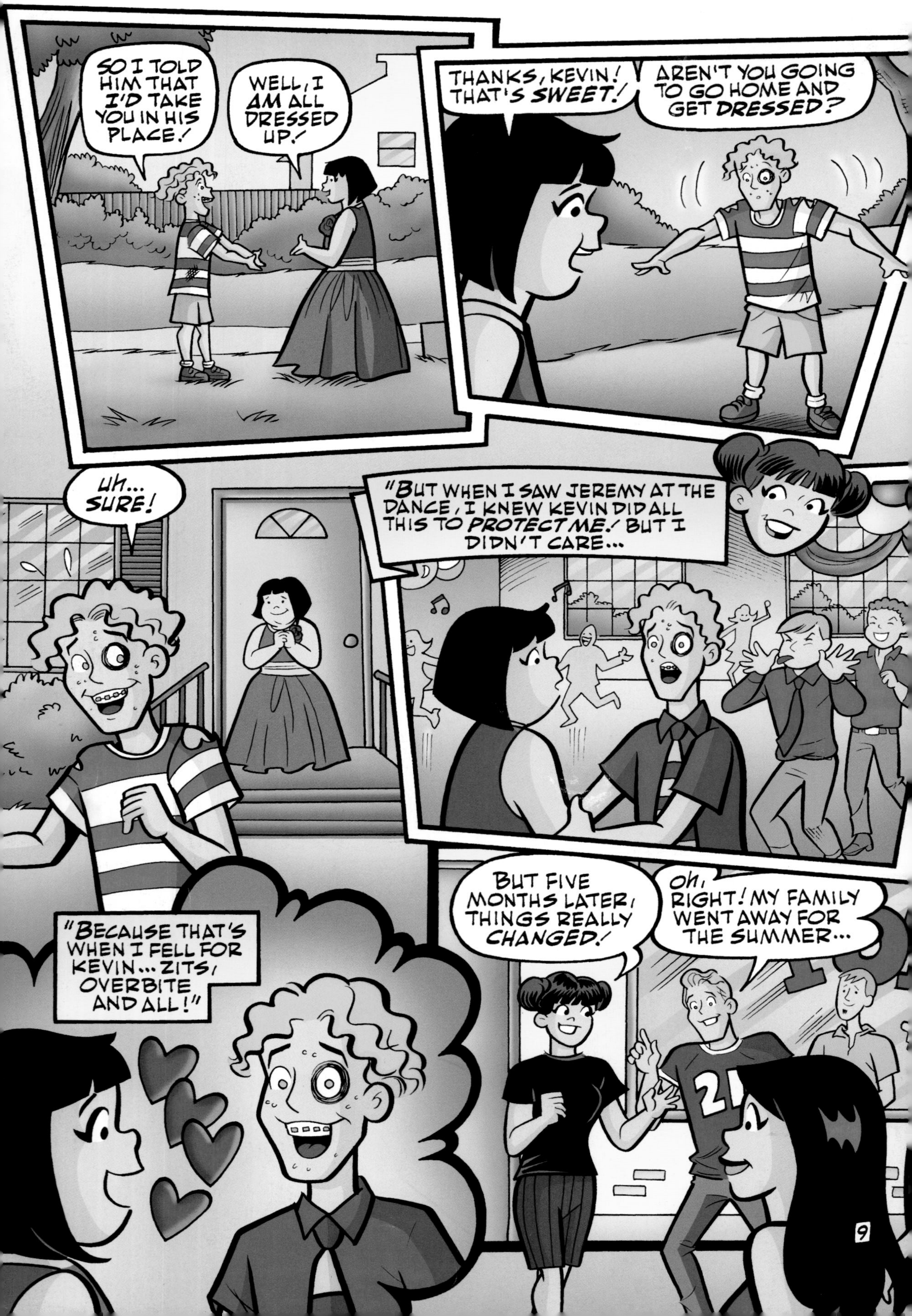
SO I TOLD HIM THAT I'D TAKE YOU IN HIS PLACE!
WELL, I AM ALL DRESSED UP!
THANKS, KEVIN! THAT'S SWEET!
AREN'T YOU GOING TO GO HOME AND GET DRESSED?
uh... SURE!
"BUT WHEN I SAW JEREMY AT THE DANCE, I KNEW KEVIN DID ALL THIS TO PROTECT ME! BUT I DIDN'T CARE...
"BECAUSE THAT'S WHEN I FELL FOR KEVIN... ZITS, OVERBITE AND ALL!"
BUT FIVE MONTHS LATER, THINGS REALLY CHANGED!
oh, RIGHT! MY FAMILY WENT AWAY FOR THE SUMMER...
21
9

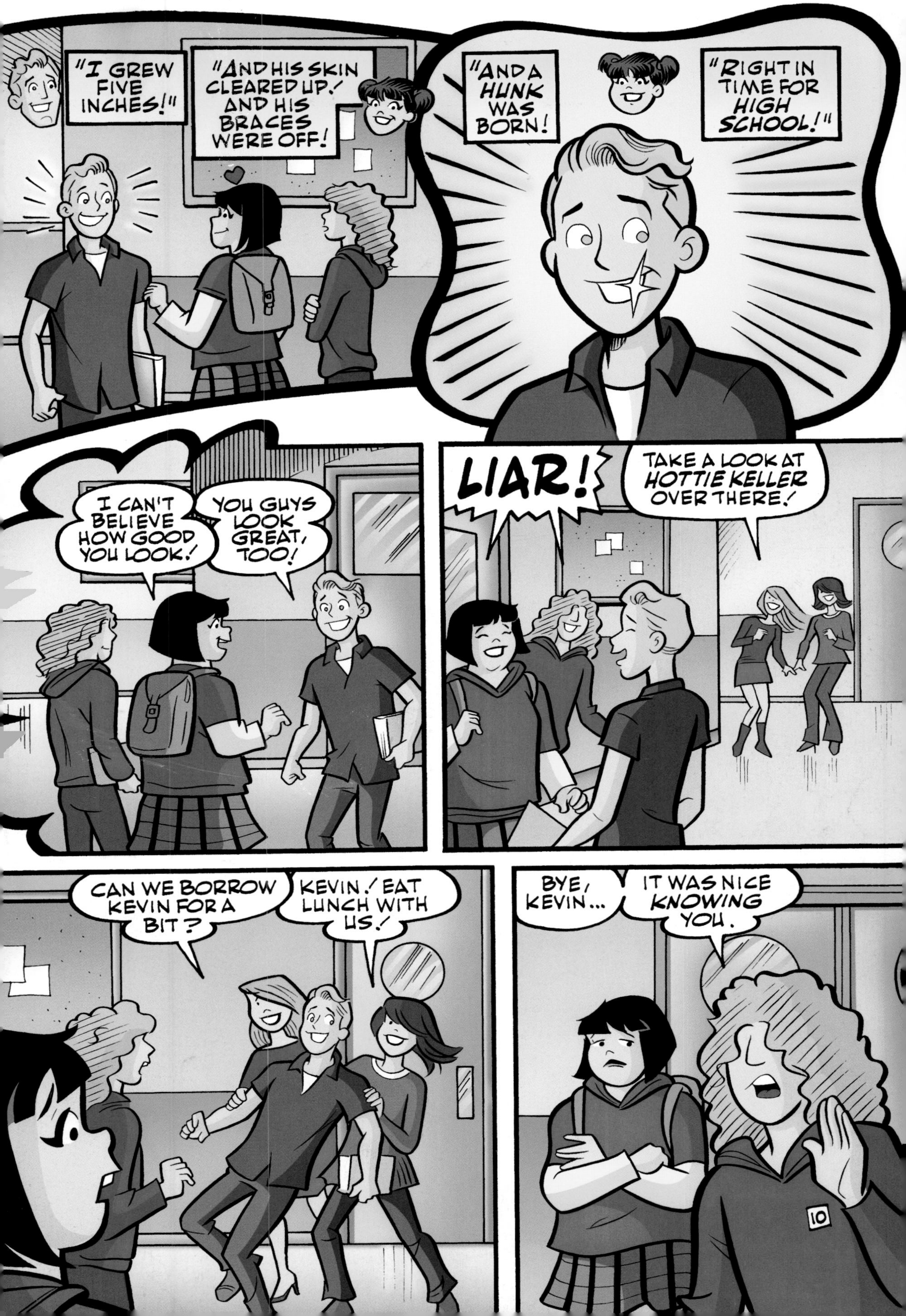
"I GREW FIVE INCHES!"
"AND HIS SKIN CLEARED UP! AND HIS BRACES WERE OFF!
"AND A HUNK WAS BORN!
"RIGHT IN TIME FOR HIGH SCHOOL!"
I CAN'T BELIEVE HOW GOOD YOU LOOK!
YOU GUYS LOOK GREAT, TOO!
LIAR!
TAKE A LOOK AT HOTTIE KELLER OVER THERE!
CAN WE BORROW KEVIN FOR A BIT?
KEVIN! EAT LUNCH WITH US!
BYE, KEVIN...
IT WAS NICE KNOWING YOU.
10

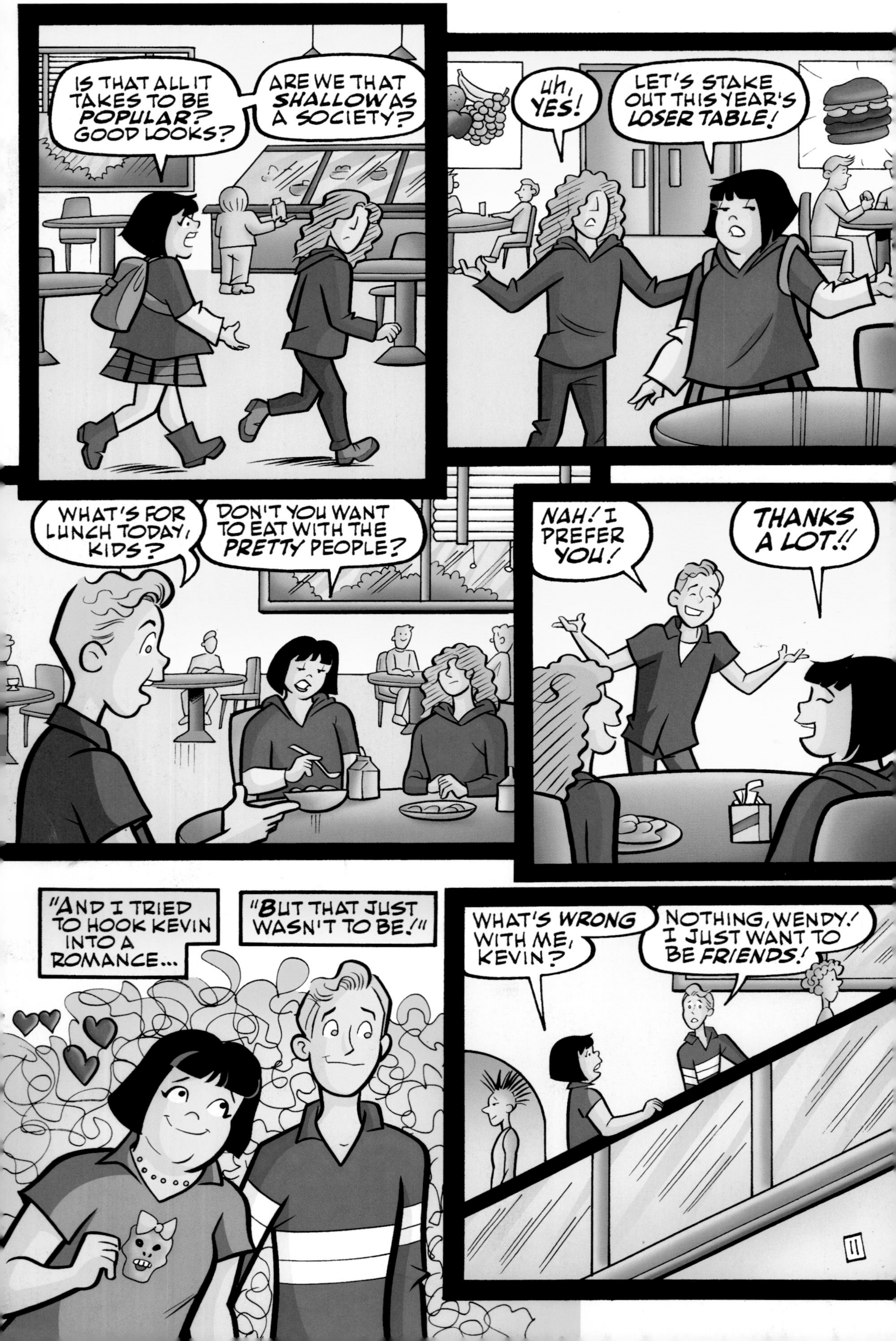
IS THAT ALL IT TAKES TO BE POPULAR? GOOD LOOKS?
ARE WE THAT SHALLOW AS A SOCIETY?
uh, YES!
LET'S STAKE OUT THIS YEAR'S LOSER TABLE!
WHAT'S FOR LUNCH TODAY, KIDS?
DON'T YOU WANT TO EAT WITH THE PRETTY PEOPLE?
NAH! I PREFER YOU!
THANKS A LOT!!
"AND I TRIED TO HOOK KEVIN INTO A ROMANCE...
"BUT THAT JUST WASN'T TO BE!"
WHAT'S WRONG WITH ME, KEVIN?
NOTHING, WENDY! I JUST WANT TO BE FRIENDS!
11

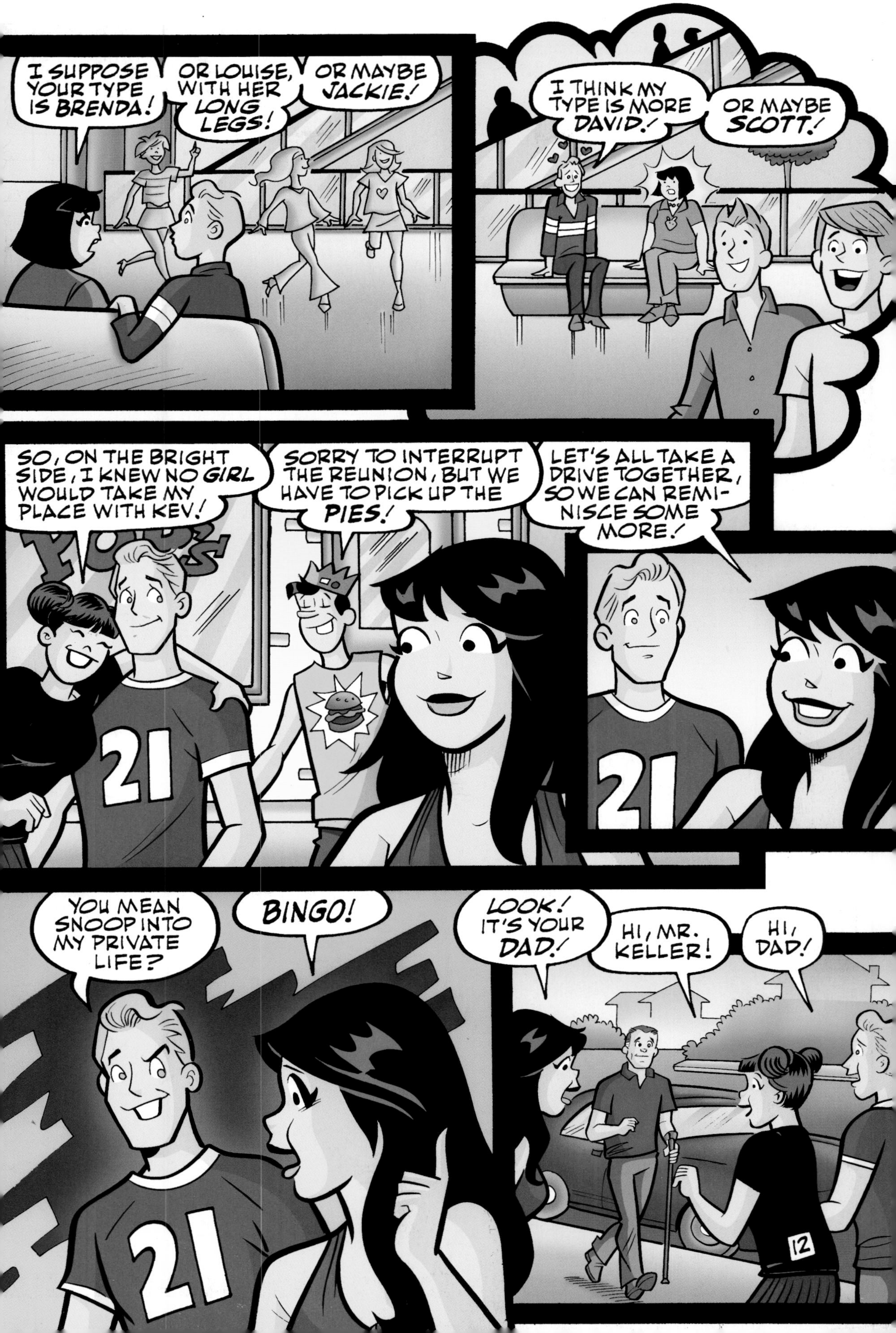

I SUPPOSE YOUR TYPE IS BRENDA!
OR LOUISE, WITH HER LONG LEGS!
OR MAYBE JACKIE!
I THINK MY TYPE IS MORE DAVID!
OR MAYBE SCOTT!
SO, ON THE BRIGHT SIDE, I KNEW NO GIRL WOULD TAKE MY PLACE WITH KEV!
SORRY TO INTERRUPT THE REUNION, BUT WE HAVE TO PICK UP THE PIES!
LET'S ALL TAKE A DRIVE TOGETHER, SO WE CAN REMI-NISCE SOME MORE!
21
21
YOU MEAN SNOOP INTO MY PRIVATE LIFE?
BINGO!
21
LOOK! IT'S YOUR DAD!
HI, MR. KELLER!
HI, DAD!
12

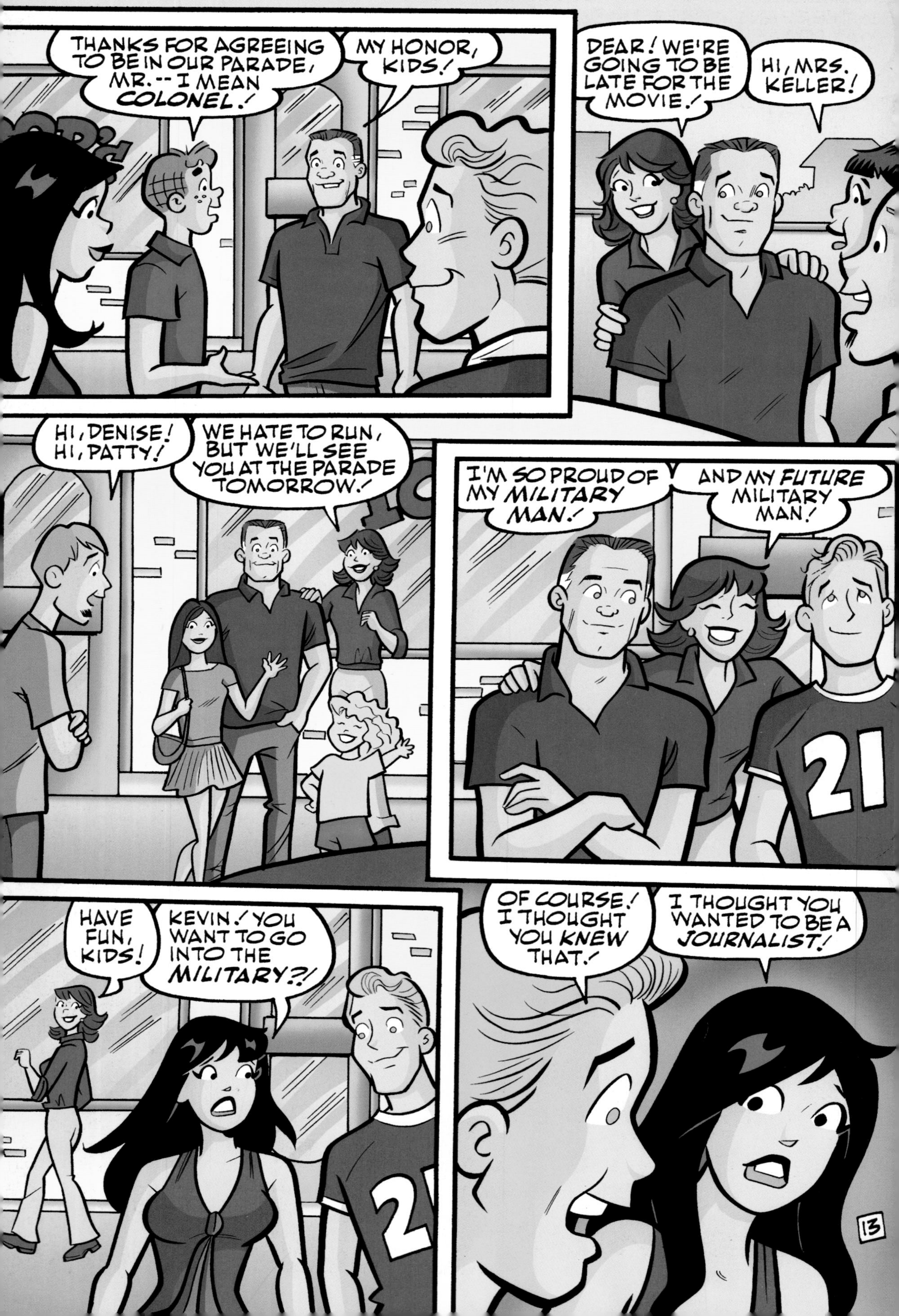

THANKS FOR AGREEING TO BE IN OUR PARADE, MR.-- I MEAN COLONEL!
MY HONOR, KIDS!
DEAR! WE'RE GOING TO BE LATE FOR THE MOVIE!
HI, MRS. KELLER!
HI, DENISE! HI, PATTY!
WE HATE TO RUN, BUT WE'LL SEE YOU AT THE PARADE TOMORROW!
I'M SO PROUD OF MY MILITARY MAN!
AND MY FUTURE MILITARY MAN!
HAVE FUN, KIDS!
KEVIN! YOU WANT TO GO INTO THE MILITARY?!
OF COURSE! I THOUGHT YOU KNEW THAT!
I THOUGHT YOU WANTED TO BE A JOURNALIST!
13

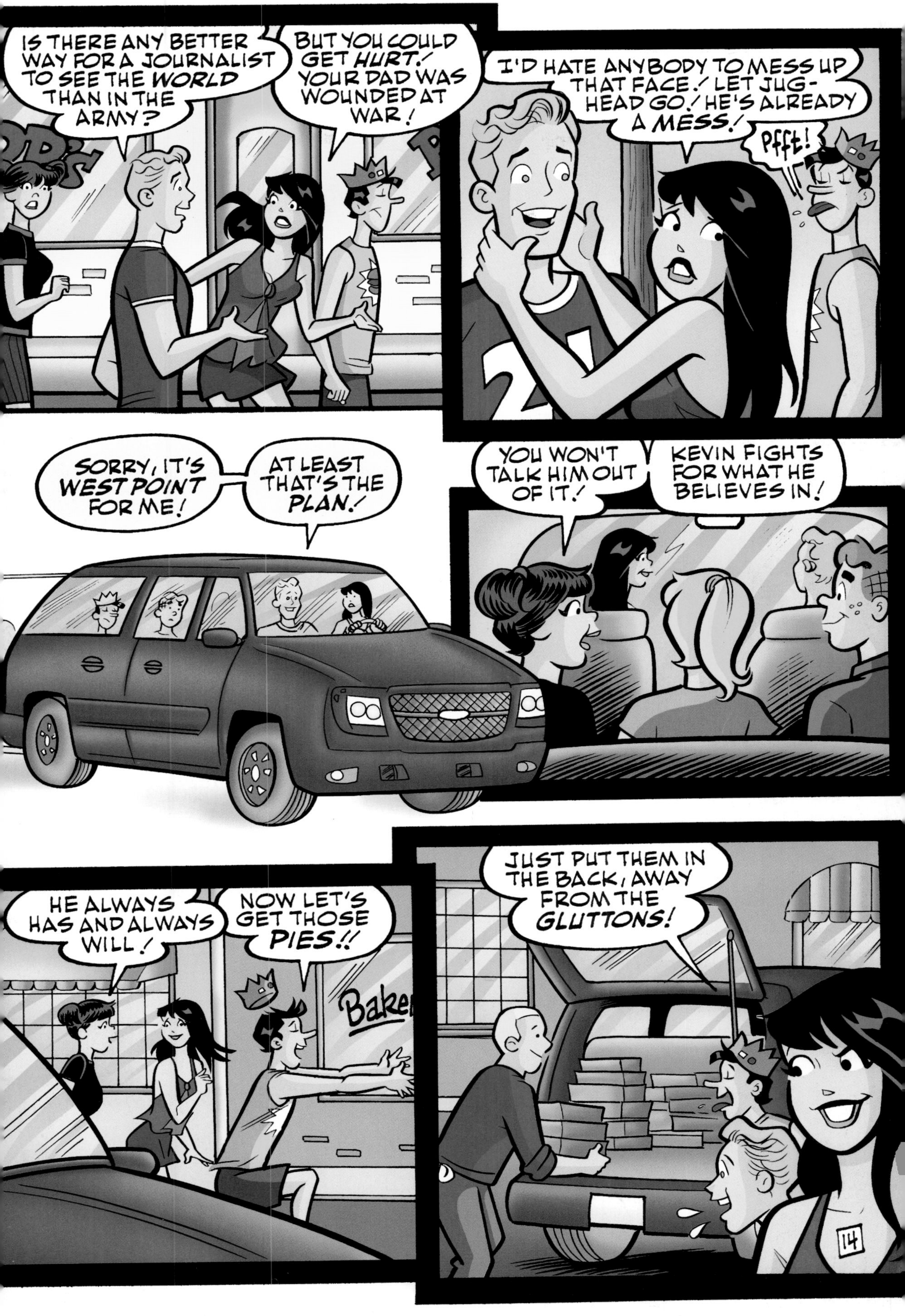
IS THERE ANY BETTER WAY FOR A JOURNALIST TO SEE THE *WORLD* THAN IN THE ARMY?
BUT YOU COULD GET *HURT*! YOUR DAD WAS WOUNDED AT WAR!
I'D HATE ANYBODY TO MESS UP THAT FACE! LET JUG-HEAD GO! HE'S ALREADY A *MESS*!
Pffft!
SORRY, IT'S *WEST POINT* FOR ME!
AT LEAST THAT'S THE *PLAN*!
YOU WON'T TALK HIM OUT OF IT!
KEVIN FIGHTS FOR WHAT HE BELIEVES IN!
HE ALWAYS HAS AND ALWAYS WILL!
NOW LET'S GET THOSE *PIES*!!
Bake
JUST PUT THEM IN THE BACK, AWAY FROM THE *GLUTTONS*!
14

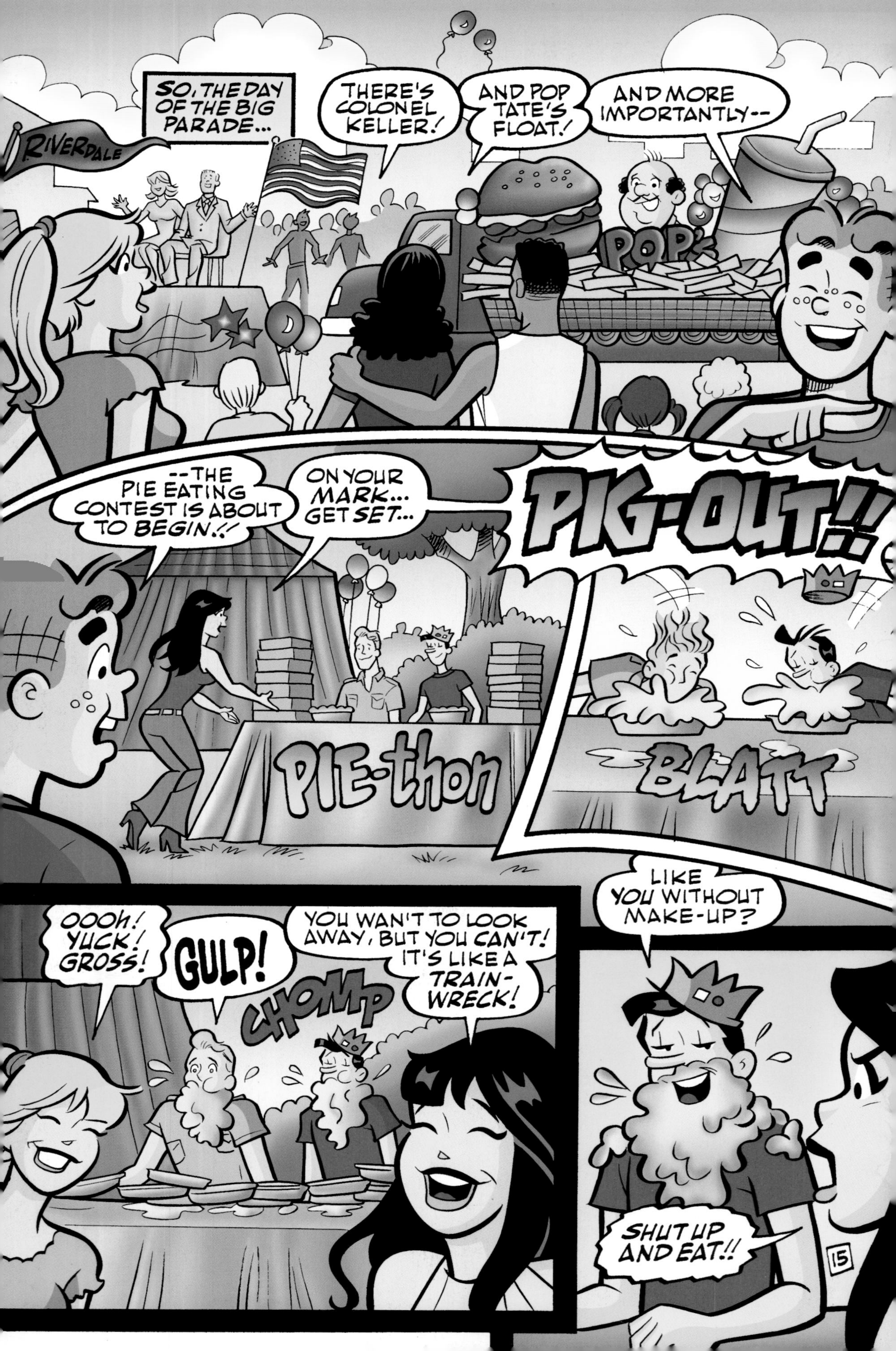
SO, THE DAY OF THE BIG PARADE...
RIVERDALE
THERE'S COLONEL KELLER!
AND POP TATE'S FLOAT!
AND MORE IMPORTANTLY--
POP'S
--THE PIE EATING CONTEST IS ABOUT TO BEGIN!
ON YOUR MARK... GET SET...
PIG-OUT!!
PIE-thon
BLATT
OOOH! YUCK! GROSS!
GULP!
YOU WAN'T TO LOOK AWAY, BUT YOU CAN'T! IT'S LIKE A TRAIN-WRECK!
CHOMP
LIKE YOU WITHOUT MAKE-UP?
SHUT UP AND EAT!!
15

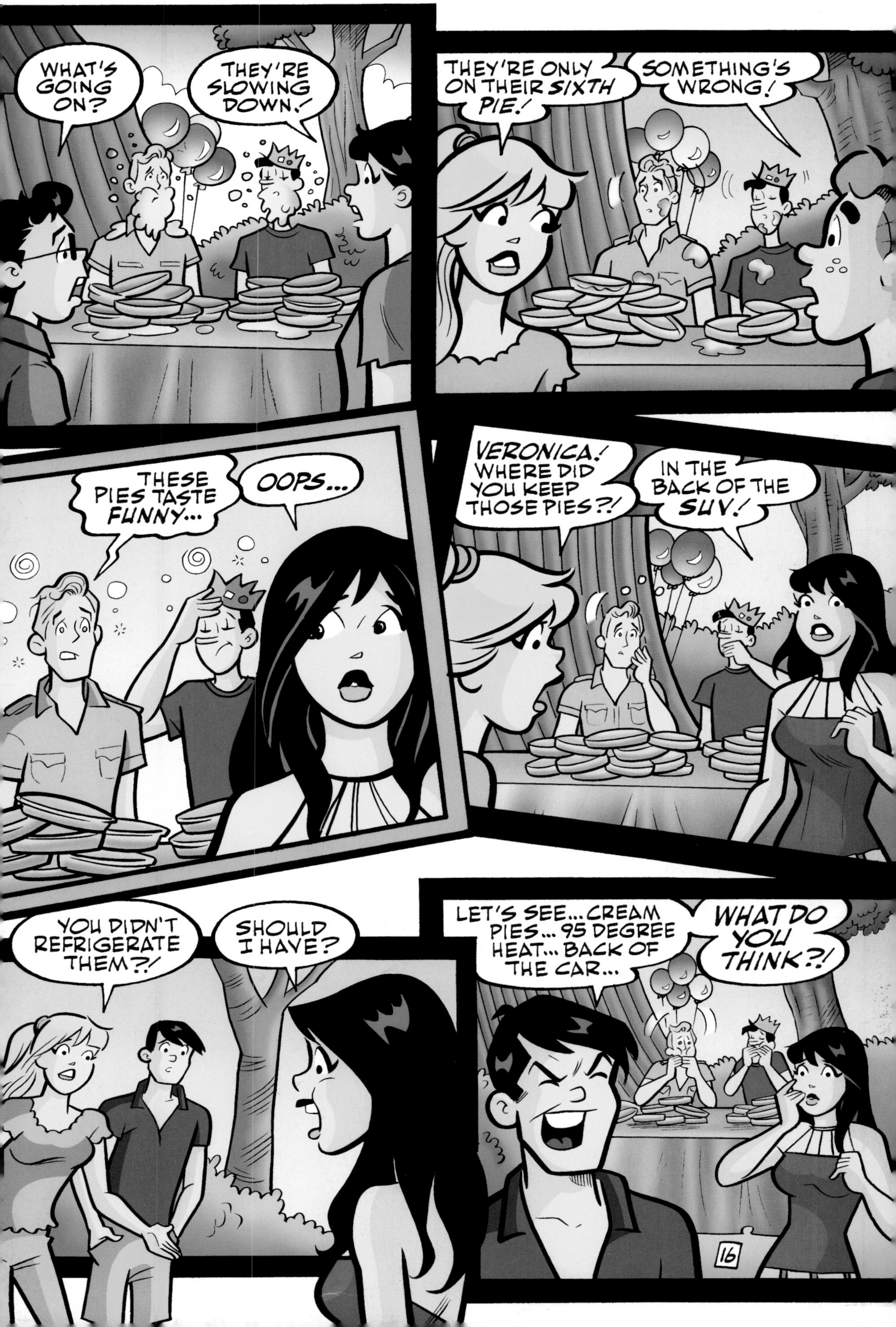
WHAT'S GOING ON?
THEY'RE SLOWING DOWN.!
THEY'RE ONLY ON THEIR SIXTH PIE.!
SOMETHING'S WRONG!
THESE PIES TASTE FUNNY...
OOPS...
VERONICA! WHERE DID YOU KEEP THOSE PIES?!
IN THE BACK OF THE SUV!
YOU DIDN'T REFRIGERATE THEM?!
SHOULD I HAVE?
LET'S SEE... CREAM PIES... 95 DEGREE HEAT... BACK OF THE CAR...
WHAT DO YOU THINK?!
16

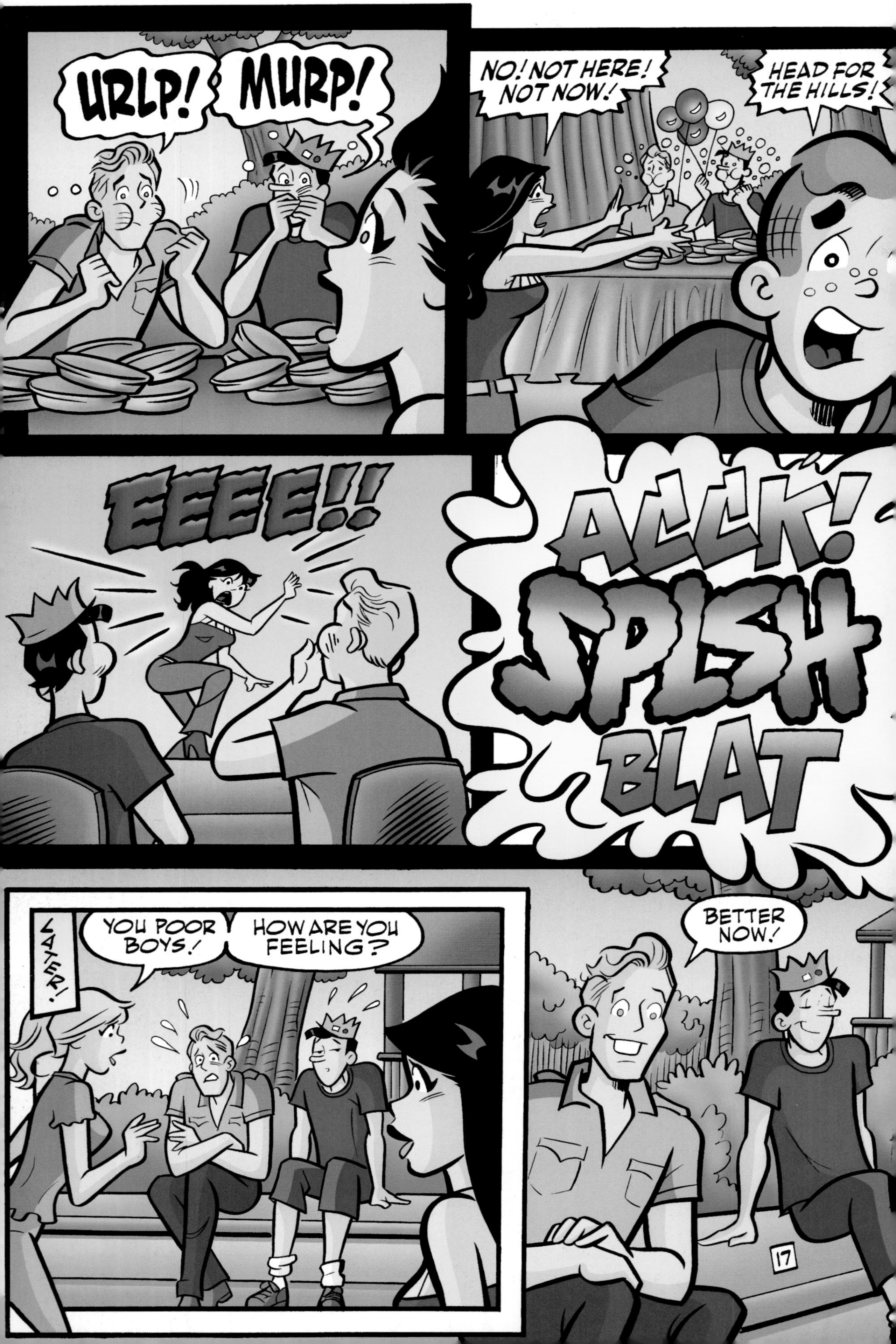
URLP!
MURP!
NO! NOT HERE! NOT NOW!
HEAD FOR THE HILLS!
EEEE!!
ACCK!
SPLSH
BLAT
LATER!
YOU POOR BOYS!
HOW ARE YOU FEELING?
BETTER NOW!
17

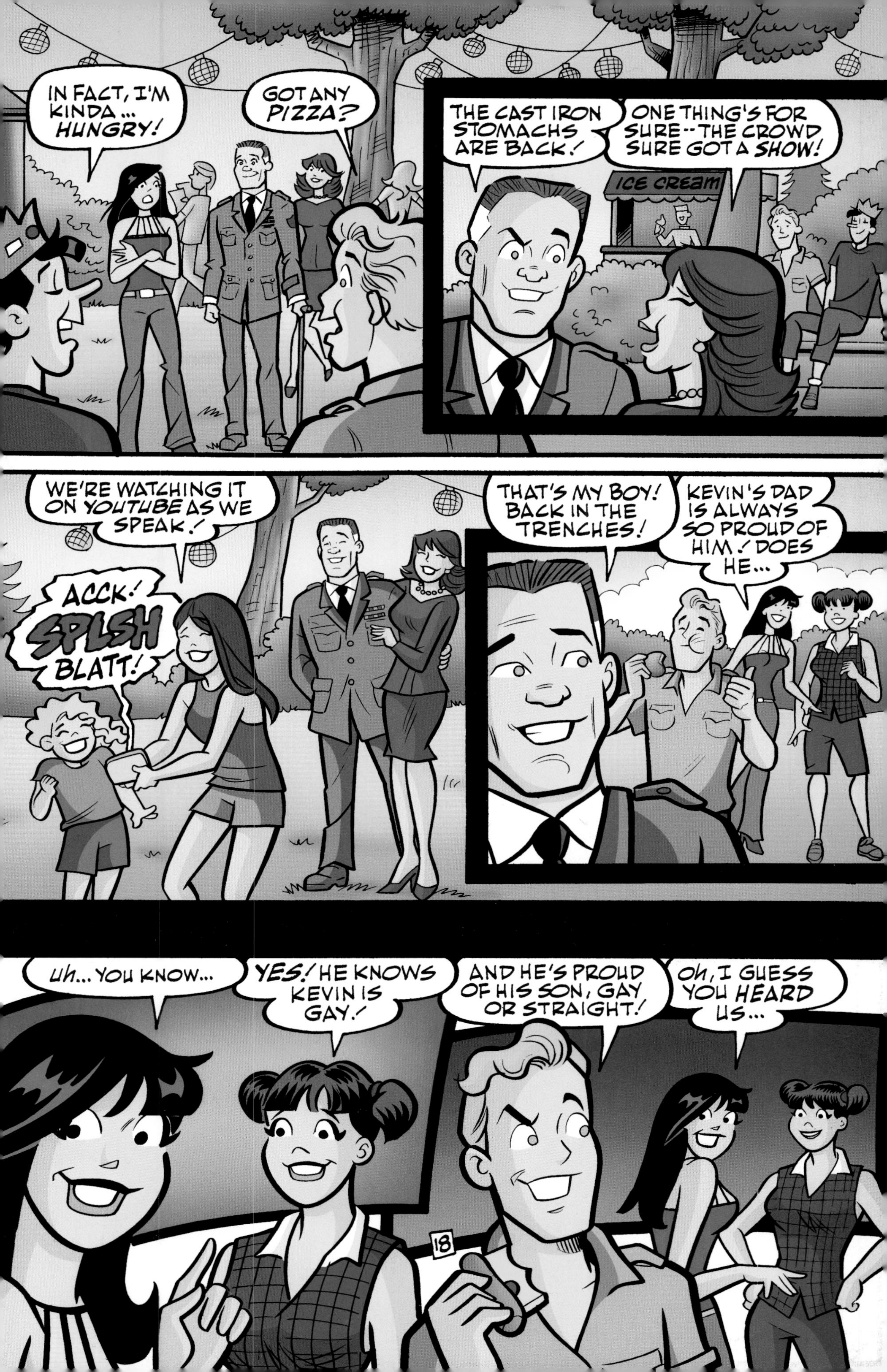
IN FACT, I'M KINDA... HUNGRY!
GOT ANY PIZZA?
THE CAST IRON STOMACHS ARE BACK!
ONE THING'S FOR SURE-- THE CROWD SURE GOT A SHOW!
ICE CREAM
WE'RE WATCHING IT ON YOUTUBE AS WE SPEAK!
ACCK! SPLSH BLATT!
THAT'S MY BOY! BACK IN THE TRENCHES!
KEVIN'S DAD IS ALWAYS SO PROUD OF HIM! DOES HE...
uh... YOU KNOW...
YES! HE KNOWS KEVIN IS GAY!
AND HE'S PROUD OF HIS SON, GAY OR STRAIGHT!
Oh, I GUESS YOU HEARD US...
18

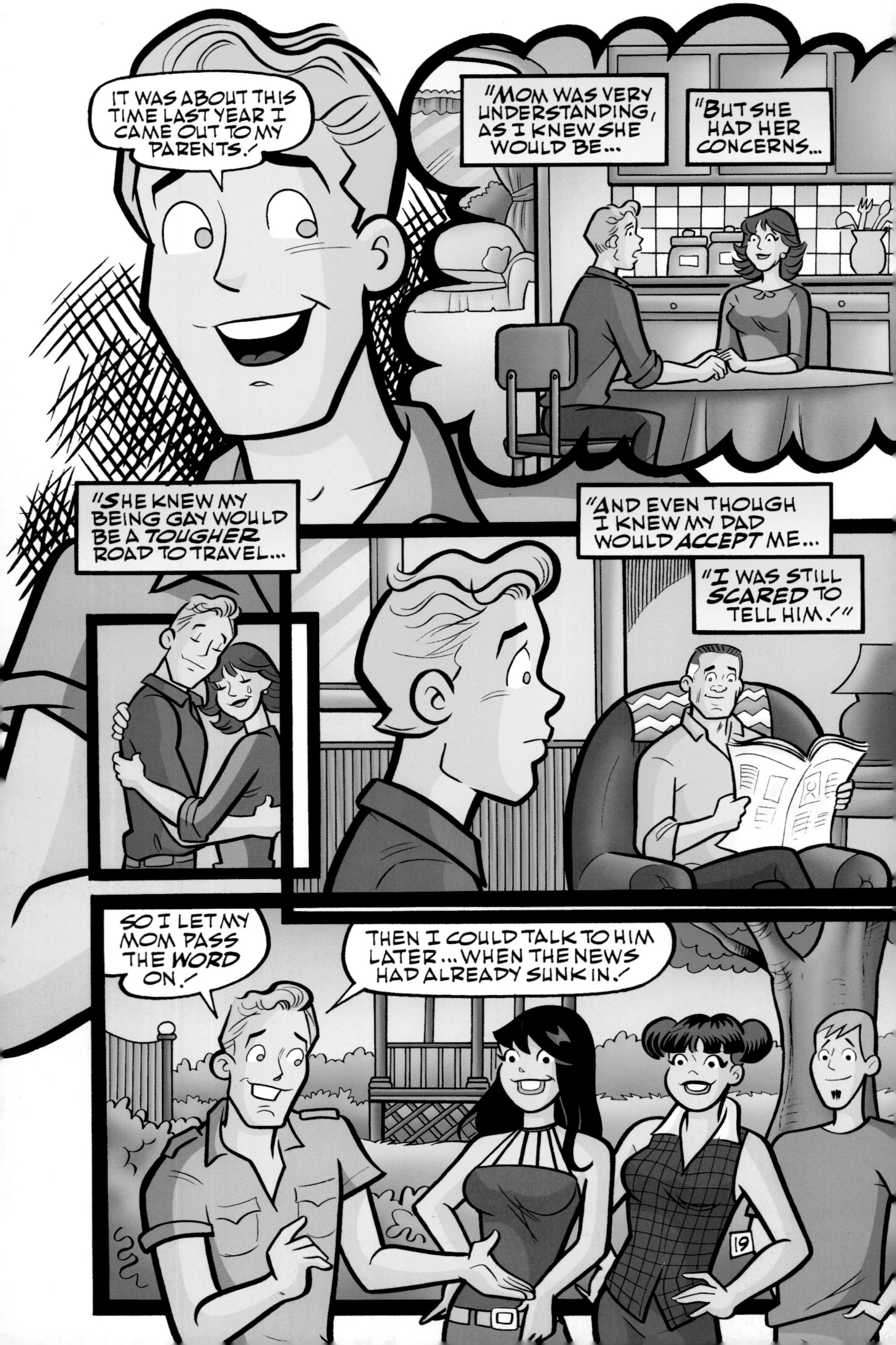
IT WAS ABOUT THIS TIME LAST YEAR I CAME OUT TO MY PARENTS!
"MOM WAS VERY UNDERSTANDING, AS I KNEW SHE WOULD BE...
"BUT SHE HAD HER CONCERNS...
"SHE KNEW MY BEING GAY WOULD BE A TOUGHER ROAD TO TRAVEL...
"AND EVEN THOUGH I KNEW MY DAD WOULD ACCEPT ME...
"I WAS STILL SCARED TO TELL HIM!"
SO I LET MY MOM PASS THE WORD ON!
THEN I COULD TALK TO HIM LATER... WHEN THE NEWS HAD ALREADY SUNK IN!
19

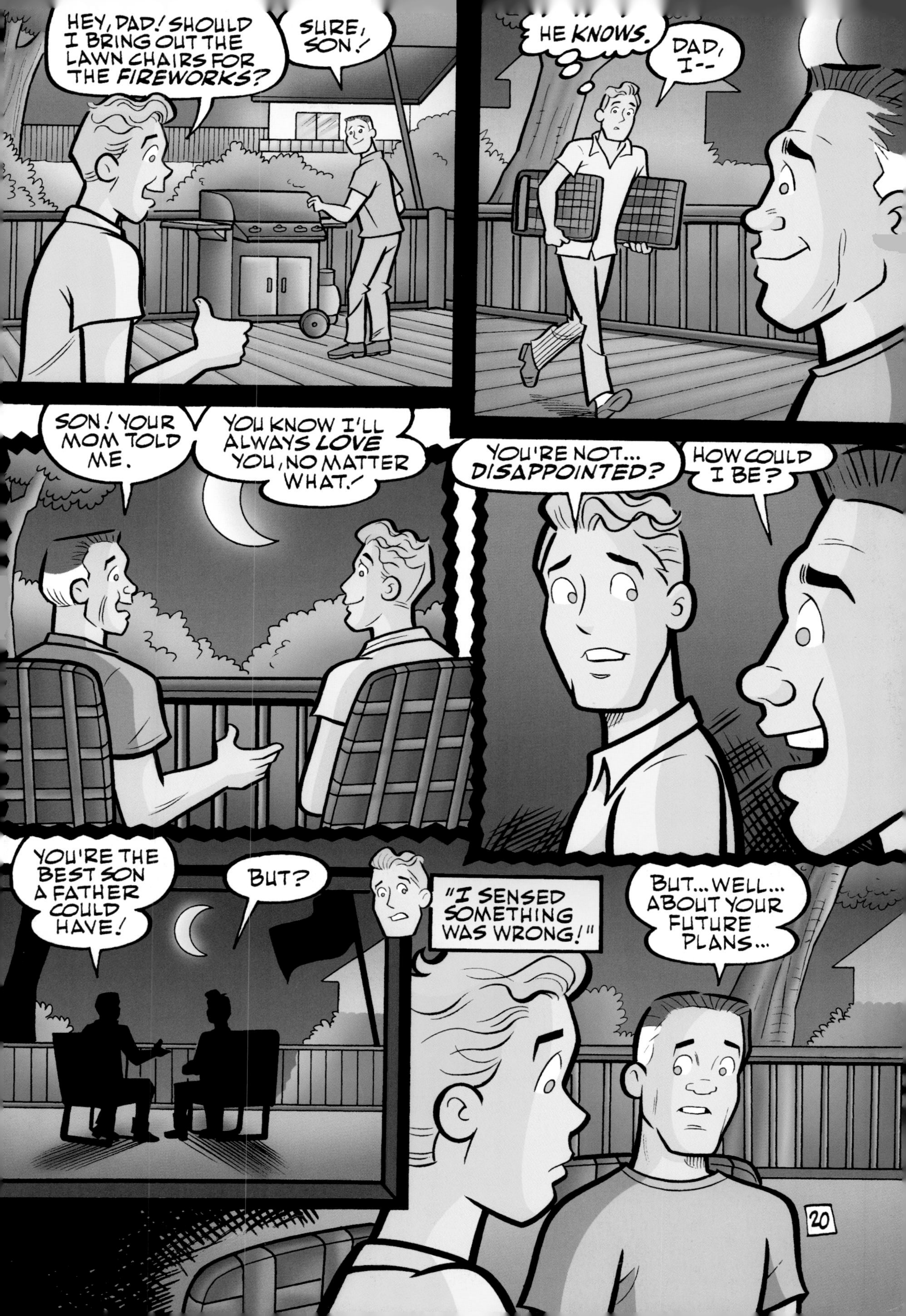

HEY, DAD! SHOULD I BRING OUT THE LAWN CHAIRS FOR THE FIREWORKS?
SURE, SON!
HE KNOWS.
DAD, I--
SON! YOUR MOM TOLD ME.
YOU KNOW I'LL ALWAYS LOVE YOU, NO MATTER WHAT!
YOU'RE NOT... DISAPPOINTED?
HOW COULD I BE?
YOU'RE THE BEST SON A FATHER COULD HAVE!
BUT?
"I SENSED SOMETHING WAS WRONG!"
BUT... WELL... ABOUT YOUR FUTURE PLANS...

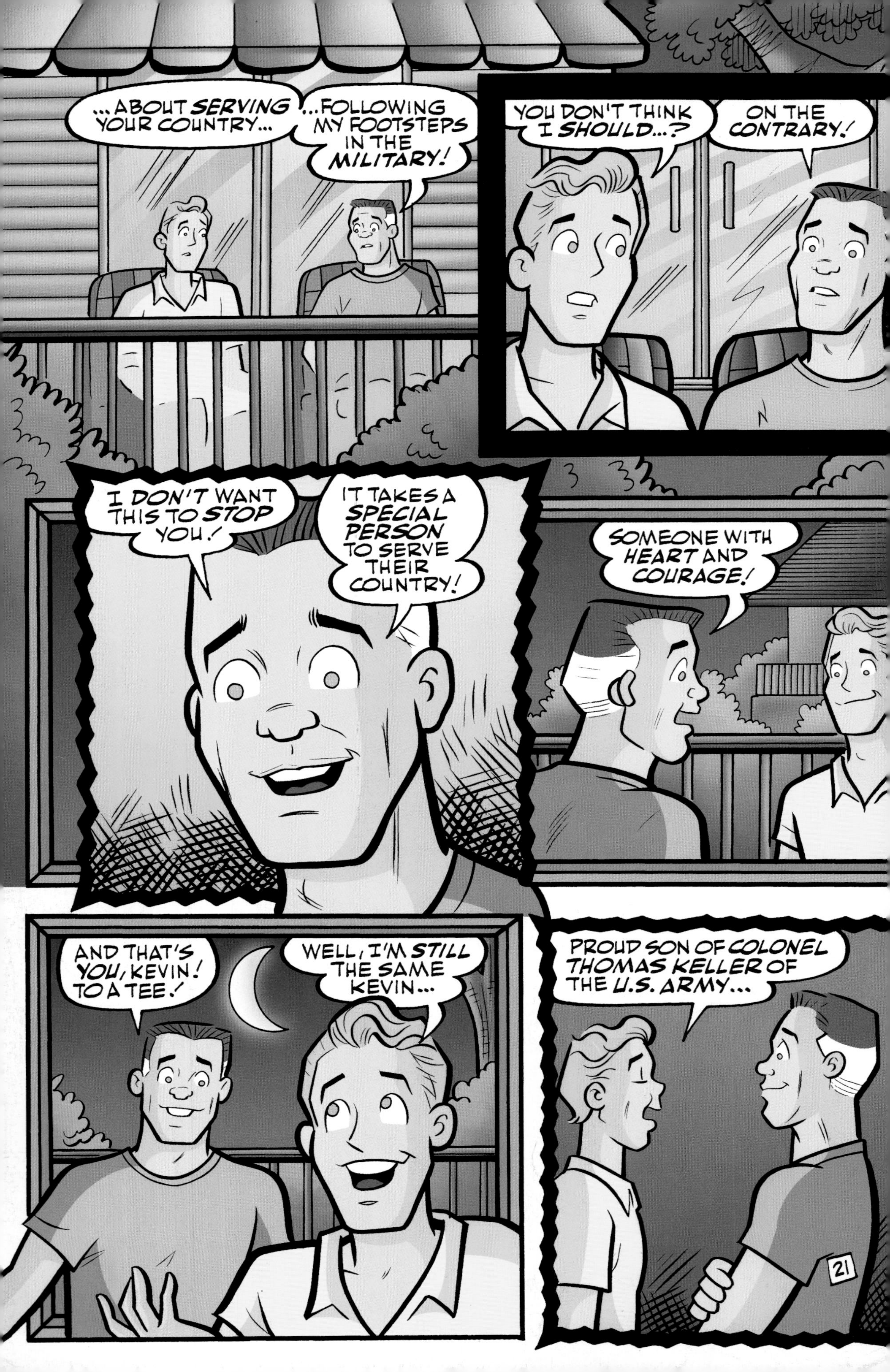
...ABOUT SERVING YOUR COUNTRY...
...FOLLOWING MY FOOTSTEPS IN THE MILITARY!
YOU DON'T THINK I SHOULD...?
ON THE CONTRARY!
I DON'T WANT THIS TO STOP YOU!
IT TAKES A SPECIAL PERSON TO SERVE THEIR COUNTRY!
SOMEONE WITH HEART AND COURAGE!
AND THAT'S YOU, KEVIN! TO A TEE!
WELL, I'M STILL THE SAME KEVIN...
PROUD SON OF COLONEL THOMAS KELLER OF THE U.S. ARMY...
21

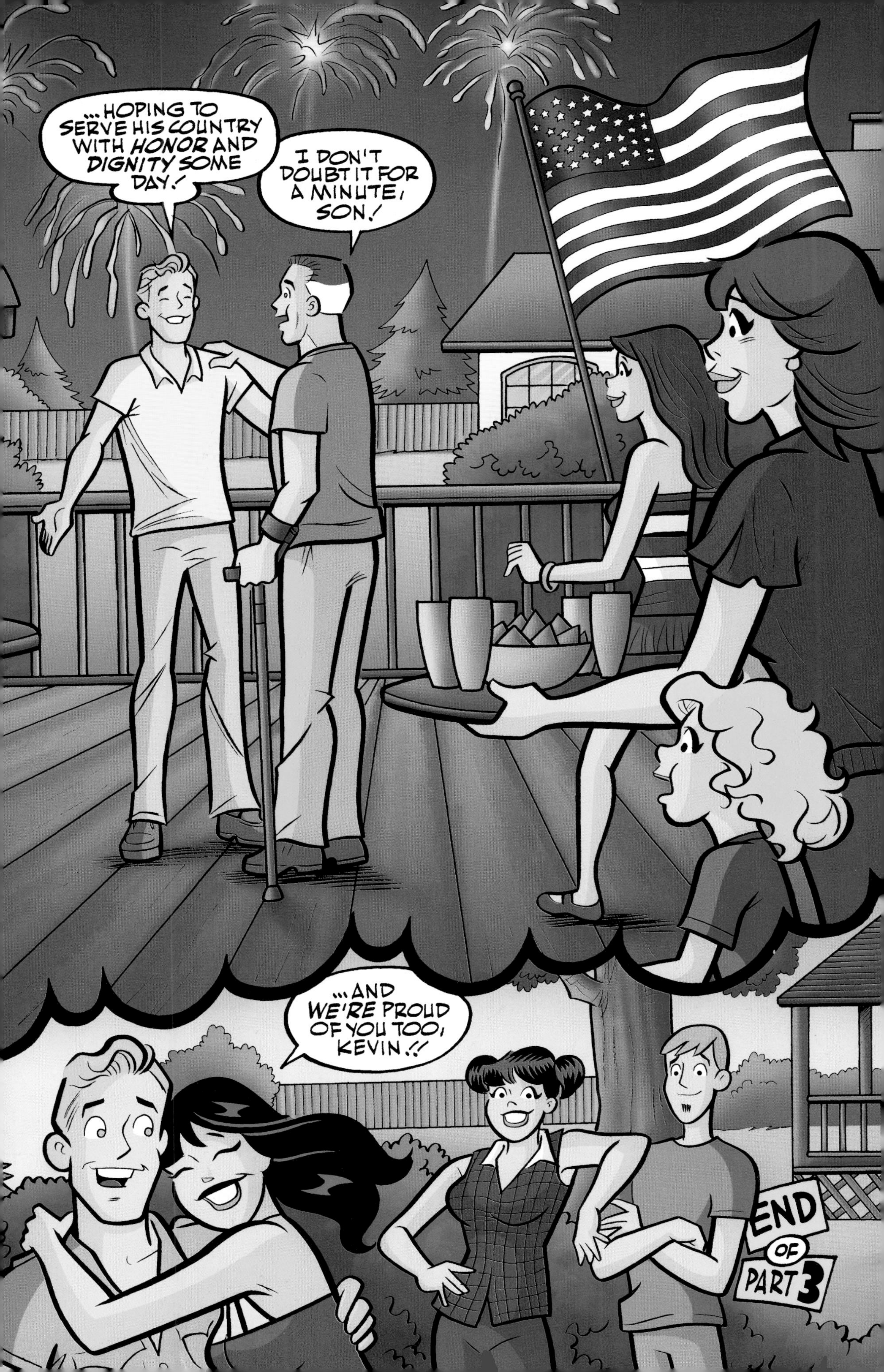
...HOPING TO SERVE HIS COUNTRY WITH *HONOR* AND *DIGNITY* SOME DAY!
I DON'T DOUBT IT FOR A MINUTE, SON!
...AND *WE'RE* PROUD OF YOU TOO, KEVIN!!
END OF PART 3

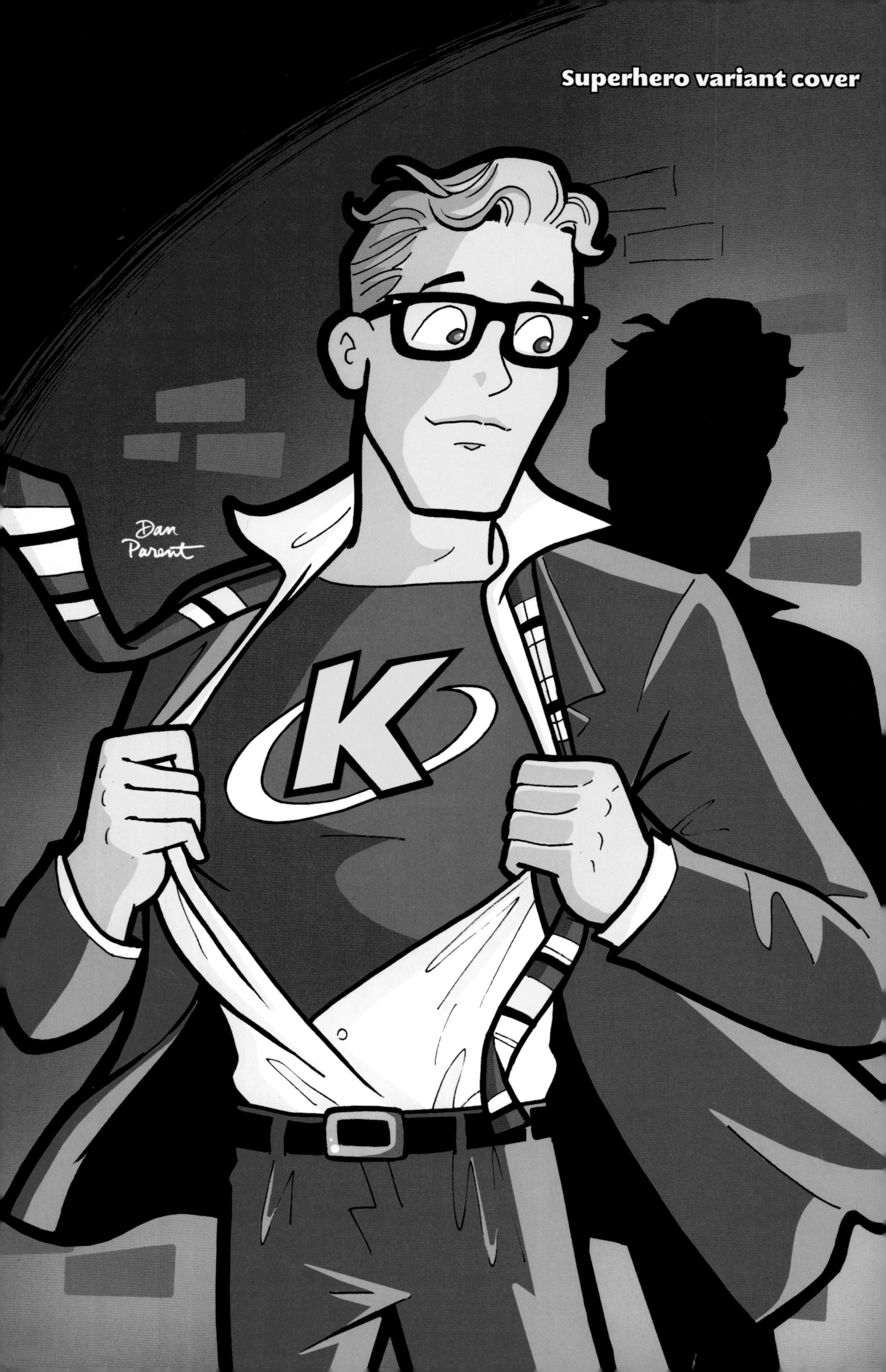
Dan Parent

Superhero variant cover

Part 4: The Write Stuff

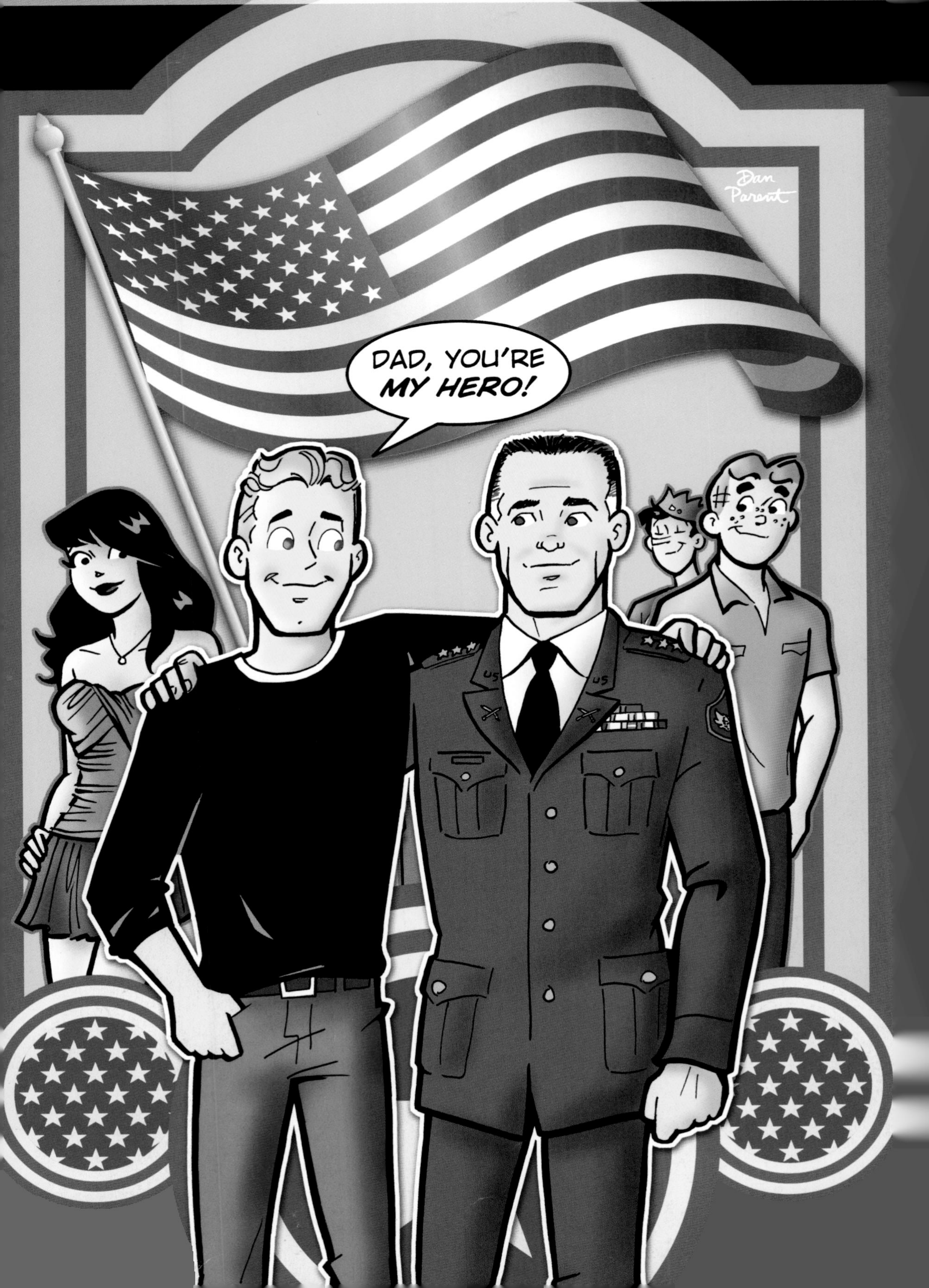

Dan Parent
DAD, YOU'RE MY HERO!

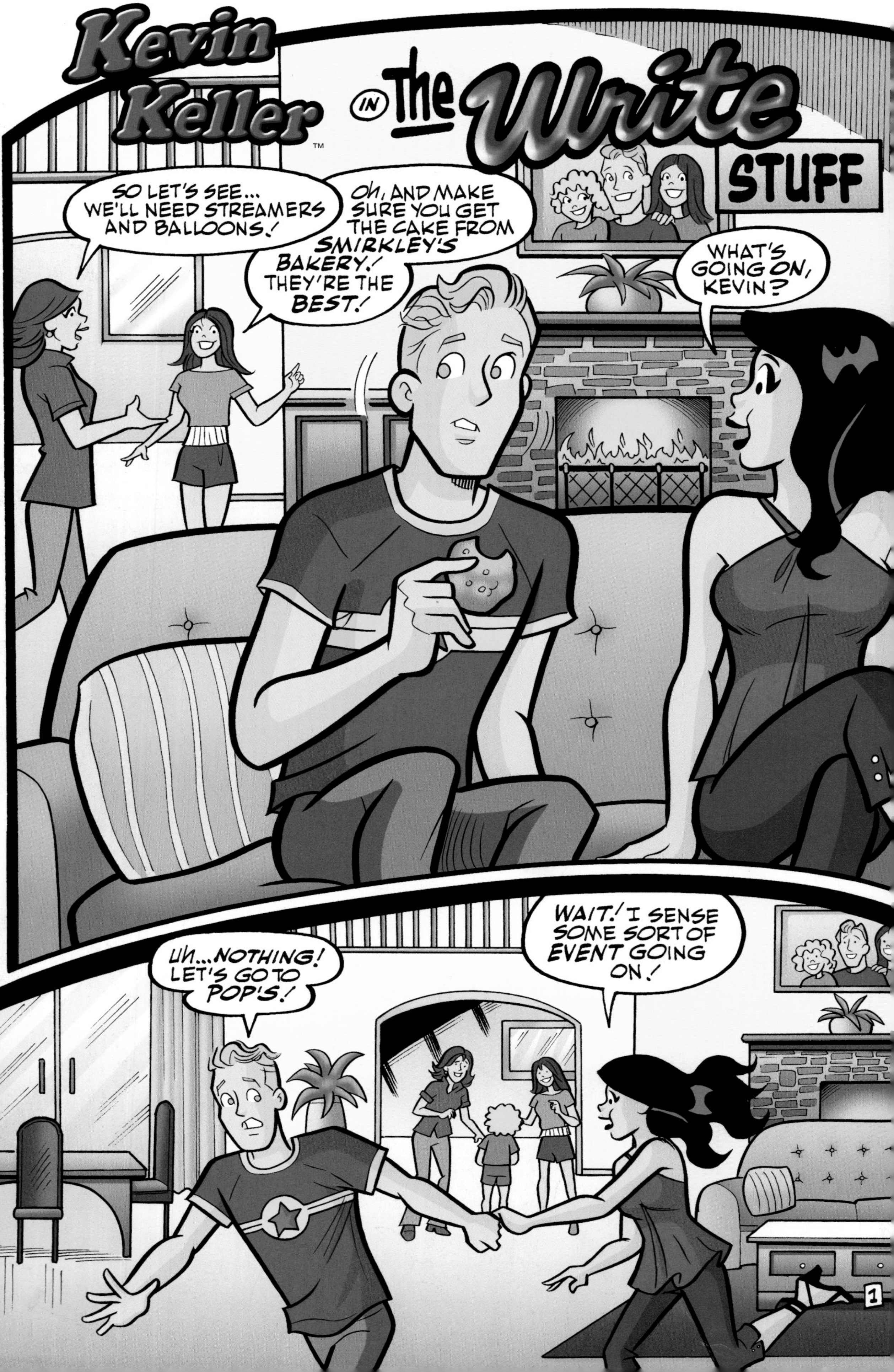
Kevin Keller™ in The Write Stuff
SO LET'S SEE... WE'LL NEED STREAMERS AND BALLOONS!
OH, AND MAKE SURE YOU GET THE CAKE FROM SMIRKLEY'S BAKERY! THEY'RE THE BEST!
WHAT'S GOING ON, KEVIN?
UH...NOTHING! LET'S GO TO POP'S!
WAIT! I SENSE SOME SORT OF EVENT GOING ON!
1

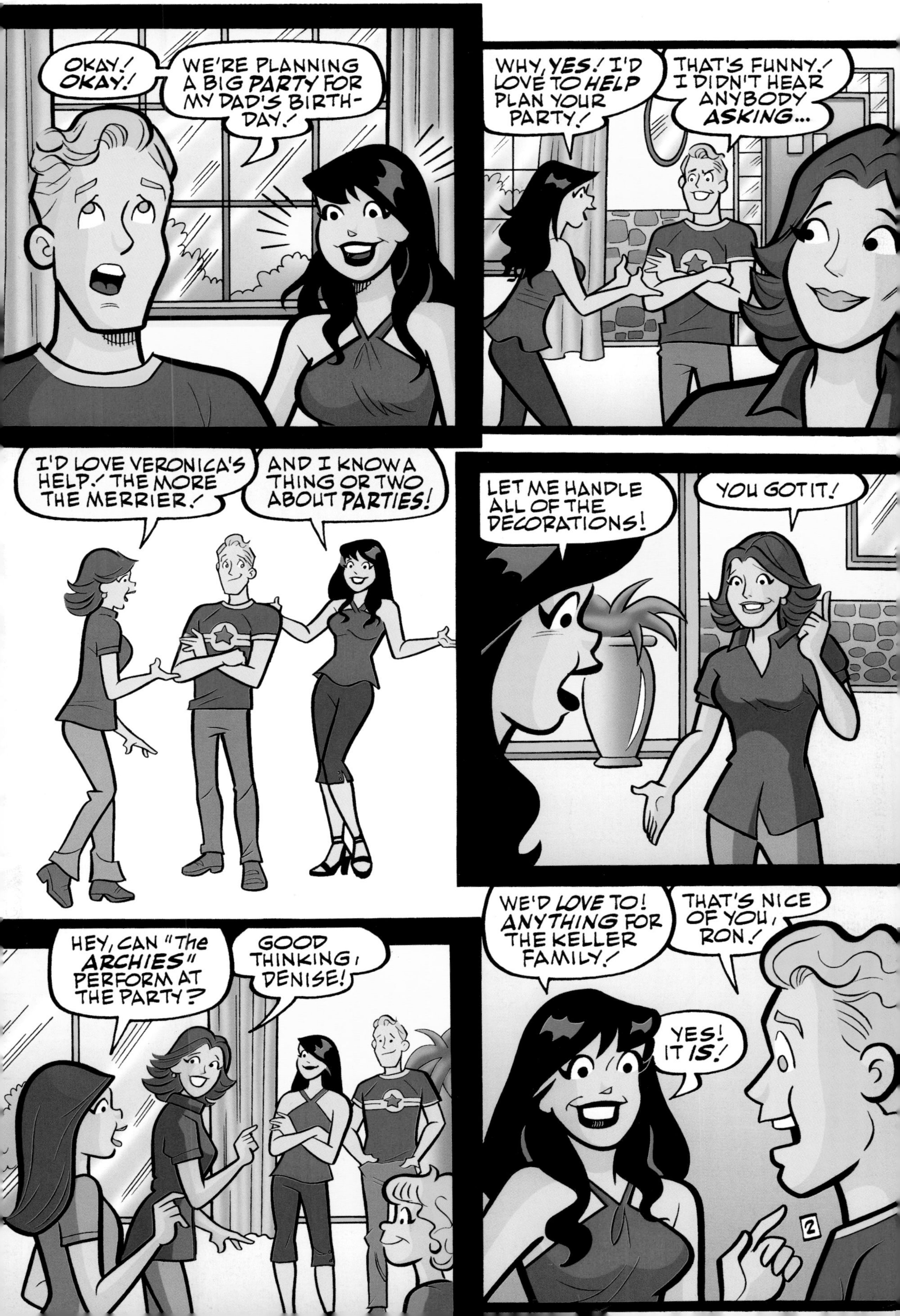
OKAY! OKAY!
WE'RE PLANNING A BIG PARTY FOR MY DAD'S BIRTH-DAY!
WHY, YES! I'D LOVE TO HELP PLAN YOUR PARTY!
THAT'S FUNNY! I DIDN'T HEAR ANYBODY ASKING...
I'D LOVE VERONICA'S HELP! THE MORE THE MERRIER!
AND I KNOW A THING OR TWO ABOUT PARTIES!
LET ME HANDLE ALL OF THE DECORATIONS!
YOU GOT IT!
HEY, CAN "The ARCHIES" PERFORM AT THE PARTY?
GOOD THINKING, DENISE!
WE'D LOVE TO! ANYTHING FOR THE KELLER FAMILY!
THAT'S NICE OF YOU, RON!
YES! IT IS!
2

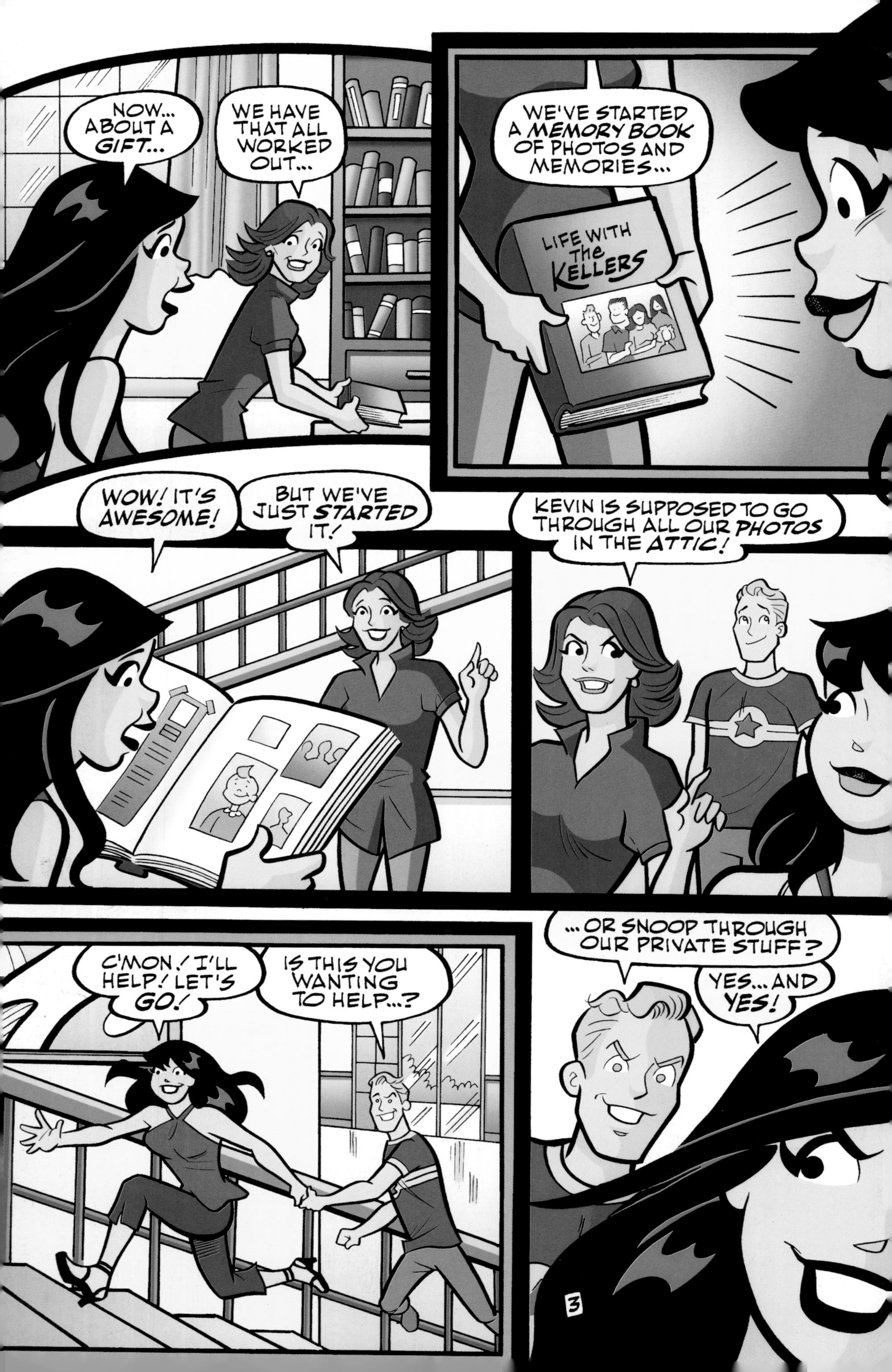
NOW... ABOUT A GIFT...
WE HAVE THAT ALL WORKED OUT...
WE'VE STARTED A MEMORY BOOK OF PHOTOS AND MEMORIES...
LIFE WITH the KELLERS
WOW! IT'S AWESOME!
BUT WE'VE JUST STARTED IT!
KEVIN IS SUPPOSED TO GO THROUGH ALL OUR PHOTOS IN THE ATTIC!
C'MON! I'LL HELP! LET'S GO!
IS THIS YOU WANTING TO HELP...?
...OR SNOOP THROUGH OUR PRIVATE STUFF?
YES... AND YES!
3

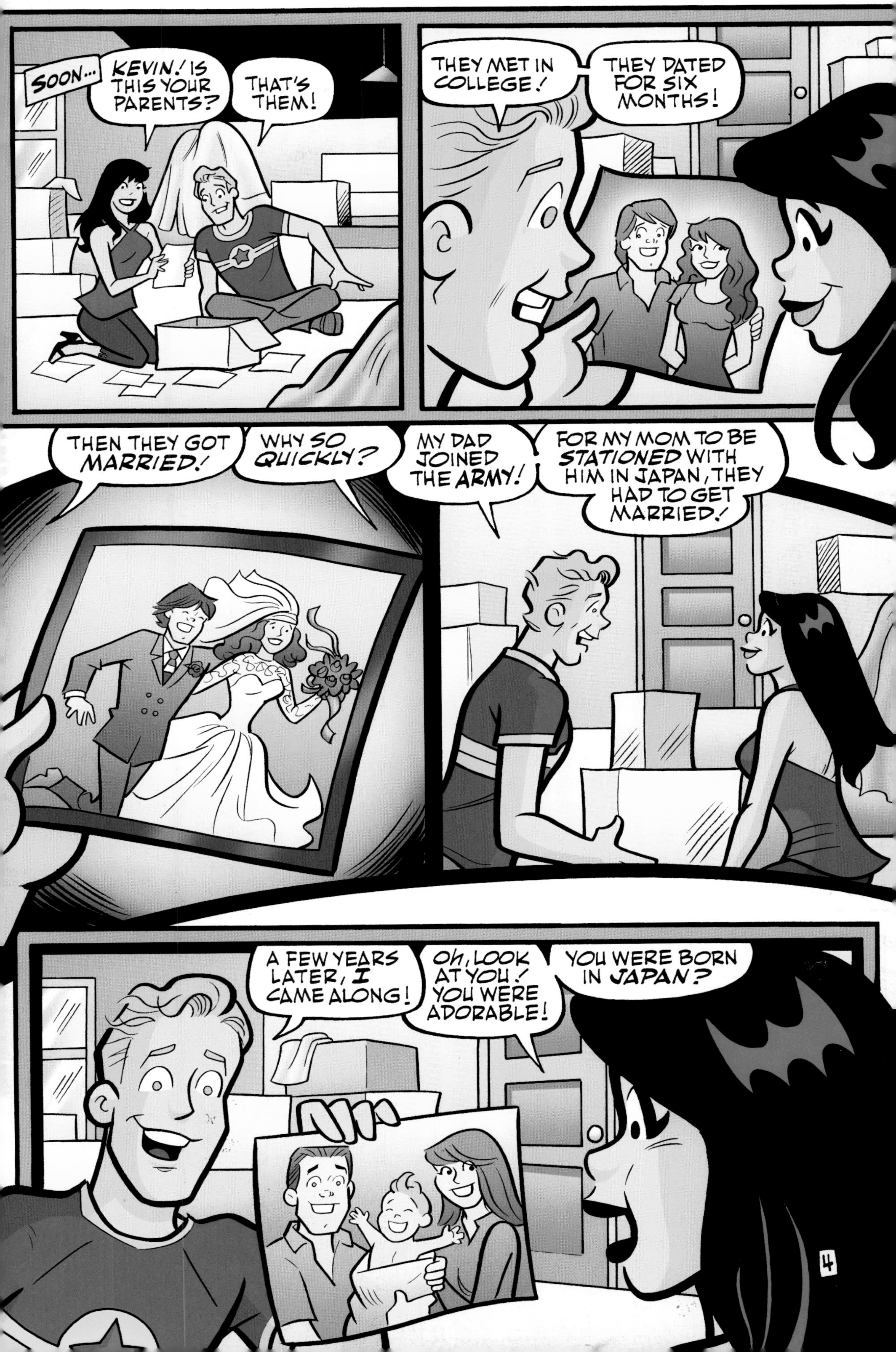
SOON...
KEVIN! IS THIS YOUR PARENTS?
THAT'S THEM!
THEY MET IN COLLEGE!
THEY DATED FOR SIX MONTHS!
THEN THEY GOT MARRIED!
WHY SO QUICKLY?
MY DAD JOINED THE ARMY!
FOR MY MOM TO BE STATIONED WITH HIM IN JAPAN, THEY HAD TO GET MARRIED!
A FEW YEARS LATER, I CAME ALONG!
Oh, LOOK AT YOU! YOU WERE ADORABLE!
YOU WERE BORN IN JAPAN?
4

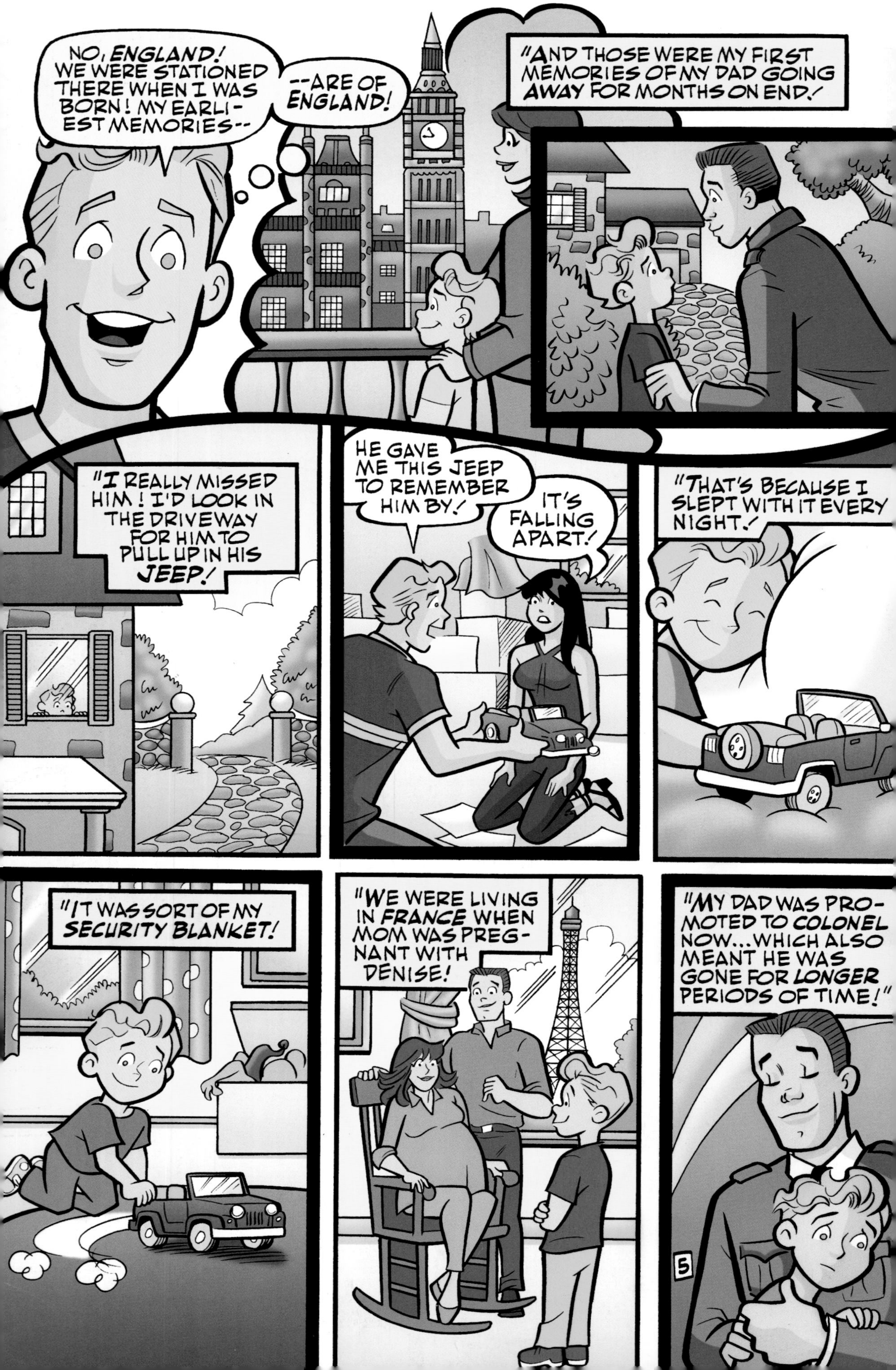
NO, ENGLAND! WE WERE STATIONED THERE WHEN I WAS BORN! MY EARLIEST MEMORIES--
--ARE OF ENGLAND!
"AND THOSE WERE MY FIRST MEMORIES OF MY DAD GOING AWAY FOR MONTHS ON END!
"I REALLY MISSED HIM! I'D LOOK IN THE DRIVEWAY FOR HIM TO PULL UP IN HIS JEEP!
HE GAVE ME THIS JEEP TO REMEMBER HIM BY!
IT'S FALLING APART!
"THAT'S BECAUSE I SLEPT WITH IT EVERY NIGHT!
"IT WAS SORT OF MY SECURITY BLANKET!
"WE WERE LIVING IN FRANCE WHEN MOM WAS PREGNANT WITH DENISE!
"MY DAD WAS PROMOTED TO COLONEL NOW...WHICH ALSO MEANT HE WAS GONE FOR LONGER PERIODS OF TIME!"
5

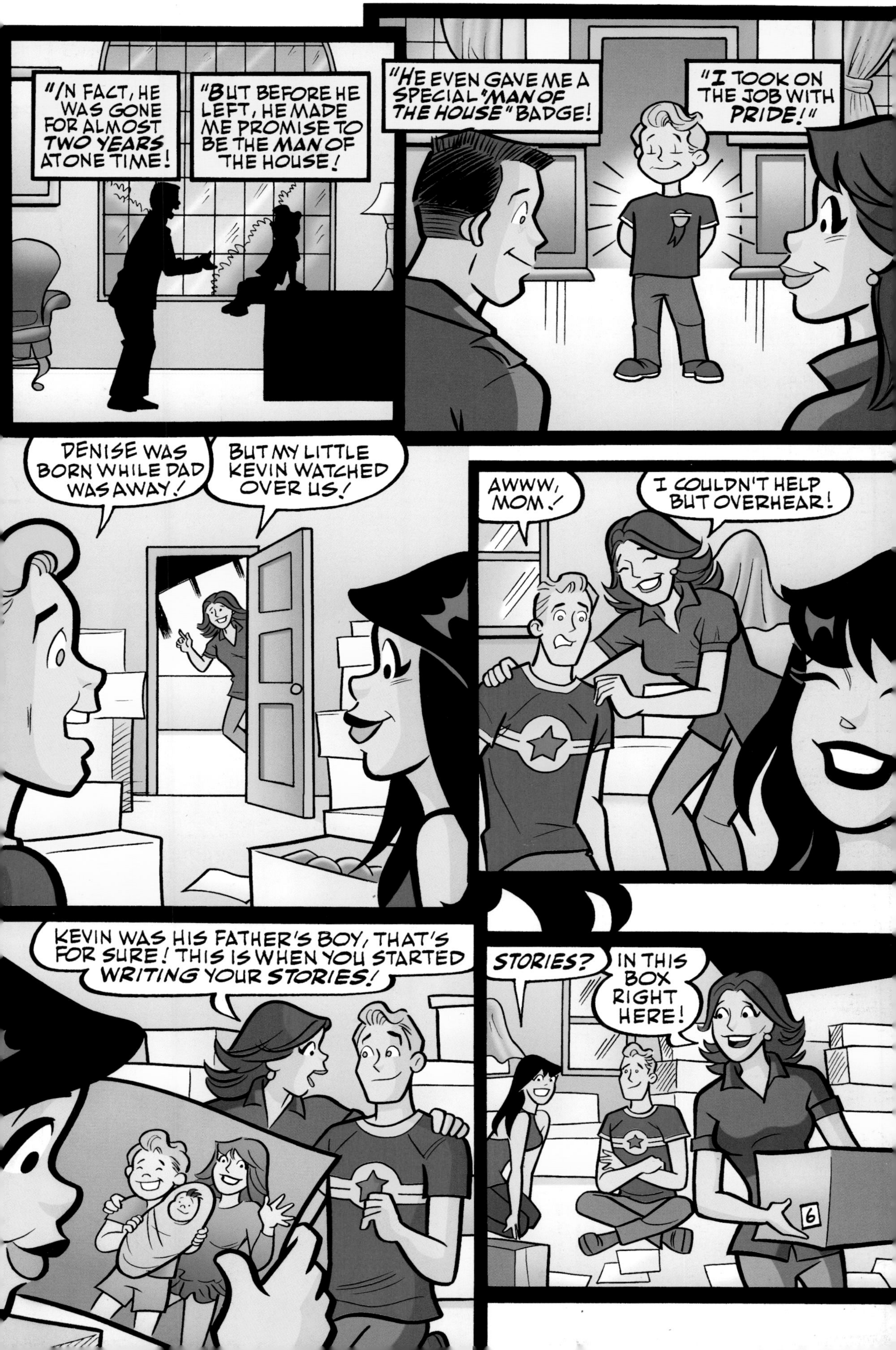
"IN FACT, HE WAS GONE FOR ALMOST TWO YEARS AT ONE TIME!
"BUT BEFORE HE LEFT, HE MADE ME PROMISE TO BE THE MAN OF THE HOUSE!
"HE EVEN GAVE ME A SPECIAL "MAN OF THE HOUSE" BADGE!
"I TOOK ON THE JOB WITH PRIDE!"
DENISE WAS BORN WHILE DAD WAS AWAY!
BUT MY LITTLE KEVIN WATCHED OVER US!
AWWW, MOM!
I COULDN'T HELP BUT OVERHEAR!
KEVIN WAS HIS FATHER'S BOY, THAT'S FOR SURE! THIS IS WHEN YOU STARTED WRITING YOUR STORIES!
STORIES?
IN THIS BOX RIGHT HERE!
6

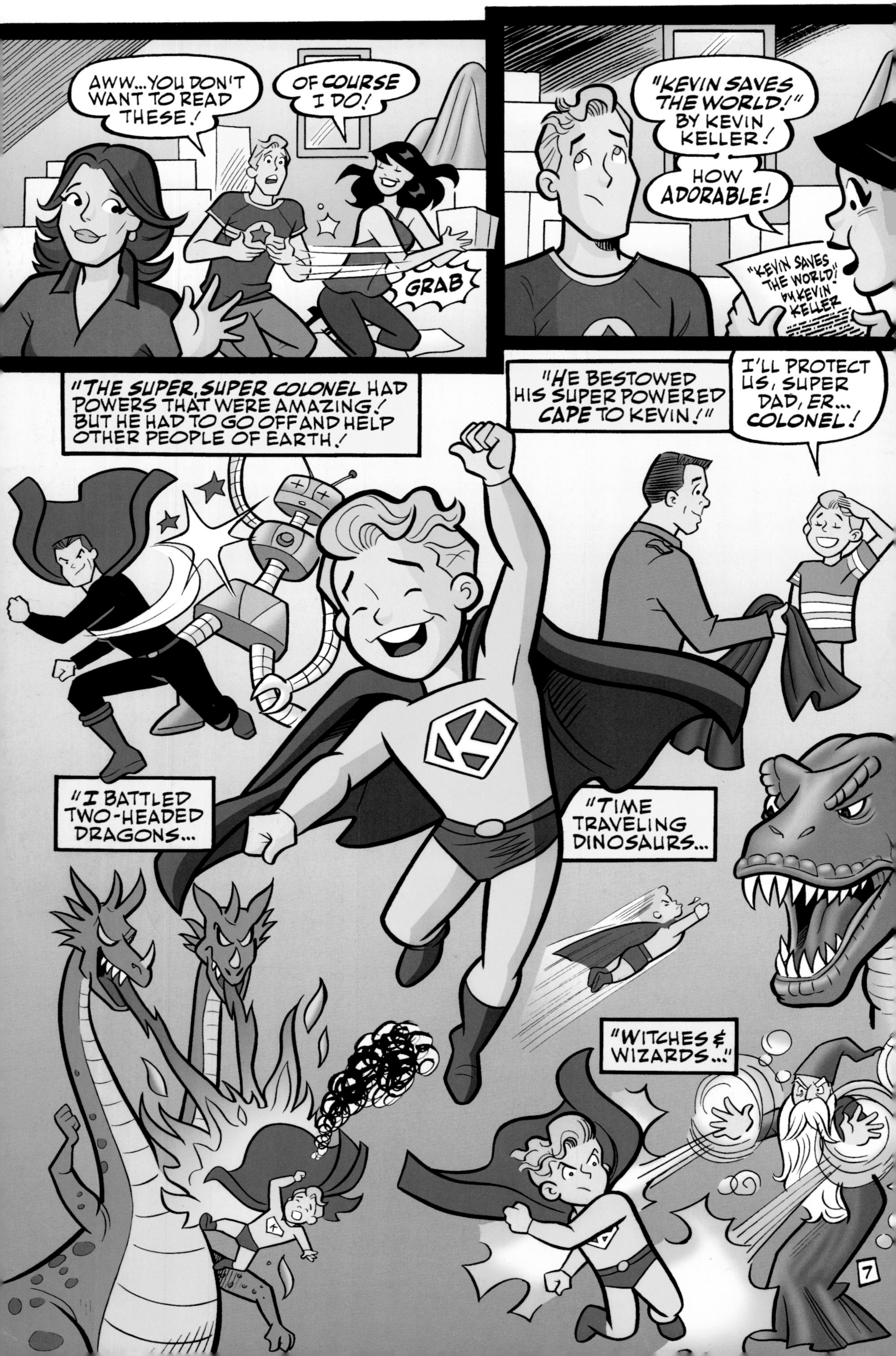
AWW...YOU DON'T WANT TO READ THESE!
OF COURSE I DO!
GRAB
"KEVIN SAVES THE WORLD!" BY KEVIN KELLER!
HOW ADORABLE!
"KEVIN SAVES THE WORLD!" by KEVIN KELLER
"THE SUPER, SUPER COLONEL HAD POWERS THAT WERE AMAZING! BUT HE HAD TO GO OFF AND HELP OTHER PEOPLE OF EARTH!
"HE BESTOWED HIS SUPER POWERED CAPE TO KEVIN!"
I'LL PROTECT US, SUPER DAD, ER... COLONEL!
"I BATTLED TWO-HEADED DRAGONS...
"TIME TRAVELING DINOSAURS...
"WITCHES & WIZARDS..."
7

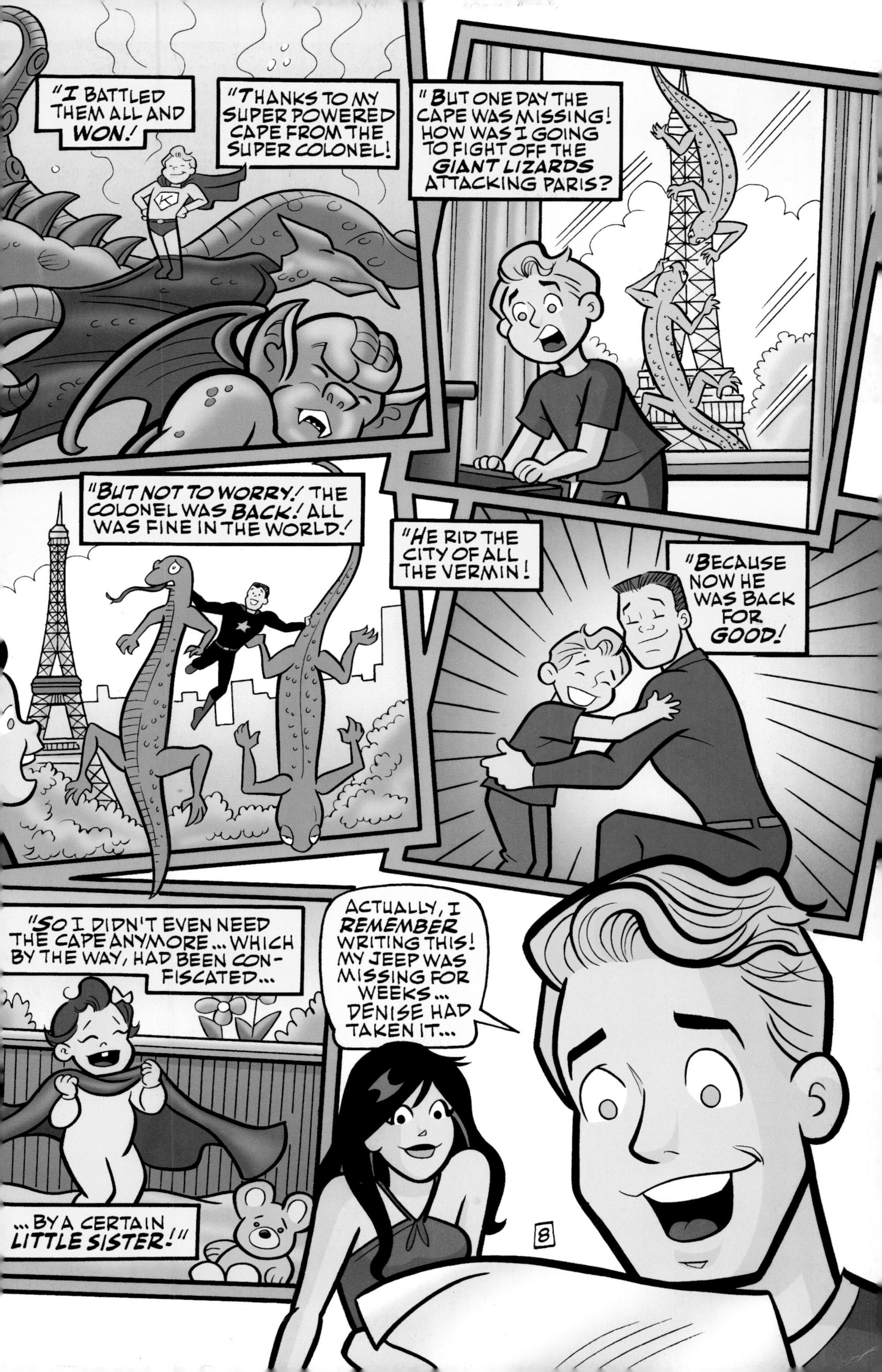
"I BATTLED THEM ALL AND WON!
"THANKS TO MY SUPER POWERED CAPE FROM THE SUPER COLONEL!
"BUT ONE DAY THE CAPE WAS MISSING! HOW WAS I GOING TO FIGHT OFF THE GIANT LIZARDS ATTACKING PARIS?
"BUT NOT TO WORRY! THE COLONEL WAS BACK! ALL WAS FINE IN THE WORLD!
"HE RID THE CITY OF ALL THE VERMIN!
"BECAUSE NOW HE WAS BACK FOR GOOD!
"SO I DIDN'T EVEN NEED THE CAPE ANYMORE... WHICH BY THE WAY, HAD BEEN CONFISCATED...
...BY A CERTAIN LITTLE SISTER!"
ACTUALLY, I REMEMBER WRITING THIS! MY JEEP WAS MISSING FOR WEEKS... DENISE HAD TAKEN IT...
8

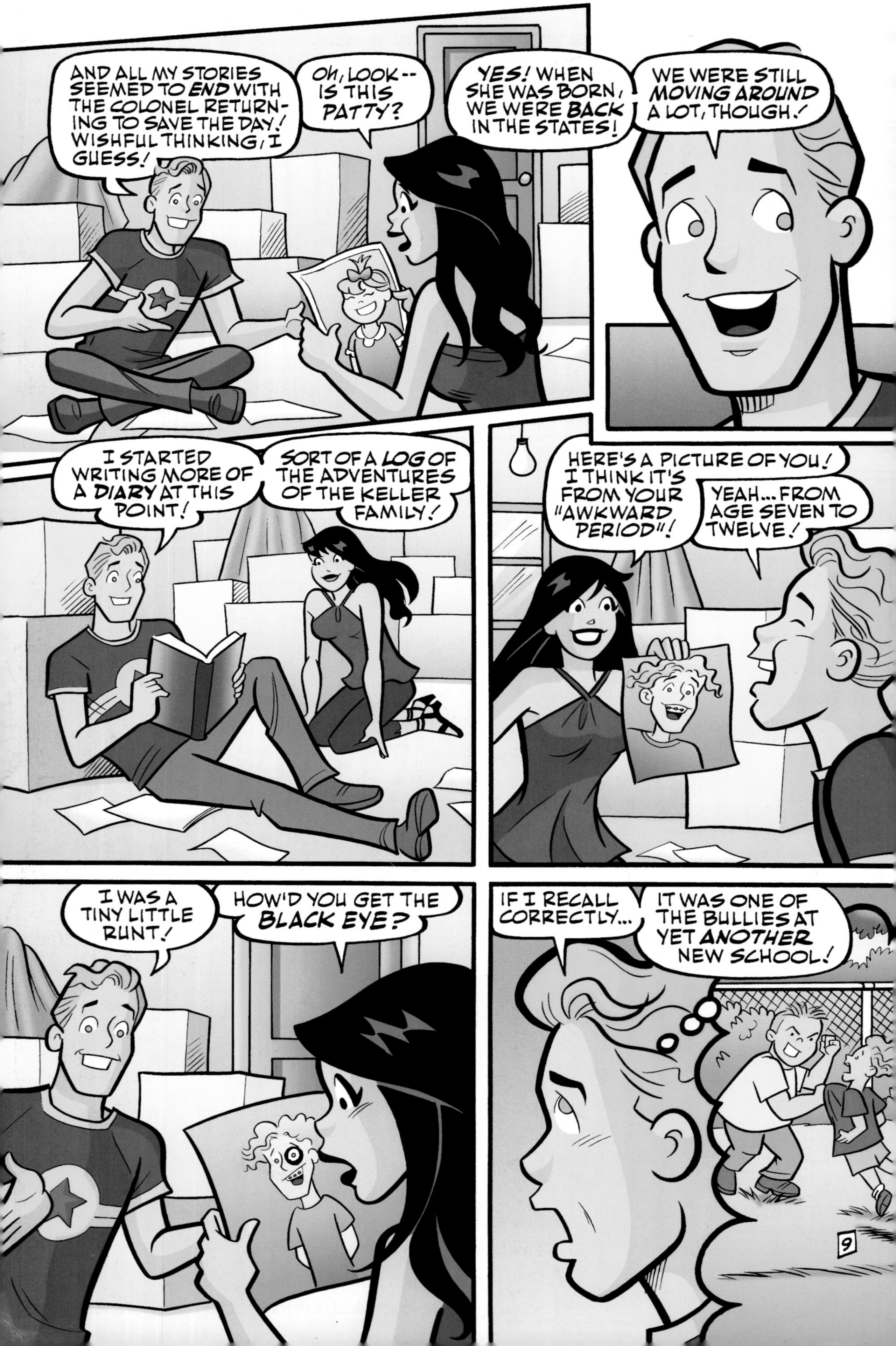
AND ALL MY STORIES SEEMED TO END WITH THE COLONEL RETURNING TO SAVE THE DAY! WISHFUL THINKING, I GUESS!
OH, LOOK-- IS THIS PATTY?
YES! WHEN SHE WAS BORN, WE WERE BACK IN THE STATES!
WE WERE STILL MOVING AROUND A LOT, THOUGH!
I STARTED WRITING MORE OF A DIARY AT THIS POINT!
SORT OF A LOG OF THE ADVENTURES OF THE KELLER FAMILY!
HERE'S A PICTURE OF YOU! I THINK IT'S FROM YOUR "AWKWARD PERIOD"!
YEAH... FROM AGE SEVEN TO TWELVE!
I WAS A TINY LITTLE RUNT!
HOW'D YOU GET THE BLACK EYE?
IF I RECALL CORRECTLY...
IT WAS ONE OF THE BULLIES AT YET ANOTHER NEW SCHOOL!
9

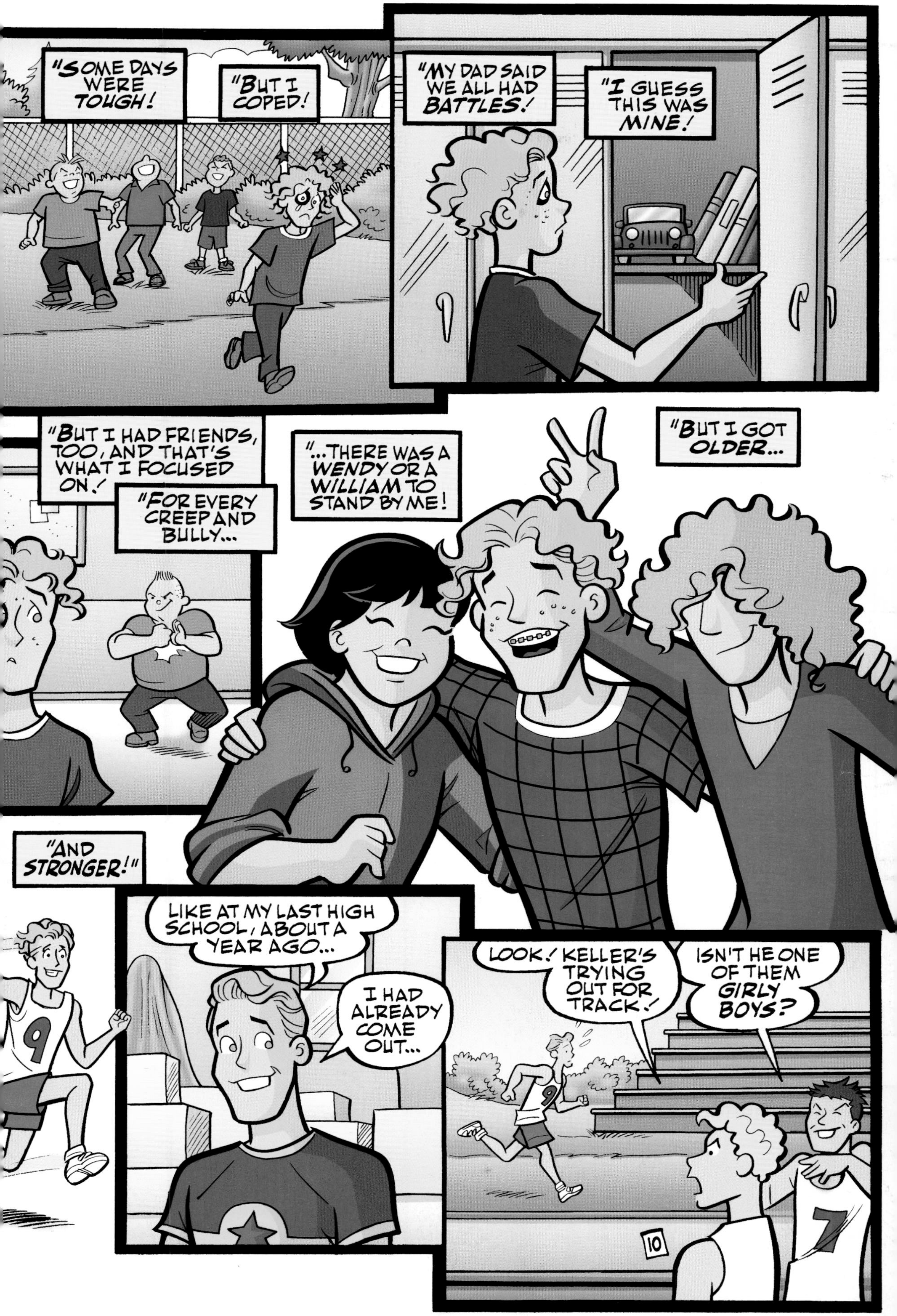
"SOME DAYS WERE TOUGH!
"BUT I COPED!
"MY DAD SAID WE ALL HAD BATTLES!
"I GUESS THIS WAS MINE!
"BUT I HAD FRIENDS, TOO, AND THAT'S WHAT I FOCUSED ON!
"FOR EVERY CREEP AND BULLY...
"...THERE WAS A WENDY OR A WILLIAM TO STAND BY ME!
"BUT I GOT OLDER...
"AND STRONGER!"
LIKE AT MY LAST HIGH SCHOOL, ABOUT A YEAR AGO...
I HAD ALREADY COME OUT...
LOOK! KELLER'S TRYING OUT FOR TRACK!
ISN'T HE ONE OF THEM GIRLY BOYS?
10

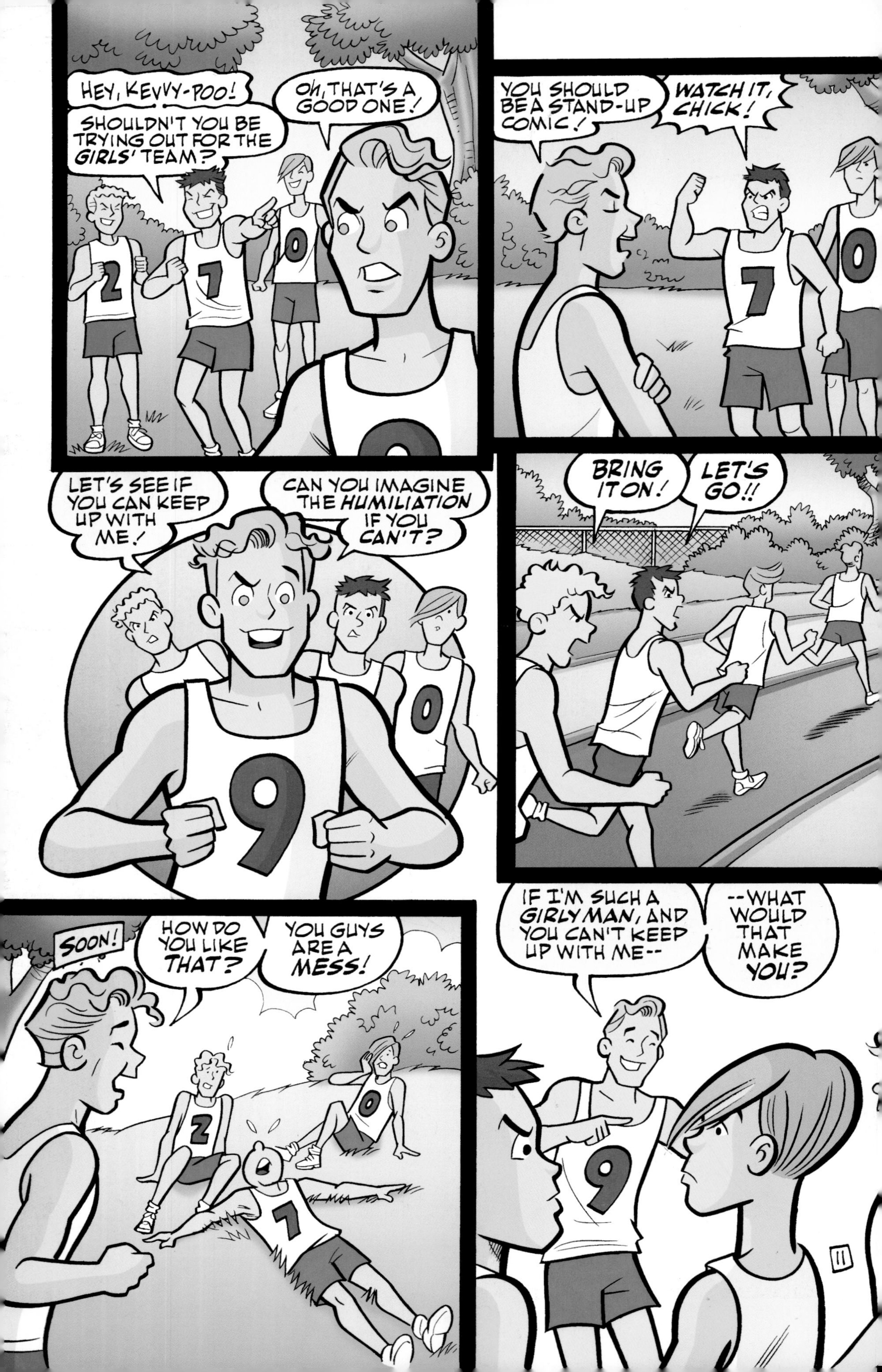
HEY, KEVVY-POO!
SHOULDN'T YOU BE TRYING OUT FOR THE GIRLS' TEAM?
OH, THAT'S A GOOD ONE!
YOU SHOULD BE A STAND-UP COMIC!
WATCH IT, CHICK!
LET'S SEE IF YOU CAN KEEP UP WITH ME!
CAN YOU IMAGINE THE HUMILIATION IF YOU CAN'T?
BRING IT ON!
LET'S GO!!
SOON!
HOW DO YOU LIKE THAT?
YOU GUYS ARE A MESS!
IF I'M SUCH A GIRLY MAN, AND YOU CAN'T KEEP UP WITH ME--
--WHAT WOULD THAT MAKE YOU?
11

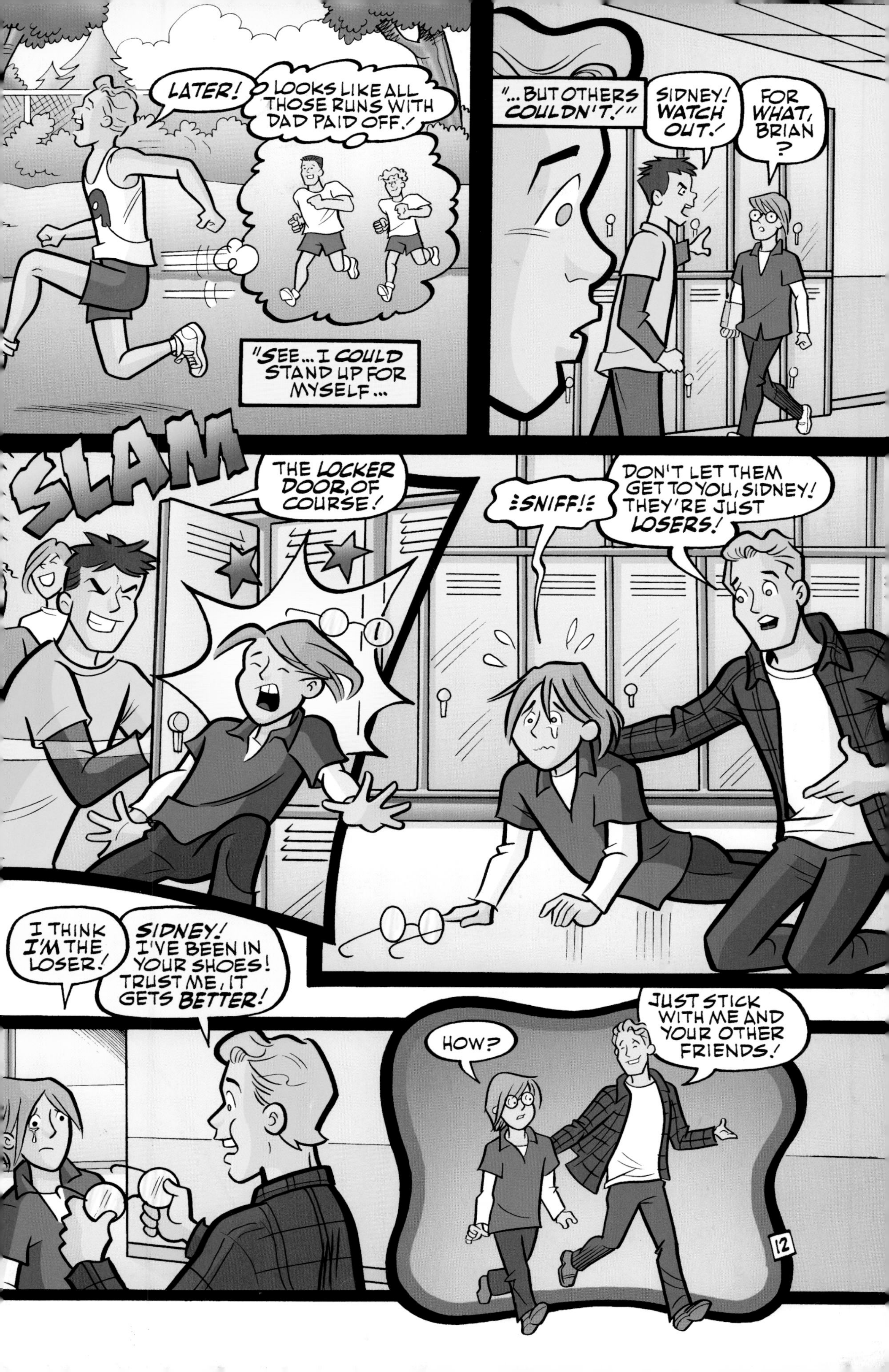
LATER!
LOOKS LIKE ALL THOSE RUNS WITH DAD PAID OFF!
"SEE... I COULD STAND UP FOR MYSELF...
"...BUT OTHERS COULDN'T!"
SIDNEY! WATCH OUT!
FOR WHAT, BRIAN?
SLAM
THE LOCKER DOOR, OF COURSE!
SNIFF!
DON'T LET THEM GET TO YOU, SIDNEY! THEY'RE JUST LOSERS!
I THINK I'M THE LOSER!
SIDNEY! I'VE BEEN IN YOUR SHOES! TRUST ME, IT GETS BETTER!
HOW?
JUST STICK WITH ME AND YOUR OTHER FRIENDS!
12

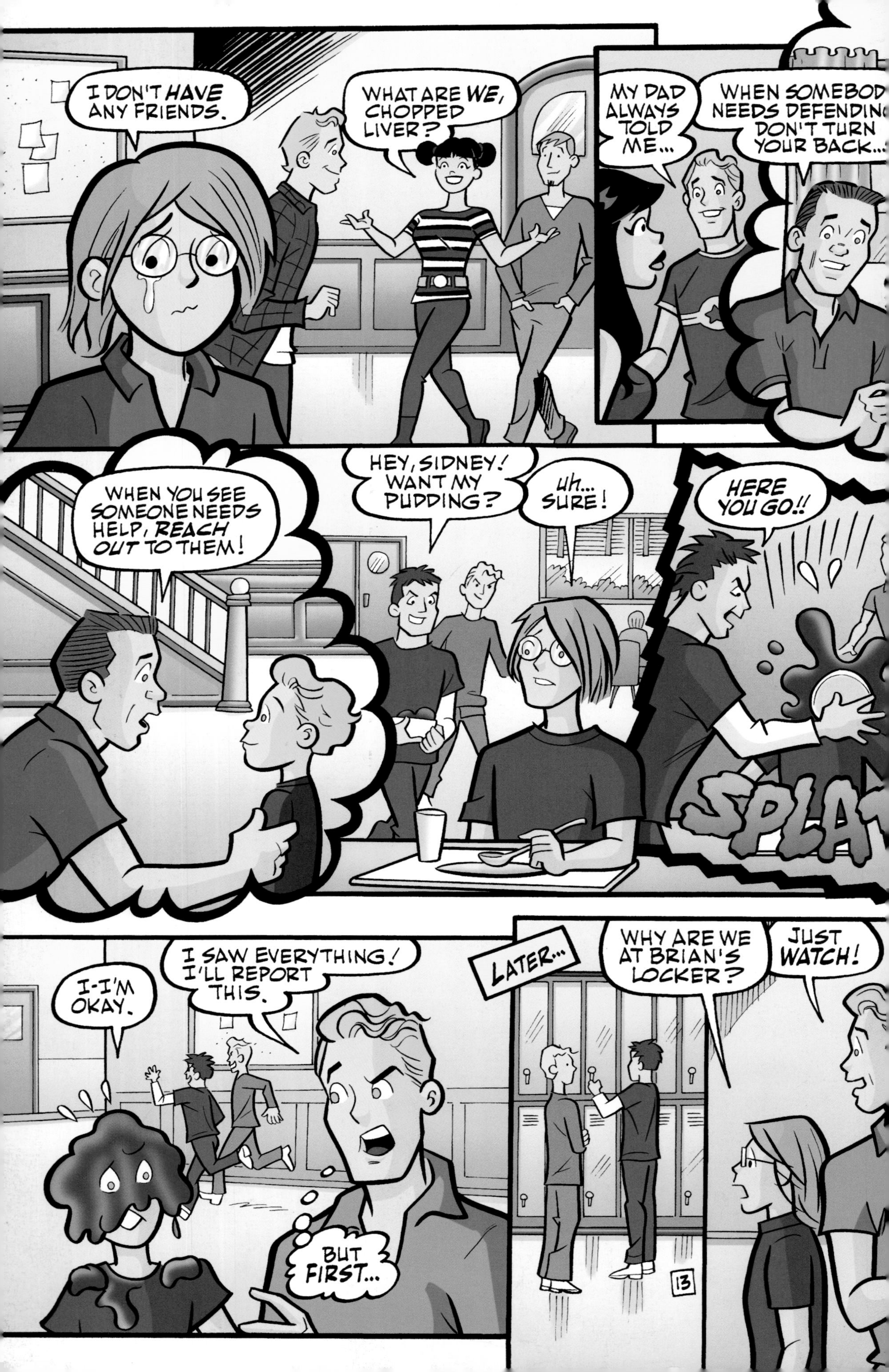
I DON'T HAVE ANY FRIENDS.
WHAT ARE WE, CHOPPED LIVER?
MY DAD ALWAYS TOLD ME...
WHEN SOMEBOD NEEDS DEFENDIN DON'T TURN YOUR BACK...
WHEN YOU SEE SOMEONE NEEDS HELP, REACH OUT TO THEM!
HEY, SIDNEY! WANT MY PUDDING?
uh... SURE!
HERE YOU GO!!
SPLAT
I-I'M OKAY.
I SAW EVERYTHING! I'LL REPORT THIS.
BUT FIRST...
LATER...
WHY ARE WE AT BRIAN'S LOCKER?
JUST WATCH!
13

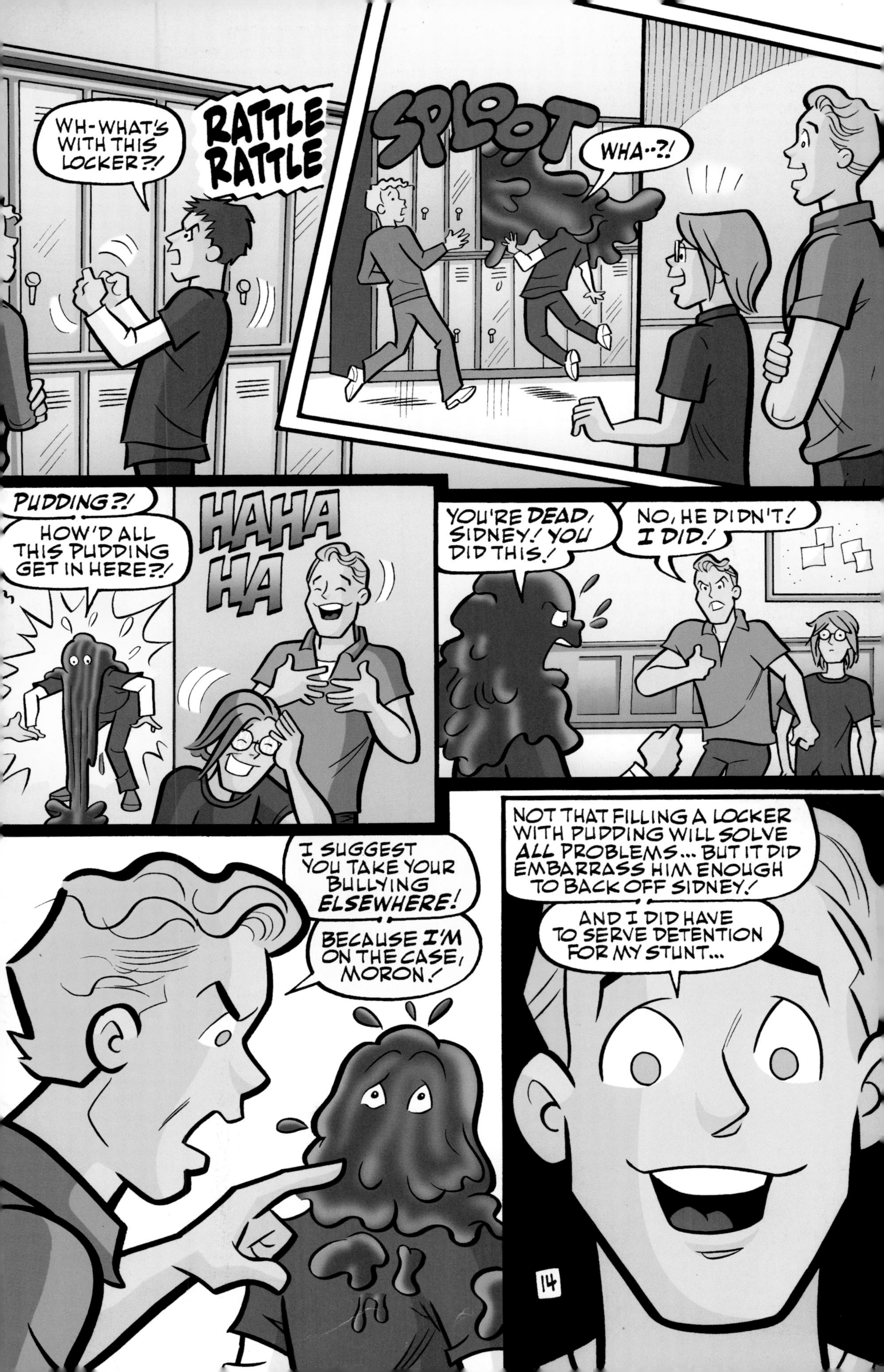
WH-WHAT'S WITH THIS LOCKER?!
RATTLE RATTLE
SPLOOT
WHA..?!
PUDDING?!
HOW'D ALL THIS PUDDING GET IN HERE?!
HAHA HA
YOU'RE DEAD, SIDNEY! YOU DID THIS!
NO, HE DIDN'T! I DID!
I SUGGEST YOU TAKE YOUR BULLYING ELSEWHERE!
BECAUSE I'M ON THE CASE, MORON!
NOT THAT FILLING A LOCKER WITH PUDDING WILL SOLVE ALL PROBLEMS... BUT IT DID EMBARRASS HIM ENOUGH TO BACK OFF SIDNEY!
AND I DID HAVE TO SERVE DETENTION FOR MY STUNT...
14

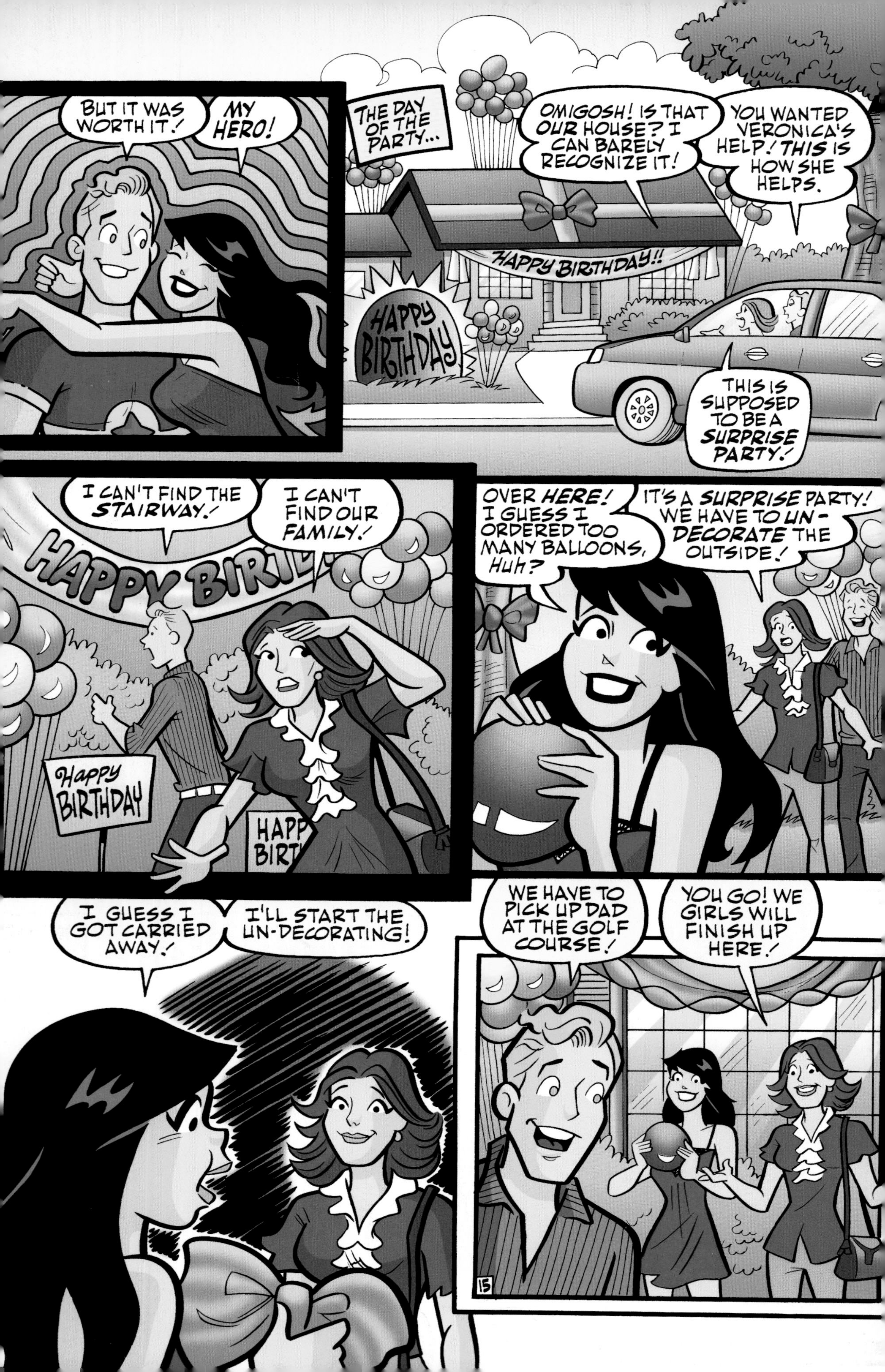
BUT IT WAS WORTH IT!
MY HERO!
THE DAY OF THE PARTY...
OMIGOSH! IS THAT OUR HOUSE? I CAN BARELY RECOGNIZE IT!
YOU WANTED VERONICA'S HELP! THIS IS HOW SHE HELPS.
HAPPY BIRTHDAY!!
HAPPY BIRTHDAY
THIS IS SUPPOSED TO BE A SURPRISE PARTY!
I CAN'T FIND THE STAIRWAY!
I CAN'T FIND OUR FAMILY!
HAPPY BIRTHDAY
OVER HERE! I GUESS I ORDERED TOO MANY BALLOONS, HUH?
IT'S A SURPRISE PARTY! WE HAVE TO UN-DECORATE THE OUTSIDE!
I GUESS I GOT CARRIED AWAY!
I'LL START THE UN-DECORATING!
WE HAVE TO PICK UP DAD AT THE GOLF COURSE!
YOU GO! WE GIRLS WILL FINISH UP HERE!
15

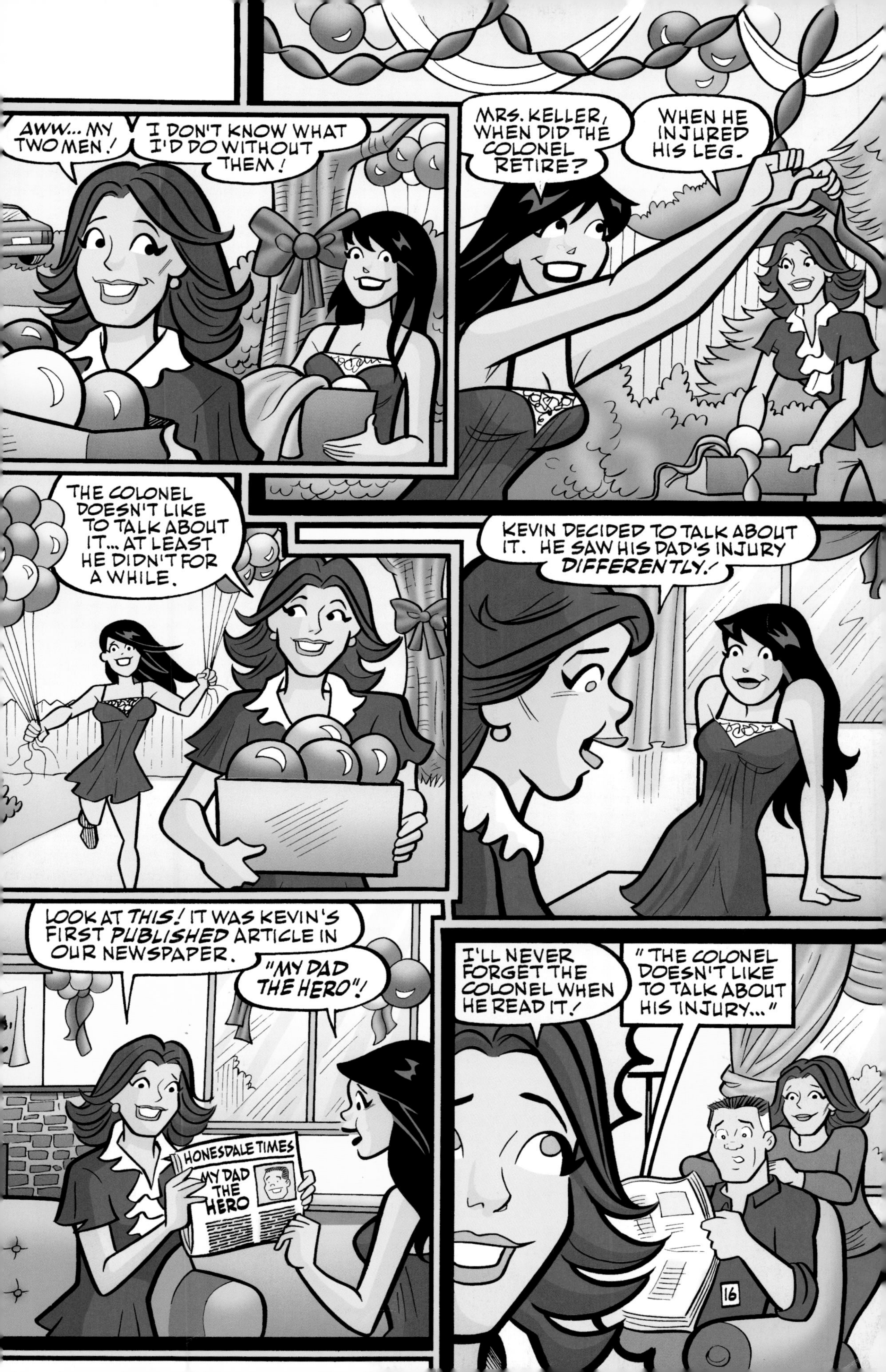
AWW... MY TWO MEN!
I DON'T KNOW WHAT I'D DO WITHOUT THEM!
MRS. KELLER, WHEN DID THE COLONEL RETIRE?
WHEN HE INJURED HIS LEG.
THE COLONEL DOESN'T LIKE TO TALK ABOUT IT... AT LEAST HE DIDN'T FOR A WHILE.
KEVIN DECIDED TO TALK ABOUT IT. HE SAW HIS DAD'S INJURY DIFFERENTLY!
LOOK AT THIS! IT WAS KEVIN'S FIRST PUBLISHED ARTICLE IN OUR NEWSPAPER.
"MY DAD THE HERO"!
HONESDALE TIMES
MY DAD THE HERO
I'LL NEVER FORGET THE COLONEL WHEN HE READ IT!
"THE COLONEL DOESN'T LIKE TO TALK ABOUT HIS INJURY..."
16

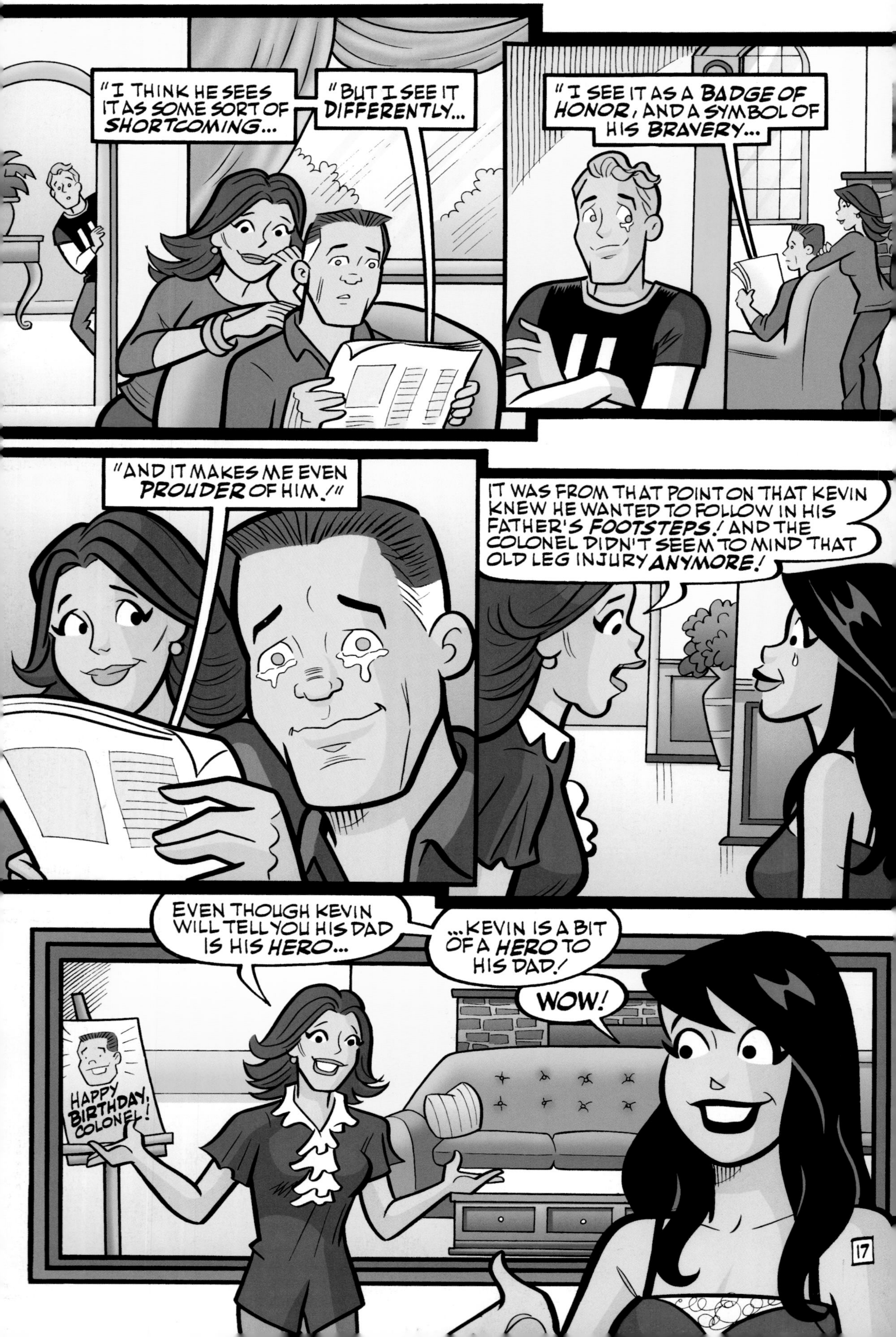
"I THINK HE SEES IT AS SOME SORT OF SHORTCOMING...
"BUT I SEE IT DIFFERENTLY...
"I SEE IT AS A BADGE OF HONOR, AND A SYMBOL OF HIS BRAVERY...
"AND IT MAKES ME EVEN PROUDER OF HIM!"
IT WAS FROM THAT POINT ON THAT KEVIN KNEW HE WANTED TO FOLLOW IN HIS FATHER'S FOOTSTEPS! AND THE COLONEL DIDN'T SEEM TO MIND THAT OLD LEG INJURY ANYMORE!
EVEN THOUGH KEVIN WILL TELL YOU HIS DAD IS HIS HERO...
...KEVIN IS A BIT OF A HERO TO HIS DAD!
WOW!
HAPPY BIRTHDAY, COLONEL!

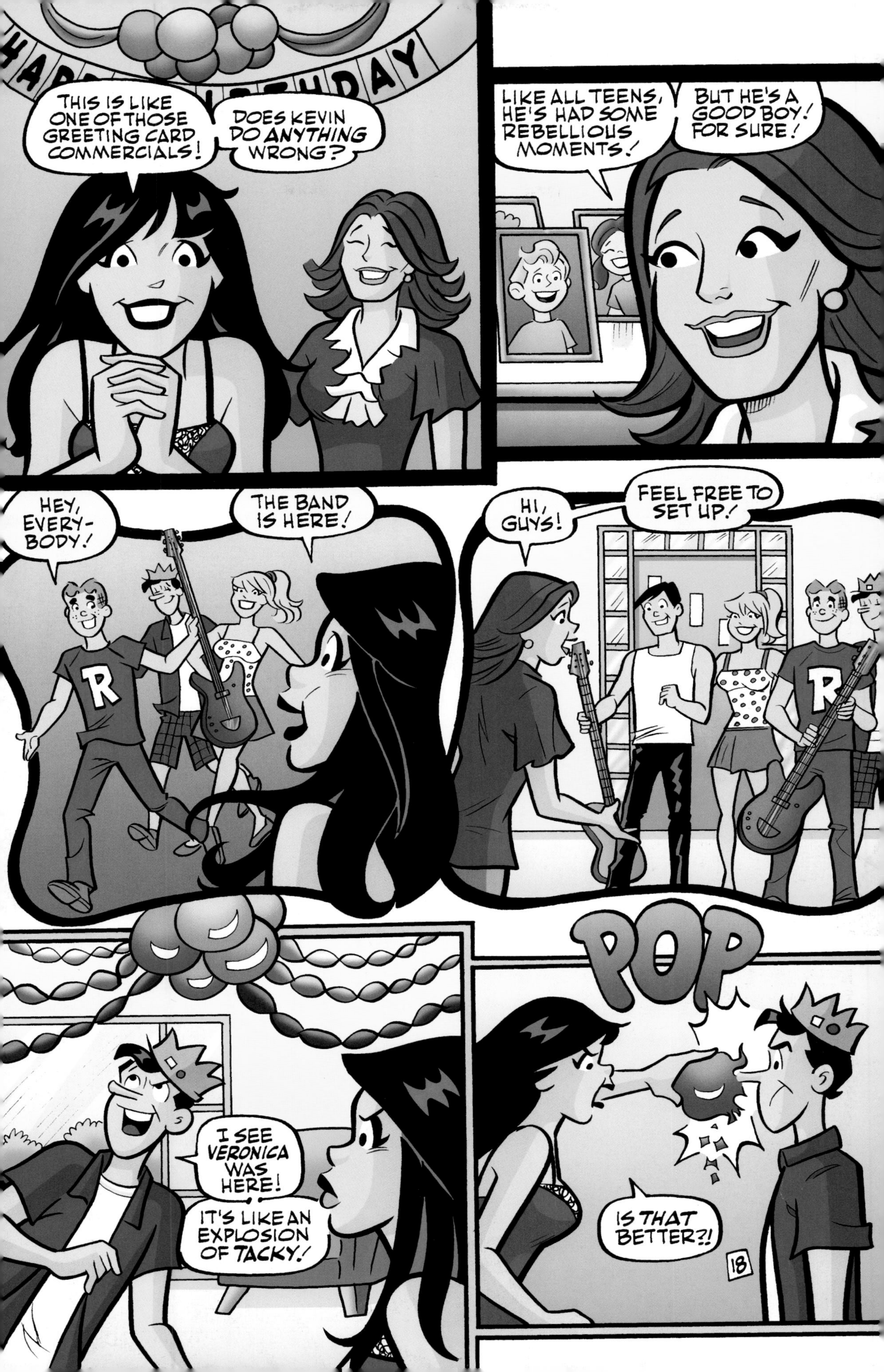
HAPPY BIRTHDAY
THIS IS LIKE ONE OF THOSE GREETING CARD COMMERCIALS!
DOES KEVIN DO ANYTHING WRONG?
LIKE ALL TEENS, HE'S HAD SOME REBELLIOUS MOMENTS!
BUT HE'S A GOOD BOY! FOR SURE!
HEY, EVERY-BODY!
THE BAND IS HERE!
HI, GUYS!
FEEL FREE TO SET UP!
I SEE VERONICA WAS HERE!
IT'S LIKE AN EXPLOSION OF TACKY!
POP
IS THAT BETTER?!
18

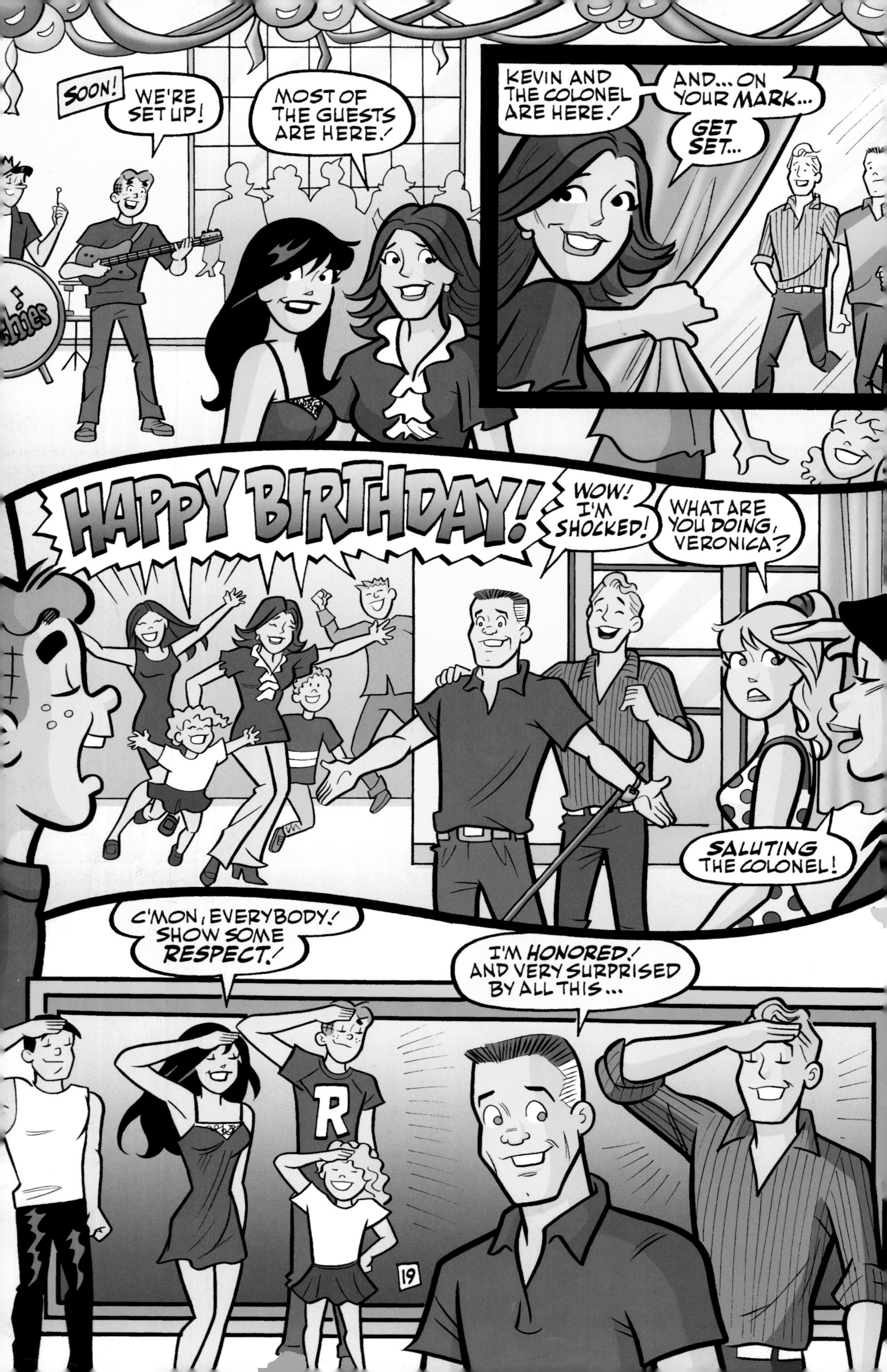
SOON!
WE'RE SET UP!
MOST OF THE GUESTS ARE HERE!
KEVIN AND THE COLONEL ARE HERE!
AND... ON YOUR MARK...
GET SET...
HAPPY BIRTHDAY!
WOW! I'M SHOCKED!
WHAT ARE YOU DOING, VERONICA?
SALUTING THE COLONEL!
C'MON, EVERYBODY! SHOW SOME RESPECT!
I'M HONORED! AND VERY SURPRISED BY ALL THIS...
19

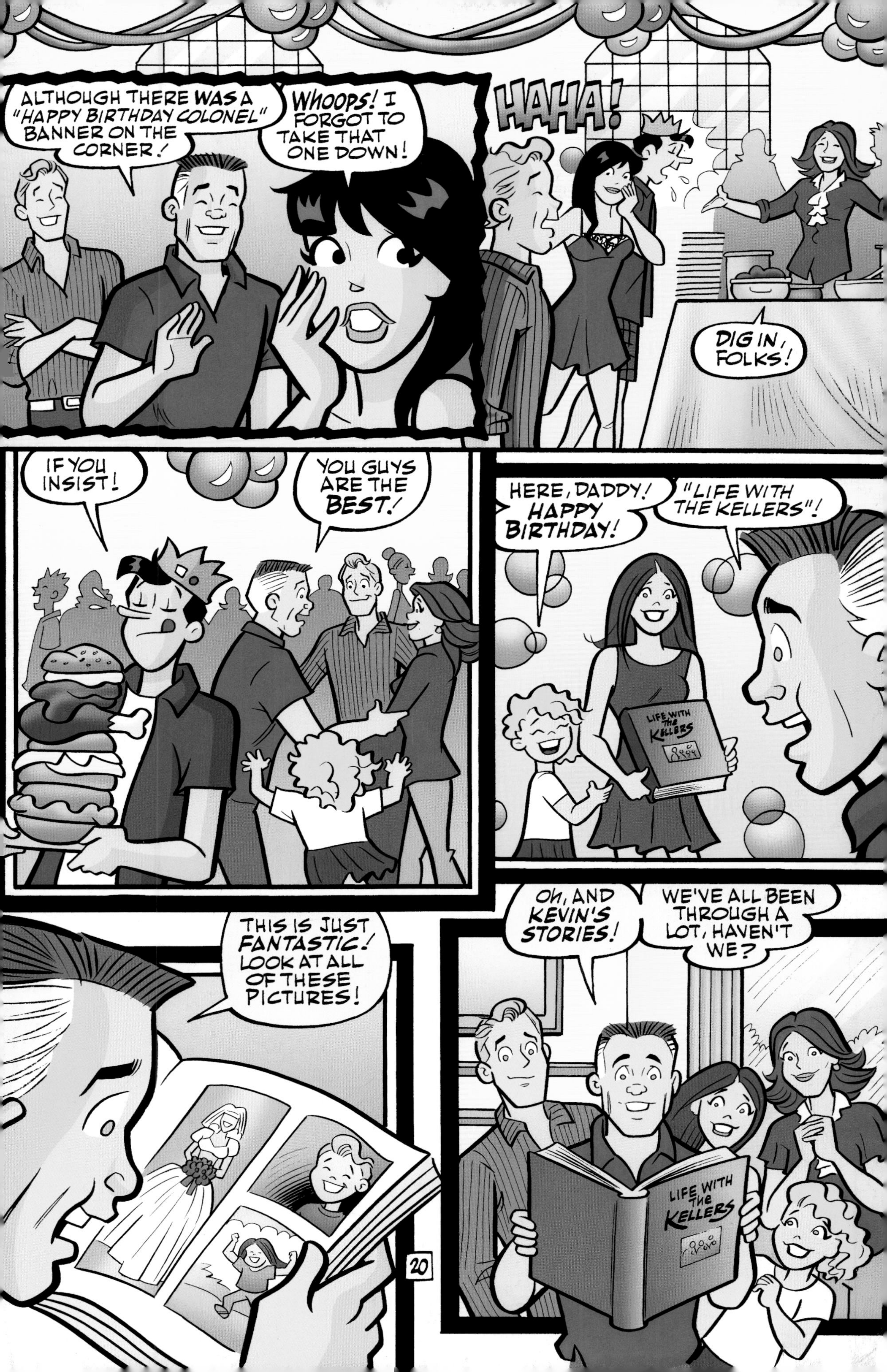
ALTHOUGH THERE WAS A "HAPPY BIRTHDAY COLONEL" BANNER ON THE CORNER!
WHOOPS! I FORGOT TO TAKE THAT ONE DOWN!
HAHA!
DIG IN, FOLKS!
IF YOU INSIST!
YOU GUYS ARE THE BEST!
HERE, DADDY! HAPPY BIRTHDAY!
"LIFE WITH THE KELLERS"!
LIFE WITH THE KELLERS
THIS IS JUST FANTASTIC! LOOK AT ALL OF THESE PICTURES!
OH, AND KEVIN'S STORIES!
WE'VE ALL BEEN THROUGH A LOT, HAVEN'T WE?
LIFE WITH THE KELLERS
20

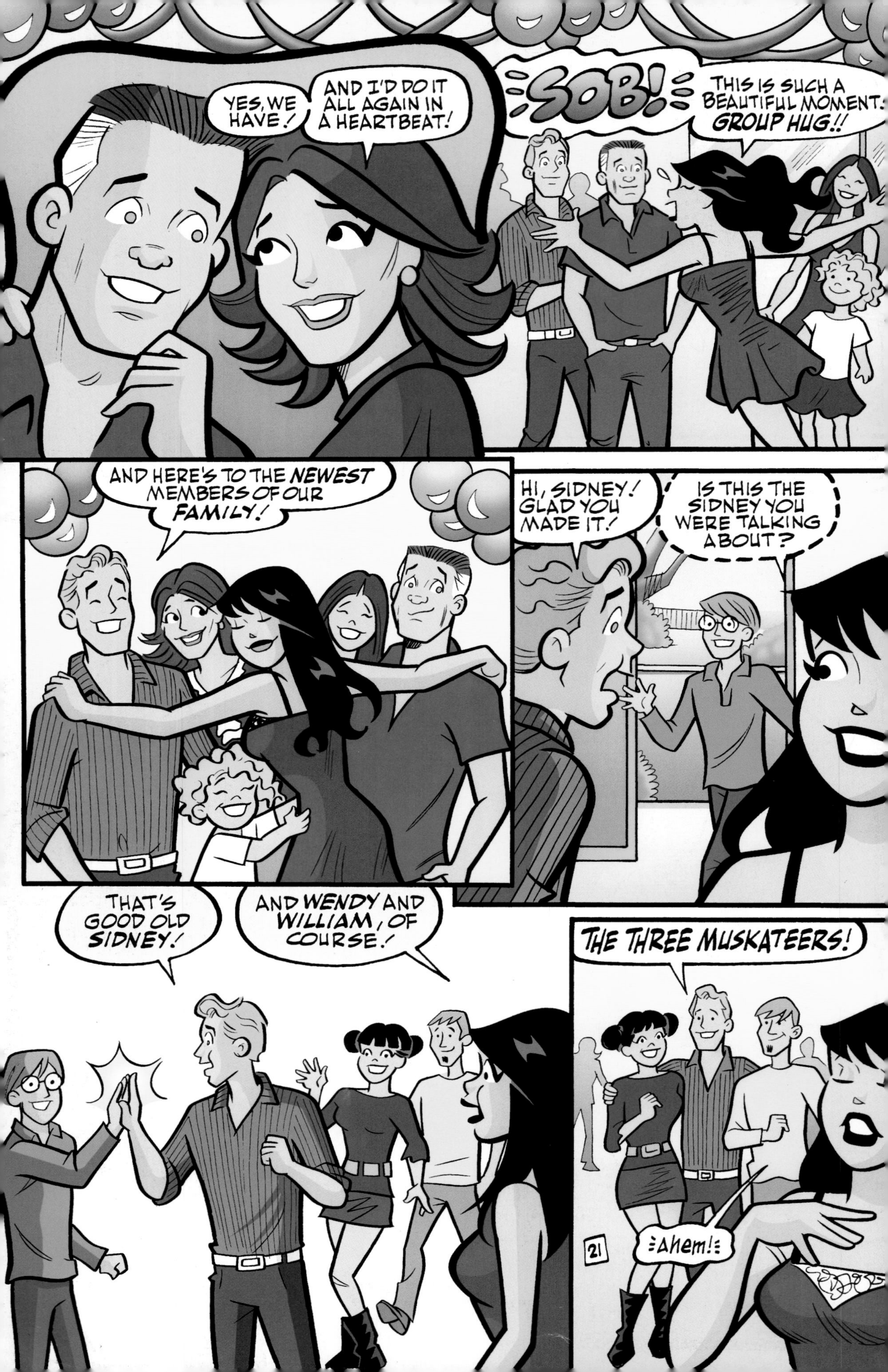
YES, WE HAVE!
AND I'D DO IT ALL AGAIN IN A HEARTBEAT!
SOB!
THIS IS SUCH A BEAUTIFUL MOMENT. GROUP HUG!!
AND HERE'S TO THE NEWEST MEMBERS OF OUR FAMILY!
HI, SIDNEY! GLAD YOU MADE IT!
IS THIS THE SIDNEY YOU WERE TALKING ABOUT?
THAT'S GOOD OLD SIDNEY!
AND WENDY AND WILLIAM, OF COURSE!
THE THREE MUSKATEERS!
AHEM!
21

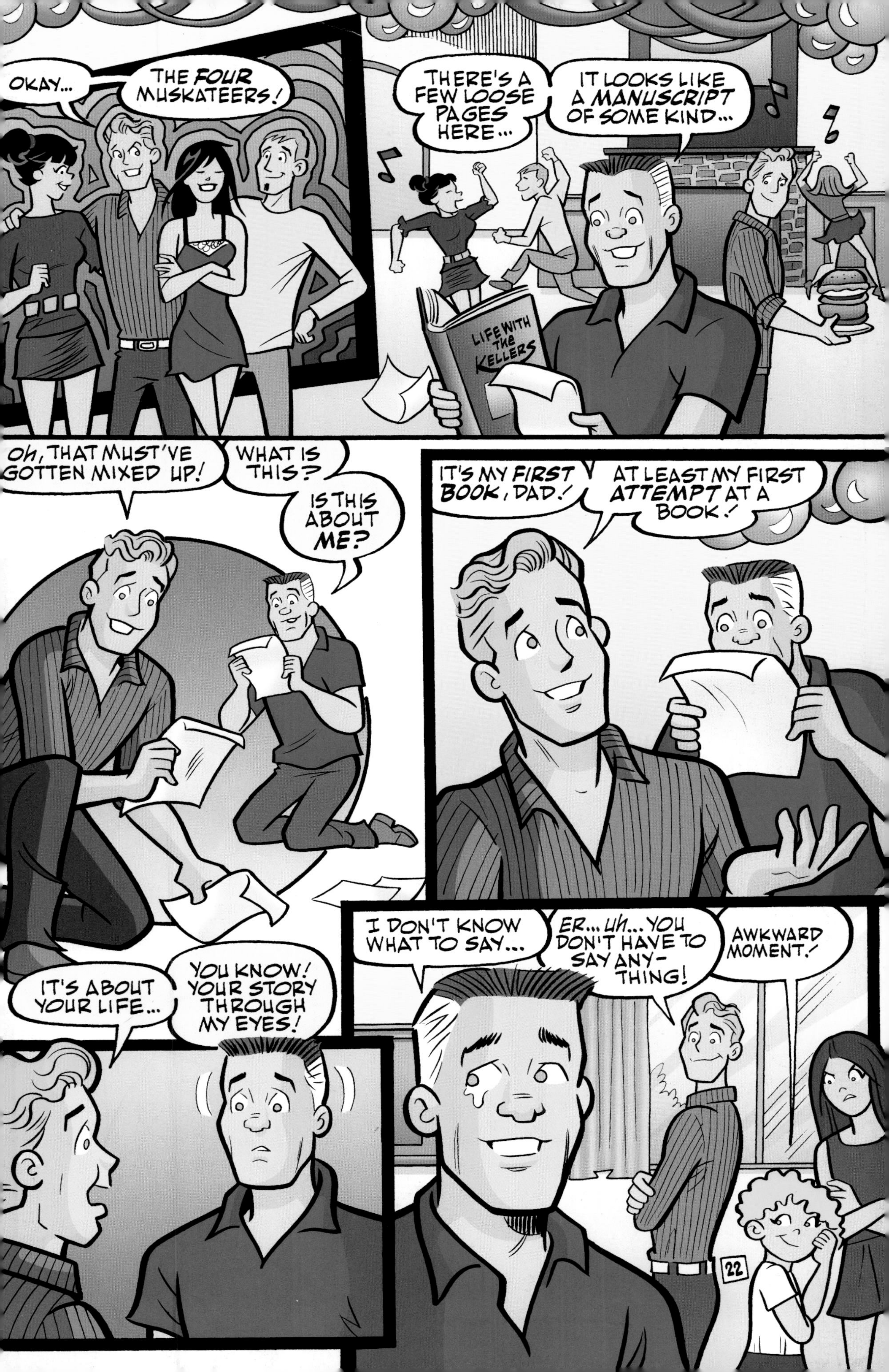

OKAY...
THE FOUR MUSKATEERS!
THERE'S A FEW LOOSE PAGES HERE...
IT LOOKS LIKE A MANUSCRIPT OF SOME KIND...
LIFE WITH The KELLERS
Oh, THAT MUST'VE GOTTEN MIXED UP!
WHAT IS THIS?
IS THIS ABOUT ME?
IT'S MY FIRST BOOK, DAD!
AT LEAST MY FIRST ATTEMPT AT A BOOK!
IT'S ABOUT YOUR LIFE...
YOU KNOW! YOUR STORY THROUGH MY EYES!
I DON'T KNOW WHAT TO SAY...
ER... Uh... YOU DON'T HAVE TO SAY ANY-THING!
AWKWARD MOMENT!
22

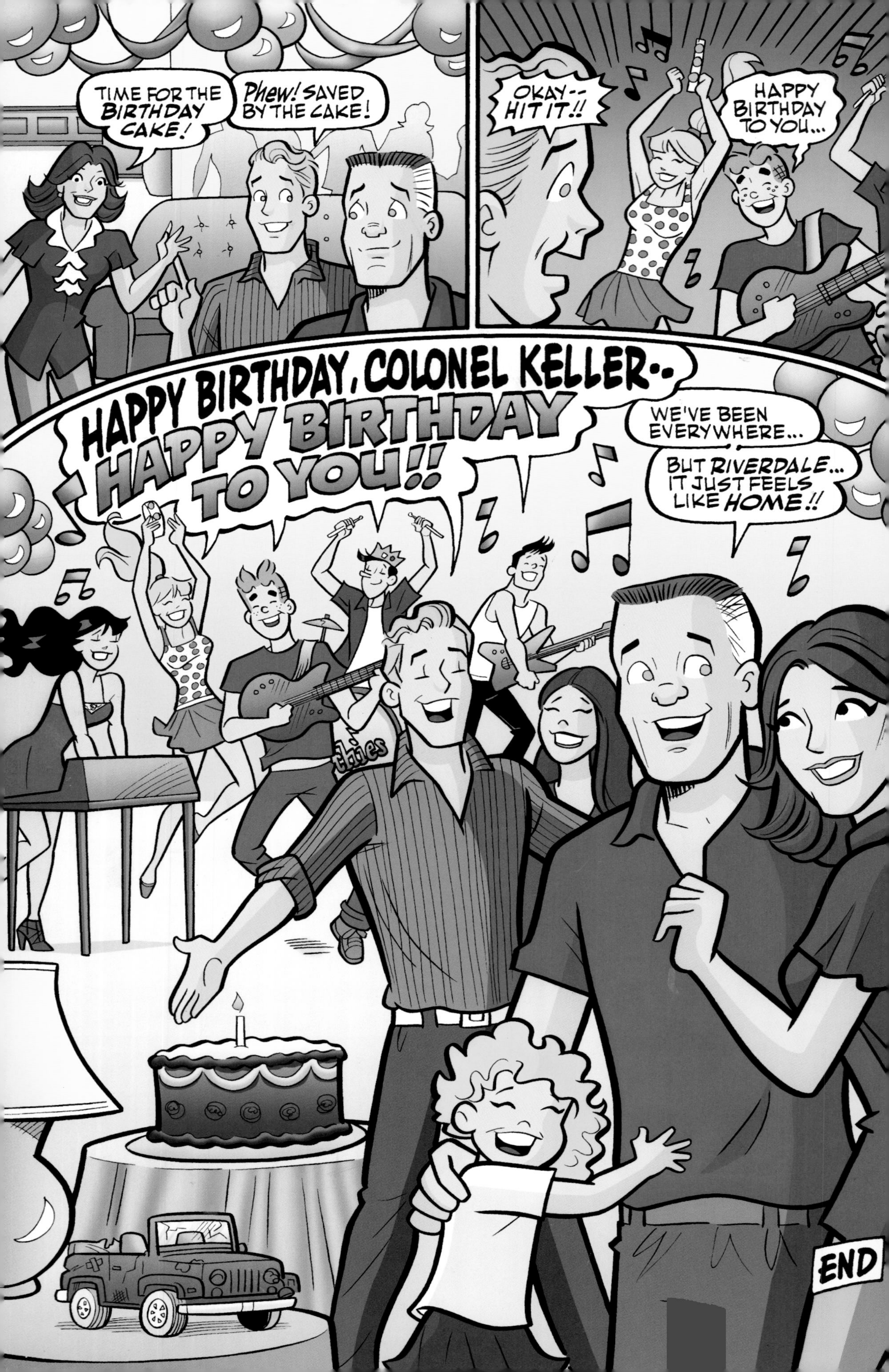
TIME FOR THE BIRTHDAY CAKE!
Phew! SAVED BY THE CAKE!
OKAY-- HIT IT!!
HAPPY BIRTHDAY TO YOU...
HAPPY BIRTHDAY, COLONEL KELLER--
HAPPY BIRTHDAY TO YOU!!
WE'VE BEEN EVERYWHERE...
BUT RIVERDALE... IT JUST FEELS LIKE HOME!!
END

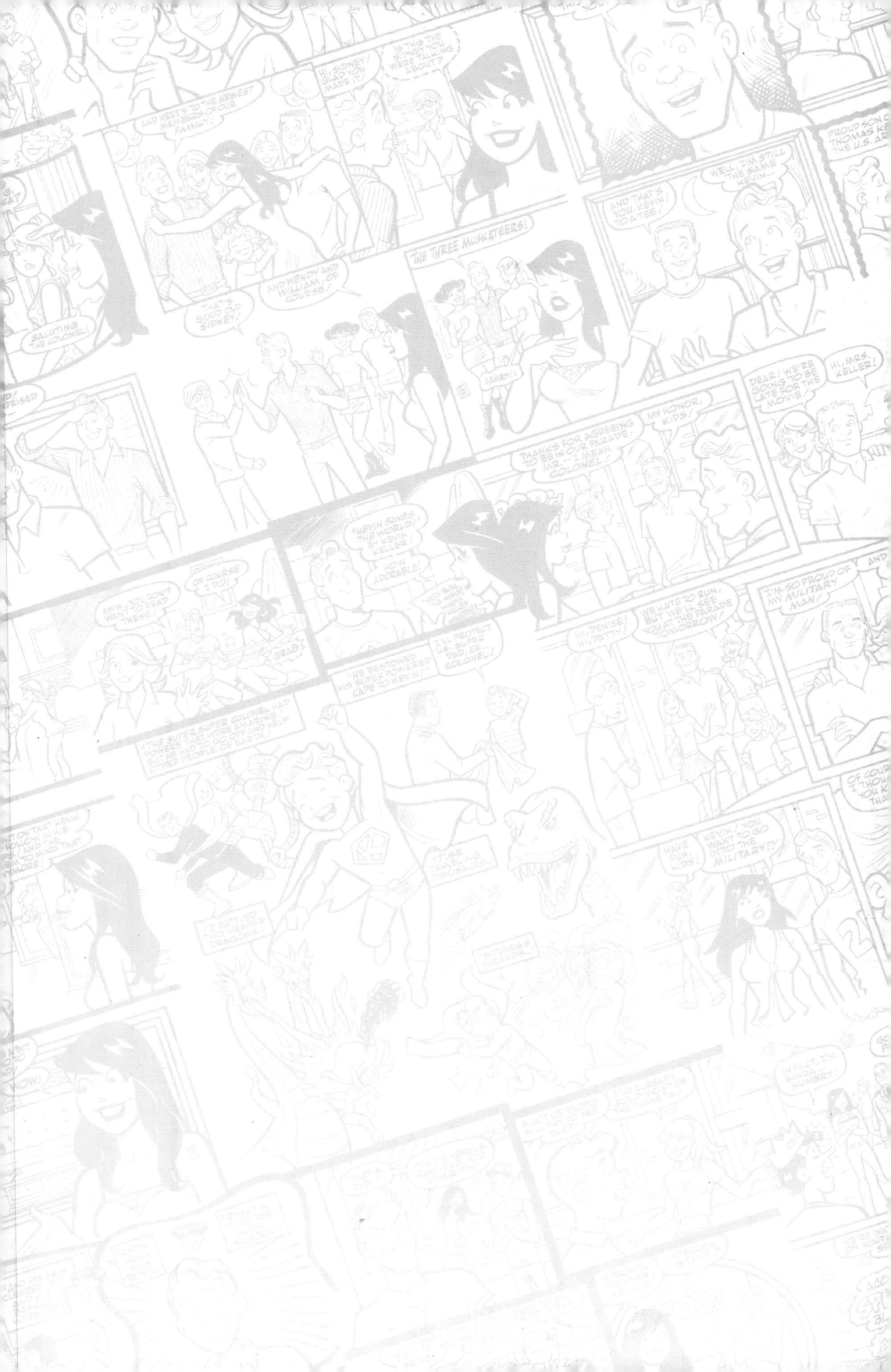
AND HERE'S TO THE NEWEST MEMBERS OF OUR FAMILY!
HI, SIDNEY! GLAD YOU MADE IT!
IS THIS THE SIDNEY YOU WERE TALKING ABOUT?
AND THAT'S YOU, KEVIN! TO A TEE!
WELL, I'M STILL THE SAME KEVIN...
SALUTING THE COLONEL!
THAT'S GOOD OLD SIDNEY!
AND WENDY AND WILLIAM, OF COURSE!
THE THREE MUSKATEERS!
DEAR! WE'RE GOING TO BE LATE FOR THE MOVIE!
HI, MRS. KELLER!
THANKS FOR AGREEING TO BE IN OUR PARADE, MR.-- I MEAN COLONEL!
MY HONOR, KIDS!
"KEVIN SAVES THE WORLD" BY KEVIN KELLER
HOW ADORABLE!
AWW, YOU DON'T WANT TO READ THESE!
OF COURSE I DO!
GRAB
HI, DENISE! HI, PATTY!
WE HATE TO RUN, BUT WE'LL SEE YOU AT THE PARADE TOMORROW!
I'M SO PROUD OF MY MILITARY MAN!
"HE BESTOWED HIS SUPER POWERED CAPE TO KEVIN!"
I'LL PROTECT US, SUPER DAD, ER... COLONEL!
"THE SUPER SUPER COLONEL HAD POWERS THAT WERE AMAZING! BUT HE HAD TO GO OFF AND HELP OTHER PEOPLE OF EARTH!"
"TIME TRAVELING DINOSAURS..."
"I BATTLED TWO-HEADED DRAGONS..."
"WITCHES & WIZARDS..."
HAVE FUN, KIDS!
KEVIN! YOU WANT TO GO INTO THE MILITARY?!
IN FACT, I'M KINDA... HUNGRY!

pop culture homage variant cover

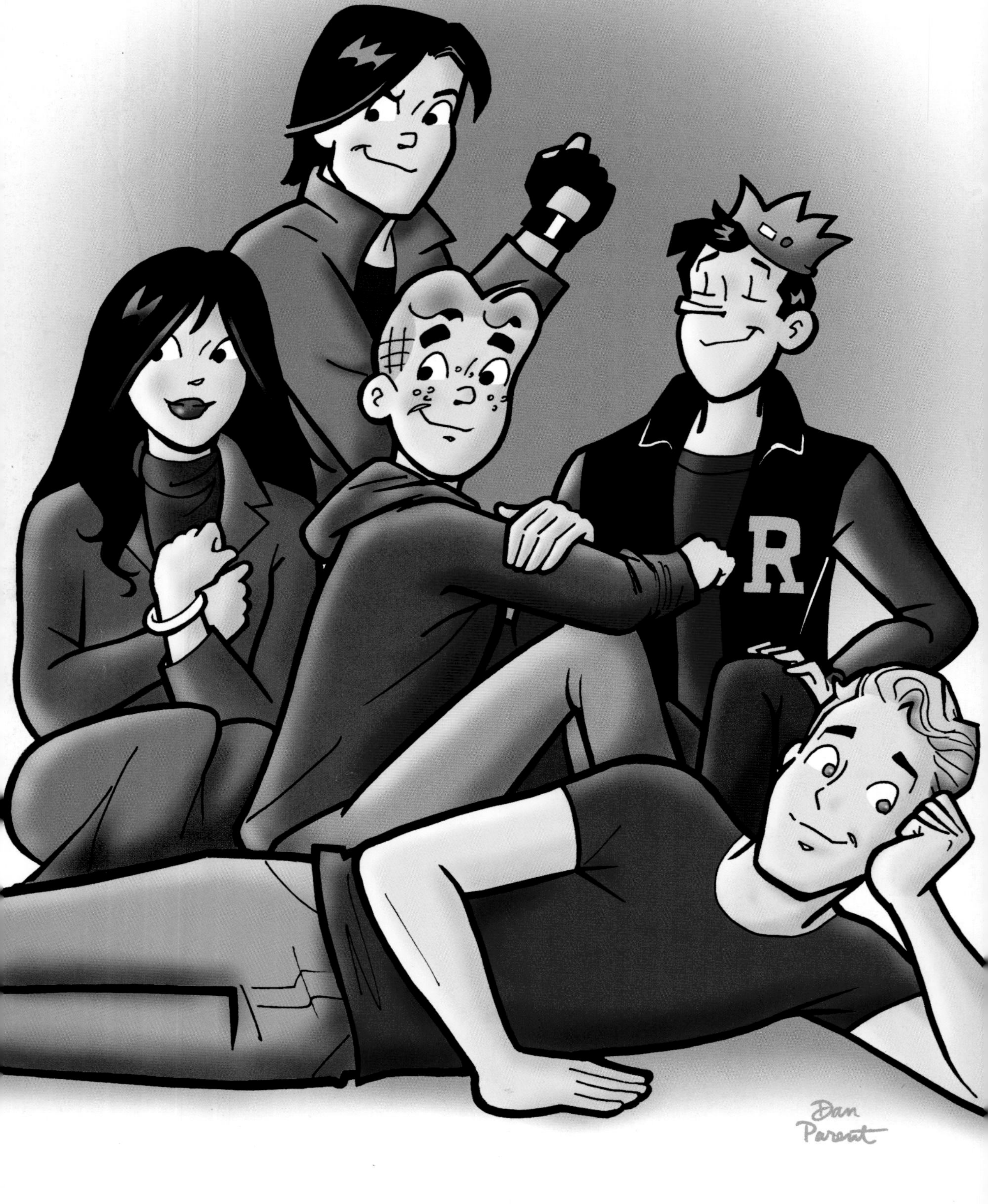
R
Dan Parent

Part 5: Let's Get It Started

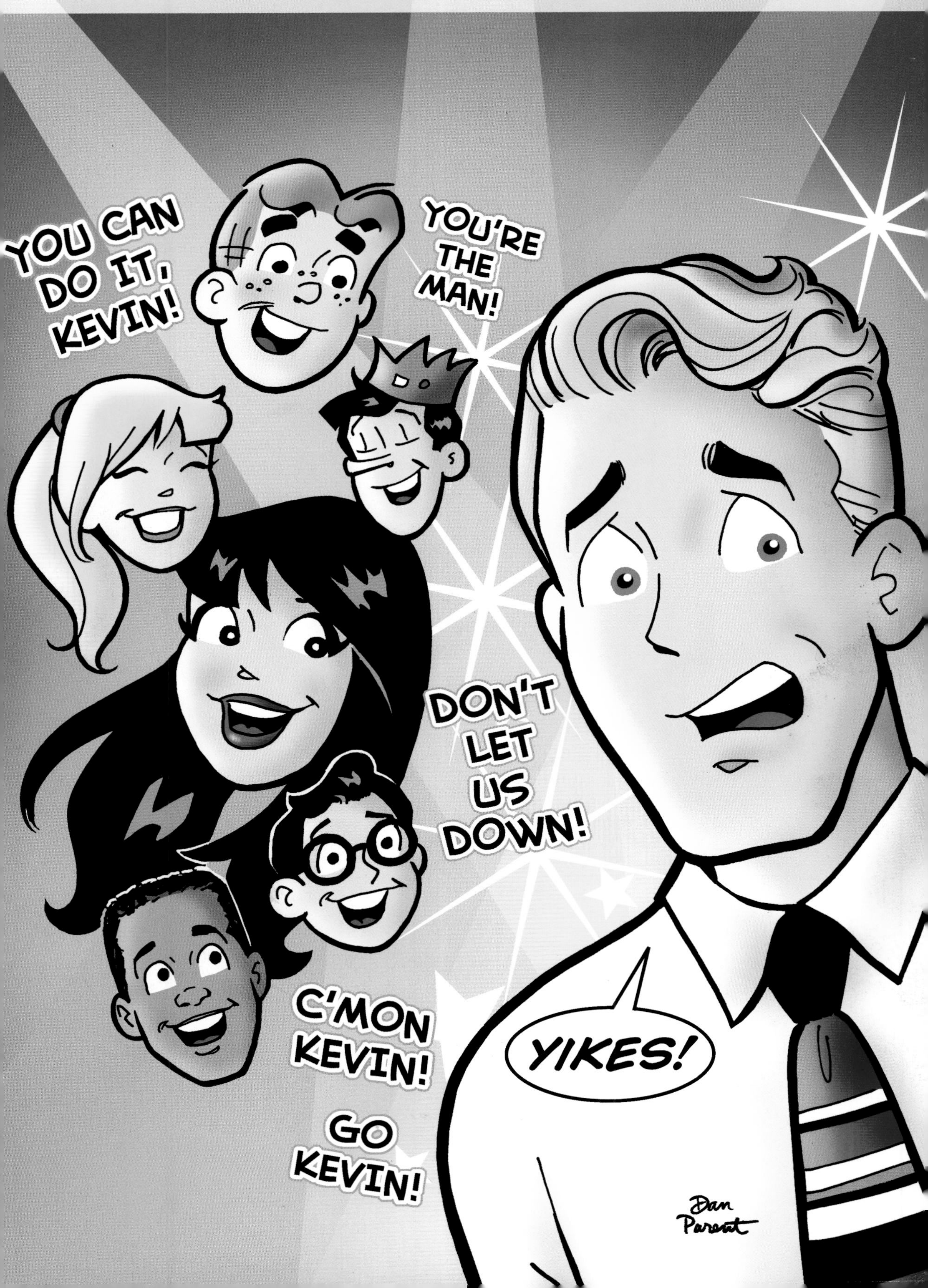
YOU CAN DO IT, KEVIN!
YOU'RE THE MAN!
DON'T LET US DOWN!
C'MON KEVIN!
GO KEVIN!
YIKES!
Dan Parent

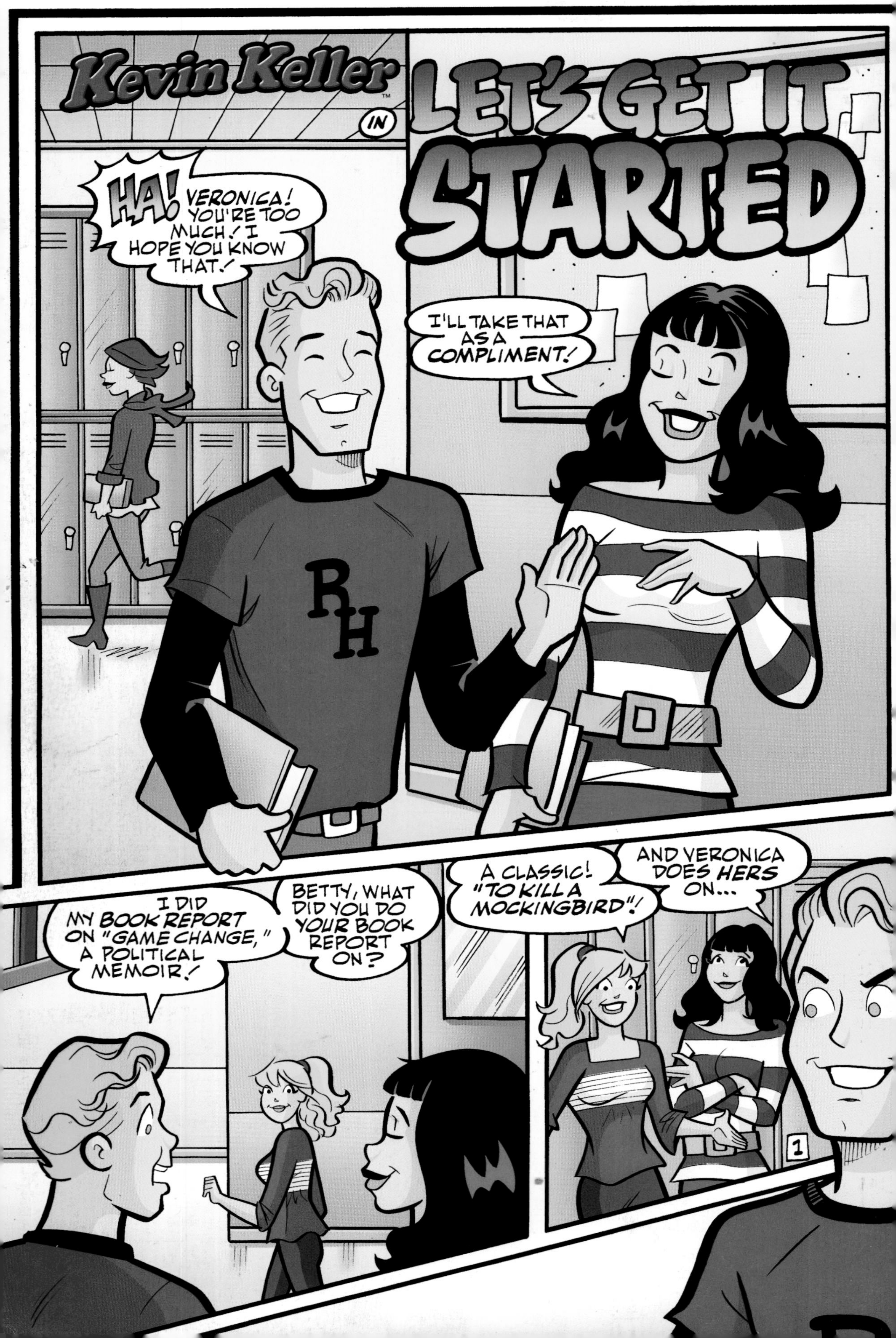
Kevin Keller™ IN
LET'S GET IT STARTED
HA! VERONICA! YOU'RE TOO MUCH! I HOPE YOU KNOW THAT!
I'LL TAKE THAT AS A COMPLIMENT!
RH
I DID MY BOOK REPORT ON "GAME CHANGE," A POLITICAL MEMOIR!
BETTY, WHAT DID YOU DO YOUR BOOK REPORT ON?
A CLASSIC! "TO KILL A MOCKINGBIRD"!
AND VERONICA DOES HERS ON...
1

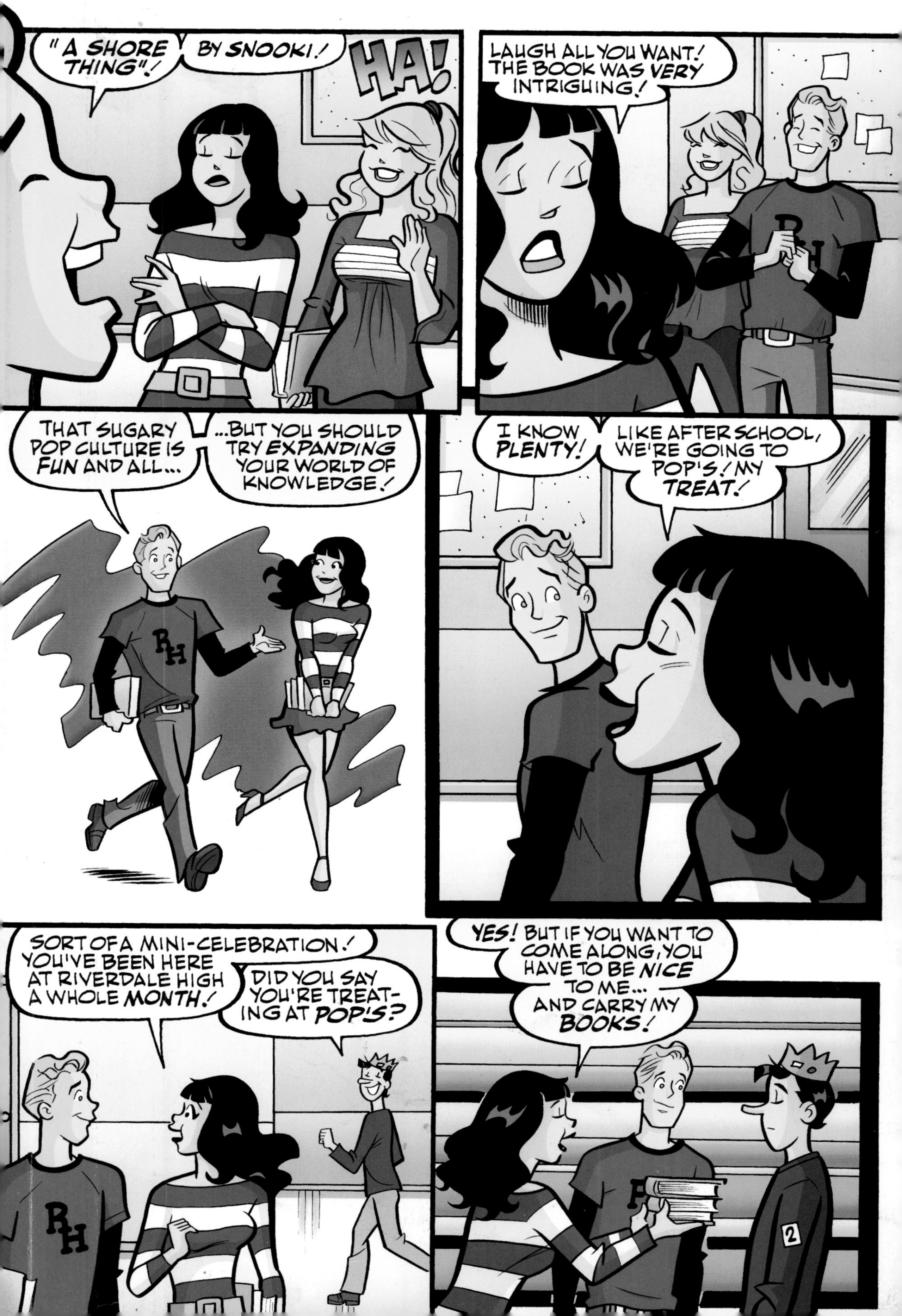
"A SHORE THING"!
BY SNOOKI!
HA!
LAUGH ALL YOU WANT! THE BOOK WAS VERY INTRIGUING!
THAT SUGARY POP CULTURE IS FUN AND ALL...
...BUT YOU SHOULD TRY EXPANDING YOUR WORLD OF KNOWLEDGE!
I KNOW PLENTY!
LIKE AFTER SCHOOL, WE'RE GOING TO POP'S! MY TREAT!
SORT OF A MINI-CELEBRATION! YOU'VE BEEN HERE AT RIVERDALE HIGH A WHOLE MONTH!
DID YOU SAY YOU'RE TREATING AT POP'S?
YES! BUT IF YOU WANT TO COME ALONG, YOU HAVE TO BE NICE TO ME... AND CARRY MY BOOKS!

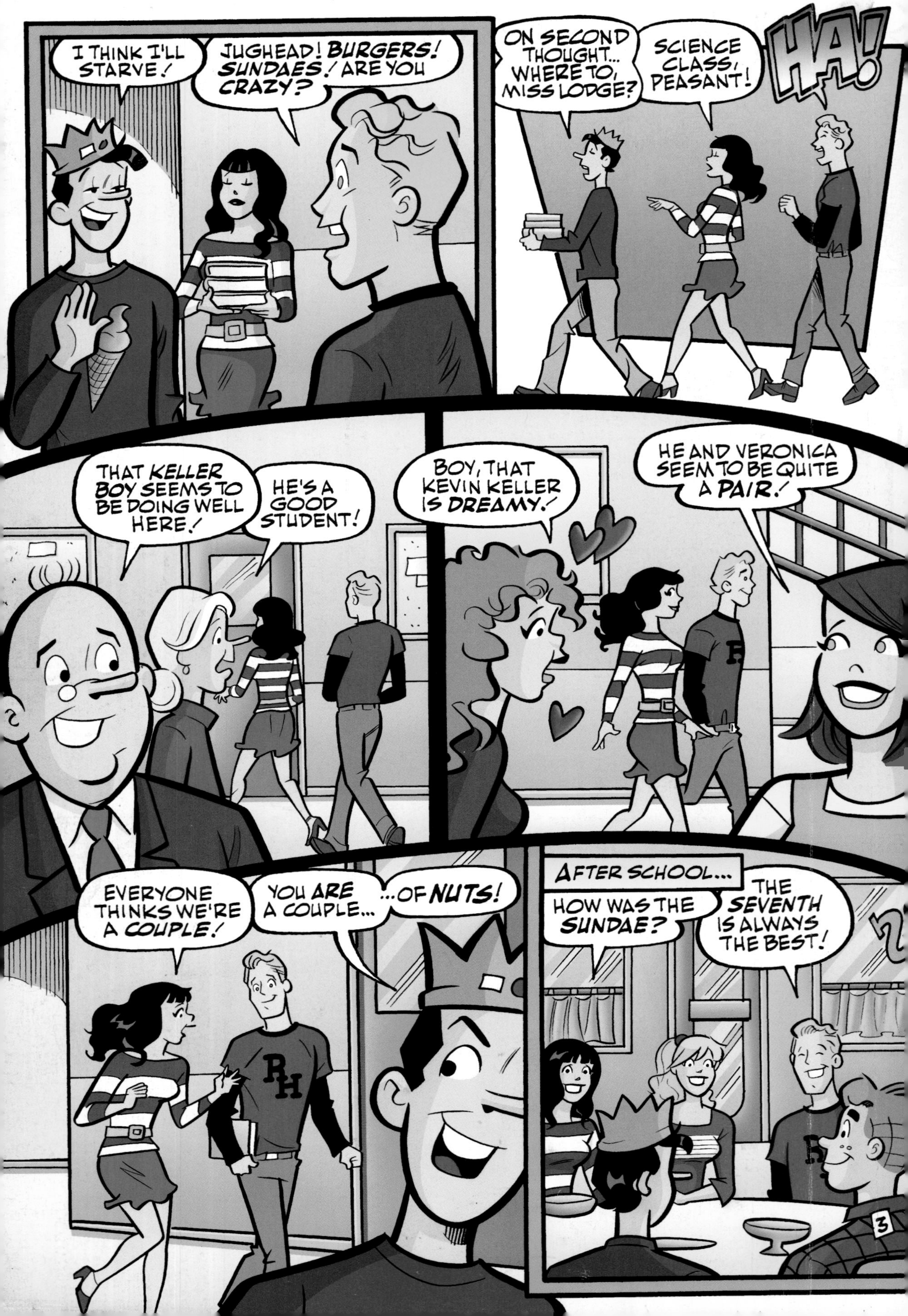
I THINK I'LL STARVE!
JUGHEAD! BURGERS! SUNDAES! ARE YOU CRAZY?
ON SECOND THOUGHT... WHERE TO, MISS LODGE?
SCIENCE CLASS, PEASANT!
HA!
THAT KELLER BOY SEEMS TO BE DOING WELL HERE!
HE'S A GOOD STUDENT!
BOY, THAT KEVIN KELLER IS DREAMY!
HE AND VERONICA SEEM TO BE QUITE A PAIR!
EVERYONE THINKS WE'RE A COUPLE!
YOU ARE A COUPLE...
...OF NUTS!
AFTER SCHOOL...
HOW WAS THE SUNDAE?
THE SEVENTH IS ALWAYS THE BEST!
3

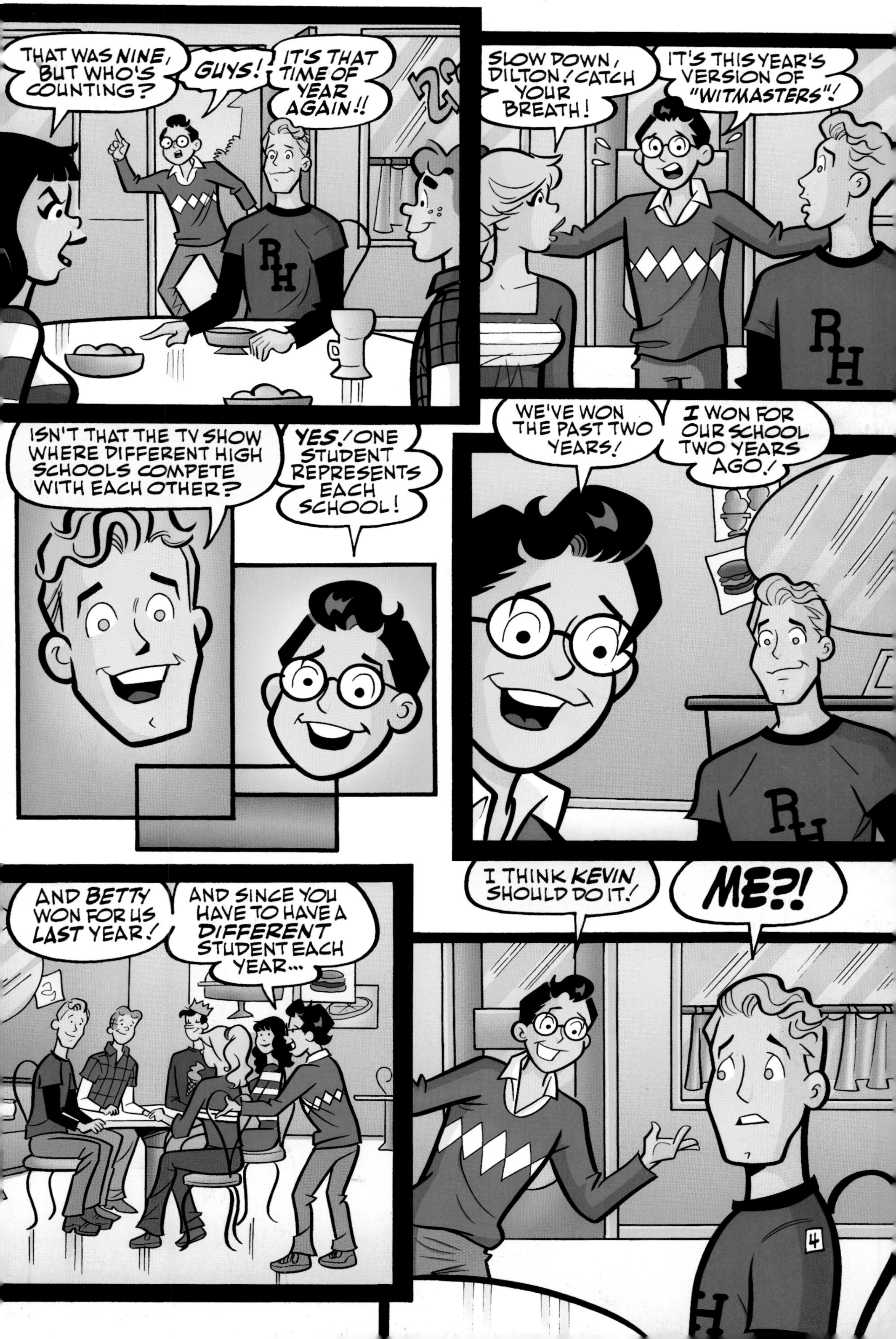
THAT WAS NINE, BUT WHO'S COUNTING?
GUYS!
IT'S THAT TIME OF YEAR AGAIN!!
SLOW DOWN, DILTON! CATCH YOUR BREATH!
IT'S THIS YEAR'S VERSION OF "WITMASTERS"!
ISN'T THAT THE TV SHOW WHERE DIFFERENT HIGH SCHOOLS COMPETE WITH EACH OTHER?
YES! ONE STUDENT REPRESENTS EACH SCHOOL!
WE'VE WON THE PAST TWO YEARS!
I WON FOR OUR SCHOOL TWO YEARS AGO!
AND BETTY WON FOR US LAST YEAR!
AND SINCE YOU HAVE TO HAVE A DIFFERENT STUDENT EACH YEAR...
I THINK KEVIN SHOULD DO IT!
ME?!
4

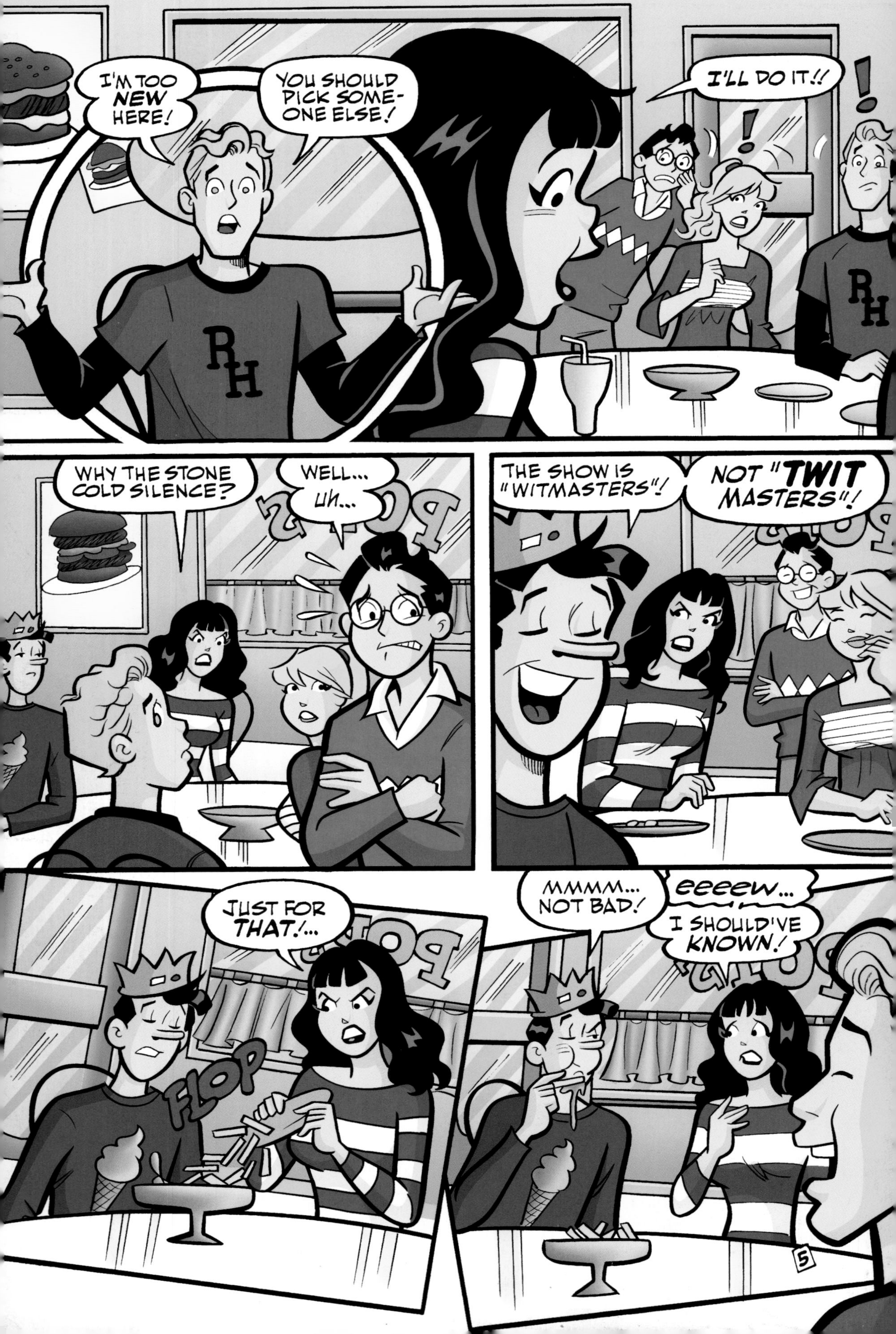
I'M TOO NEW HERE!
YOU SHOULD PICK SOME-ONE ELSE!
I'LL DO IT!!
!
!
WHY THE STONE COLD SILENCE?
WELL... uh...
THE SHOW IS "WITMASTERS"!
NOT "TWIT MASTERS"!
JUST FOR THAT!...
FLOP
MMMM... NOT BAD!
eeeew...
I SHOULD'VE KNOWN!
5

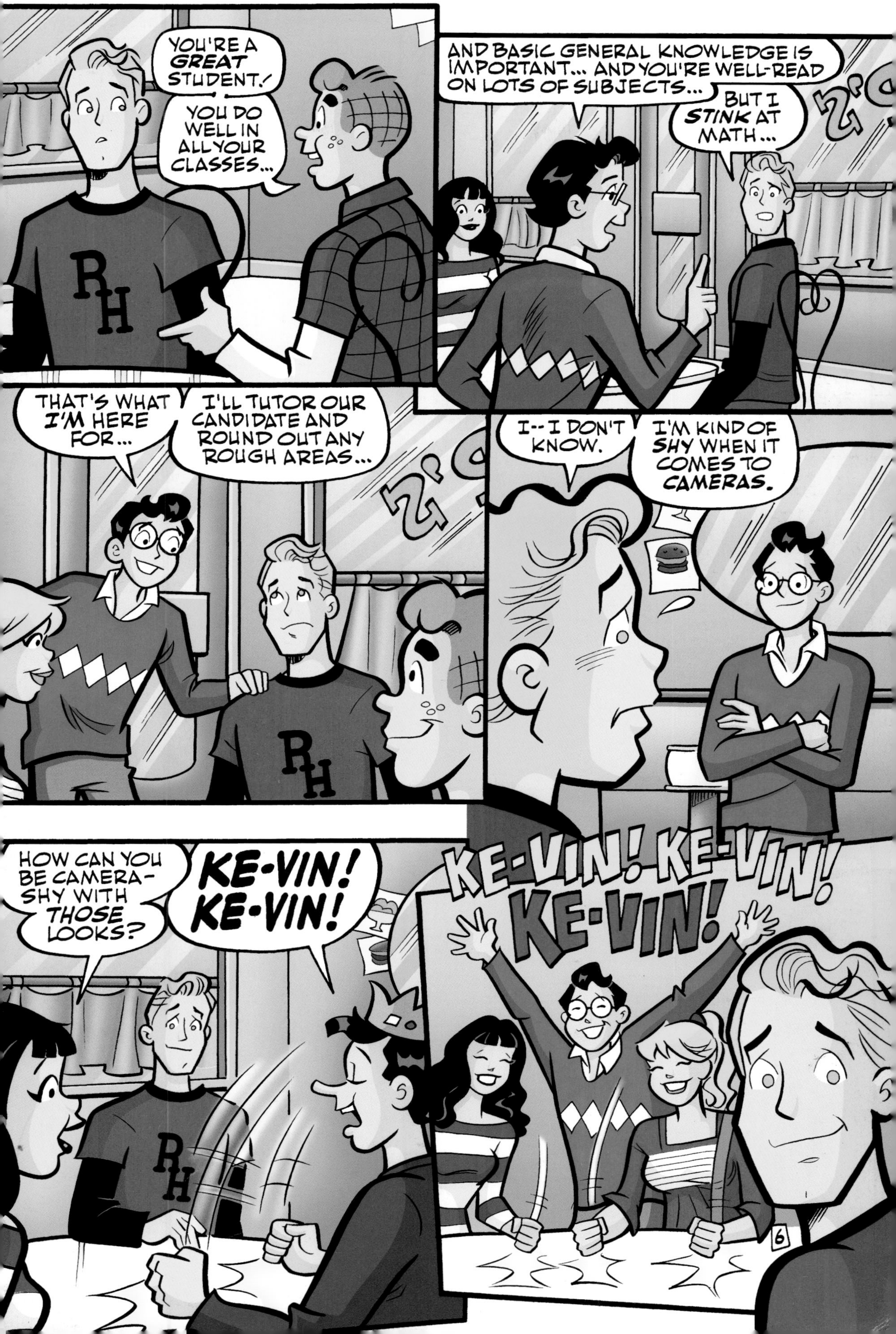

YOU'RE A GREAT STUDENT!
YOU DO WELL IN ALL YOUR CLASSES...
AND BASIC GENERAL KNOWLEDGE IS IMPORTANT... AND YOU'RE WELL-READ ON LOTS OF SUBJECTS...
BUT I STINK AT MATH...
THAT'S WHAT I'M HERE FOR...
I'LL TUTOR OUR CANDIDATE AND ROUND OUT ANY ROUGH AREAS...
I-- I DON'T KNOW.
I'M KIND OF SHY WHEN IT COMES TO CAMERAS.
HOW CAN YOU BE CAMERA-SHY WITH THOSE LOOKS?
KE-VIN! KE-VIN!
KE-VIN! KE-VIN! KE-VIN!
6

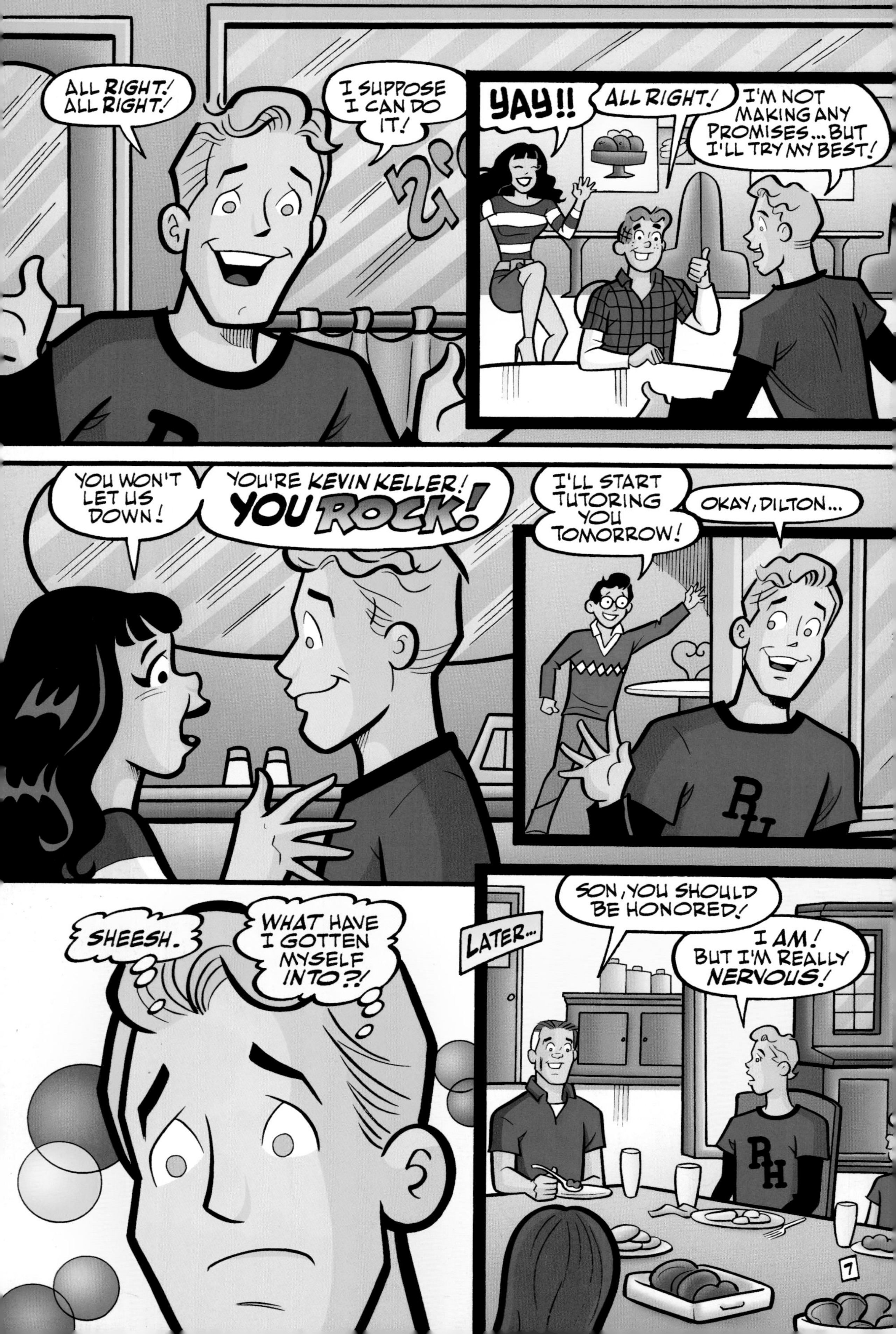
ALL RIGHT! ALL RIGHT!
I SUPPOSE I CAN DO IT!
YAY!!
ALL RIGHT!
I'M NOT MAKING ANY PROMISES... BUT I'LL TRY MY BEST!
YOU WON'T LET US DOWN!
YOU'RE KEVIN KELLER! YOU ROCK!
I'LL START TUTORING YOU TOMORROW!
OKAY, DILTON...
SHEESH.
WHAT HAVE I GOTTEN MYSELF INTO?!
LATER...
SON, YOU SHOULD BE HONORED!
I AM! BUT I'M REALLY NERVOUS!
7

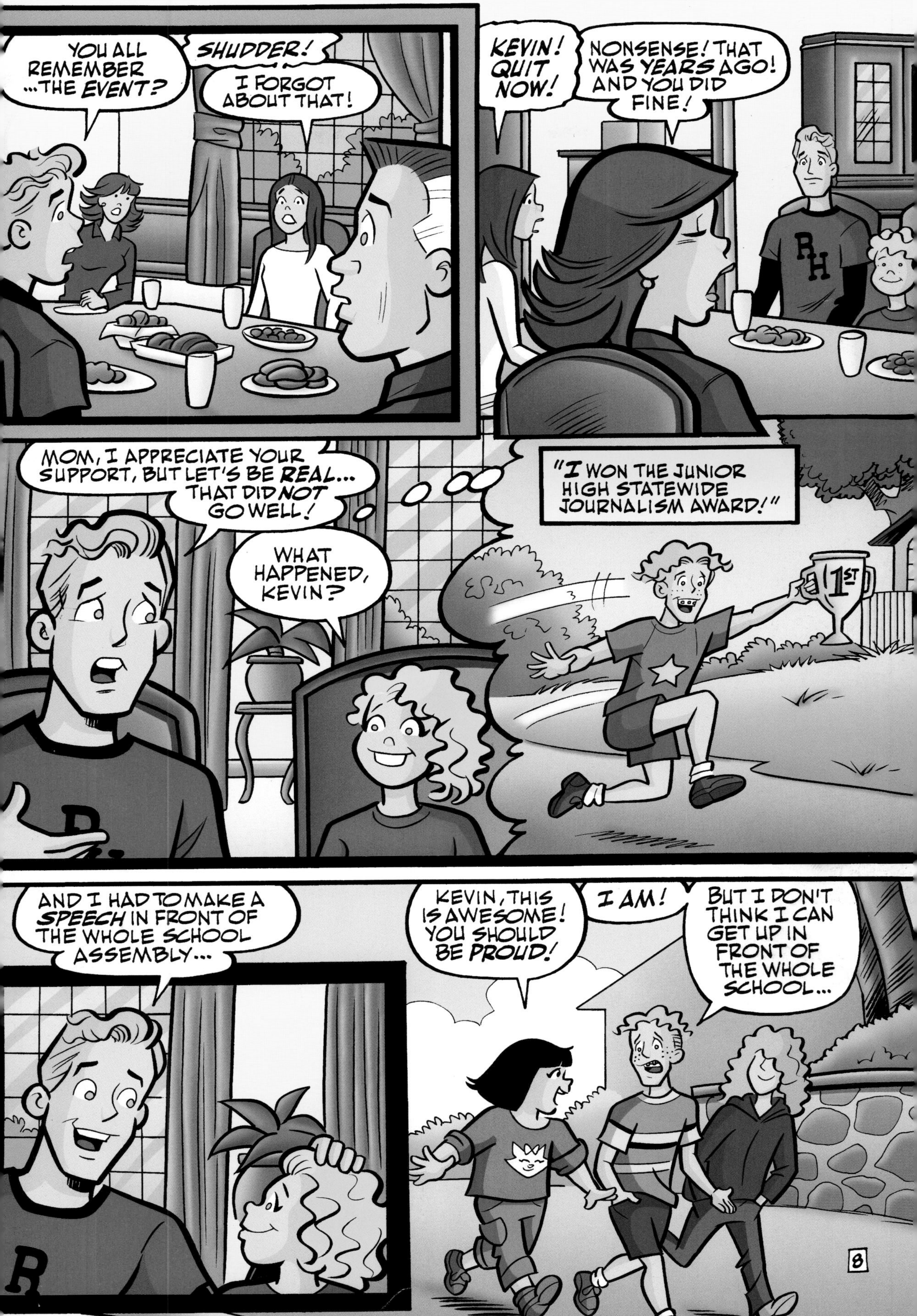
YOU ALL REMEMBER ...THE EVENT?
SHUDDER!
I FORGOT ABOUT THAT!
KEVIN! QUIT NOW!
NONSENSE! THAT WAS YEARS AGO! AND YOU DID FINE!
MOM, I APPRECIATE YOUR SUPPORT, BUT LET'S BE REAL... THAT DID NOT GO WELL!
WHAT HAPPENED, KEVIN?
"I WON THE JUNIOR HIGH STATEWIDE JOURNALISM AWARD!"
1ST
RH
AND I HAD TO MAKE A SPEECH IN FRONT OF THE WHOLE SCHOOL ASSEMBLY...
KEVIN, THIS IS AWESOME! YOU SHOULD BE PROUD!
I AM!
BUT I DON'T THINK I CAN GET UP IN FRONT OF THE WHOLE SCHOOL...
8

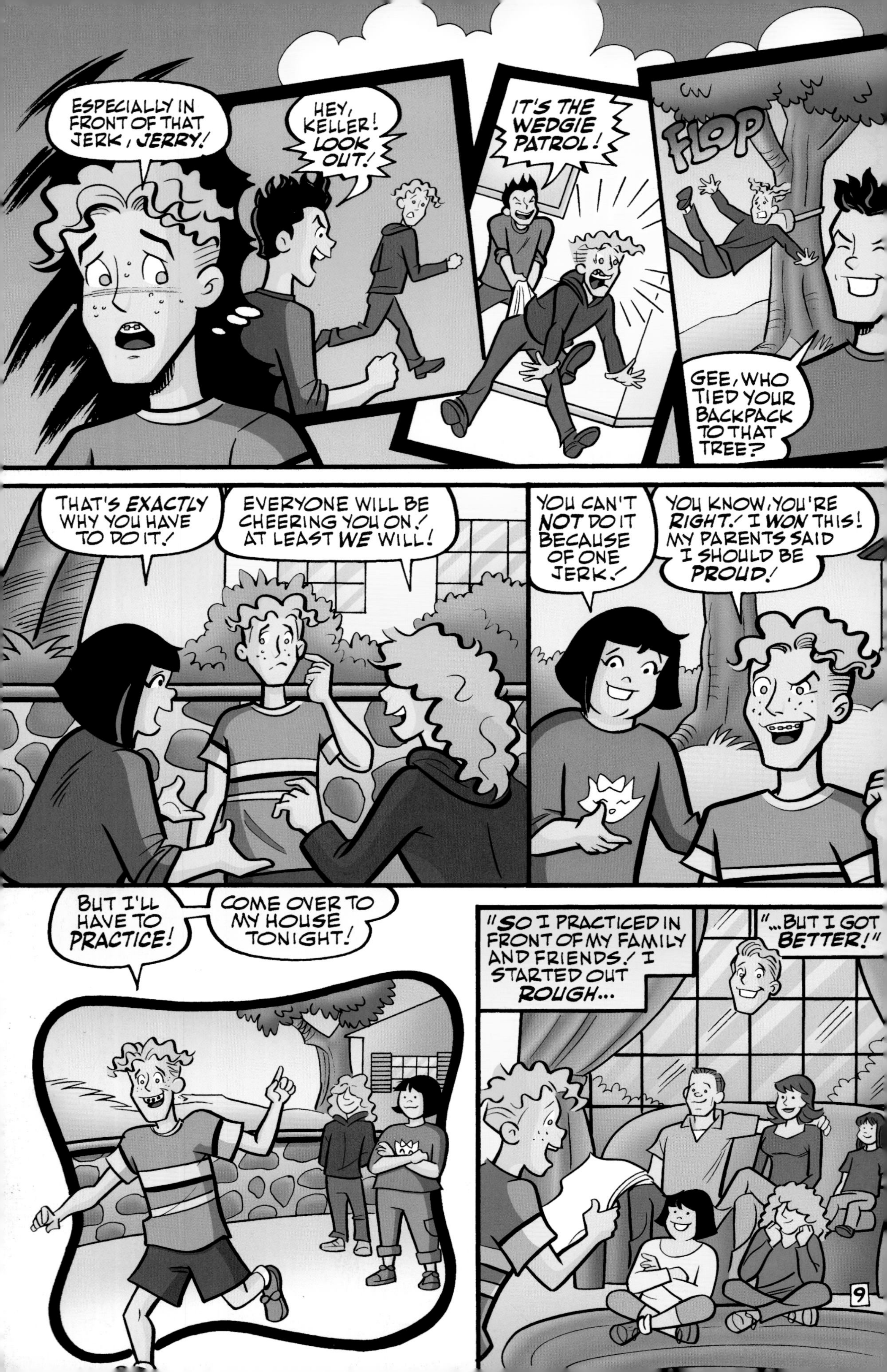
ESPECIALLY IN FRONT OF THAT JERK, JERRY!
HEY, KELLER! LOOK OUT!
IT'S THE WEDGIE PATROL!
FLOP
GEE, WHO TIED YOUR BACKPACK TO THAT TREE?
THAT'S EXACTLY WHY YOU HAVE TO DO IT!
EVERYONE WILL BE CHEERING YOU ON! AT LEAST WE WILL!
YOU CAN'T NOT DO IT BECAUSE OF ONE JERK!
YOU KNOW, YOU'RE RIGHT! I WON THIS! MY PARENTS SAID I SHOULD BE PROUD!
BUT I'LL HAVE TO PRACTICE!
COME OVER TO MY HOUSE TONIGHT!
"SO I PRACTICED IN FRONT OF MY FAMILY AND FRIENDS! I STARTED OUT ROUGH...
"...BUT I GOT BETTER!"

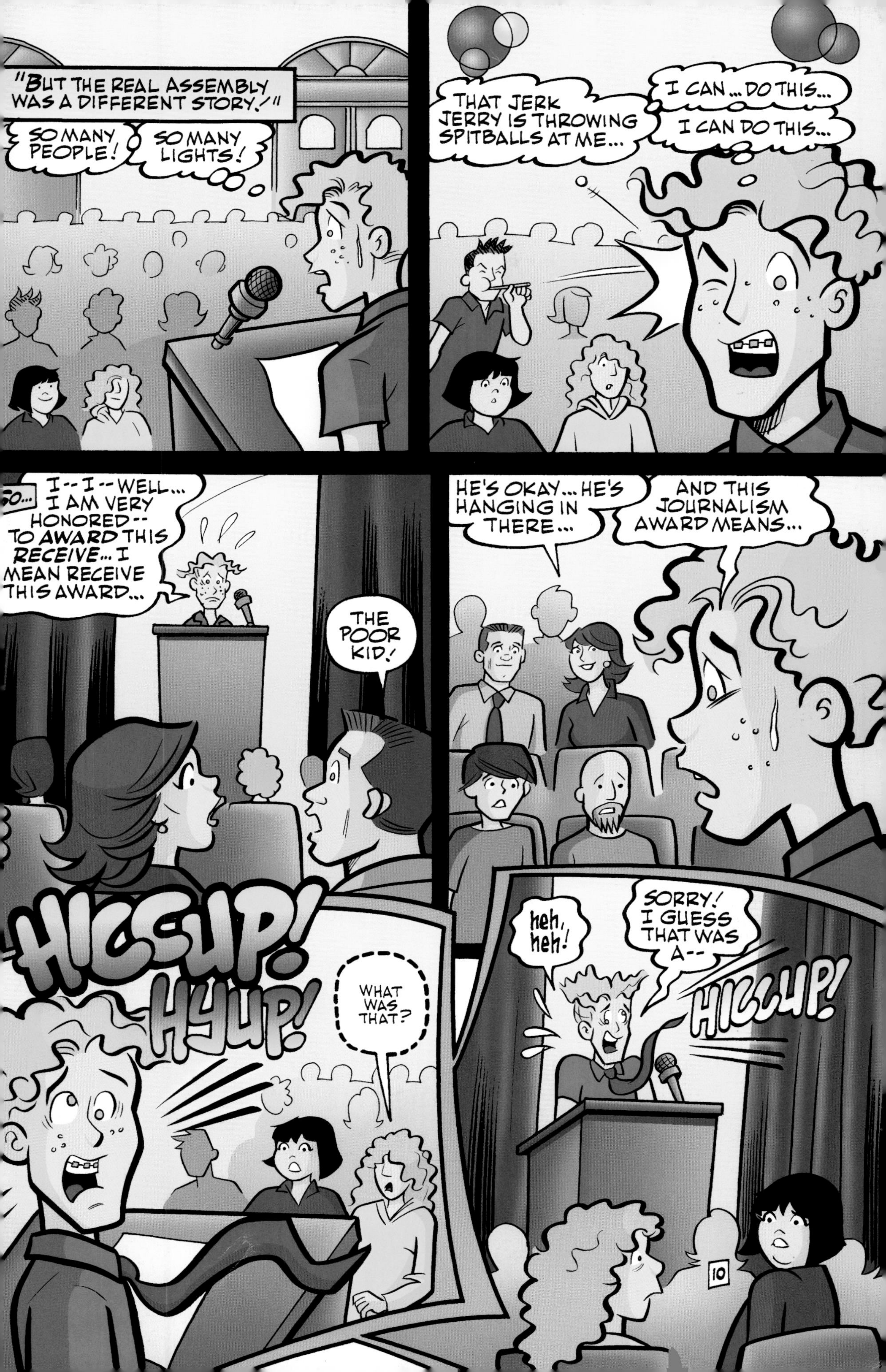

"BUT THE REAL ASSEMBLY WAS A DIFFERENT STORY!"
SO MANY PEOPLE!
SO MANY LIGHTS!
THAT JERK JERRY IS THROWING SPITBALLS AT ME...
I CAN... DO THIS...
I CAN DO THIS...
I-- I-- WELL... I AM VERY HONORED-- TO AWARD THIS RECEIVE... I MEAN RECEIVE THIS AWARD...
THE POOR KID!
HE'S OKAY... HE'S HANGING IN THERE...
AND THIS JOURNALISM AWARD MEANS...
HICCUP!
HYUP!
WHAT WAS THAT?
heh, heh!
SORRY! I GUESS THAT WAS A--
HICCUP!
10

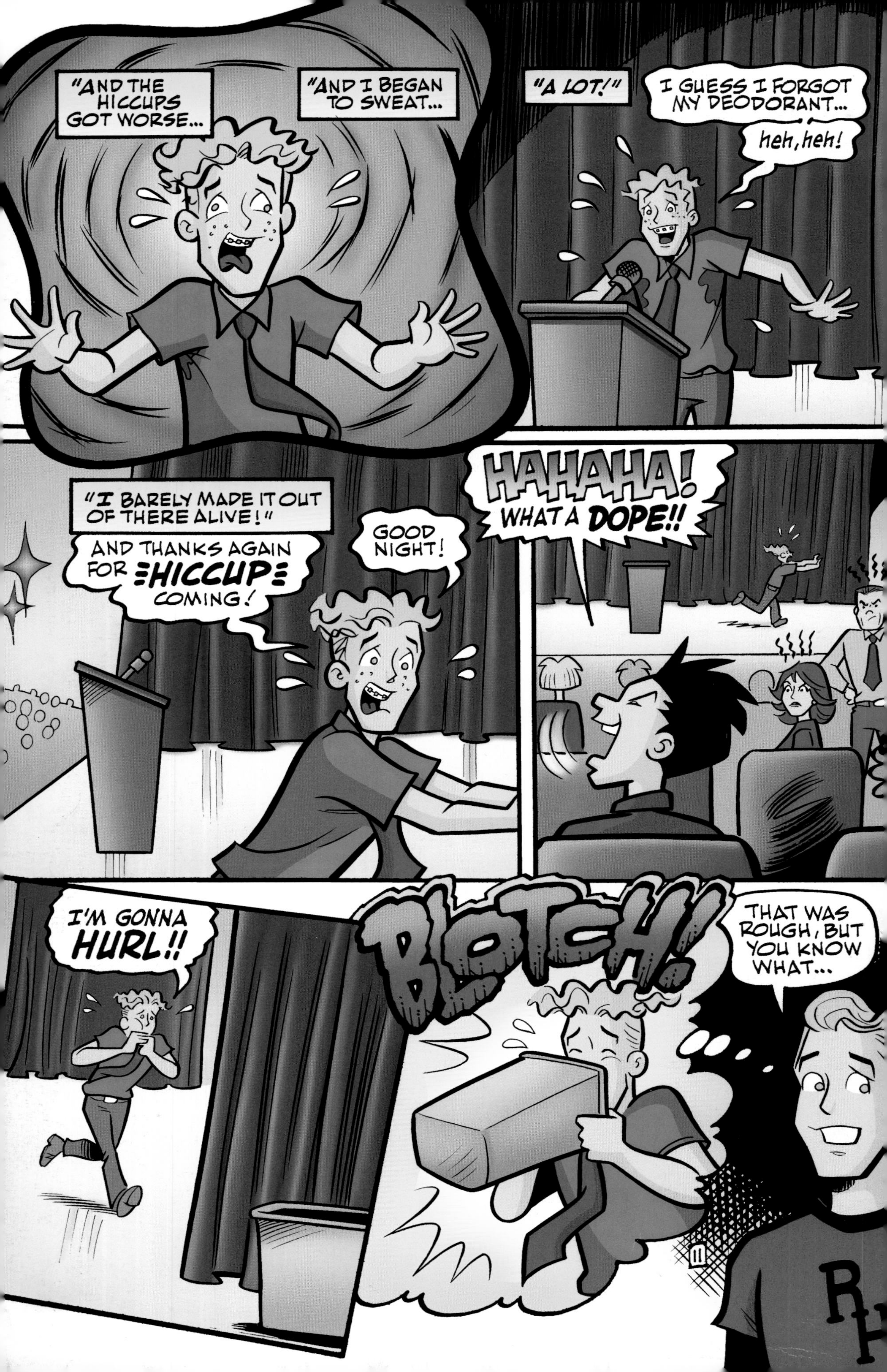
"AND THE HICCUPS GOT WORSE...
"AND I BEGAN TO SWEAT...
"A LOT!"
I GUESS I FORGOT MY DEODORANT...
heh, heh!
"I BARELY MADE IT OUT OF THERE ALIVE!"
AND THANKS AGAIN FOR HICCUP COMING!
GOOD NIGHT!
HAHAHA! WHAT A DOPE!!
I'M GONNA HURL!!
BLOTCH!!
THAT WAS ROUGH, BUT YOU KNOW WHAT...
11

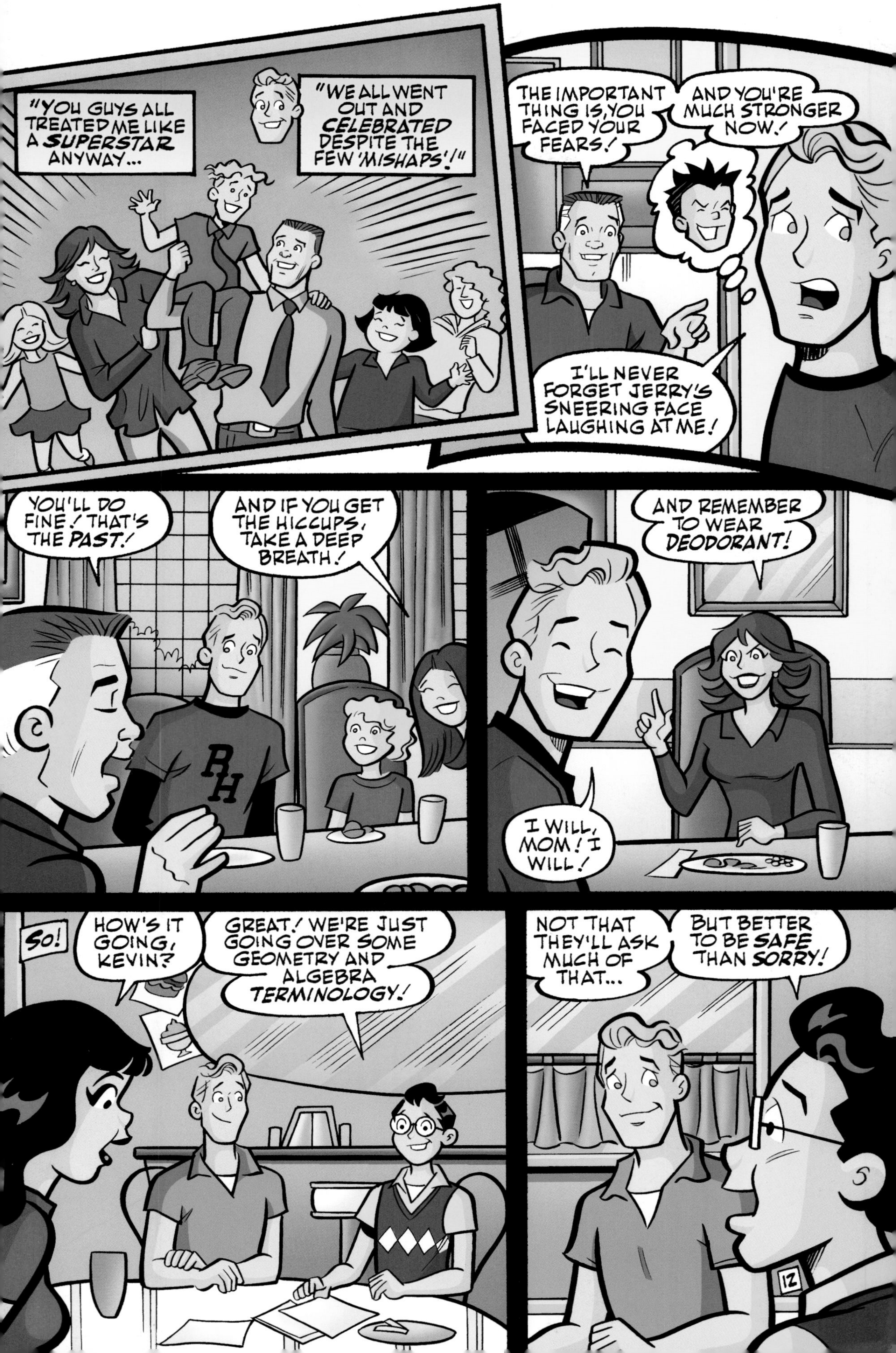
"YOU GUYS ALL TREATED ME LIKE A SUPERSTAR ANYWAY...
"WE ALL WENT OUT AND CELEBRATED DESPITE THE FEW 'MISHAPS'!"
THE IMPORTANT THING IS, YOU FACED YOUR FEARS!
AND YOU'RE MUCH STRONGER NOW!
I'LL NEVER FORGET JERRY'S SNEERING FACE LAUGHING AT ME!
YOU'LL DO FINE! THAT'S THE PAST!
AND IF YOU GET THE HICCUPS, TAKE A DEEP BREATH!
AND REMEMBER TO WEAR DEODORANT!
I WILL, MOM! I WILL!
SO!
HOW'S IT GOING, KEVIN?
GREAT! WE'RE JUST GOING OVER SOME GEOMETRY AND ALGEBRA TERMINOLOGY!
NOT THAT THEY'LL ASK MUCH OF THAT...
BUT BETTER TO BE SAFE THAN SORRY!
12

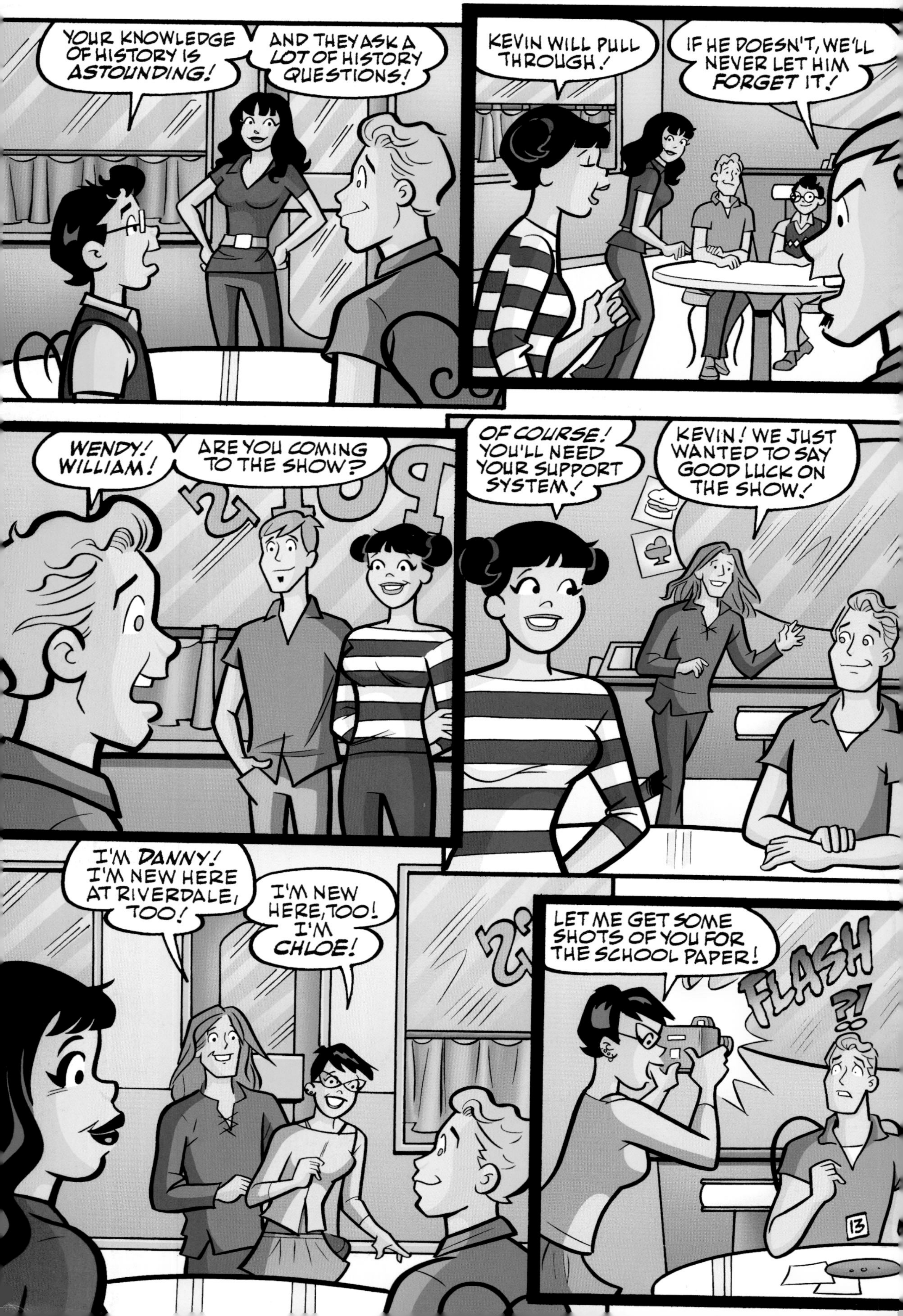

YOUR KNOWLEDGE OF HISTORY IS ASTOUNDING!
AND THEY ASK A LOT OF HISTORY QUESTIONS!
KEVIN WILL PULL THROUGH!
IF HE DOESN'T, WE'LL NEVER LET HIM FORGET IT!
WENDY! WILLIAM!
ARE YOU COMING TO THE SHOW?
OF COURSE! YOU'LL NEED YOUR SUPPORT SYSTEM!
KEVIN! WE JUST WANTED TO SAY GOOD LUCK ON THE SHOW!
I'M DANNY! I'M NEW HERE AT RIVERDALE, TOO!
I'M NEW HERE, TOO! I'M CHLOE!
LET ME GET SOME SHOTS OF YOU FOR THE SCHOOL PAPER!
FLASH
?!
13

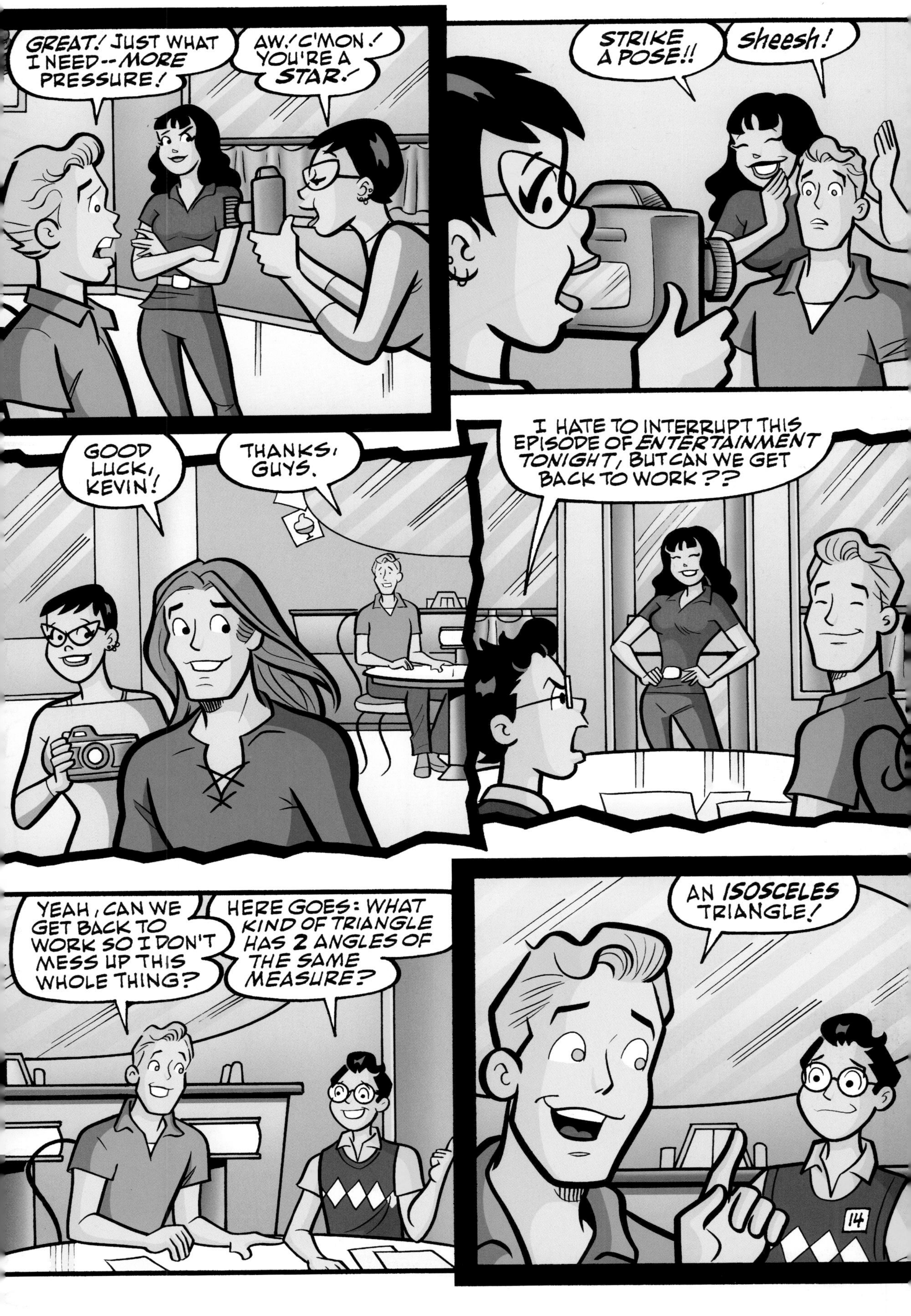
GREAT! JUST WHAT I NEED--MORE PRESSURE!
AW! C'MON! YOU'RE A STAR!
STRIKE A POSE!!
Sheesh!
GOOD LUCK, KEVIN!
THANKS, GUYS.
I HATE TO INTERRUPT THIS EPISODE OF ENTERTAINMENT TONIGHT, BUT CAN WE GET BACK TO WORK??
YEAH, CAN WE GET BACK TO WORK SO I DON'T MESS UP THIS WHOLE THING?
HERE GOES: WHAT KIND OF TRIANGLE HAS 2 ANGLES OF THE SAME MEASURE?
AN ISOSCELES TRIANGLE!
14

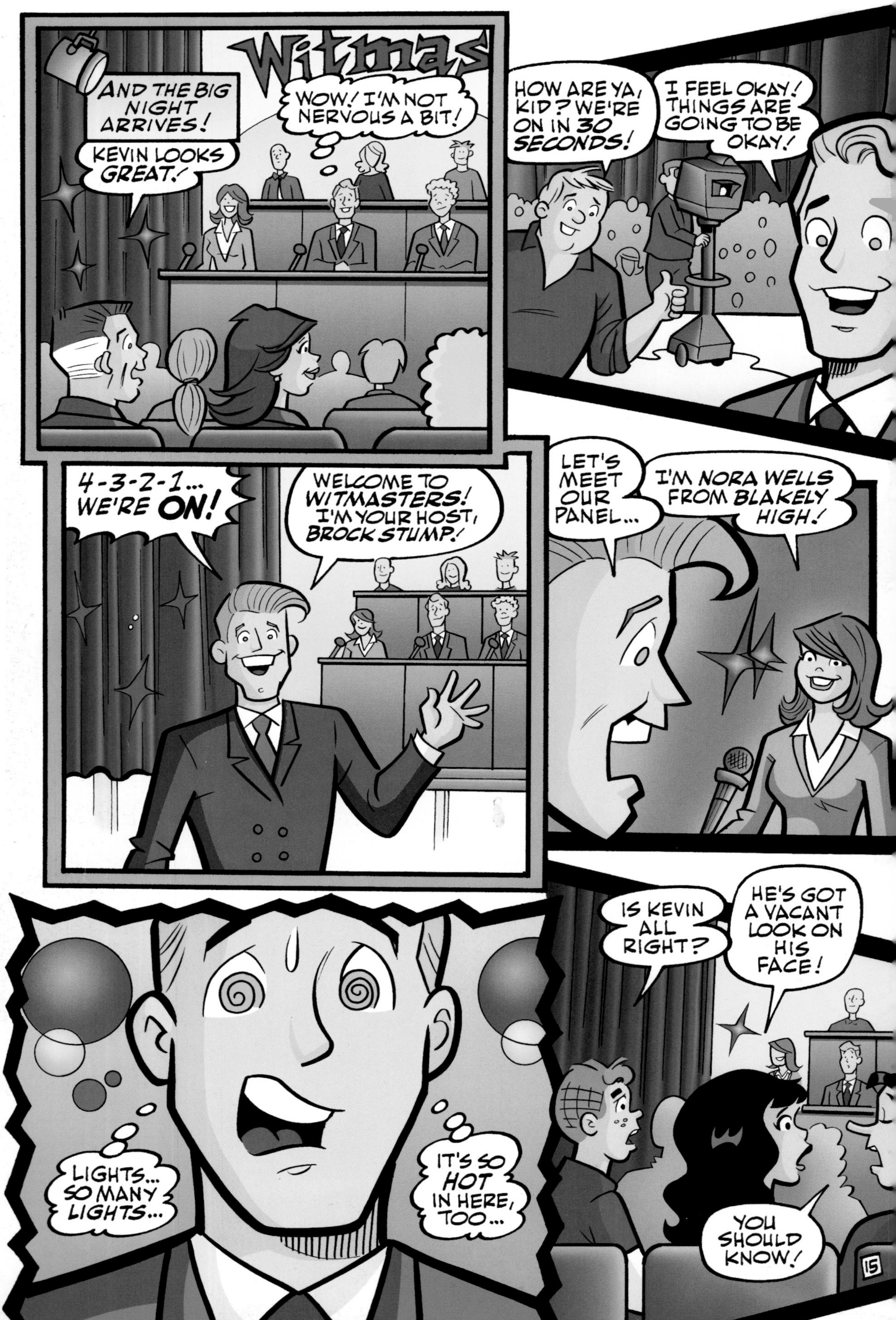
Witmas
AND THE BIG NIGHT ARRIVES!
KEVIN LOOKS GREAT!
WOW! I'M NOT NERVOUS A BIT!
HOW ARE YA, KID? WE'RE ON IN 30 SECONDS!
I FEEL OKAY! THINGS ARE GOING TO BE OKAY!
4-3-2-1... WE'RE ON!
WELCOME TO WITMASTERS! I'M YOUR HOST, BROCK STUMP!
LET'S MEET OUR PANEL...
I'M NORA WELLS FROM BLAKELY HIGH!
LIGHTS... SO MANY LIGHTS...
IT'S SO HOT IN HERE, TOO...
IS KEVIN ALL RIGHT?
HE'S GOT A VACANT LOOK ON HIS FACE!
YOU SHOULD KNOW!

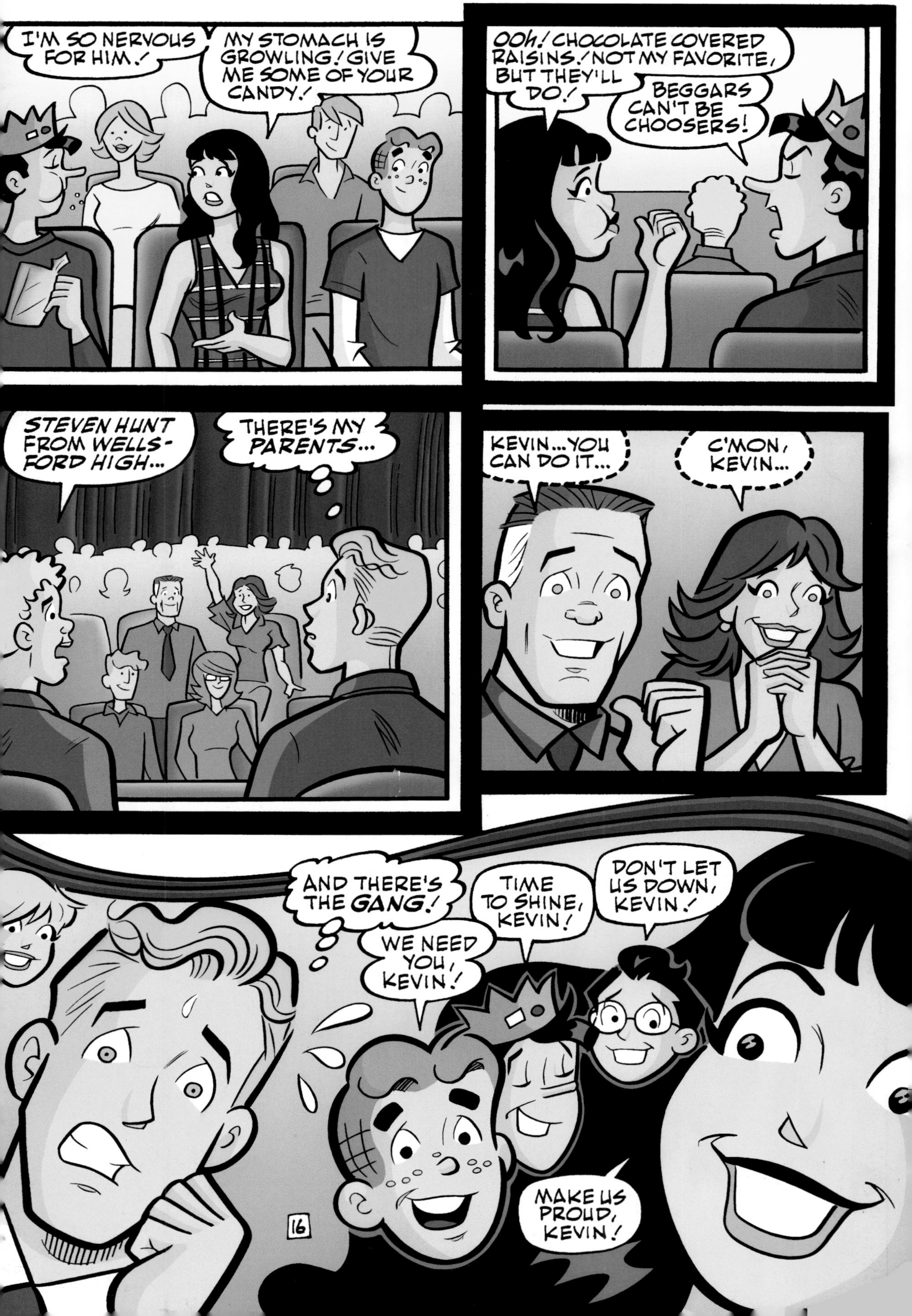

I'M SO NERVOUS FOR HIM!
MY STOMACH IS GROWLING! GIVE ME SOME OF YOUR CANDY!
Ooh! CHOCOLATE COVERED RAISINS! NOT MY FAVORITE, BUT THEY'LL DO!
BEGGARS CAN'T BE CHOOSERS!
STEVEN HUNT FROM WELLS-FORD HIGH...
THERE'S MY PARENTS...
KEVIN... YOU CAN DO IT...
C'MON, KEVIN...
AND THERE'S THE GANG!
WE NEED YOU, KEVIN!
TIME TO SHINE, KEVIN!
DON'T LET US DOWN, KEVIN!
MAKE US PROUD, KEVIN!
16

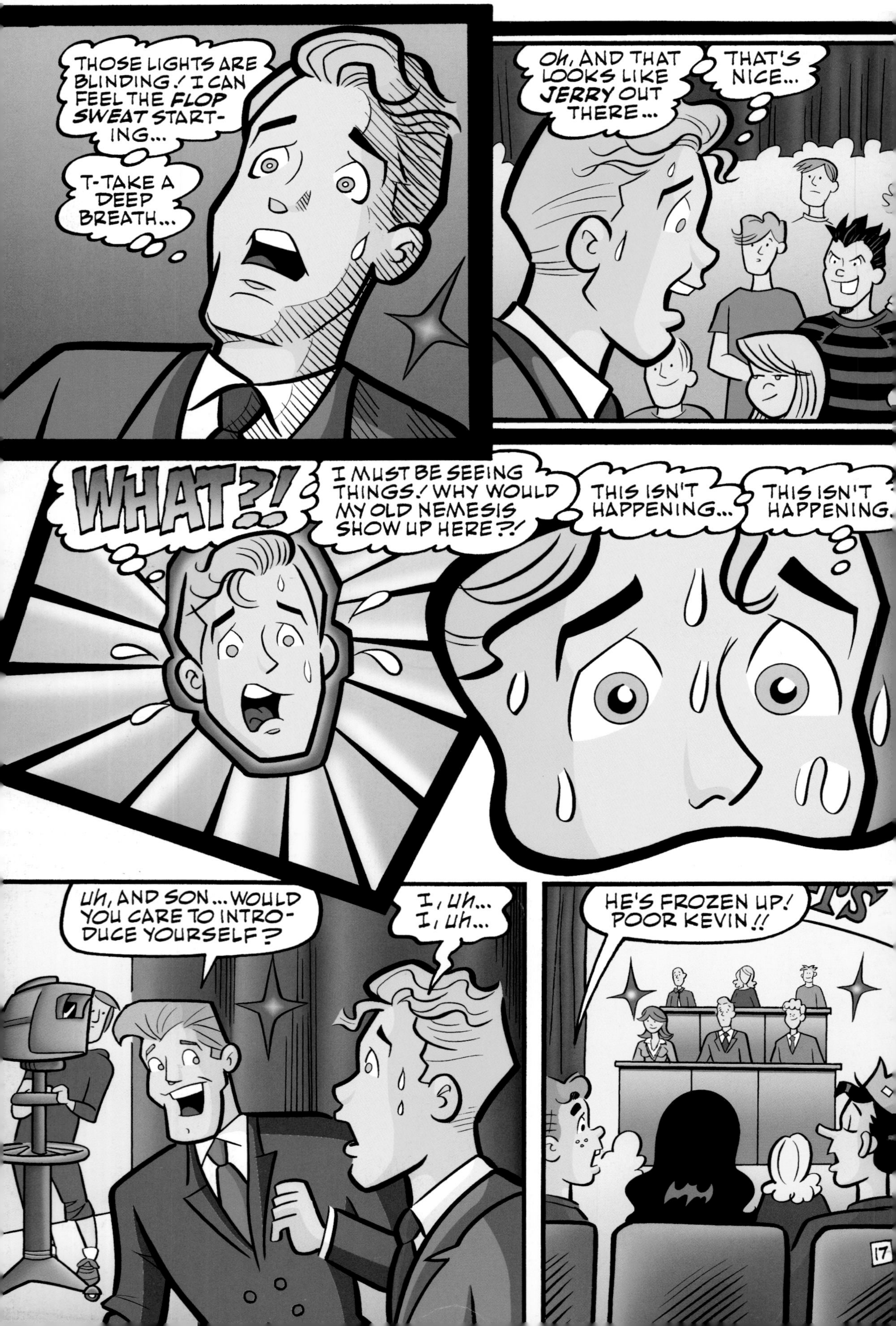
THOSE LIGHTS ARE BLINDING! I CAN FEEL THE FLOP SWEAT STARTING...
T-TAKE A DEEP BREATH...
OH, AND THAT LOOKS LIKE JERRY OUT THERE...
THAT'S NICE...
WHAT?!
I MUST BE SEEING THINGS! WHY WOULD MY OLD NEMESIS SHOW UP HERE?!
THIS ISN'T HAPPENING...
THIS ISN'T HAPPENING.
UH, AND SON... WOULD YOU CARE TO INTRODUCE YOURSELF?
I, UH... I, UH...
HE'S FROZEN UP! POOR KEVIN!!

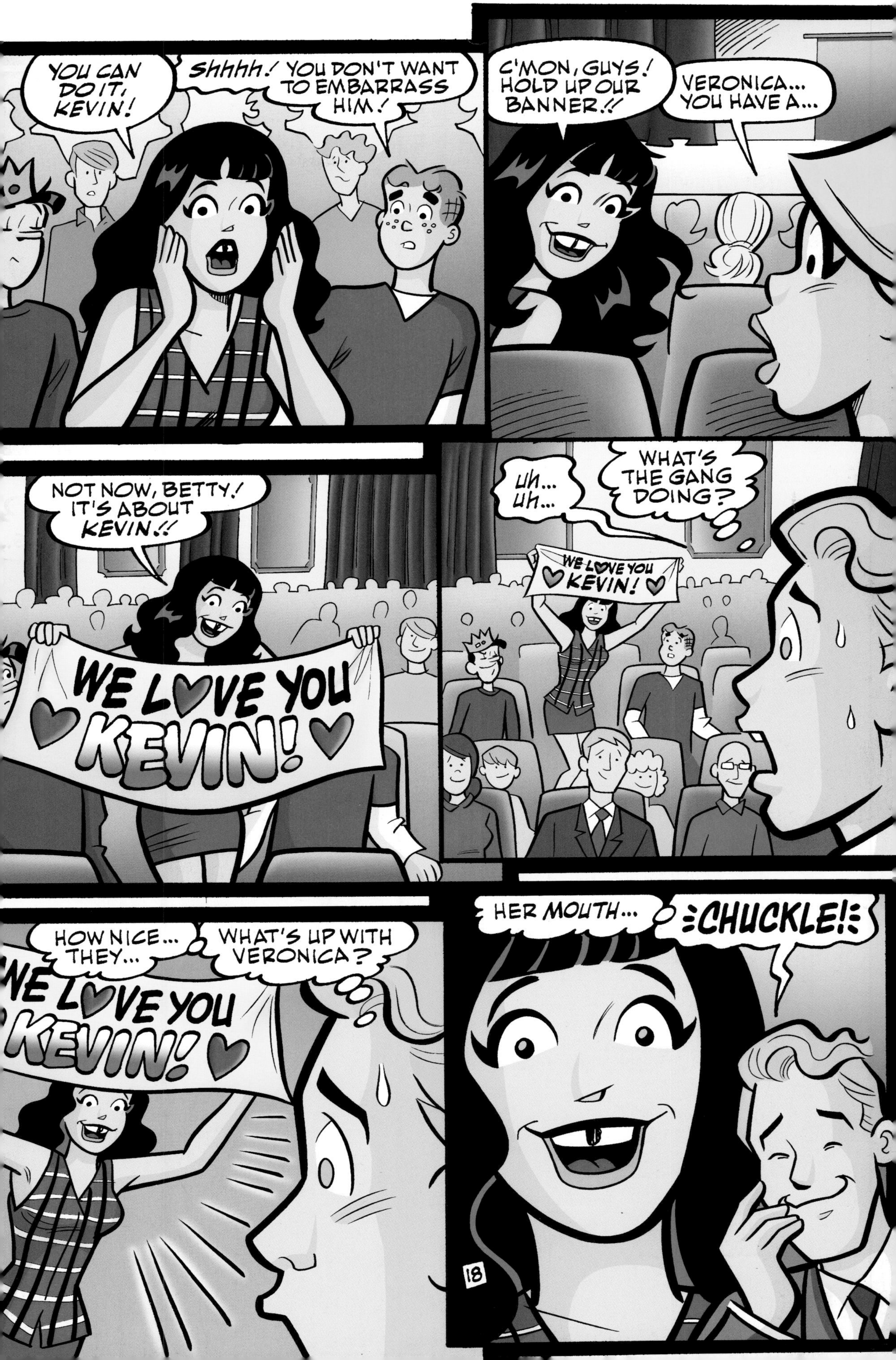
YOU CAN DO IT, KEVIN!
Shhhh! YOU DON'T WANT TO EMBARRASS HIM!
C'MON, GUYS! HOLD UP OUR BANNER!!
VERONICA... YOU HAVE A...
NOT NOW, BETTY! IT'S ABOUT KEVIN!!
WE LOVE YOU KEVIN!
UH... UH...
WHAT'S THE GANG DOING?
WE LOVE YOU KEVIN!
HOW NICE... THEY...
WHAT'S UP WITH VERONICA?
WE LOVE YOU KEVIN!
HER MOUTH...
CHUCKLE!
18

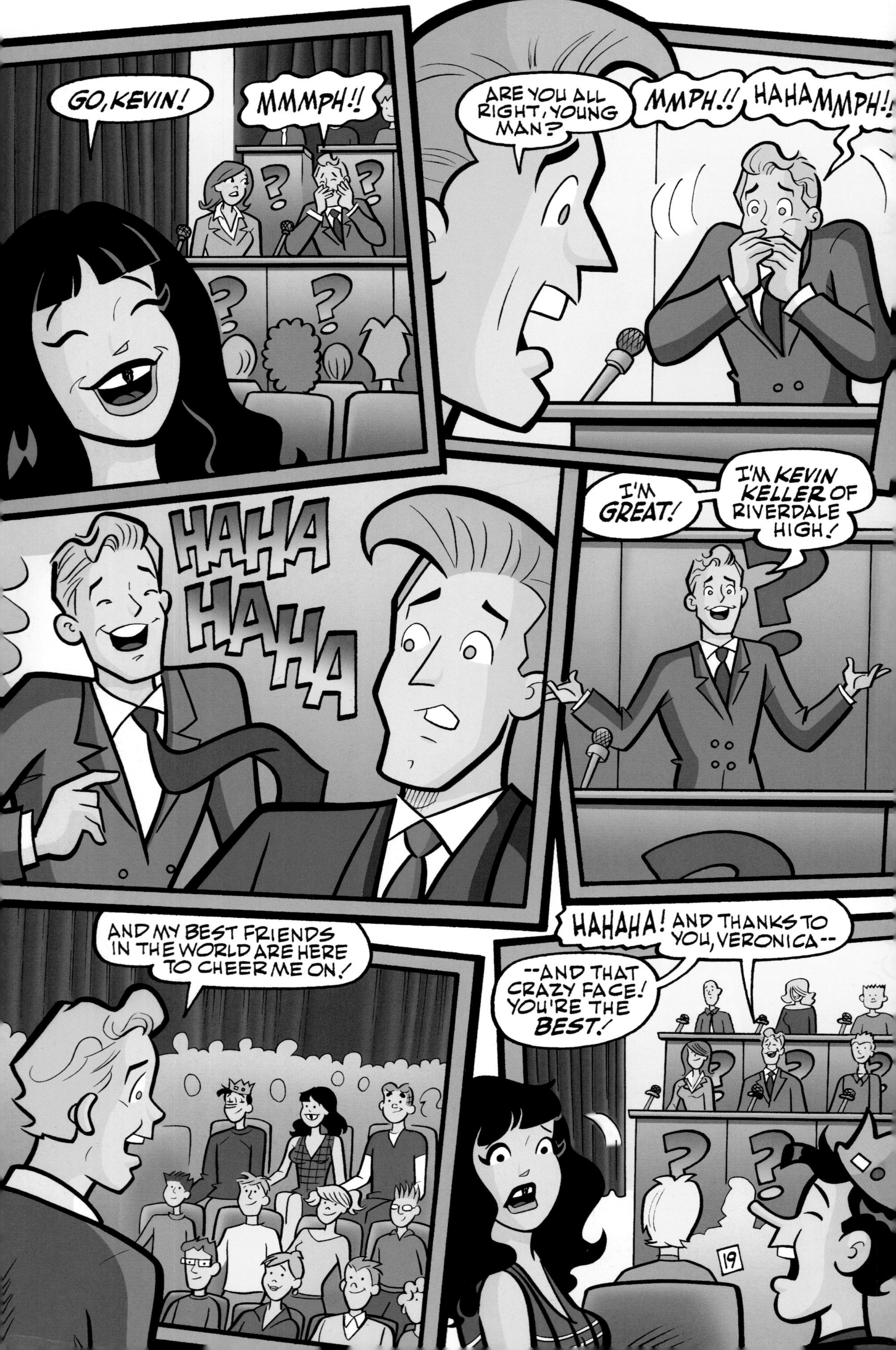
GO, KEVIN!
MMMPH!!
ARE YOU ALL RIGHT, YOUNG MAN?
MMPH!!
HAHAMMPH!!
HAHA HAHAHA
I'M GREAT!
I'M KEVIN KELLER OF RIVERDALE HIGH!
AND MY BEST FRIENDS IN THE WORLD ARE HERE TO CHEER ME ON!
HAHAHA!
AND THANKS TO YOU, VERONICA--
--AND THAT CRAZY FACE! YOU'RE THE BEST!
19

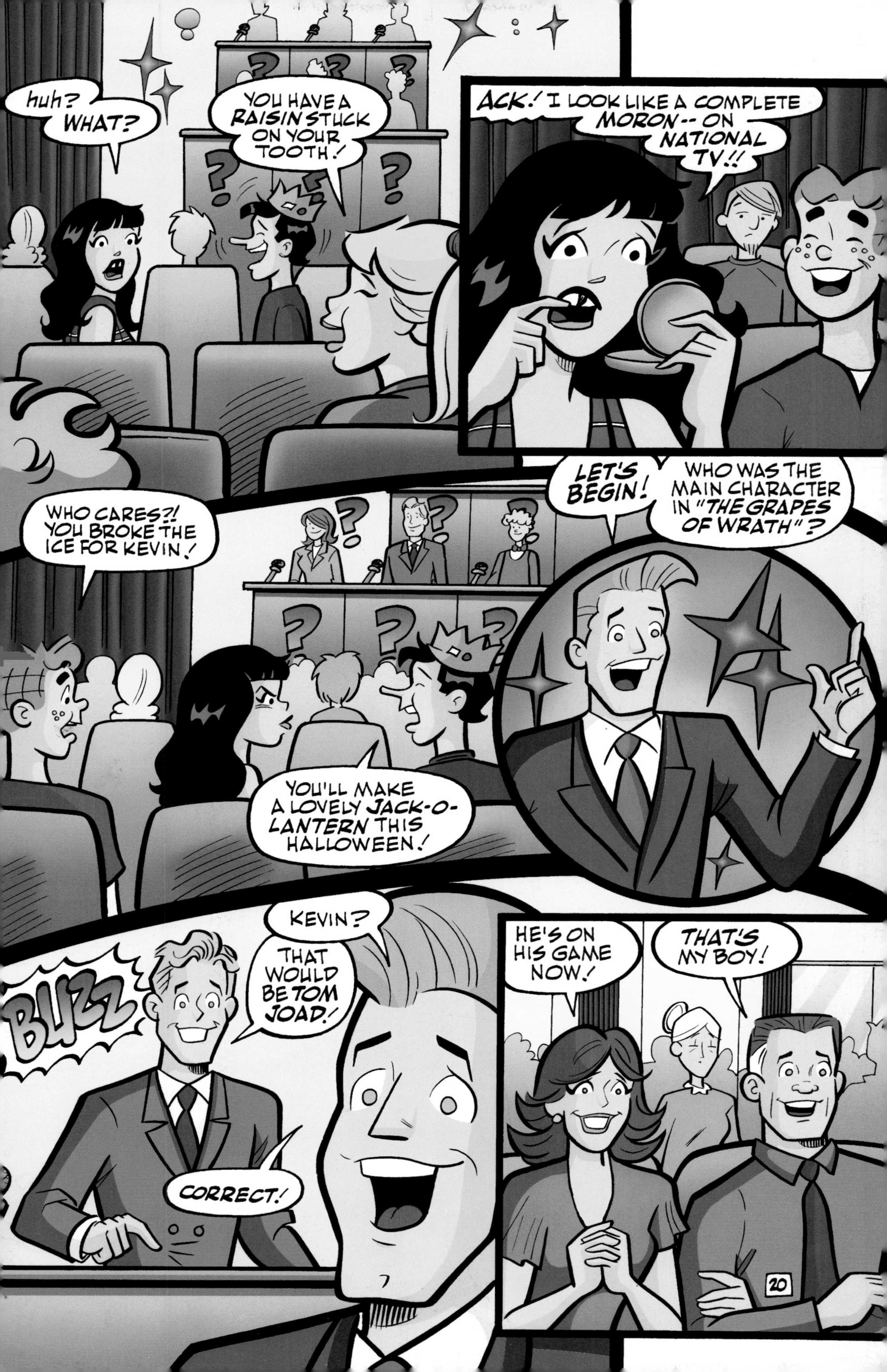
huh? WHAT?
YOU HAVE A RAISIN STUCK ON YOUR TOOTH!
ACK! I LOOK LIKE A COMPLETE MORON -- ON NATIONAL TV!!
WHO CARES?! YOU BROKE THE ICE FOR KEVIN!
YOU'LL MAKE A LOVELY JACK-O-LANTERN THIS HALLOWEEN!
LET'S BEGIN!
WHO WAS THE MAIN CHARACTER IN "THE GRAPES OF WRATH"?
BUZZ
KEVIN?
THAT WOULD BE TOM JOAD!
CORRECT!
HE'S ON HIS GAME NOW!
THAT'S MY BOY!
20

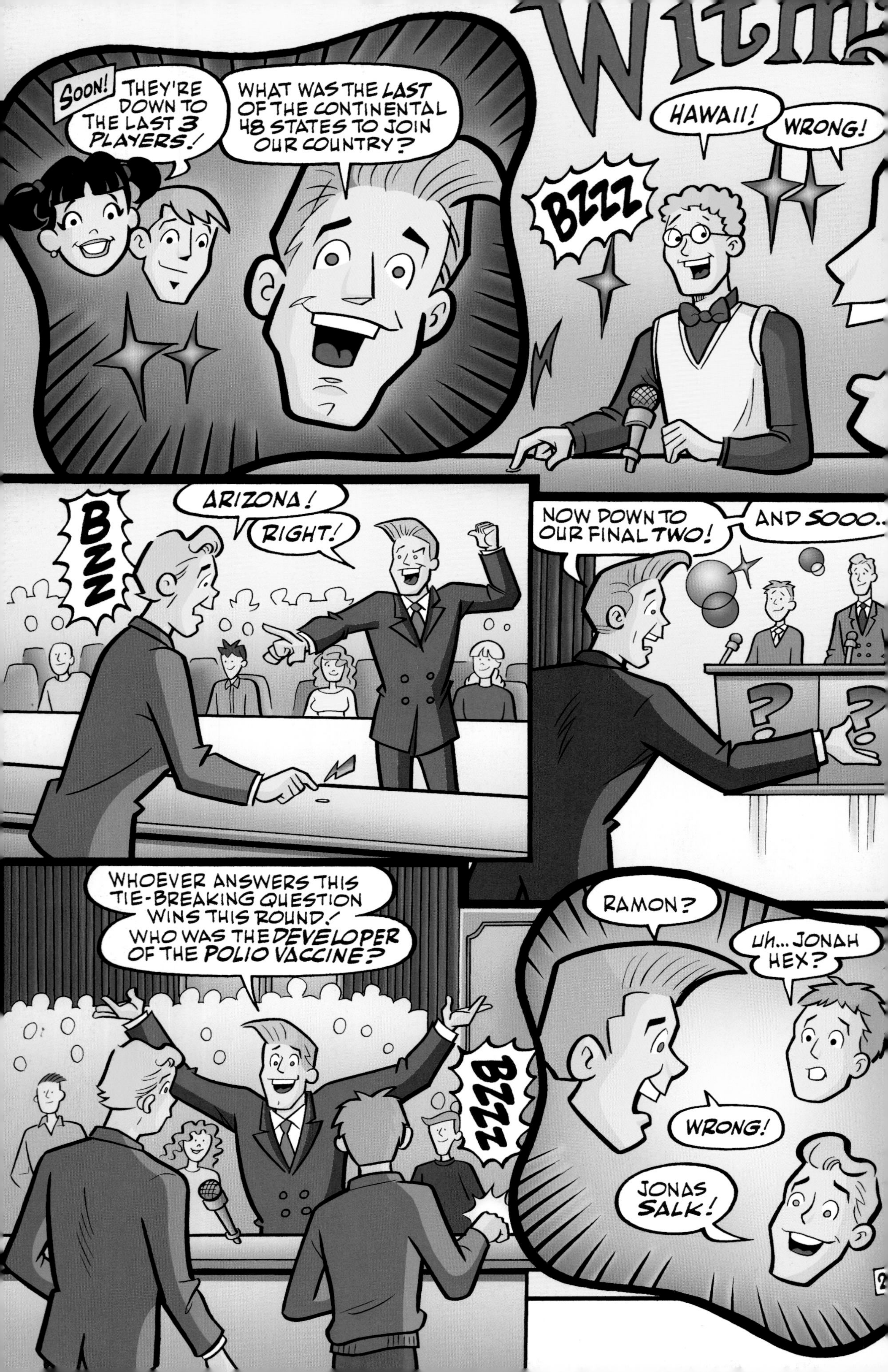
Witm
SOON!
THEY'RE DOWN TO THE LAST 3 PLAYERS!
WHAT WAS THE LAST OF THE CONTINENTAL 48 STATES TO JOIN OUR COUNTRY?
HAWAII!
WRONG!
BZZZ
BZZ
ARIZONA!
RIGHT!
NOW DOWN TO OUR FINAL TWO!
AND SOOO...
WHOEVER ANSWERS THIS TIE-BREAKING QUESTION WINS THIS ROUND! WHO WAS THE DEVELOPER OF THE POLIO VACCINE?
BZZZ
RAMON?
UH... JONAH HEX?
WRONG!
JONAS SALK!

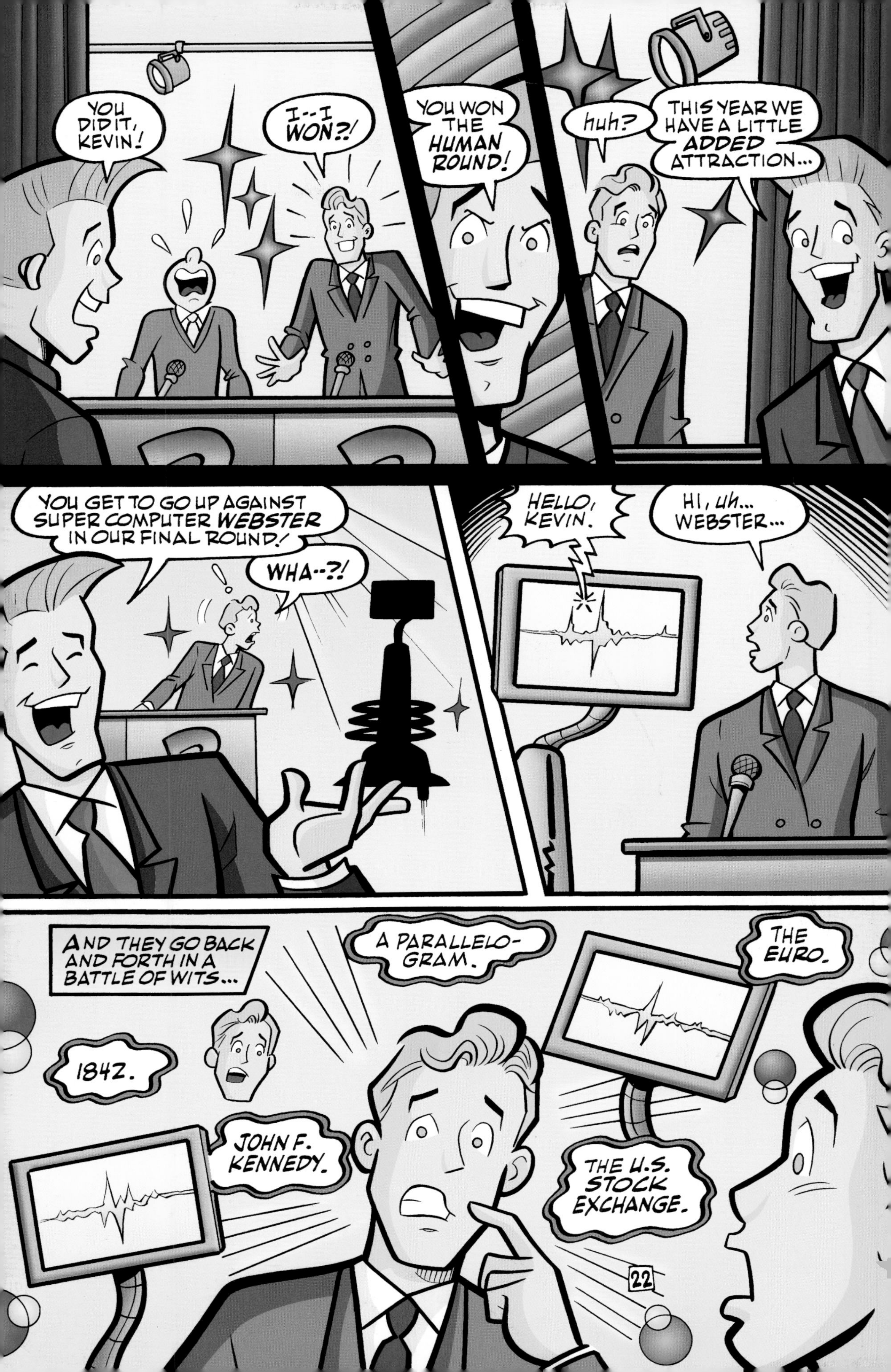
YOU DID IT, KEVIN!
I--I WON?!
YOU WON THE HUMAN ROUND!
huh?
THIS YEAR WE HAVE A LITTLE ADDED ATTRACTION...
YOU GET TO GO UP AGAINST SUPER COMPUTER WEBSTER IN OUR FINAL ROUND!
WHA--?!
HELLO, KEVIN.
HI, uh... WEBSTER...
AND THEY GO BACK AND FORTH IN A BATTLE OF WITS...
A PARALLELO-GRAM.
THE EURO.
1842.
JOHN F. KENNEDY.
THE U.S. STOCK EXCHANGE.
22

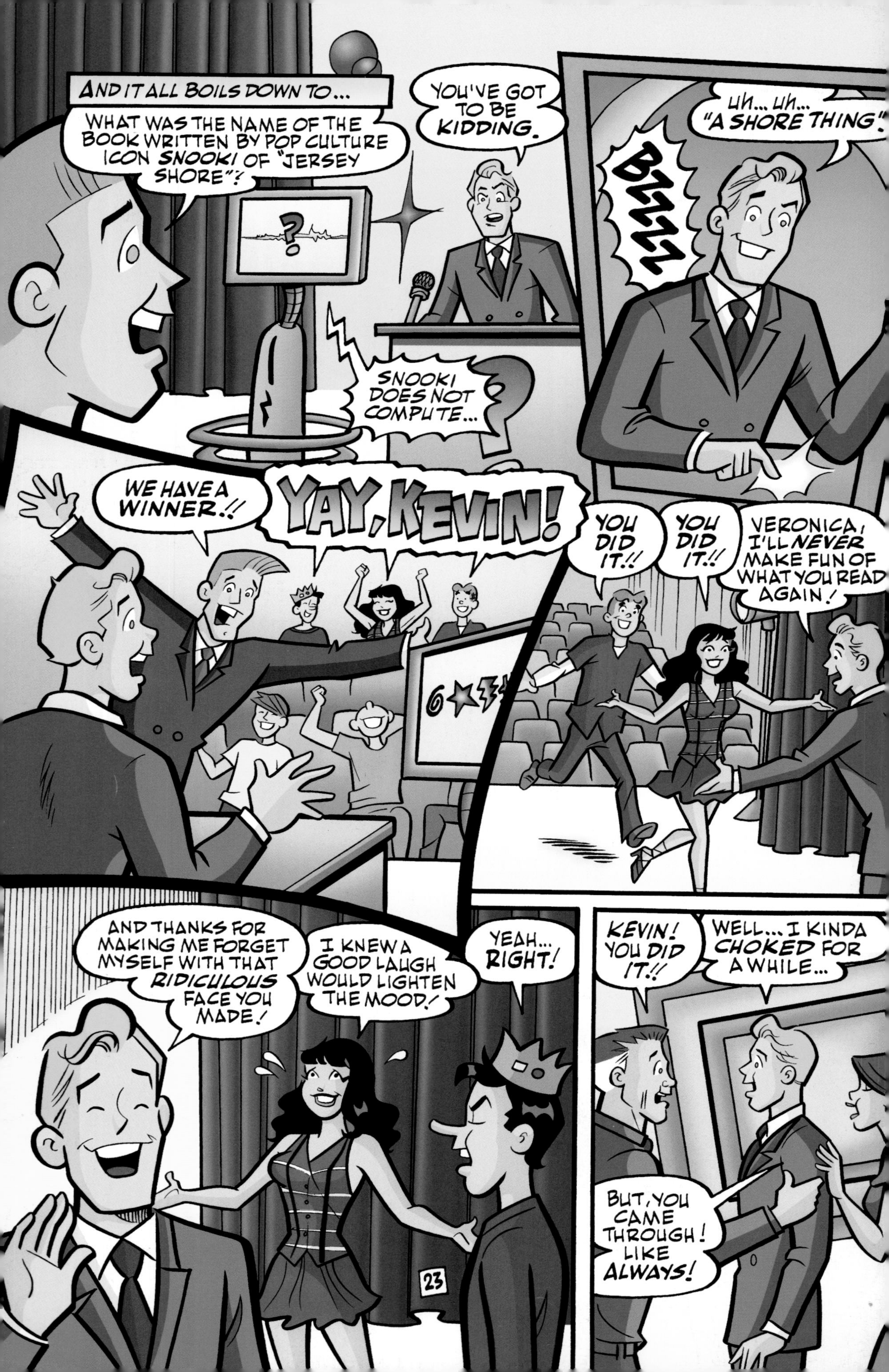
AND IT ALL BOILS DOWN TO...
WHAT WAS THE NAME OF THE BOOK WRITTEN BY POP CULTURE ICON SNOOKI OF "JERSEY SHORE"?
YOU'VE GOT TO BE KIDDING.
SNOOKI DOES NOT COMPUTE...
UH... UH... "A SHORE THING".
BZZZZ
WE HAVE A WINNER.!!
YAY, KEVIN!
YOU DID IT.!!
YOU DID IT.!!
VERONICA, I'LL NEVER MAKE FUN OF WHAT YOU READ AGAIN!
AND THANKS FOR MAKING ME FORGET MYSELF WITH THAT RIDICULOUS FACE YOU MADE!
I KNEW A GOOD LAUGH WOULD LIGHTEN THE MOOD!
YEAH... RIGHT!
KEVIN! YOU DID IT.!!
WELL... I KINDA CHOKED FOR A WHILE...
BUT, YOU CAME THROUGH! LIKE ALWAYS!

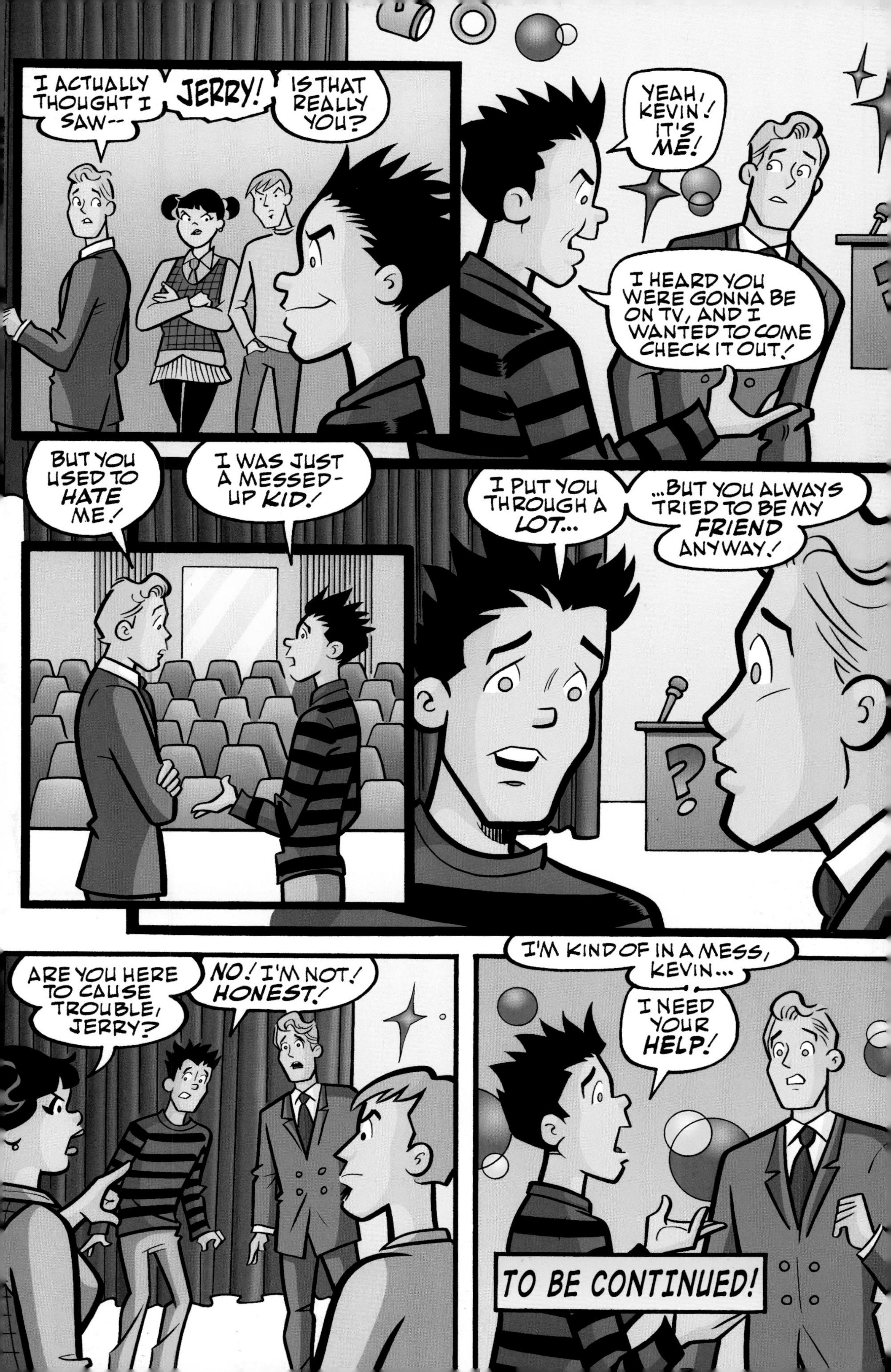
I ACTUALLY THOUGHT I SAW--
JERRY!
IS THAT REALLY YOU?
YEAH, KEVIN! IT'S ME!
I HEARD YOU WERE GONNA BE ON TV, AND I WANTED TO COME CHECK IT OUT!
BUT YOU USED TO HATE ME!
I WAS JUST A MESSED-UP KID!
I PUT YOU THROUGH A LOT...
...BUT YOU ALWAYS TRIED TO BE MY FRIEND ANYWAY!
ARE YOU HERE TO CAUSE TROUBLE, JERRY?
NO! I'M NOT! HONEST!
I'M KIND OF IN A MESS, KEVIN...
I NEED YOUR HELP!
TO BE CONTINUED!

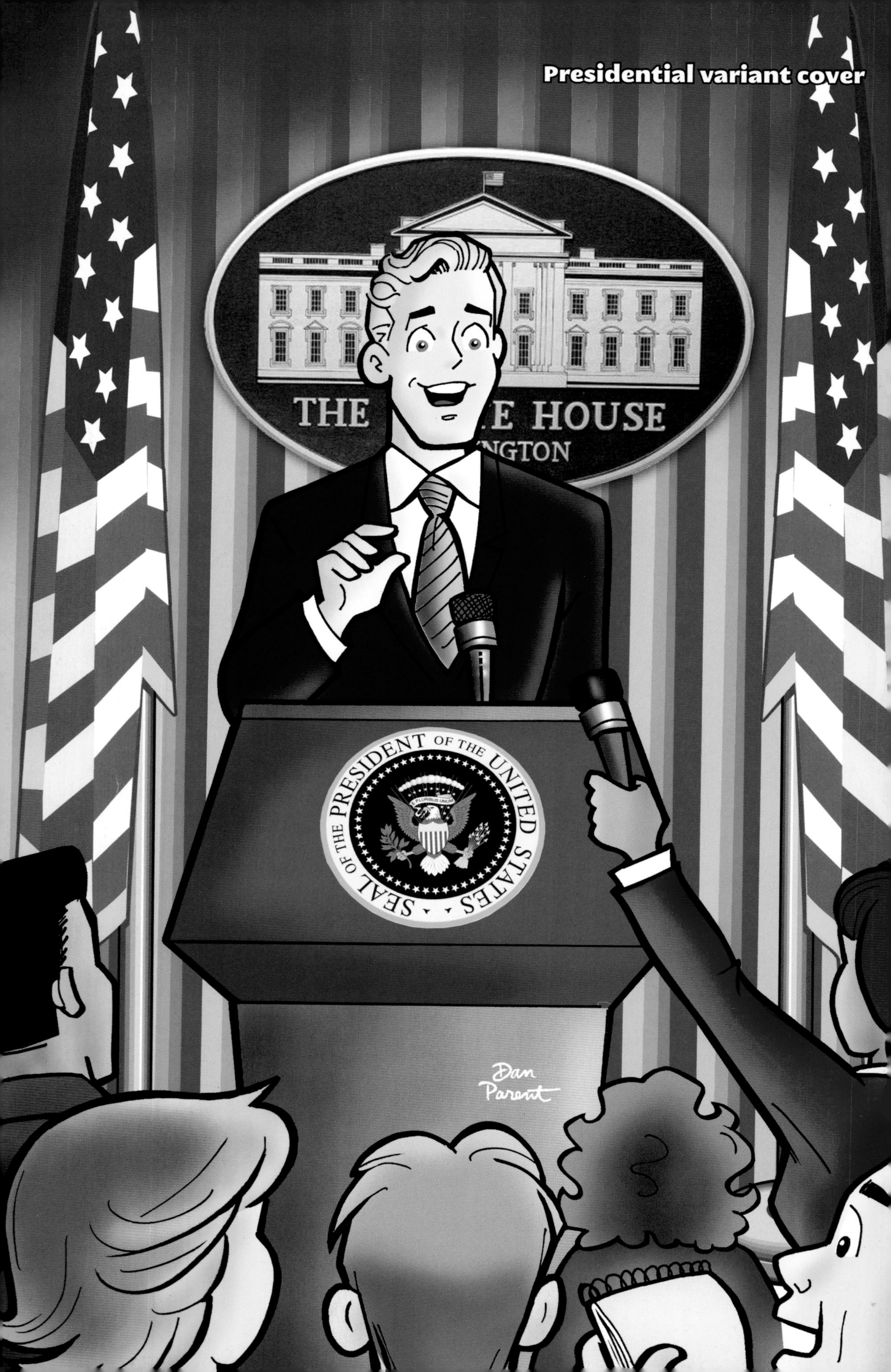
SEAL OF THE PRESIDENT OF THE UNITED STATES
Dan Parent
Presidential variant cover

Part 6: Taking the Lead

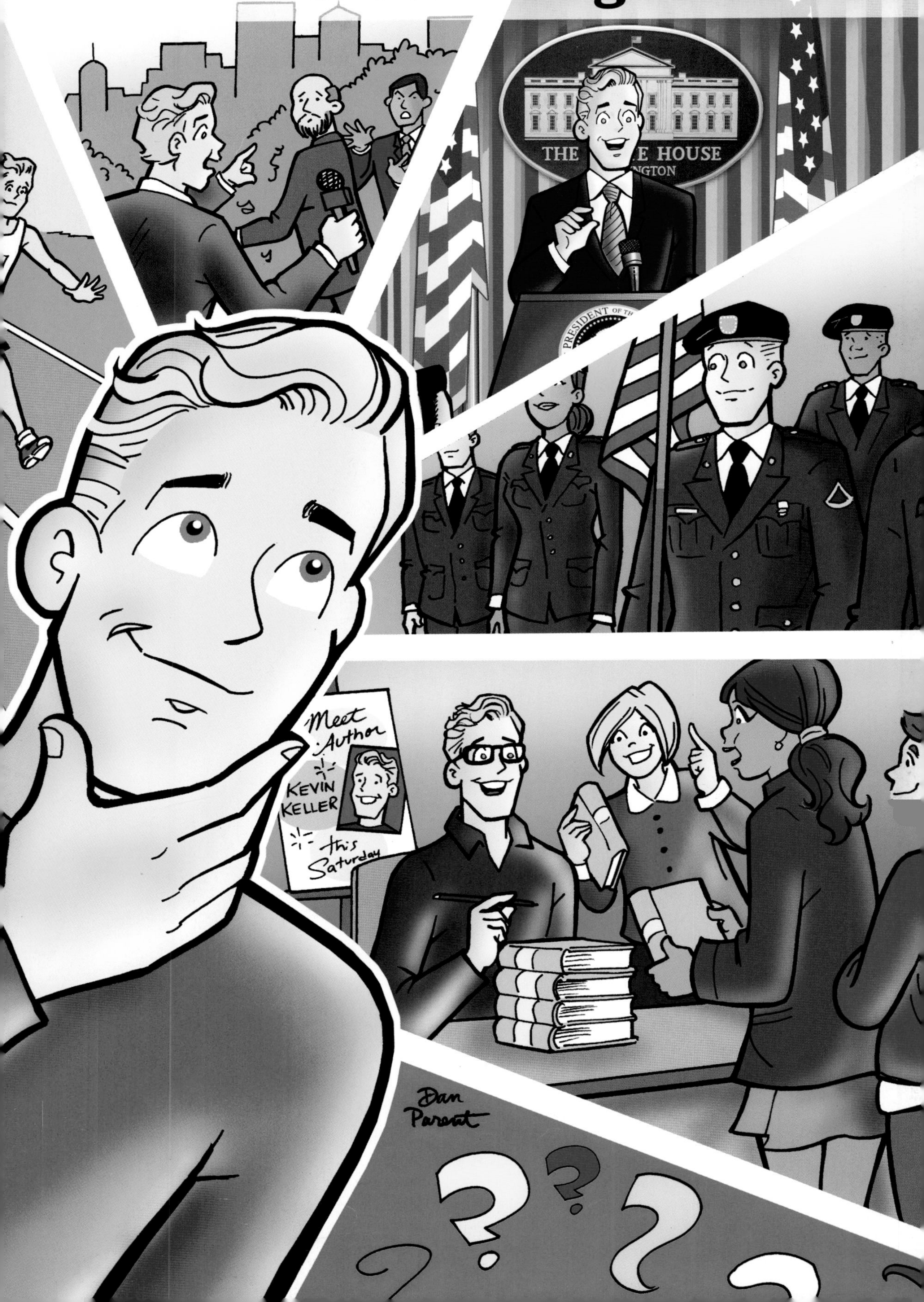
THE [...]E HOUSE
Meet Author
KEVIN KELLER
this Saturday
Dan Parent

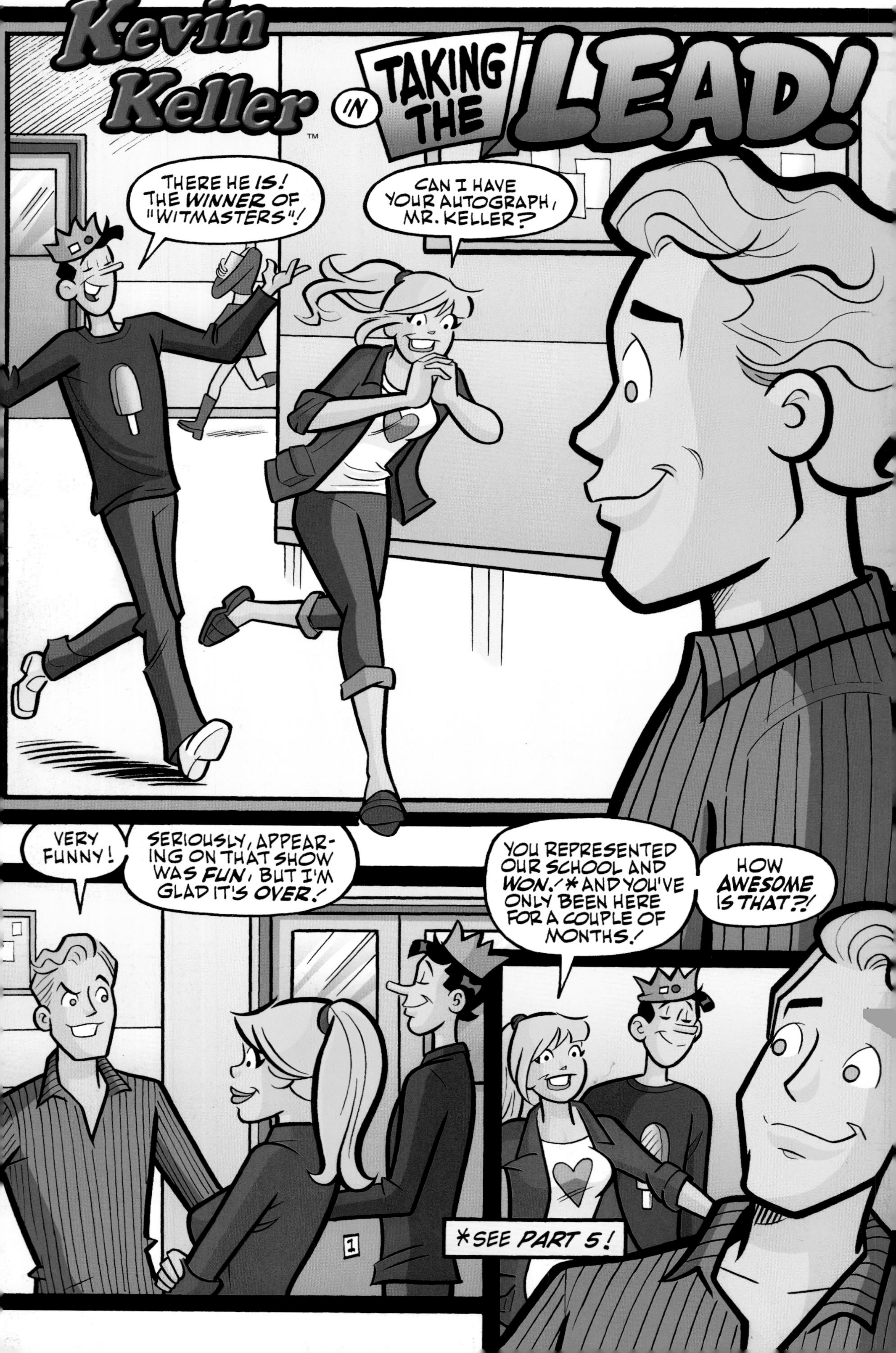
Kevin Keller™ in TAKING THE LEAD!
THERE HE IS! THE WINNER OF "WITMASTERS"!
CAN I HAVE YOUR AUTOGRAPH, MR. KELLER?
VERY FUNNY!
SERIOUSLY, APPEARING ON THAT SHOW WAS FUN, BUT I'M GLAD IT'S OVER!
YOU REPRESENTED OUR SCHOOL AND WON! * AND YOU'VE ONLY BEEN HERE FOR A COUPLE OF MONTHS!
HOW AWESOME IS THAT?!
* SEE PART 5!
1

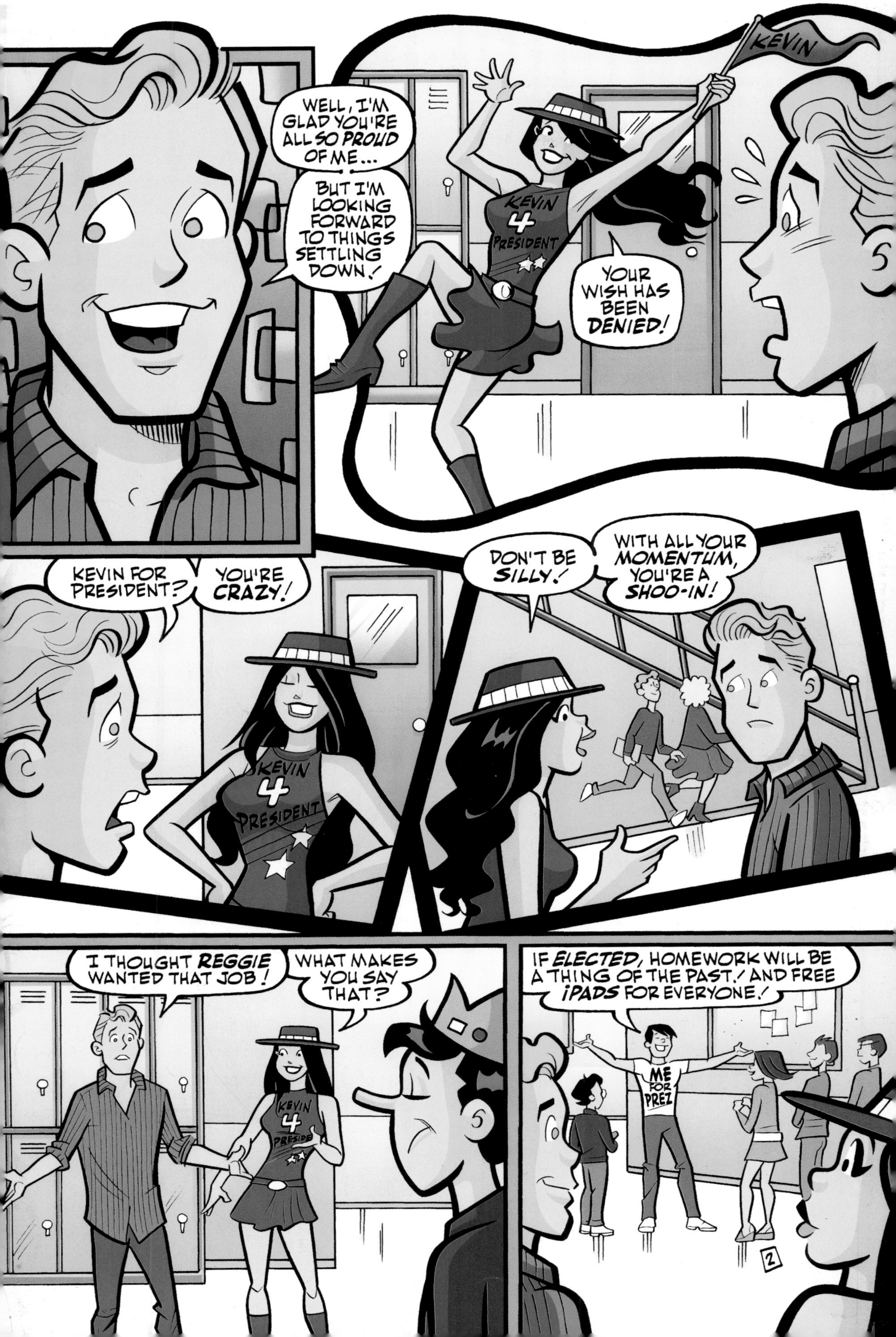
KEVIN
WELL, I'M GLAD YOU'RE ALL SO PROUD OF ME...
BUT I'M LOOKING FORWARD TO THINGS SETTLING DOWN!
YOUR WISH HAS BEEN DENIED!
KEVIN 4 PRESIDENT
KEVIN FOR PRESIDENT?
YOU'RE CRAZY!
DON'T BE SILLY!
WITH ALL YOUR MOMENTUM, YOU'RE A SHOO-IN!
I THOUGHT REGGIE WANTED THAT JOB!
WHAT MAKES YOU SAY THAT?
IF ELECTED, HOMEWORK WILL BE A THING OF THE PAST! AND FREE iPADS FOR EVERYONE!
ME FOR PREZ
2

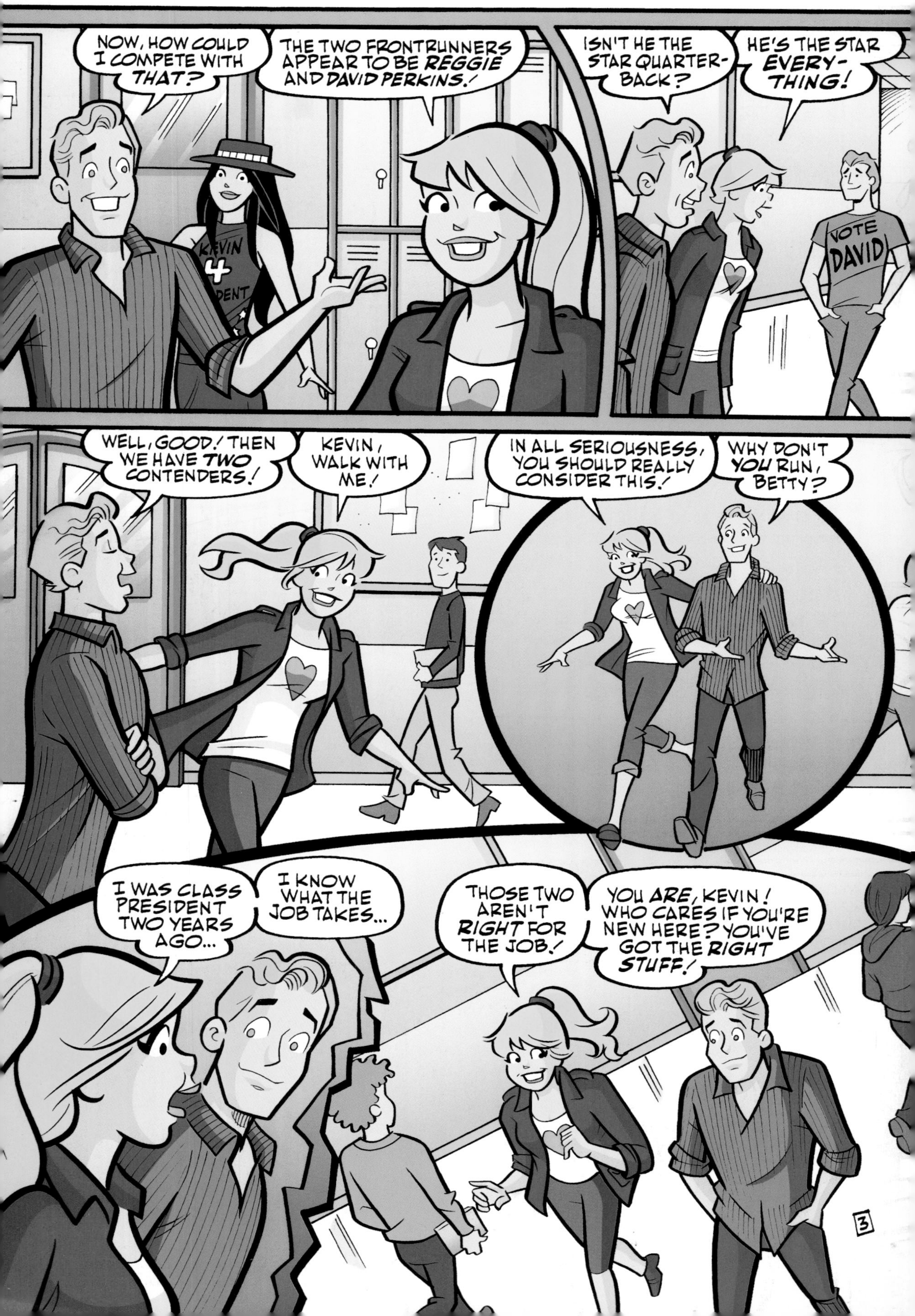
NOW, HOW COULD I COMPETE WITH THAT?
THE TWO FRONTRUNNERS APPEAR TO BE REGGIE AND DAVID PERKINS!
ISN'T HE THE STAR QUARTER-BACK?
HE'S THE STAR EVERY-THING!
VOTE DAVID
WELL, GOOD! THEN WE HAVE TWO CONTENDERS!
KEVIN, WALK WITH ME!
IN ALL SERIOUSNESS, YOU SHOULD REALLY CONSIDER THIS!
WHY DON'T YOU RUN, BETTY?
I WAS CLASS PRESIDENT TWO YEARS AGO...
I KNOW WHAT THE JOB TAKES...
THOSE TWO AREN'T RIGHT FOR THE JOB!
YOU ARE, KEVIN! WHO CARES IF YOU'RE NEW HERE? YOU'VE GOT THE RIGHT STUFF!

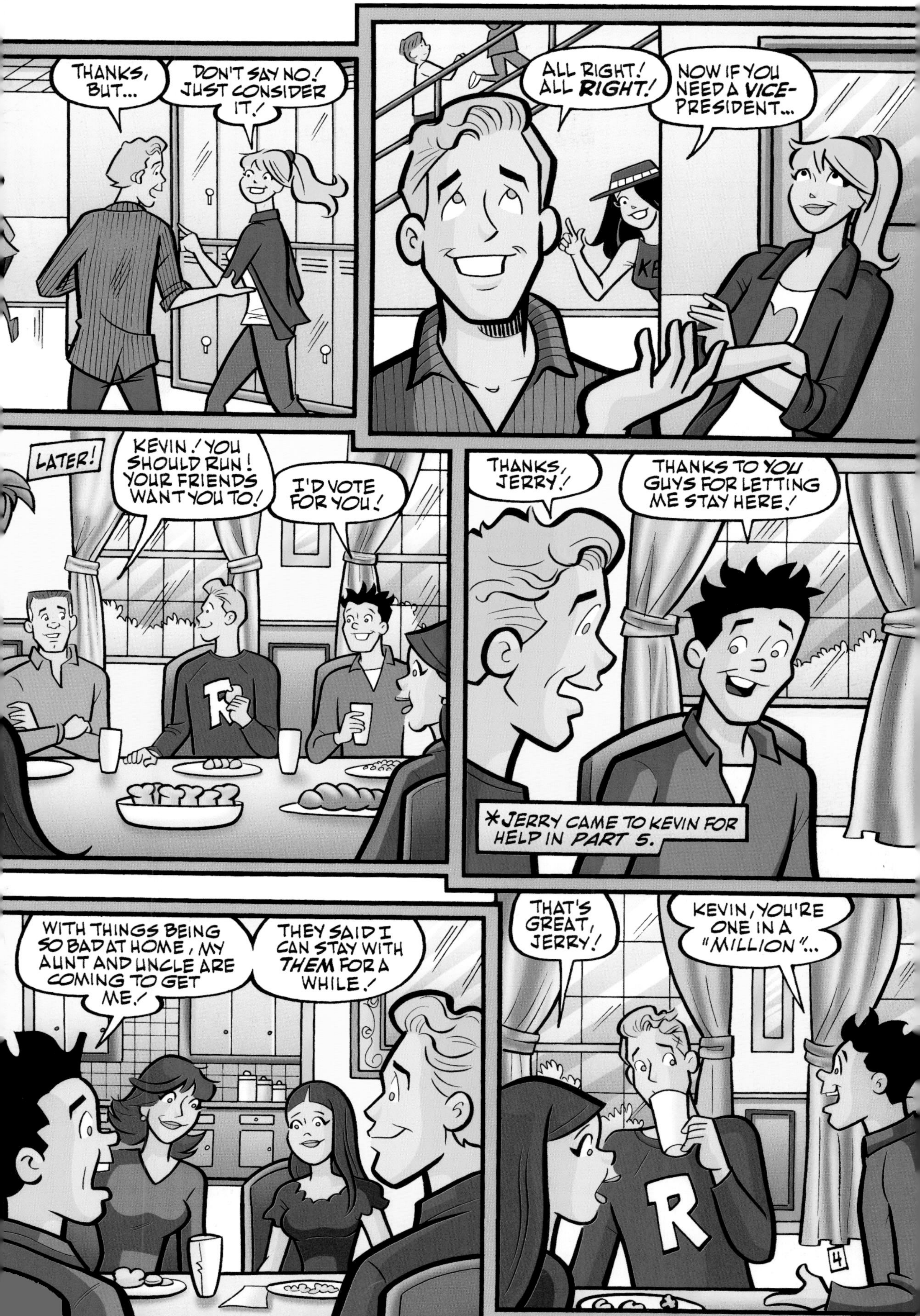
THANKS, BUT...
DON'T SAY NO! JUST CONSIDER IT!
ALL RIGHT! ALL RIGHT!
NOW IF YOU NEED A VICE-PRESIDENT...
LATER!
KEVIN! YOU SHOULD RUN! YOUR FRIENDS WANT YOU TO!
I'D VOTE FOR YOU!
THANKS, JERRY!
THANKS TO YOU GUYS FOR LETTING ME STAY HERE!
*JERRY CAME TO KEVIN FOR HELP IN PART 5.
WITH THINGS BEING SO BAD AT HOME, MY AUNT AND UNCLE ARE COMING TO GET ME!
THEY SAID I CAN STAY WITH THEM FOR A WHILE!
THAT'S GREAT, JERRY!
KEVIN, YOU'RE ONE IN A "MILLION"...
4

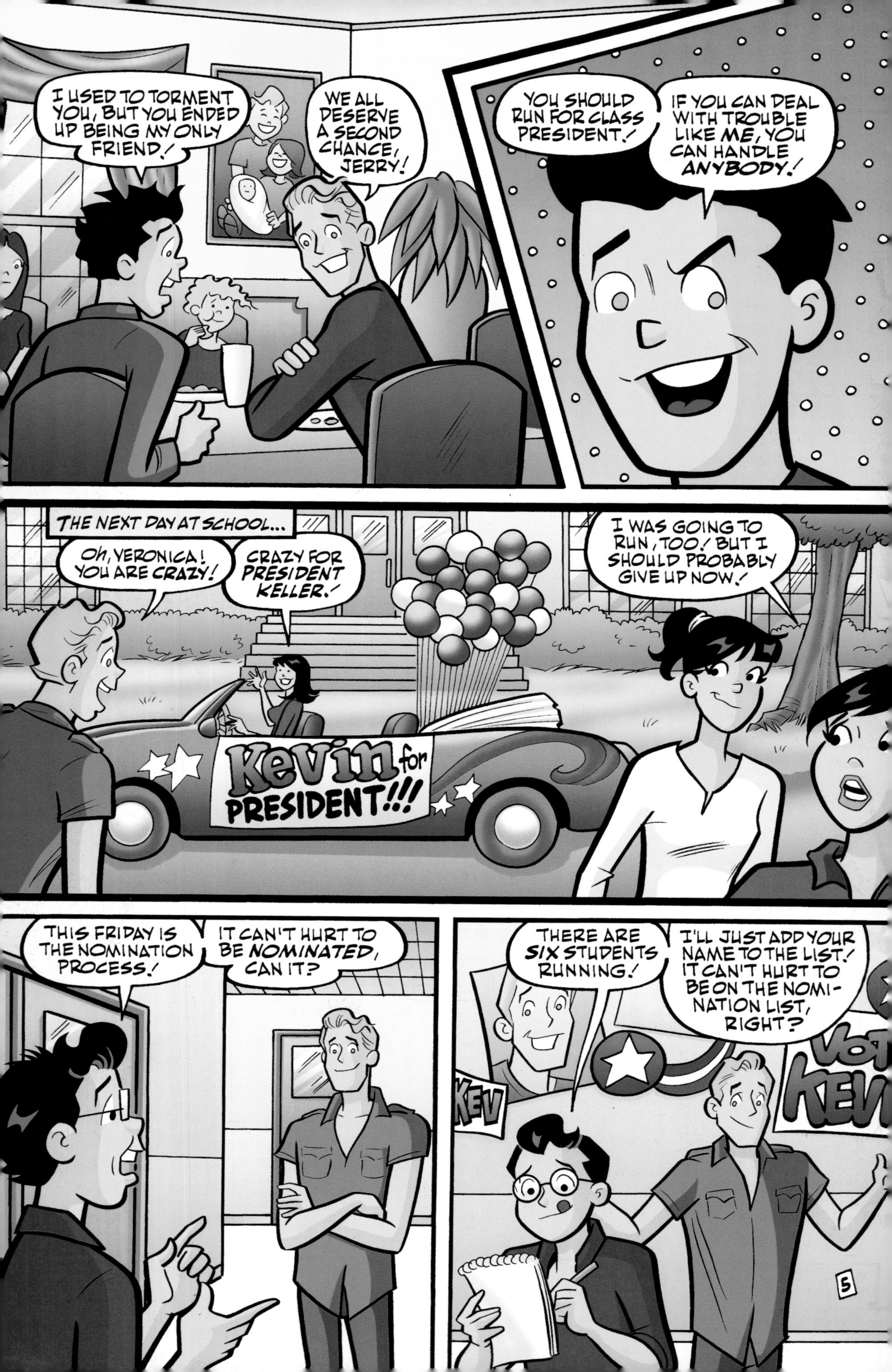
I USED TO TORMENT YOU, BUT YOU ENDED UP BEING MY ONLY FRIEND!
WE ALL DESERVE A SECOND CHANCE, JERRY!
YOU SHOULD RUN FOR CLASS PRESIDENT!
IF YOU CAN DEAL WITH TROUBLE LIKE ME, YOU CAN HANDLE ANYBODY!
THE NEXT DAY AT SCHOOL...
Oh, VERONICA! YOU ARE CRAZY!
CRAZY FOR PRESIDENT KELLER!
Kevin for PRESIDENT!!!
I WAS GOING TO RUN, TOO! BUT I SHOULD PROBABLY GIVE UP NOW!
THIS FRIDAY IS THE NOMINATION PROCESS!
IT CAN'T HURT TO BE NOMINATED, CAN IT?
THERE ARE SIX STUDENTS RUNNING!
I'LL JUST ADD YOUR NAME TO THE LIST! IT CAN'T HURT TO BE ON THE NOMINATION LIST, RIGHT?
KEV
5

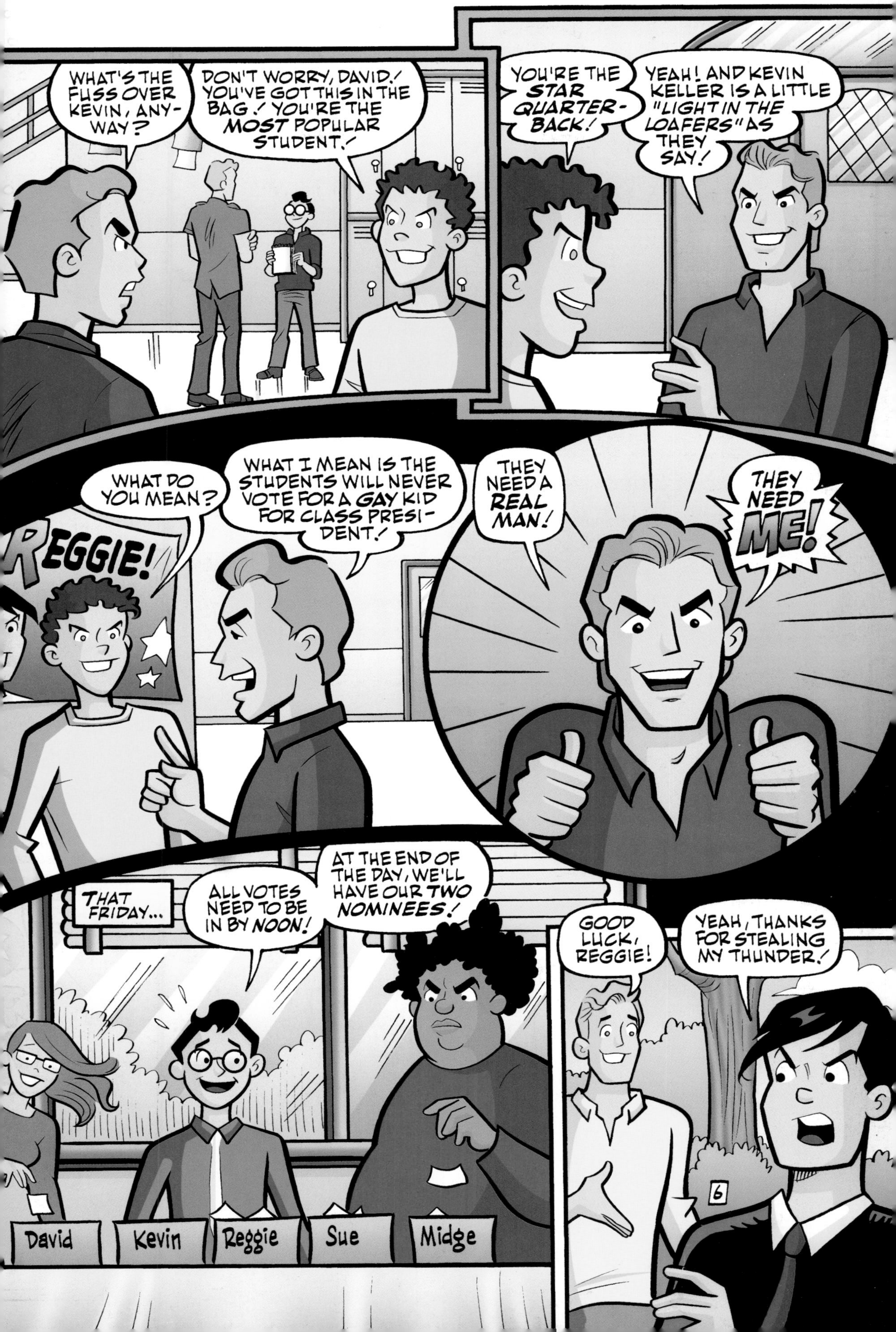
WHAT'S THE FUSS OVER KEVIN, ANY-WAY?
DON'T WORRY, DAVID! YOU'VE GOT THIS IN THE BAG! YOU'RE THE MOST POPULAR STUDENT!
YOU'RE THE STAR QUARTER-BACK!
YEAH! AND KEVIN KELLER IS A LITTLE "LIGHT IN THE LOAFERS" AS THEY SAY!
WHAT DO YOU MEAN?
REGGIE!
WHAT I MEAN IS THE STUDENTS WILL NEVER VOTE FOR A GAY KID FOR CLASS PRESI-DENT!
THEY NEED A REAL MAN!
THEY NEED ME!
THAT FRIDAY...
ALL VOTES NEED TO BE IN BY NOON!
AT THE END OF THE DAY, WE'LL HAVE OUR TWO NOMINEES!
David
Kevin
Reggie
Sue
Midge
GOOD LUCK, REGGIE!
YEAH, THANKS FOR STEALING MY THUNDER!
6

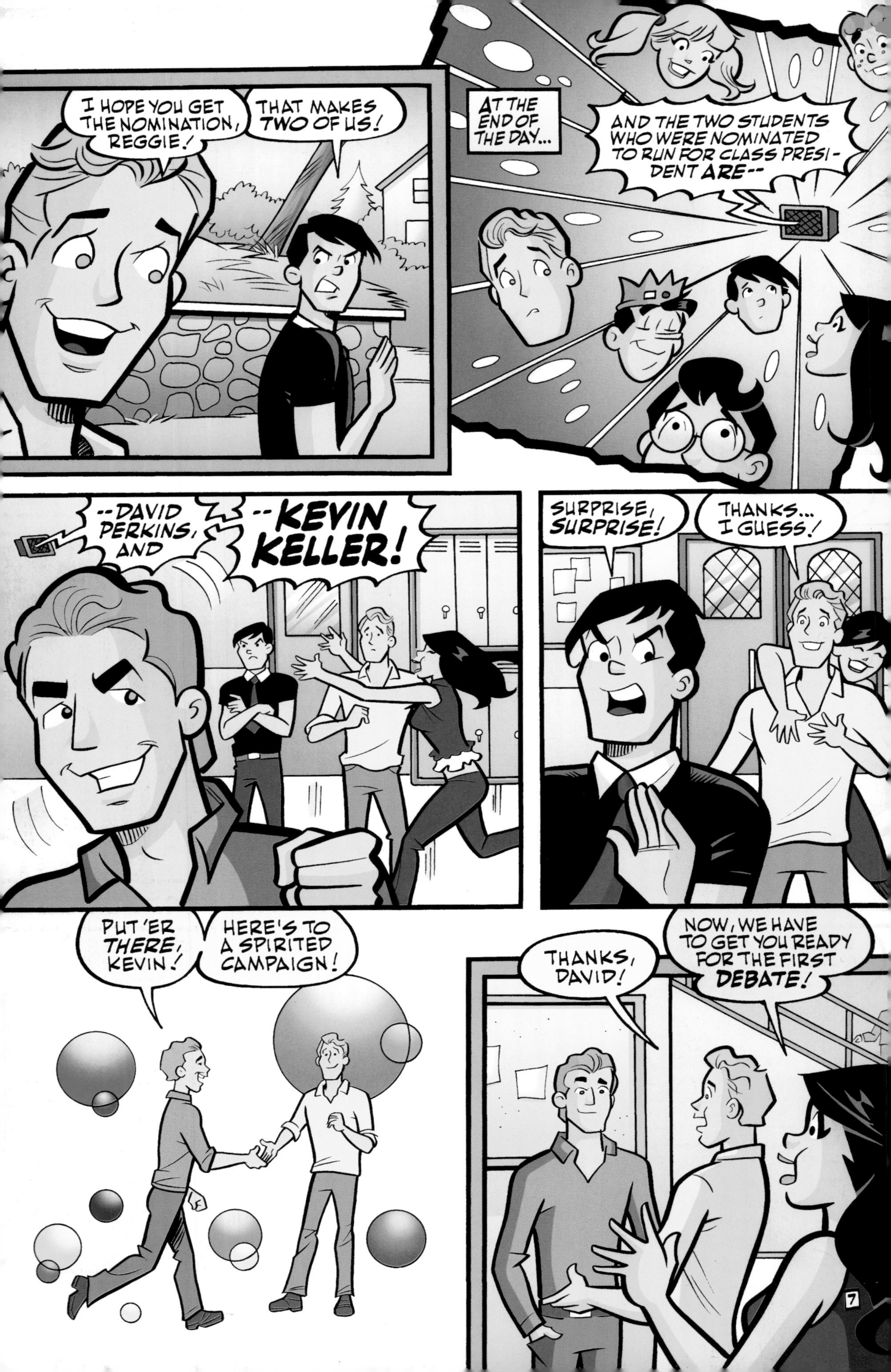
I HOPE YOU GET THE NOMINATION, REGGIE!
THAT MAKES TWO OF US!
AT THE END OF THE DAY...
AND THE TWO STUDENTS WHO WERE NOMINATED TO RUN FOR CLASS PRESI-DENT ARE--
--DAVID PERKINS, AND
--KEVIN KELLER!
SURPRISE, SURPRISE!
THANKS... I GUESS!
PUT 'ER THERE, KEVIN!
HERE'S TO A SPIRITED CAMPAIGN!
THANKS, DAVID!
NOW, WE HAVE TO GET YOU READY FOR THE FIRST DEBATE!

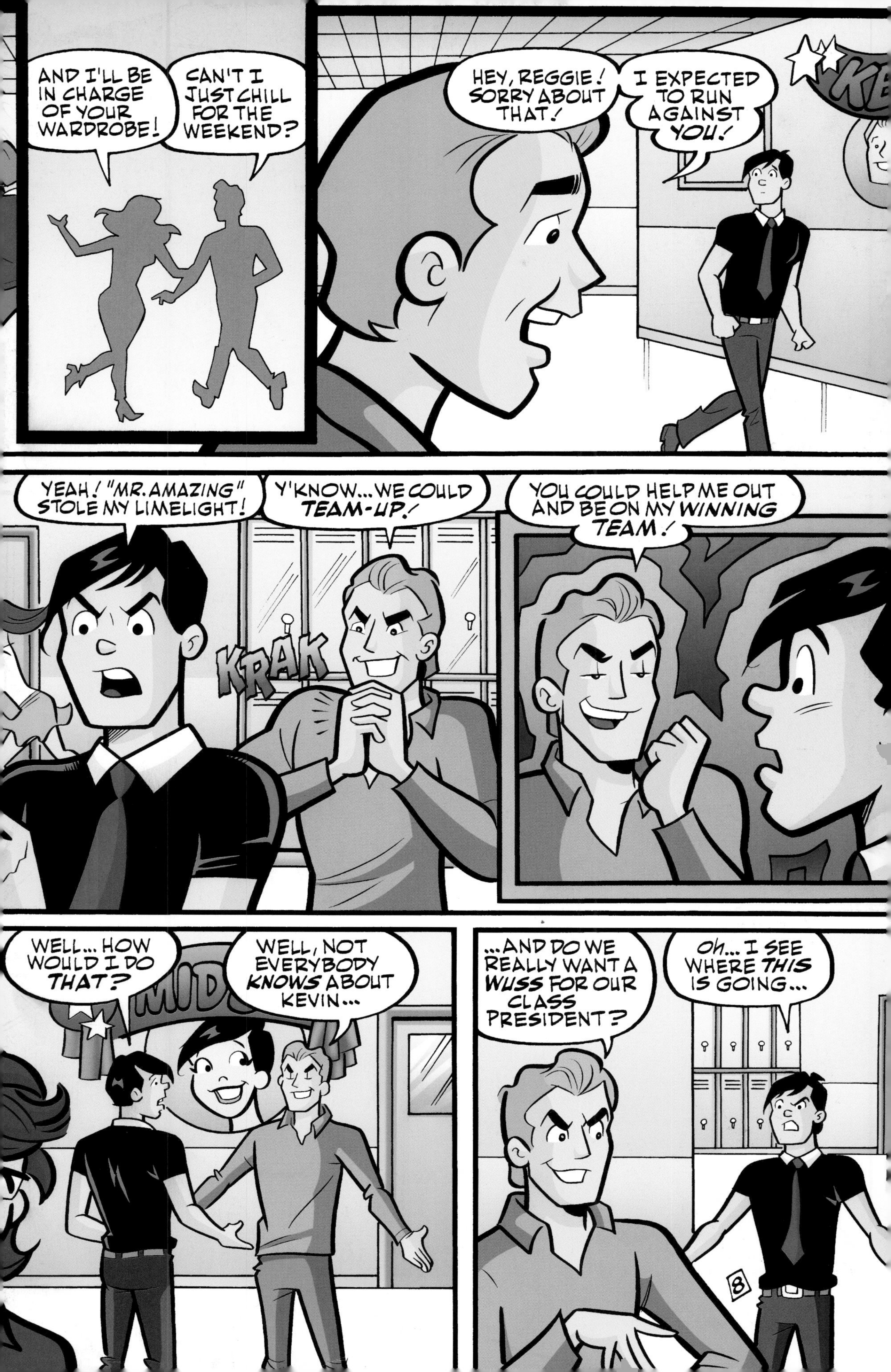

AND I'LL BE IN CHARGE OF YOUR WARDROBE!
CAN'T I JUST CHILL FOR THE WEEKEND?
HEY, REGGIE! SORRY ABOUT THAT!
I EXPECTED TO RUN AGAINST *YOU*!
YEAH! "MR. AMAZING" STOLE MY LIMELIGHT!
Y'KNOW... WE COULD *TEAM-UP*!
KRAK
YOU COULD HELP ME OUT AND BE ON MY *WINNING TEAM*!
WELL... HOW WOULD I DO *THAT*?
WELL, NOT EVERYBODY *KNOWS* ABOUT KEVIN...
...AND DO WE REALLY WANT A *WUSS* FOR OUR CLASS PRESIDENT?
Oh... I SEE WHERE *THIS* IS GOING...
8

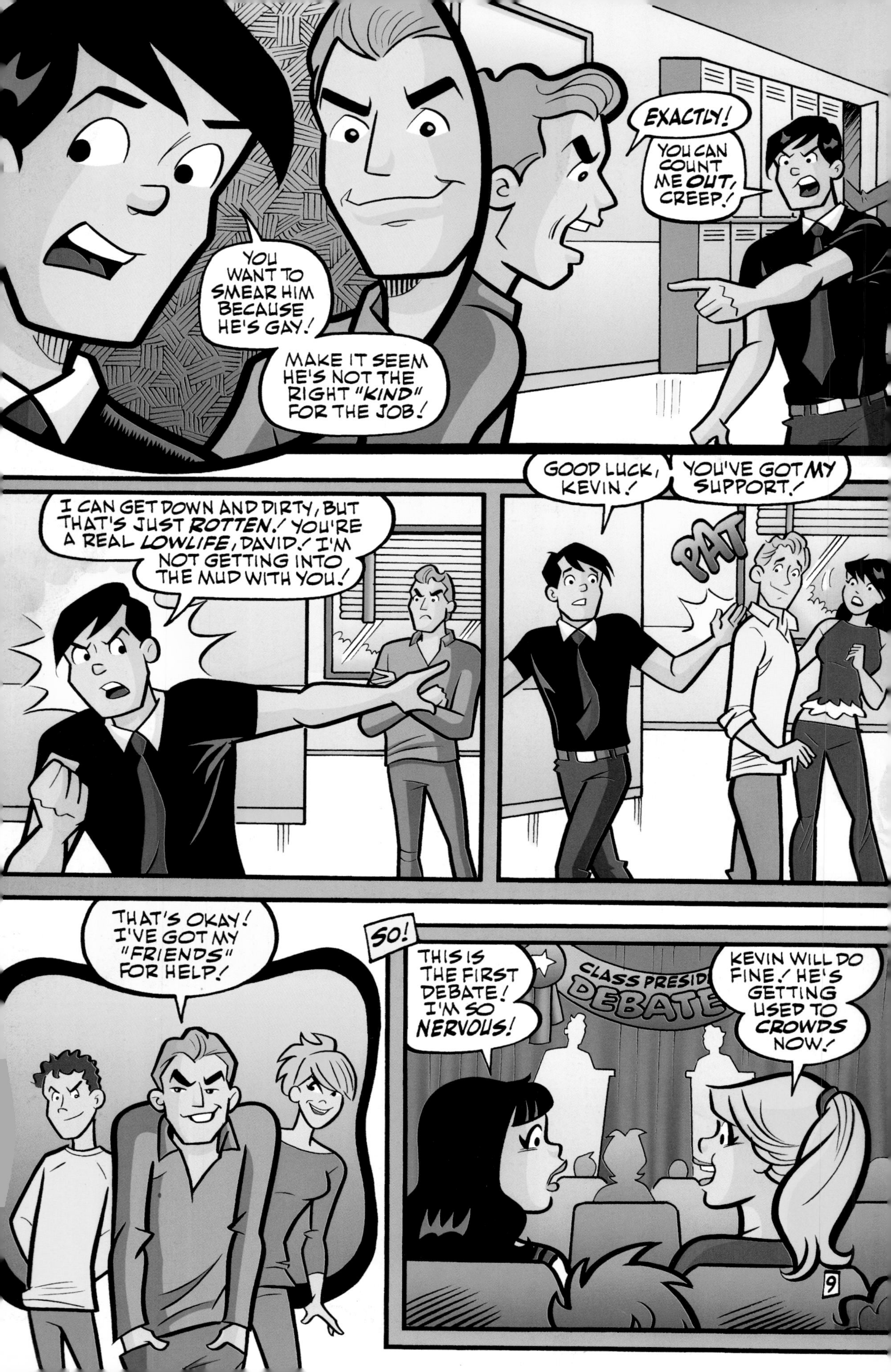
YOU WANT TO SMEAR HIM BECAUSE HE'S GAY!
MAKE IT SEEM HE'S NOT THE RIGHT "KIND" FOR THE JOB!
EXACTLY!
YOU CAN COUNT ME OUT, CREEP!
I CAN GET DOWN AND DIRTY, BUT THAT'S JUST ROTTEN! YOU'RE A REAL LOWLIFE, DAVID! I'M NOT GETTING INTO THE MUD WITH YOU!
GOOD LUCK, KEVIN!
YOU'VE GOT MY SUPPORT!
PAT
THAT'S OKAY! I'VE GOT MY "FRIENDS" FOR HELP!
SO!
CLASS PRESID
DEBATE
THIS IS THE FIRST DEBATE! I'M SO NERVOUS!
KEVIN WILL DO FINE! HE'S GETTING USED TO CROWDS NOW!
9

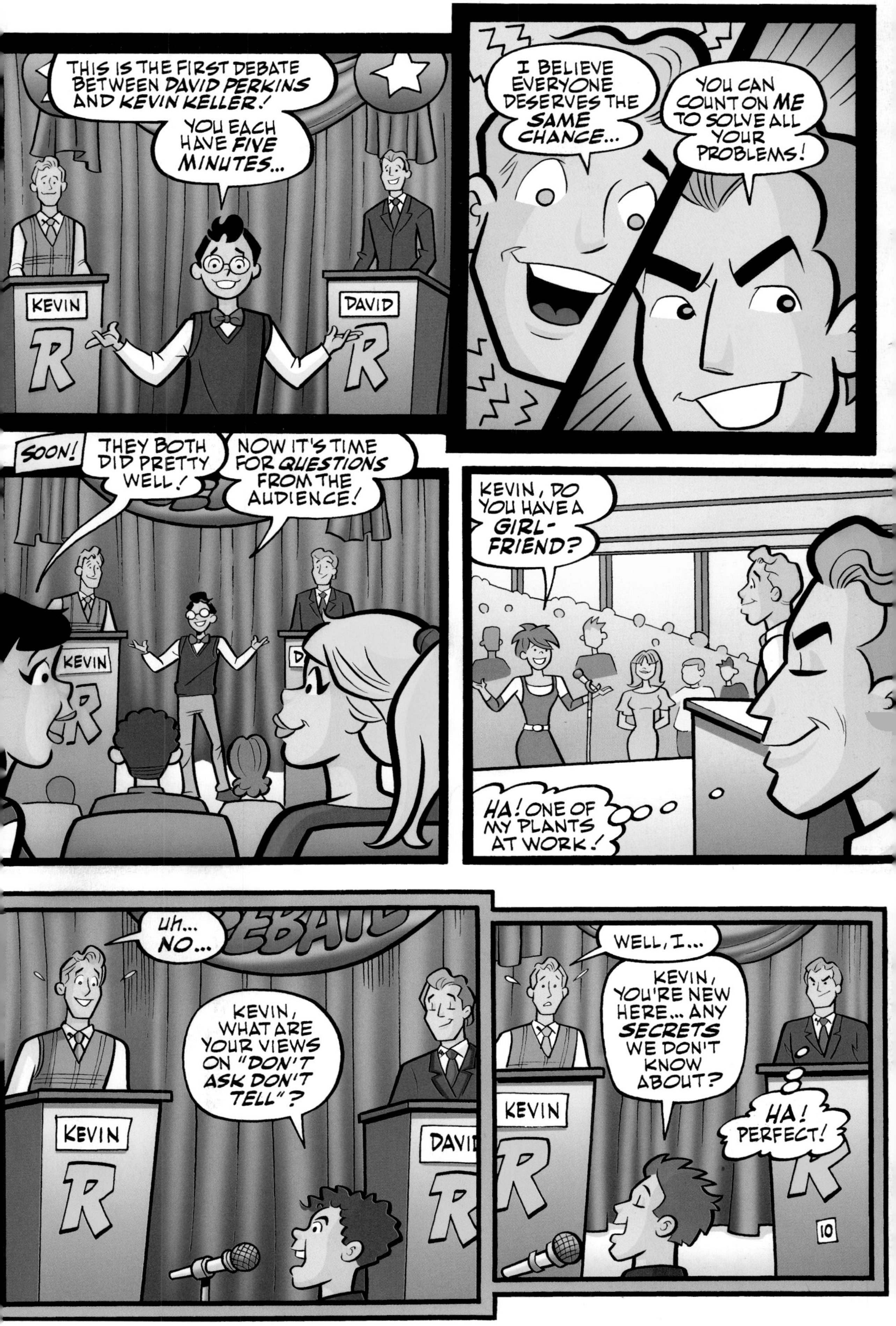
THIS IS THE FIRST DEBATE BETWEEN DAVID PERKINS AND KEVIN KELLER!
YOU EACH HAVE FIVE MINUTES...
KEVIN
DAVID
I BELIEVE EVERYONE DESERVES THE SAME CHANCE...
YOU CAN COUNT ON ME TO SOLVE ALL YOUR PROBLEMS!
SOON!
THEY BOTH DID PRETTY WELL!
NOW IT'S TIME FOR QUESTIONS FROM THE AUDIENCE!
KEVIN
KEVIN, DO YOU HAVE A GIRL-FRIEND?
HA! ONE OF MY PLANTS AT WORK!
UH... NO...
KEVIN, WHAT ARE YOUR VIEWS ON "DON'T ASK DON'T TELL"?
KEVIN
WELL, I...
KEVIN, YOU'RE NEW HERE... ANY SECRETS WE DON'T KNOW ABOUT?
HA! PERFECT!
KEVIN
10

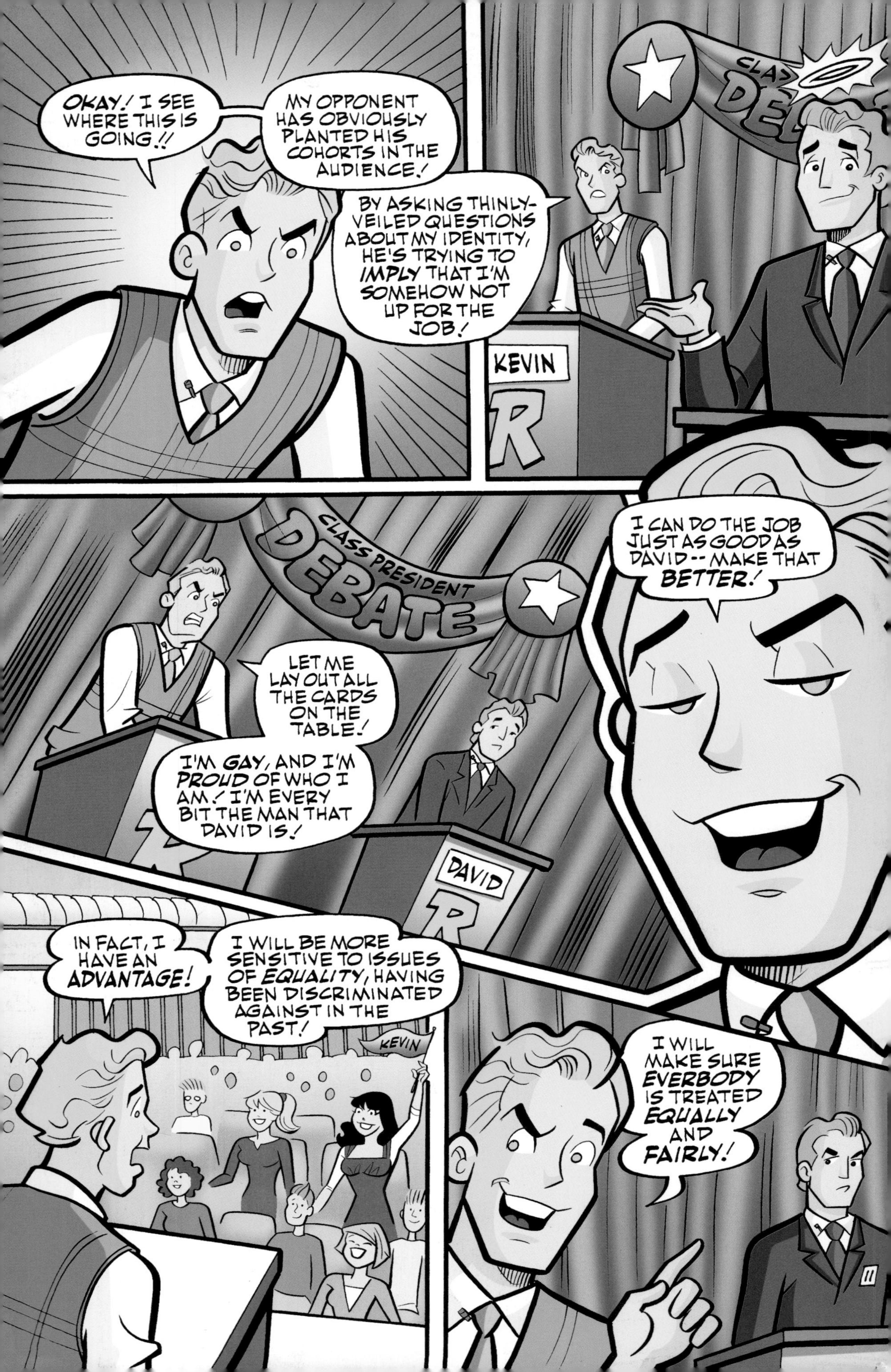
OKAY! I SEE WHERE THIS IS GOING!!
MY OPPONENT HAS OBVIOUSLY PLANTED HIS COHORTS IN THE AUDIENCE!
BY ASKING THINLY-VEILED QUESTIONS ABOUT MY IDENTITY, HE'S TRYING TO IMPLY THAT I'M SOMEHOW NOT UP FOR THE JOB!
CLASS
KEVIN
R
CLASS PRESIDENT DEBATE
LET ME LAY OUT ALL THE CARDS ON THE TABLE!
I'M GAY, AND I'M PROUD OF WHO I AM! I'M EVERY BIT THE MAN THAT DAVID IS!
DAVID
R
I CAN DO THE JOB JUST AS GOOD AS DAVID -- MAKE THAT BETTER!
IN FACT, I HAVE AN ADVANTAGE!
I WILL BE MORE SENSITIVE TO ISSUES OF EQUALITY, HAVING BEEN DISCRIMINATED AGAINST IN THE PAST!
KEVIN
I WILL MAKE SURE EVERBODY IS TREATED EQUALLY AND FAIRLY!

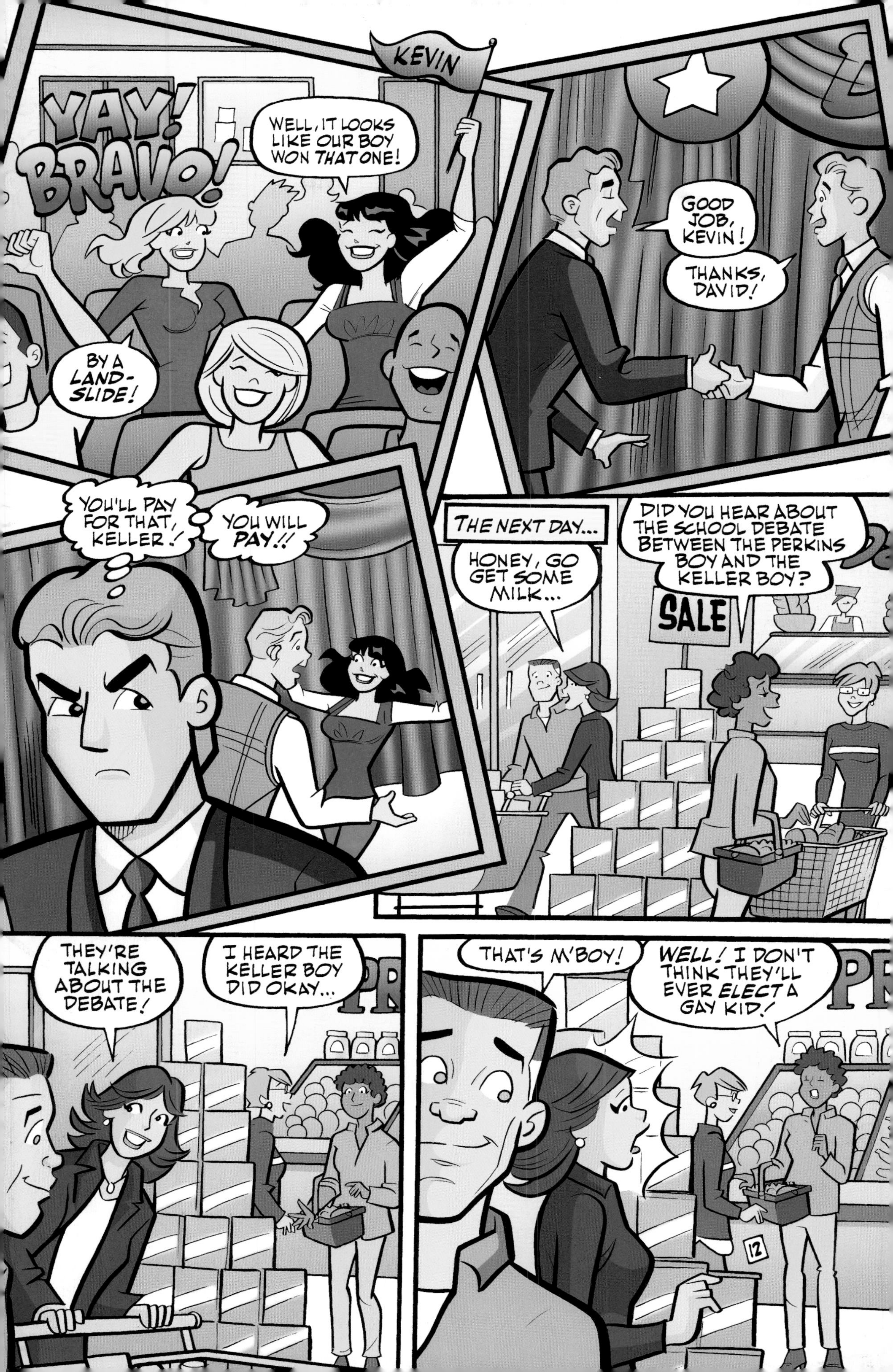
KEVIN
YAY! BRAVO!
WELL, IT LOOKS LIKE OUR BOY WON THAT ONE!
BY A LAND-SLIDE!
GOOD JOB, KEVIN!
THANKS, DAVID!
YOU'LL PAY FOR THAT, KELLER!
YOU WILL PAY!!
THE NEXT DAY...
HONEY, GO GET SOME MILK...
DID YOU HEAR ABOUT THE SCHOOL DEBATE BETWEEN THE PERKINS BOY AND THE KELLER BOY?
SALE
THEY'RE TALKING ABOUT THE DEBATE!
I HEARD THE KELLER BOY DID OKAY...
THAT'S M'BOY!
WELL! I DON'T THINK THEY'LL EVER ELECT A GAY KID!
12

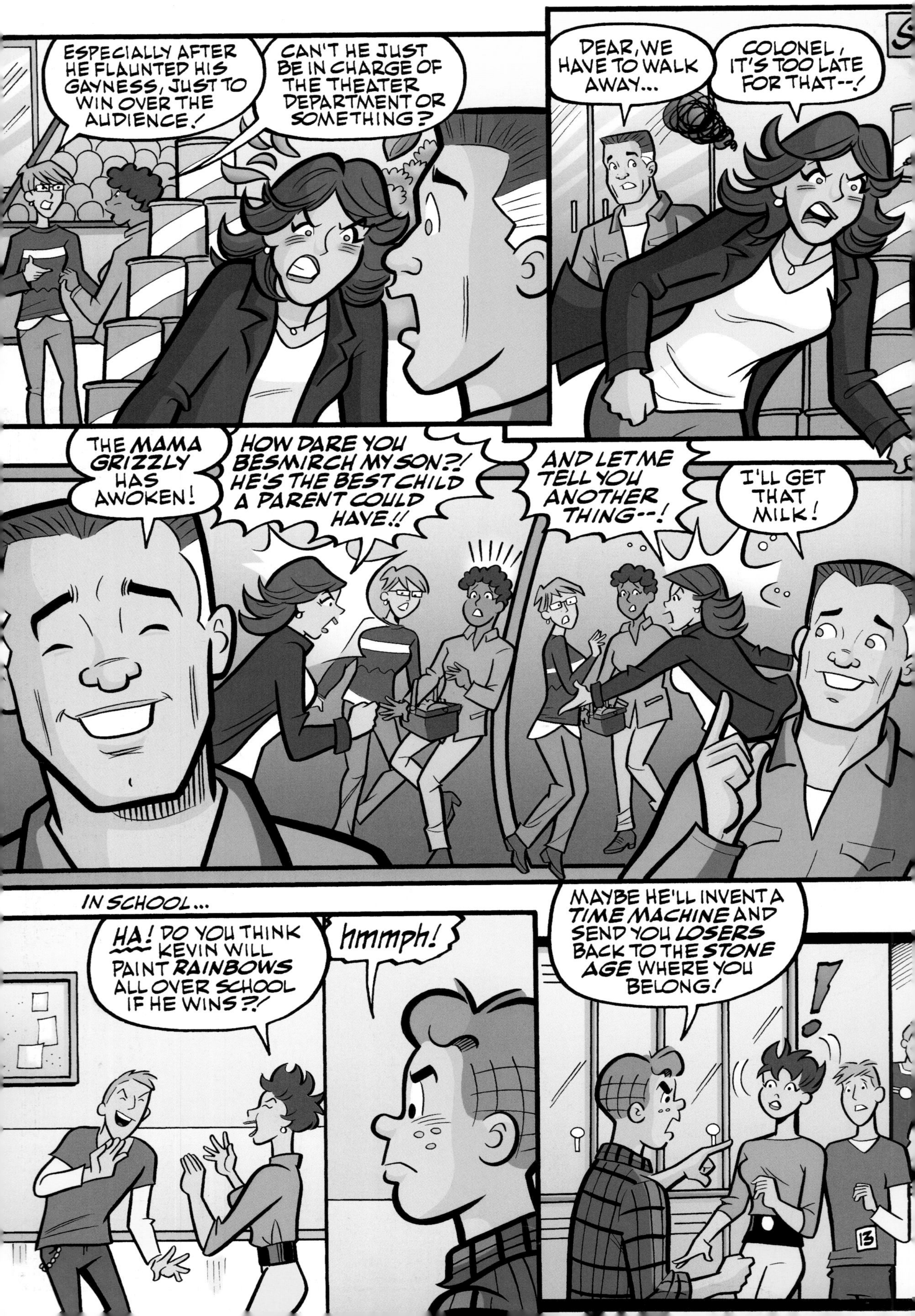
ESPECIALLY AFTER HE FLAUNTED HIS GAYNESS, JUST TO WIN OVER THE AUDIENCE!
CAN'T HE JUST BE IN CHARGE OF THE THEATER DEPARTMENT OR SOMETHING?
DEAR, WE HAVE TO WALK AWAY...
COLONEL, IT'S TOO LATE FOR THAT--!
THE MAMA GRIZZLY HAS AWOKEN!
HOW DARE YOU BESMIRCH MY SON?! HE'S THE BEST CHILD A PARENT COULD HAVE!!
AND LET ME TELL YOU ANOTHER THING--!
I'LL GET THAT MILK!
IN SCHOOL...
HA! DO YOU THINK KEVIN WILL PAINT RAINBOWS ALL OVER SCHOOL IF HE WINS?!
hmmph!
MAYBE HE'LL INVENT A TIME MACHINE AND SEND YOU LOSERS BACK TO THE STONE AGE WHERE YOU BELONG!
13

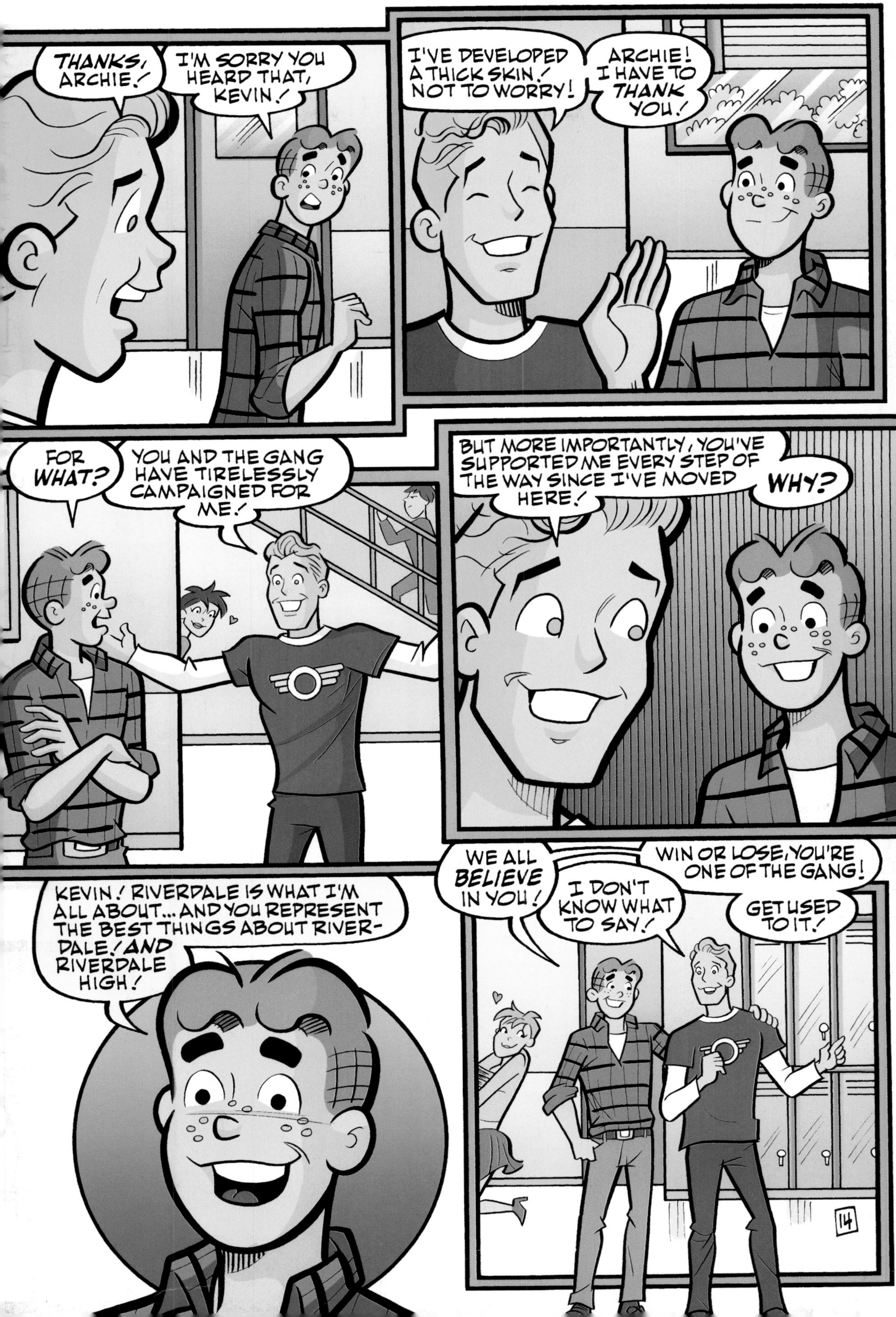
THANKS, ARCHIE!
I'M SORRY YOU HEARD THAT, KEVIN!
I'VE DEVELOPED A THICK SKIN! NOT TO WORRY!
ARCHIE! I HAVE TO THANK YOU!
FOR WHAT?
YOU AND THE GANG HAVE TIRELESSLY CAMPAIGNED FOR ME!
BUT MORE IMPORTANTLY, YOU'VE SUPPORTED ME EVERY STEP OF THE WAY SINCE I'VE MOVED HERE!
WHY?
KEVIN! RIVERDALE IS WHAT I'M ALL ABOUT... AND YOU REPRESENT THE BEST THINGS ABOUT RIVER-DALE! AND RIVERDALE HIGH!
WE ALL BELIEVE IN YOU!
WIN OR LOSE, YOU'RE ONE OF THE GANG!
I DON'T KNOW WHAT TO SAY!
GET USED TO IT!
14

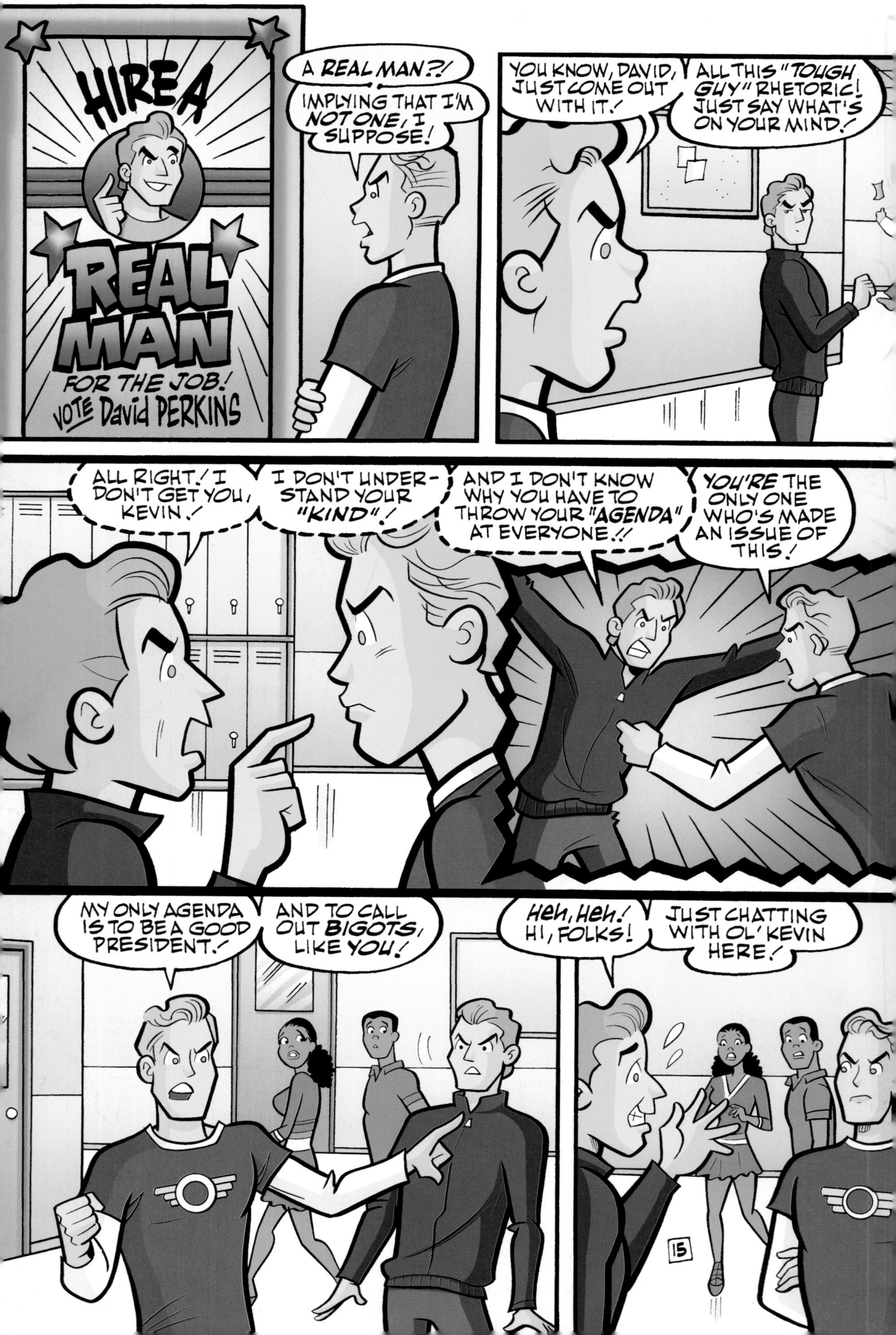
HIRE A
REAL MAN
FOR THE JOB!
VOTE David PERKINS
A REAL MAN?!
IMPLYING THAT I'M NOT ONE, I SUPPOSE!
YOU KNOW, DAVID, JUST COME OUT WITH IT!
ALL THIS "TOUGH GUY" RHETORIC! JUST SAY WHAT'S ON YOUR MIND!
ALL RIGHT! I DON'T GET YOU, KEVIN!
I DON'T UNDER-STAND YOUR "KIND"!
AND I DON'T KNOW WHY YOU HAVE TO THROW YOUR "AGENDA" AT EVERYONE!!
YOU'RE THE ONLY ONE WHO'S MADE AN ISSUE OF THIS!
MY ONLY AGENDA IS TO BE A GOOD PRESIDENT!
AND TO CALL OUT BIGOTS, LIKE YOU!
Heh, Heh! HI, FOLKS!
JUST CHATTING WITH OL' KEVIN HERE!
15

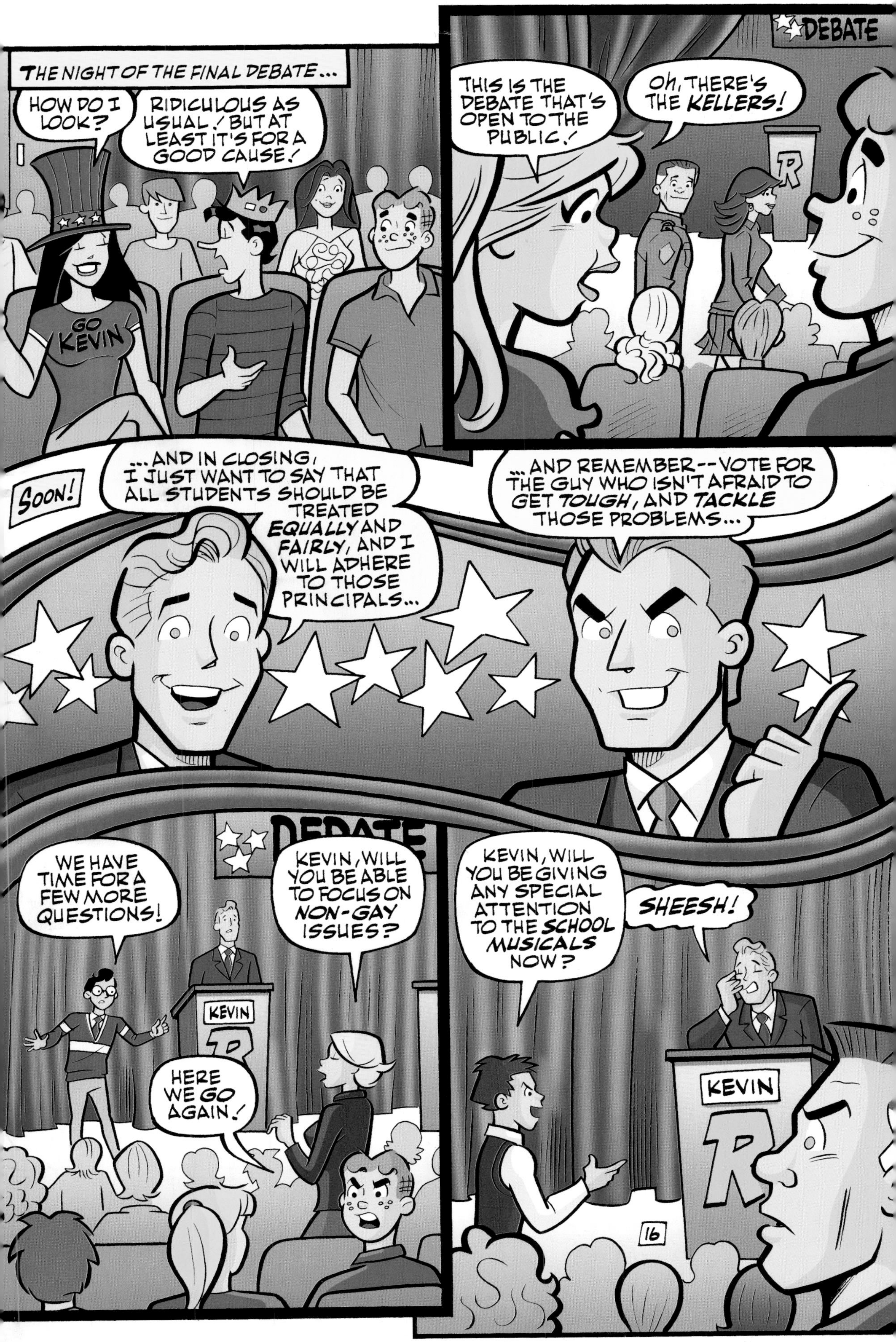
THE NIGHT OF THE FINAL DEBATE...
HOW DO I LOOK?
RIDICULOUS AS USUAL! BUT AT LEAST IT'S FOR A GOOD CAUSE!
GO KEVIN
DEBATE
THIS IS THE DEBATE THAT'S OPEN TO THE PUBLIC!
Oh, THERE'S THE KELLERS!
SOON!
...AND IN CLOSING, I JUST WANT TO SAY THAT ALL STUDENTS SHOULD BE TREATED EQUALLY AND FAIRLY, AND I WILL ADHERE TO THOSE PRINCIPALS...
...AND REMEMBER--VOTE FOR THE GUY WHO ISN'T AFRAID TO GET TOUGH, AND TACKLE THOSE PROBLEMS...
WE HAVE TIME FOR A FEW MORE QUESTIONS!
KEVIN, WILL YOU BE ABLE TO FOCUS ON NON-GAY ISSUES?
KEVIN
HERE WE GO AGAIN!
KEVIN, WILL YOU BE GIVING ANY SPECIAL ATTENTION TO THE SCHOOL MUSICALS NOW?
SHEESH!
KEVIN
16

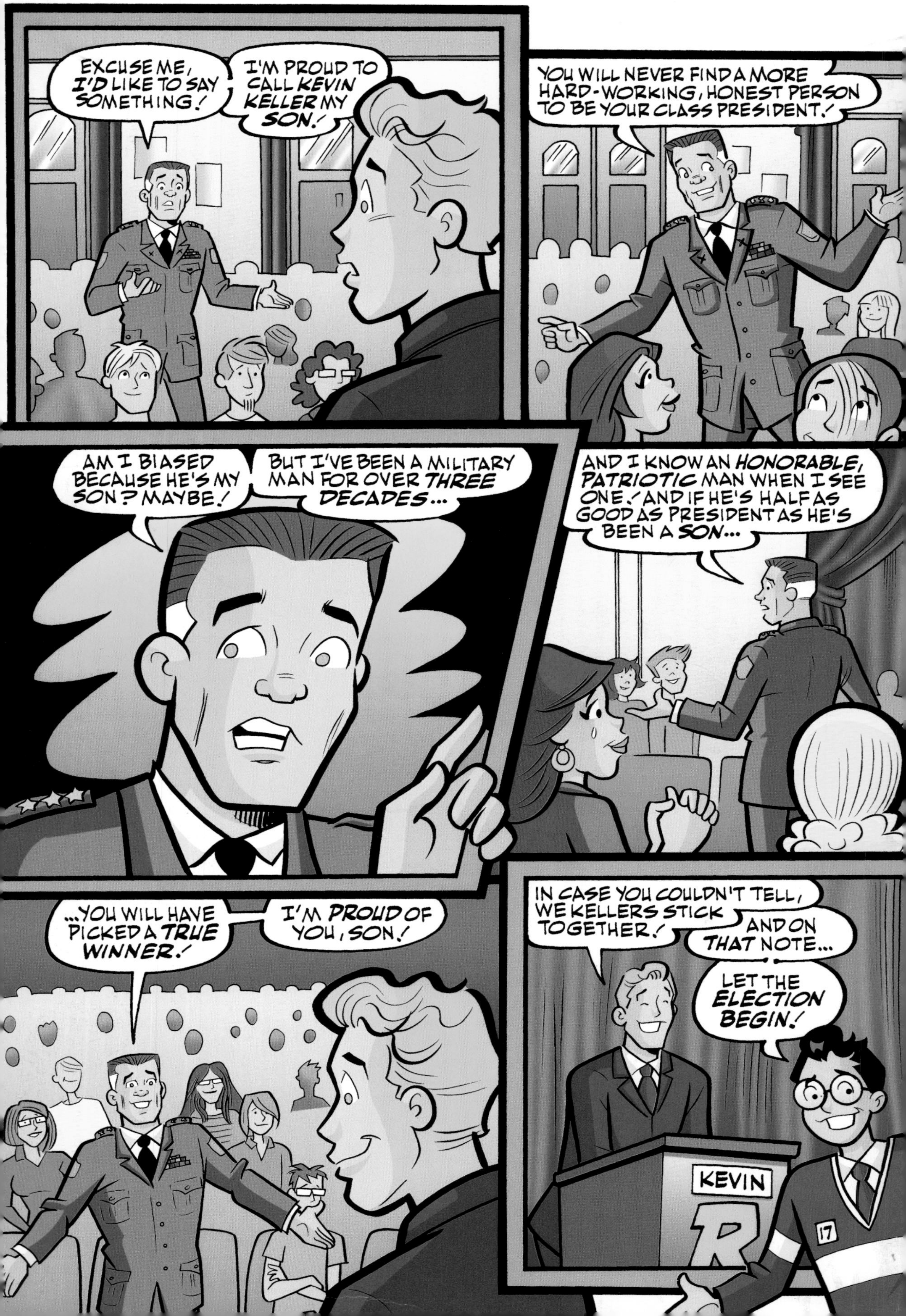
EXCUSE ME, I'D LIKE TO SAY SOMETHING!
I'M PROUD TO CALL KEVIN KELLER MY SON!
YOU WILL NEVER FIND A MORE HARD-WORKING, HONEST PERSON TO BE YOUR CLASS PRESIDENT!
AM I BIASED BECAUSE HE'S MY SON? MAYBE!
BUT I'VE BEEN A MILITARY MAN FOR OVER THREE DECADES...
AND I KNOW AN HONORABLE, PATRIOTIC MAN WHEN I SEE ONE! AND IF HE'S HALF AS GOOD AS PRESIDENT AS HE'S BEEN A SON...
...YOU WILL HAVE PICKED A TRUE WINNER!
I'M PROUD OF YOU, SON!
IN CASE YOU COULDN'T TELL, WE KELLERS STICK TOGETHER!
AND ON THAT NOTE...
LET THE ELECTION BEGIN!
KEVIN
R
17

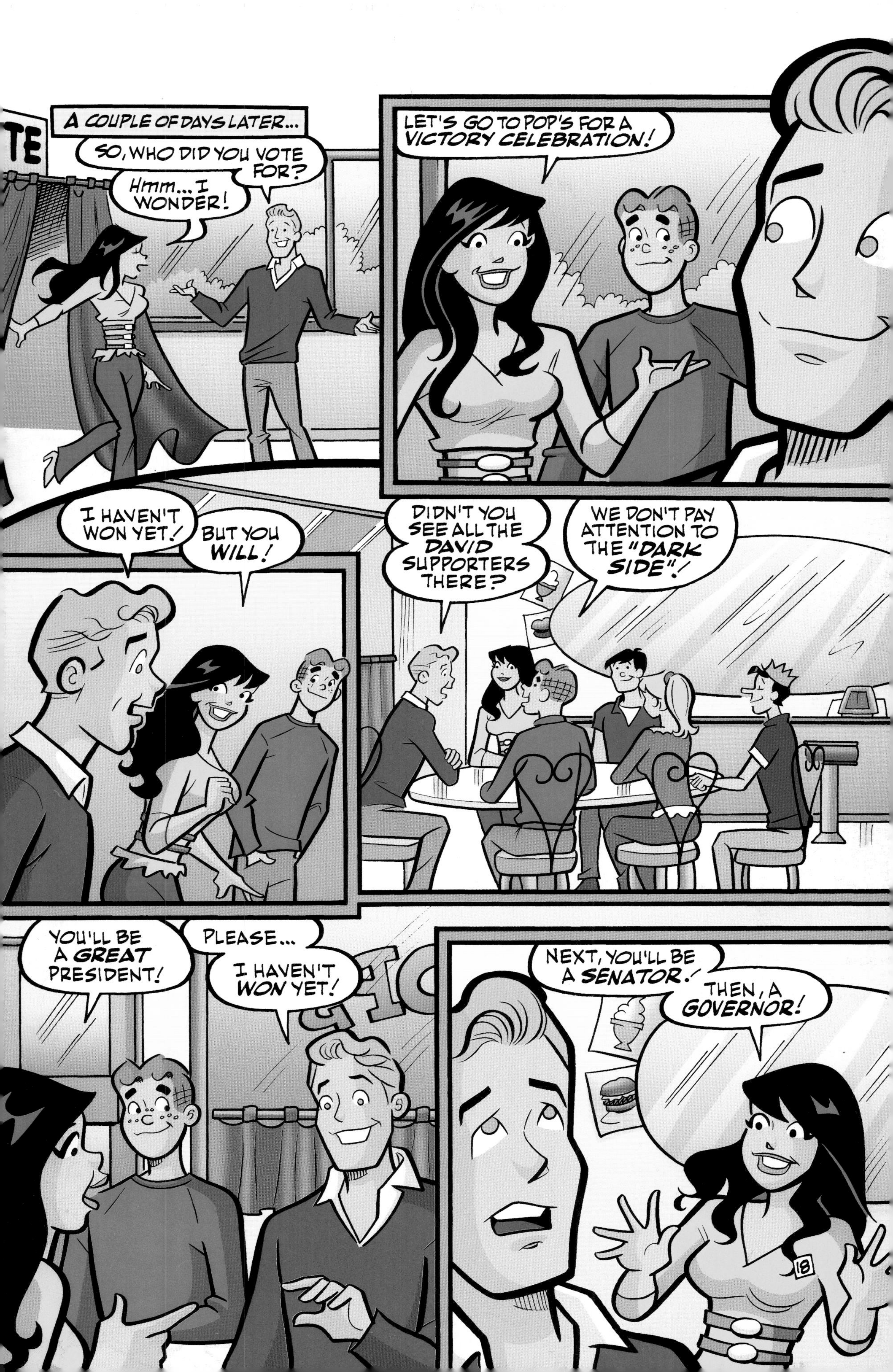
TE
A COUPLE OF DAYS LATER...
SO, WHO DID YOU VOTE FOR?
Hmm... I WONDER!
LET'S GO TO POP'S FOR A VICTORY CELEBRATION!
I HAVEN'T WON YET!
BUT YOU WILL!
DIDN'T YOU SEE ALL THE DAVID SUPPORTERS THERE?
WE DON'T PAY ATTENTION TO THE "DARK SIDE"!
YOU'LL BE A GREAT PRESIDENT!
PLEASE...
I HAVEN'T WON YET!
NEXT, YOU'LL BE A SENATOR!
THEN, A GOVERNOR!
18

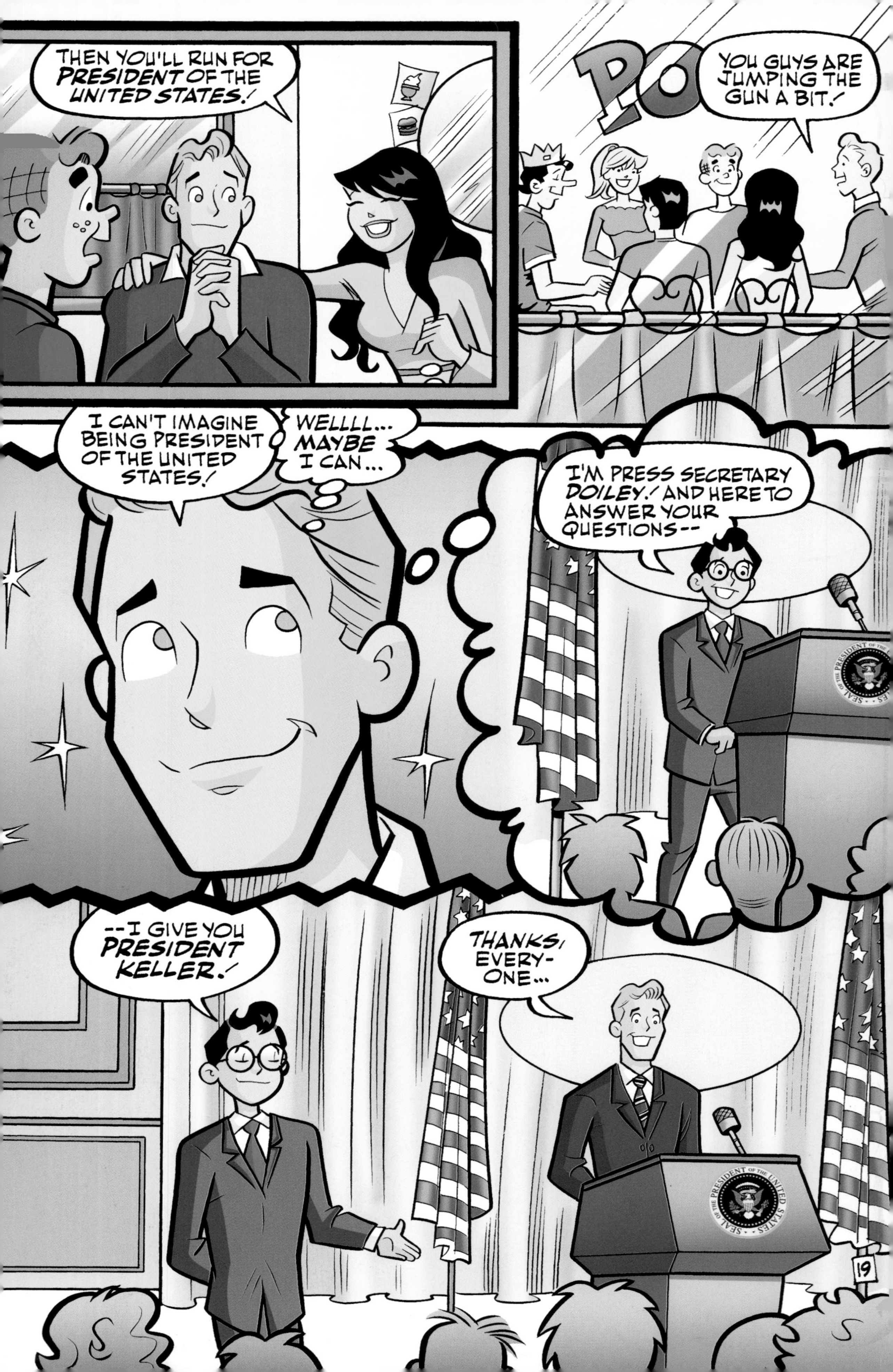
THEN YOU'LL RUN FOR PRESIDENT OF THE UNITED STATES!
PO
YOU GUYS ARE JUMPING THE GUN A BIT!
I CAN'T IMAGINE BEING PRESIDENT OF THE UNITED STATES!
WELLLL... MAYBE I CAN...
I'M PRESS SECRETARY DOILEY! AND HERE TO ANSWER YOUR QUESTIONS--
--I GIVE YOU PRESIDENT KELLER!
THANKS, EVERY-ONE...
SEAL OF THE PRESIDENT OF THE UNITED STATES

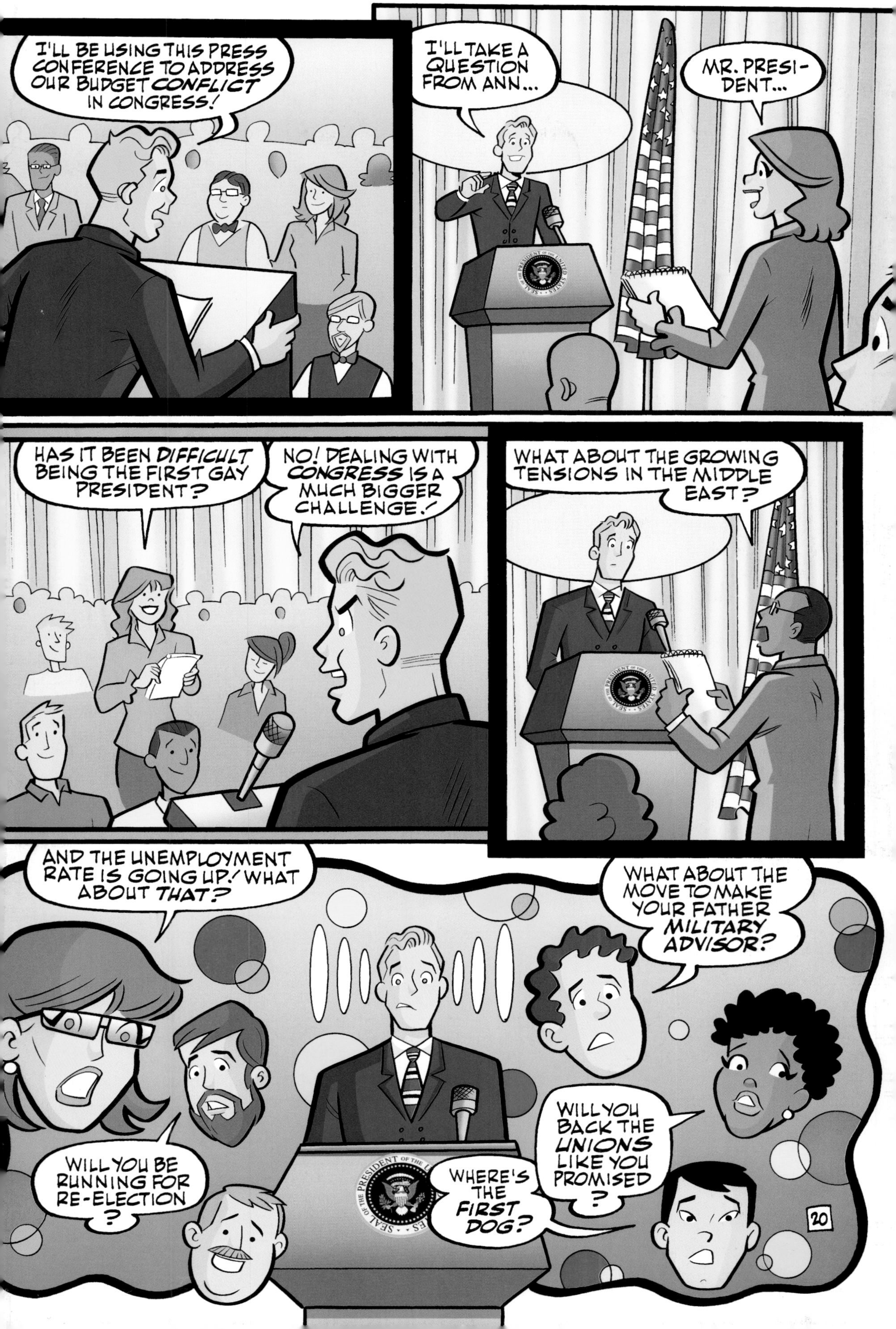
I'LL BE USING THIS PRESS CONFERENCE TO ADDRESS OUR BUDGET CONFLICT IN CONGRESS!
I'LL TAKE A QUESTION FROM ANN...
MR. PRESI-DENT...
HAS IT BEEN DIFFICULT BEING THE FIRST GAY PRESIDENT?
NO! DEALING WITH CONGRESS IS A MUCH BIGGER CHALLENGE!
WHAT ABOUT THE GROWING TENSIONS IN THE MIDDLE EAST?
AND THE UNEMPLOYMENT RATE IS GOING UP! WHAT ABOUT THAT?
WHAT ABOUT THE MOVE TO MAKE YOUR FATHER MILITARY ADVISOR?
WILL YOU BE RUNNING FOR RE-ELECTION?
WHERE'S THE FIRST DOG?
WILL YOU BACK THE UNIONS LIKE YOU PROMISED?
20

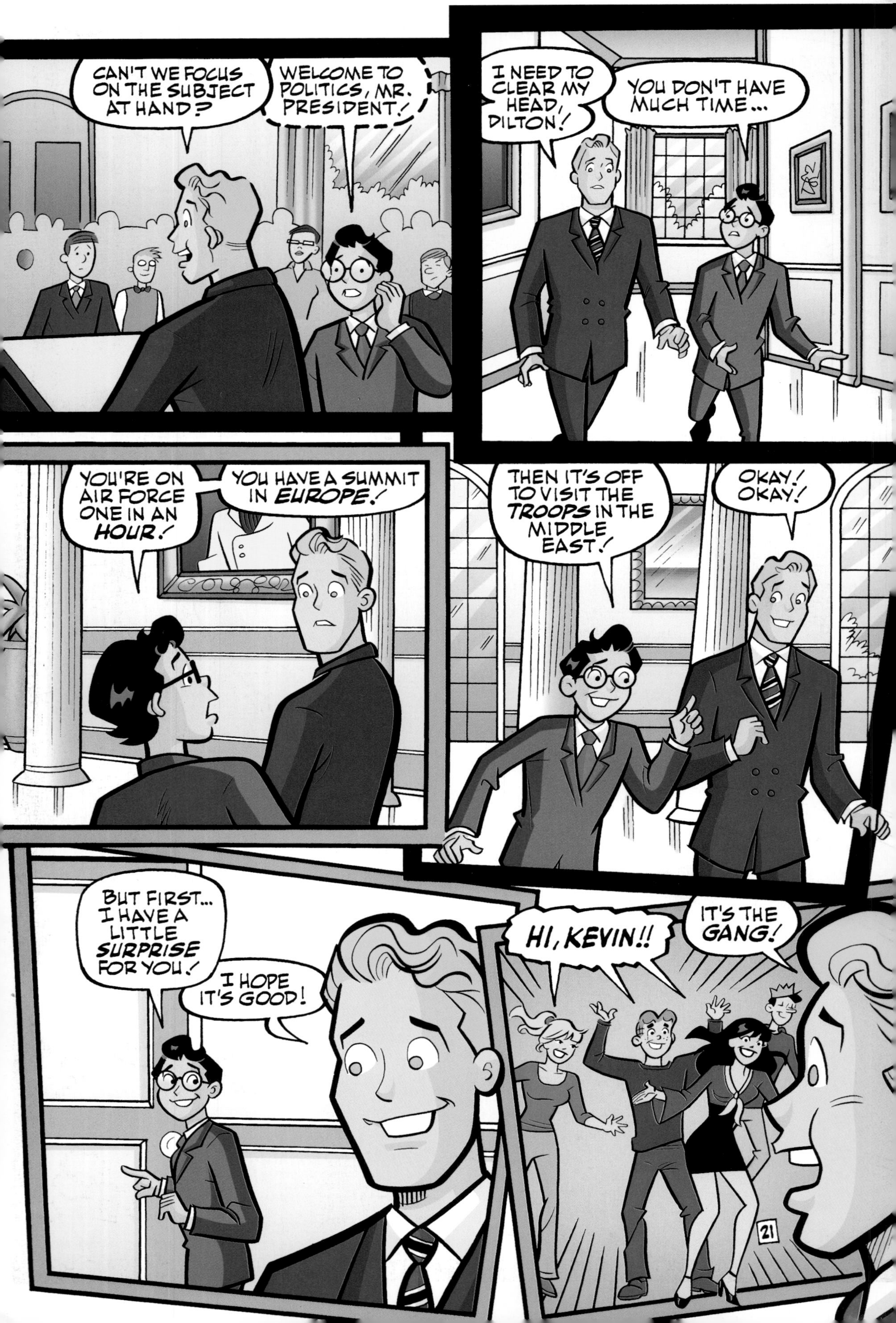

CAN'T WE FOCUS ON THE SUBJECT AT HAND?
WELCOME TO POLITICS, MR. PRESIDENT!
I NEED TO CLEAR MY HEAD, DILTON!
YOU DON'T HAVE MUCH TIME...
YOU'RE ON AIR FORCE ONE IN AN HOUR!
YOU HAVE A SUMMIT IN EUROPE!
THEN IT'S OFF TO VISIT THE TROOPS IN THE MIDDLE EAST!
OKAY! OKAY!
BUT FIRST... I HAVE A LITTLE SURPRISE FOR YOU!
I HOPE IT'S GOOD!
HI, KEVIN!!
IT'S THE GANG!

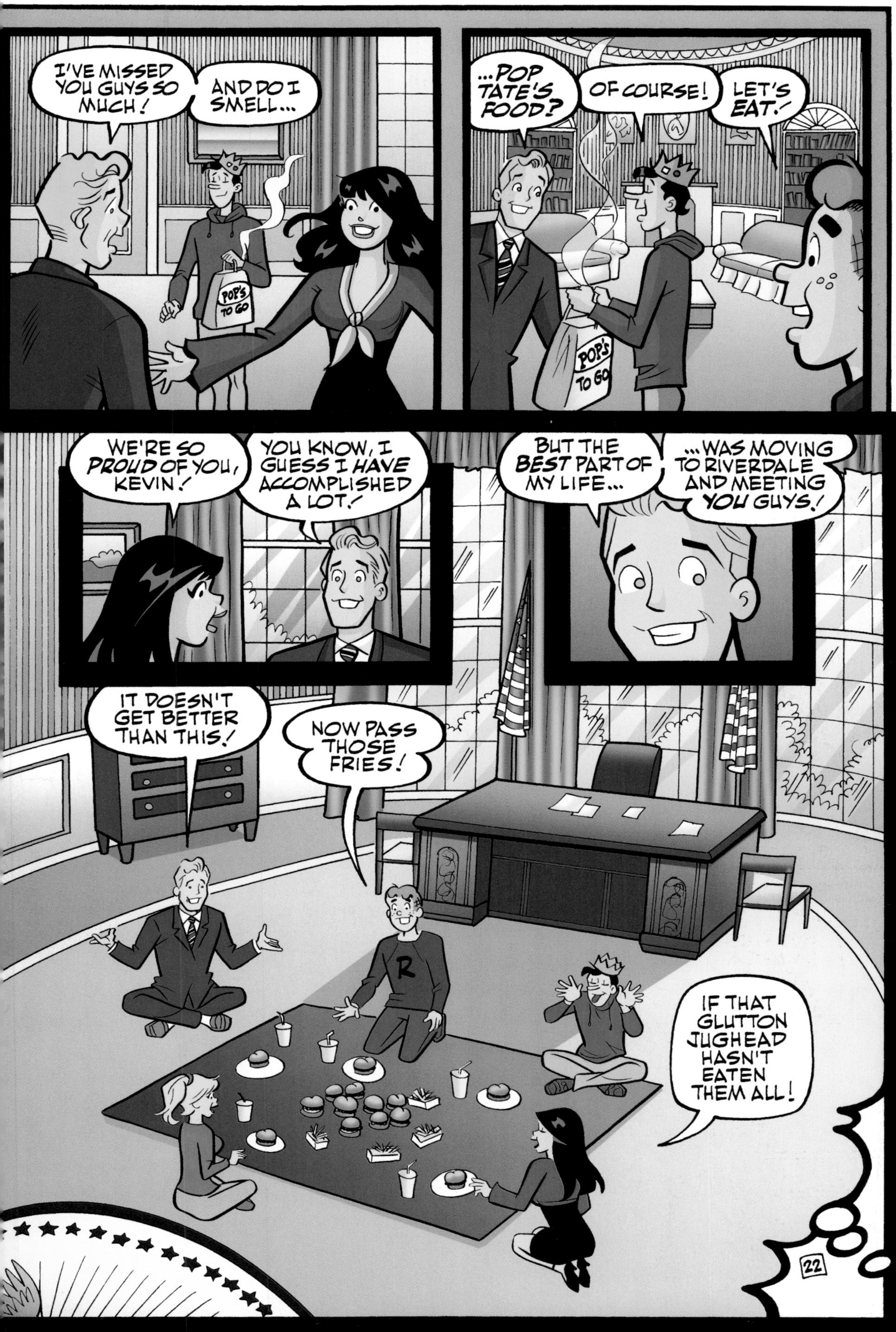
I'VE MISSED YOU GUYS SO MUCH!
AND DO I SMELL...
...POP TATE'S FOOD?
OF COURSE!
LET'S EAT!
POP'S TO GO
WE'RE SO PROUD OF YOU, KEVIN!
YOU KNOW, I GUESS I HAVE ACCOMPLISHED A LOT!
BUT THE BEST PART OF MY LIFE...
...WAS MOVING TO RIVERDALE AND MEETING YOU GUYS!
IT DOESN'T GET BETTER THAN THIS!
NOW PASS THOSE FRIES!
IF THAT GLUTTON JUGHEAD HASN'T EATEN THEM ALL!

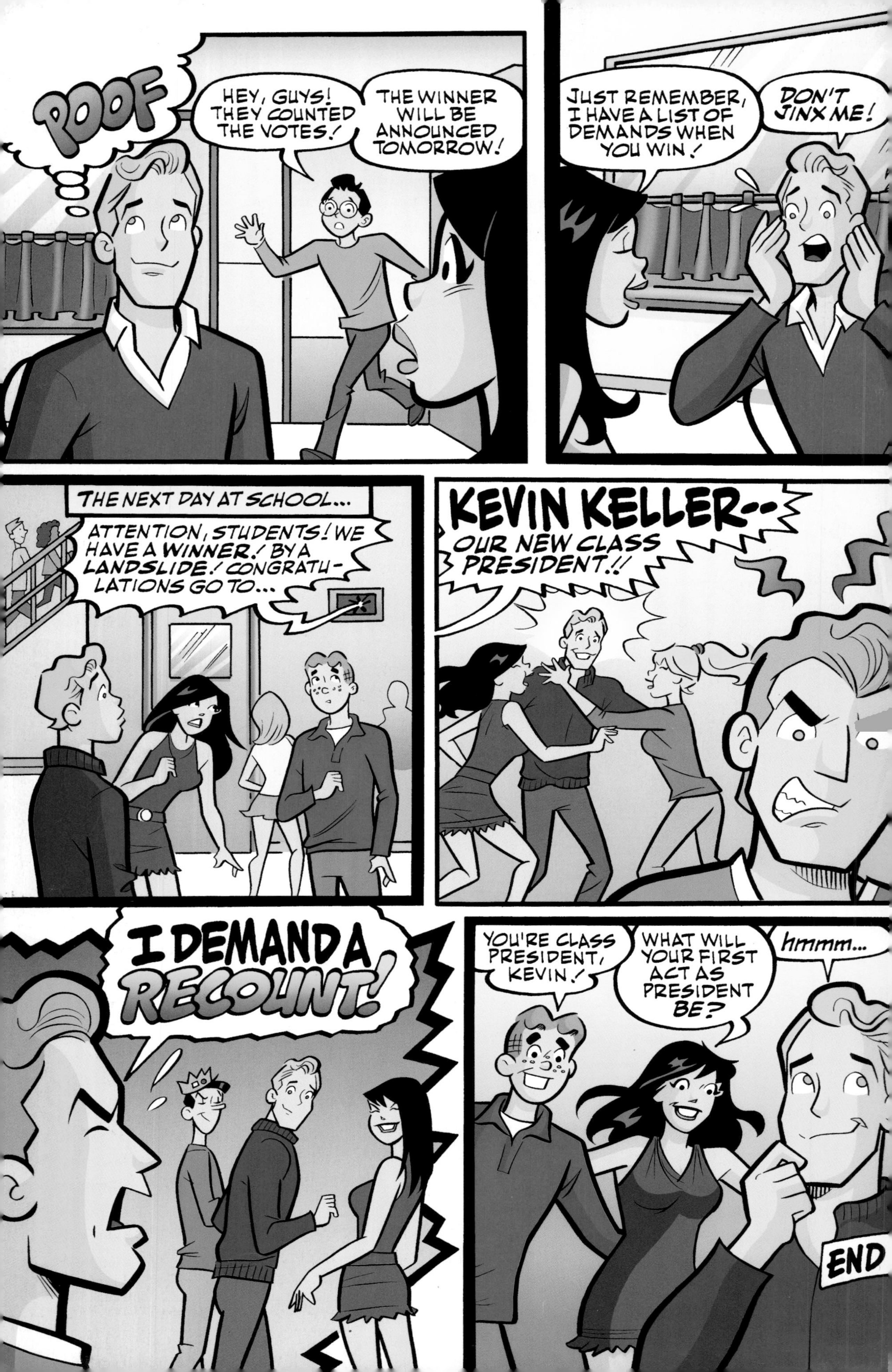
POOF
HEY, GUYS! THEY COUNTED THE VOTES!
THE WINNER WILL BE ANNOUNCED TOMORROW!
JUST REMEMBER, I HAVE A LIST OF DEMANDS WHEN YOU WIN!
DON'T JINX ME!
THE NEXT DAY AT SCHOOL...
ATTENTION, STUDENTS! WE HAVE A WINNER! BY A LANDSLIDE! CONGRATU-LATIONS GO TO...
KEVIN KELLER-- OUR NEW CLASS PRESIDENT!!
I DEMAND A RECOUNT!
YOU'RE CLASS PRESIDENT, KEVIN!
WHAT WILL YOUR FIRST ACT AS PRESIDENT BE?
hmmm...
END

AN INTERVIEW WITH KEVIN Keller™

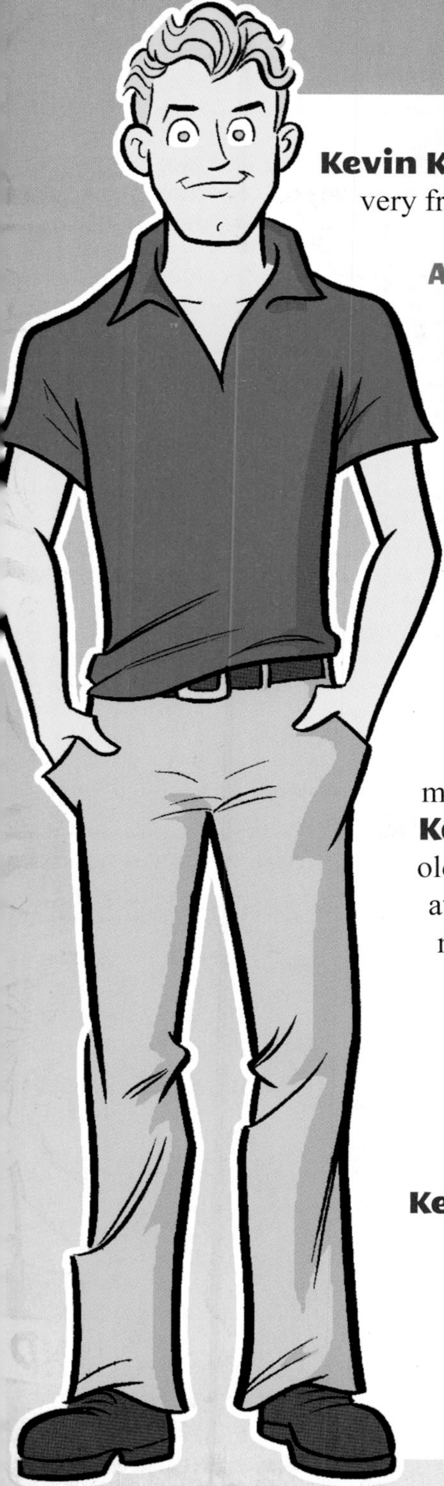

ARCHIE COMICS: What do you think of Riverdale?
Kevin Keller: So far, so good. The people of Riverdale have been very friendly and I'm enjoying being a student at Riverdale High.

AC: What did you think of Veronica when you first met her?
Kevin: Veronica is one in a million! She's a riot! It's cute how much she's crushing on me, but I think we all know she's not my type. Did you know that she once talked for fifteen minutes before she realized I wasn't there?

AC: What do you think of the relationship between Archie, Betty, and Veronica? Have you ever seen anything like it?
Kevin: It's a very interesting relationship. In my hometown you never would see two girls staying best friends while fighting over the same guy. It's a great story. I kind of want to write about it.

AC: Being an aspiring writer, do you prefer the traditional method of journalism or are you embracing digital methods?
Kevin: Writing is my passion. I worked for the paper in my old hometown, and I'm working for the Blue and Gold paper at Riverdale High. Eventhough I've been published in a few magazines, I would love to write the great American novel! As far as journalism, I'm old school. Don't get me wrong, I like blogging and I'm not opposed to the current trend of digital media, but I prefer holding a book or a newspaper in my hands.

AC: How has your family adjusted to living in Riverdale?
Kevin: They love it. My parents love their jobs, and my two little sisters are tearing it up!

AC: Well Kevin, here's to a great first year in Riverdale!
Kevin: Thanks! Now if you'll excuse me, I have a pizza waiting for me down at Pop's, and I need to get to it before Jughead does!

CONTINUE THE FUN WITH ARCHIE COMICS' GRAPHIC NOVEL LIBRARY!

Archie
THE MARRIED LIFE
TWO WORLDS. TWO LOVES. TWO DESTINIES.

Archie: The Married Life Book One

Collecting the first 6 parts of the critically acclaimed Archie Marries Betty and Archie Marries Veronica storylines.

ISBN: 978-1-879794-01-3

Archie
THE MARRIED LIFE
TWO WORLDS. TWO LOVES. TWO DESTINIES.

Archie: The Married Life Book Two

Collecting parts 7-12 of the critically acclaimed Archie Marries Betty and Archie Marries Veronica storylines.

ISBN: 978-1-879794-99-3

THE ARCHIE WEDDING
Archie
WILL YOU MARRY ME?

The Archie Wedding: Will you Marry Me?

Archie has finally chosen! The winner is... BOTH OF THEM!

ISBN: 978-1-879794-51-1

JINX
torres • burchett • austin

Jinx

Jinx isn't so "Li'l" anymore! She's all grown up and off to high school.

ISBN: 978-1-879794-91-7

Betty and Veronica
BEST FRIENDS FOREVER

Betty & Veronica: Best Friends Forever

Betty & Veronica prove that when it comes to BFFs they're among the best!

ISBN: 978-1-879794-76-4

Archie
CYBER ADVENTURES

Archie: Cyber Adventures

Archie and friends go on an adventure through the world of video games!

ISBN: 978-1-879794-73-3

The Best of
Sabrina
THE TEENAGE WITCH

The Magic of Sabrina the Teenage Witch

Sabrina will keep you spellbound with this magical collection.

ISBN: 978-1-879794-67-2

Archie
OBAMA & PALIN IN RIVERDALE

Archie: Obama & Palin in Riverdale

It's an election for the ages when two of the most important political figures of the 21st century clash in Riverdale.

ISBN: 978-1-879794-68-9

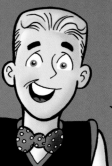

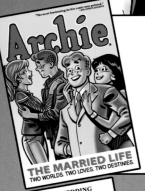

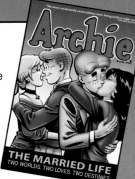

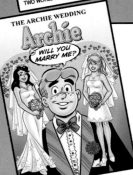

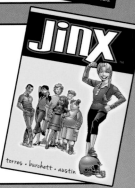

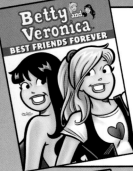

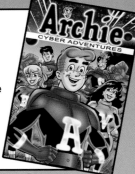

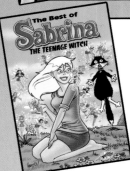

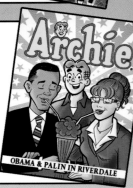

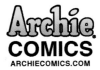

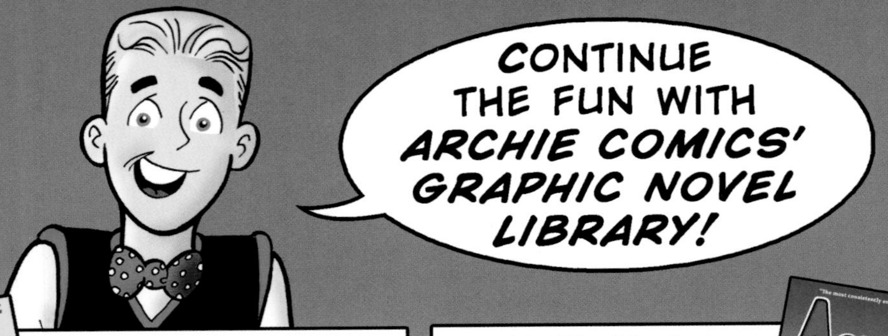

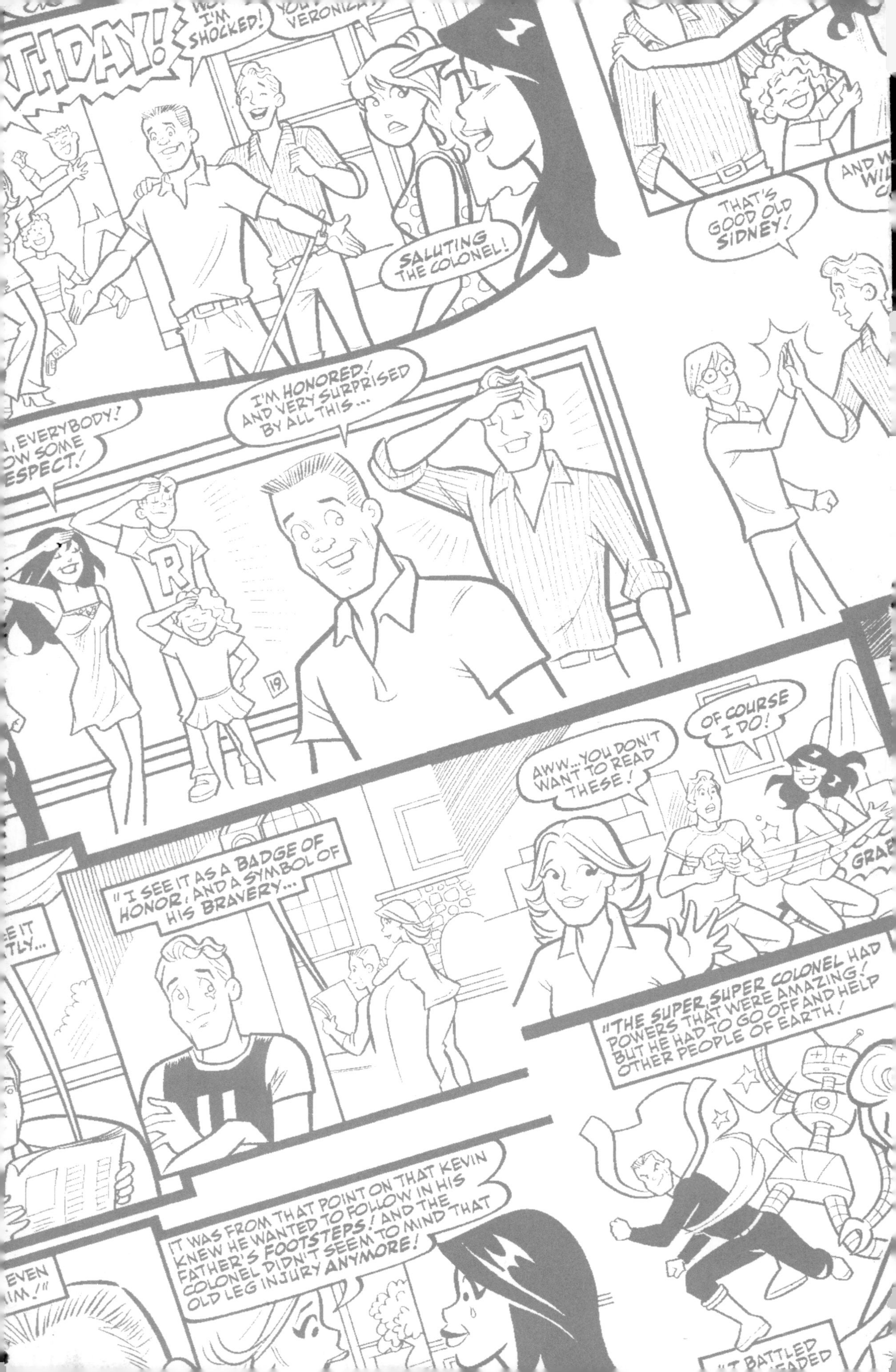
I'M SHOCKED!
SALUTING THE COLONEL!
THAT'S GOOD OLD SIDNEY!
I'M HONORED! AND VERY SURPRISED BY ALL THIS...
19
"I SEE IT AS A BADGE OF HONOR, AND A SYMBOL OF HIS BRAVERY...
AWW...YOU DON'T WANT TO READ THESE!
OF COURSE I DO!
"THE SUPER, SUPER COLONEL HAD POWERS THAT WERE AMAZING! BUT HE HAD TO GO OFF AND HELP OTHER PEOPLE OF EARTH!
IT WAS FROM THAT POINT ON THAT KEVIN KNEW HE WANTED TO FOLLOW IN HIS FATHER'S FOOTSTEPS! AND THE COLONEL DIDN'T SEEM TO MIND THAT OLD LEG INJURY ANYMORE!